A DARK MOON RAGING

She stood immobile for so long that William scrambled to his feet. Looking out to see what she was watching, he could see nothing. Only the grey slate roofs of the houses below, and beyond them the mist-shrouded outlines of mill chimneys in the valley. Apart from a coal barge with its weary grey horse moving slowly along a leaden canal, there was nothing of interest.

'What are you looking at, Connie? What do you see?'

Her dark eyes were veiled in thought. 'I see the moors, the great wide spaces where one is free, not the smoky town down there. Up there, the other way, the air is clean and beautiful, the heather springs under your feet and the wind whistles round the rocks. We'll go there soon, William, you and I.'

He did not care for her in this mood, her gaze abstracted and far-away. She was still his adored Connie, of course, but something in her manner inspired awe in him, fear even, for he could not understand.

A DARK MOON RAGING

AILEEN ARMITAGE

Hamlyn Paperbacks

A DARK MOON RAGING
ISBN 0 600 20556 8

First published in Great Britain 1982
by Hamlyn Paperbacks
Copyright © 1982 by Aileen Armitage

Hamlyn Paperbacks are published by
The Hamlyn Publishing Group Ltd.,
Astronaut House,
Feltham, Middlesex, England.

Printed and bound in Great Britain by
Cox & Wyman Ltd, Reading

'Misled by fancy's meteor ray,
By passion driven;
But yet the light that led astray
Was light from Heaven.'

Jeremiah Burroughs: *The Vision*

1 : 1844

Snow drifted gently, fine and white, out of the February night, cloaking the harsh stone outlines of Thwaite Lodge in a silent white shroud. The lodge stood alone, aloof, on the outskirts of Hawksmoor, where Royal Lane curled its way up to the watchtower on the ridge of the hill.

Although well past midnight two windows in the lodge still glowed with light, one upstairs and one down. In the parlour Samuel Lumb, Inspector of Factories, sat gloomily by the low fire, a glass of brandy and water at his elbow and a copy of *The Times* lying unread on his lap. If ever a man was sorely vexed with troubles, it was he.

It was not his work that troubled him, but Adeline. Frail and petite when he had married her fourteen years ago, she was now even more fragile and far from well. Childbearing had not come as easily to her as to other women, and at this very moment she was upstairs endeavouring feebly to give birth for the eighth time. God grant she would be more successful this time, he prayed inwardly. Four babies in the past five years had been either stillborn or had lived all too briefly, and at thirty-eight Adeline was no longer young.

'Mr Lumb, sir?'

He looked up in surprise, not having heard the tap at the door. Miss Platt was standing there, her normally smoothly-coiled dark hair escaping in wisps from its pins. Her young face looked pale and drawn.

'Mr Lumb, I really don't think you need to wait up any longer, sir. Mrs Lumb is sleeping now. It won't arrive before morning, the midwife says, so there's really no need for you to miss a night's sleep.'

'Thank you, Miss Platt. I must confess I was dozing off where I sit. Hard going, is it?'

'So the midwife says, though, as you know, sir, I have no experience of confinements. I am sure all will be well in Mrs Dawson's capable hands, however.'

'I'm sure you're right. Goodnight, Miss Platt.'

When she had gone he drew his hunter wearily from his waistcoat pocket and bent closer to the light of the oil lamp. With difficulty he focussed on the hands of the watch. He was growing long-sighted, he realised sadly. He too was ageing. He must go and visit the spectacle-maker in Hawksmoor as soon as time and pressing business allowed.

A quarter to two. Miss Platt was right. He could still have a few hours' sleep before he would have to rise and go to the factory. She was a sensible girl, Cecily Platt, and he felt reassured by her capable presence. It was a lucky stroke finding her. Advertising for a nanny held its dangers, however good a woman's references might be, for her personality might not fit one's household, but Cecily Platt was a godsend. A farmer's daughter, she had all the calm, efficient competence he would expect of a girl brought up in the country, but she had the added attraction of having a mother who was gently-born. Hence the girl had been given a good education, and it was clear from her natural grace and refinement that she owed much to inherited gentility.

The doctor in Brighouse for whom she had last worked gave her an excellent reference, and in the six weeks she had been at Thwaite Lodge her behaviour had borne out every syllable. She had a firm, superior manner with the servants that was at the same time polite, and to her employers she was always deferential without losing her lady-like poise. During her mistress's indisposition she had run the menage so smoothly and efficiently that Samuel had hardly noticed any change. Indeed, if Miss Platt could care for the child that seemed so reluctant to be born as well as she did everything else, he would account himself a very fortunate man indeed.

He rose stiffly from his chair, lit a candle from the lamp and left the parlour. As he climbed the stairs, pulling his weight with the help of the sturdy mahogany balustrade, it occurred to him that if, God forbid, Adeline were not to survive this latest onslaught on her delicate frame, then Miss Platt would have the full responsibility of running his home. He would have to appoint her as housekeeper; that way Mrs Roebuck, the cook, would be obliged to accept her instructions. It was sad to have to plan for such an eventuality but one must be practical and prepare oneself. One had to face possibilities, however unpleasant. After all, if Adeline were to die, then it was God's will.

Once on the landing, Samuel Lumb headed as usual towards his own bedroom. At the doorway he remembered: while Adeline was occupied in childbirth he was relegated to the spare room. He sighed. The feather bed in the spare room was lumpy compared to that of the marital bed, and it was cold without Adeline at his side. He bent one ear close to the door and could hear deep, stertorous breathing. At that moment the door opened and the plump figure of Mrs Dawson emerged. She was wiping her hands on her apron, and with relief he saw that the apron was not bloodstained.

Mrs Dawson gave a tired smile. 'There's nowt happening yet, Mr Lumb. I've given Mrs Lumb a draught of laudanum and she'll sleep soundly till morning now. Then maybe it'll come.'

He looked at her warily. 'She's not in trouble, is she? I can soon send over for Dr Ramsden if he's needed.'

He saw the look of slight that leapt into the woman's eyes. 'Nay, there's no need, Mr Lumb. It's rest she needs, that's all, after all she's been trying. She's not strong, you know, and it took many an hour for the last one, if you recall.'

He did recall, and how puny and weak the creature was when he did arrive, so feeble he only lived five hours. Whether Mrs Dawson's professional pride was offended or not, he'd send for the doctor first thing in the morning, he decided, if Adeline still had not succeeded in bringing the child forth on her own. There was no shame in have recourse to the forceps.

'You go on to bed, sir,' Mrs Dawson urged. 'Miss Platt is sitting with the mistress while I go down to the kitchen to make a cup of tea. One of us will be close by all night and we'll

9

see you're called if there's owt happens.'

He lingered by the door. Despite her words he still felt uneasy. 'She's sleeping now, you say? How was she before she fell asleep? In much pain?' he asked stiffly. It was embarrassing for a man to have to talk about such feminine mysteries as childbirth.

'Well, as you know, sir, it's never easy for Mrs Lumb,' the midwife answered cautiously. 'The pains were coming fast and I thought we were on our way, but then she started to ramble, as if she'd forgotten what she was about. That's why I gave her the sleeping draught.'

'Rambling?' repeated Samuel Lumb in alarm. That was the very thing he dreaded. His wife's physical weakness he had learnt to accept, but just lately she had been showing signs of a weakness no man in his right mind would want to admit even to his closest friends. Absent-mindedness, he preferred to call it, when Adeline accused the chambermaid of stealing a lace-edged handkerchief which she later found in her own reticule. And again the day she drove in the carriage into Hawksmoor with Mary Jane and Elizabeth, sent the coachman home and then lost herself completely. Luckily a shopkeeper had sent word to Mr Lumb, who was able to fetch her, but he recalled how distracted she was, unable to remember her own name and not even recognising her own two little daughters. By the next day it was all forgotten and she was back to normal, but her little attacks of absent-mindedness did seem to recur more and more frequently these days.

'Rambling?' he repeated.

'Oh, only a little delirious because of the pains, sir. Women are often like that when they're having bad pain. She'll be fine by morning, you'll see. Could I have a light from your candle, sir?'

She took up a candlestick from the landing table and held it towards him. Samuel Lumb tilted his candle to light hers, and then turned away.

'Goodnight, sir. Sleep well,' Mrs Dawson called.

The spare room was small and sparsely furnished compared to his own room with the handsome white ash furniture he had had specially made for his wedding to Adeline. This was a cold room too, north-facing and exposed to that silent white onslaught of snow outside. No fire blazed in the tiny hearth, but under the bedcovers, he was relieved to find, Miss Platt had had the foresight to place two stone hot-water bottles. He undressed quickly and climbed into the high bed.

Beyond the reach of the hot-water bottles the sheets stretched cold, almost damp. Samuel curled his portly weight into as small an area as he could, hugging the warmth. Poor Adeline, he thought. Much as he missed her body's warmth close to his, he could feel pity for her in her plight, far worse than his. At this moment she slept in a brief respite from the pain and torment, but by morning her struggles would be renewed and there was nothing he could do to help her. Poor little woman, too frail for the fight. God grant her sufficient strength to endure and survive, he prayed. After all, the children needed her. Mary Jane at thirteen and Elizabeth a year younger had need of a mother yet, even though she was at times a little confused. Edward at ten was nearing the age to go away to school and did not need her so much, but the girls . . . He thought fondly of his two daughters, the elder so lively and pretty, the younger charming in her elfin way. But it was Edward who afforded him most joy. Adeline had done well then, providing Samuel with a son at last and one so sturdy and capable too. Edward would be a credit to him one day and with luck perhaps he would have a brother before long.

So long as it was not a baby brother who would soon join the other four babies in Longwood churchyard, thought Samuel. The little plot was filling rapidly with tiny unnamed Lumbs.

Samuel Lumb eventually drifted off into uneasy sleep. Dawn was peering through the tall, narrow window when he awoke and heard urgent voices in the passage outside. He rolled out of bed and pulled on his dressing gown before opening the door. Miss Platt, already dressed, was speaking to Mrs Dawson in a low, firm tone. In her hand she held a steel kitchen knife, long and pointed. She caught sight of her master across the midwife's shoulder. From behind the closed door of the bedroom came the low sound of Mrs Lumb moaning.

'You return to your patient, Mrs Dawson, and I'll put on the kettle. Good morning, Mr Lumb.'

The midwife's head swivelled around rapidly to face him. 'Oh, good morning, sir. You'll be glad to hear there are signs the baby is on his way at last. Shouldn't be long now.'

She bustled back into the bedroom. Miss Platt turned towards the stairs. 'Your breakfast will be ready in ten minutes, sir. I'll send Gladys up with your hot water.'

As he poured the water into the basin to wash, Samuel could hear his wife's moans. He must reach the factory by nine, but there was time to call at the doctor's house on the way and ask him to visit Thwaite Lodge. No harm in making sure, even if Mrs Dawson was offended. He stropped his razor and lifted it to his chin. The gleam of steel reminded him of the knife in Miss Platt's hand, and he shuddered. It must have been sharpened and brought upstairs for whatever the ritual was in birth, cutting the cord between mother and child he had heard. He was thankful he was a man, an engineer and not a doctor and thus spared the gory details of childbirth. Someone would find him at the mill to give him the news or he would hear when he climbed back up Royal Lane tonight.

Shaving completed, he dressed and went downstairs. The aroma of kippers and bacon filled the dining room and he lifted the tureens to sniff appreciatively. A man needed a good breakfast inside him before riding out in foul weather such as this.

It was at the moment that Samuel Lumb was sitting down at the table in the Pack Horse Inn in Hawksmoor to tuck into a succulent meat pasty for his lunch that Mrs Dawson drew forth the tiny child. She cut the cord with her scissors and handed it over quickly to Cecily Platt.

'Here, you take him. Mrs Lumb's pretty weak.'

She bent again to minister to her patient, who by now was almost unconscious. Cecily Platt looked at the minute, bloodstained creature in her hands in alarm. It was limp, pallid and not yet breathing.

'Slap him, for goodness' sake,' Mrs Dawson exhorted. 'Make him breathe, though for the life of me I can't see that one living for long. Like the last, I reckon.'

Cecily lifted one hand and slapped the tiny back. It seemed almost inhuman to hit a thing so fragile. At once a feeble squeak began, and the little limbs started to quiver. She could see pulsations under its skin as the blood flowed. It was a repulsive creature, naked like a newborn hairless rat and just as ugly. There was a gap in the bony skull where its brain throbbed visibly.

'It's a girl,' she told the midwife. 'She's breathing.'

Having cleaned the baby and wrapped her in a warm piece of blanket lying ready by the fire, she laid her in the wicker cot. Mrs Dawson paid the infant no more attention until her ministrations to the newly-delivered mother were complete. Mrs Lumb lay still now, struggles ended and her pale face wreathed in a vacant smile.

'You have a daughter, Mrs Lumb,' the midwife said loudly close to her ear. 'Another little daughter, three daughters now.'

Mrs Lumb's expression did not change. The midwife shrugged. 'It's no use, Miss Platt. She doesn't hear me. She could be drunk or drugged for all she knows of what's going on. Not built for it, you know. Three days in labour have driven her half-crazy and she were never quite all there before, if you ask me.'

She crossed to the cot and drew back the blanket to survey the baby. 'Wouldn't waste your time sewing or owt for this one, Miss Platt. She'll not last long. Why, she can't be more than four pounds or so. Too puny for this hard winter — she'll not survive it.'

Cecily Platt's chin rose. 'This may be my first confinement and first baby to care for, but if it's in my power to tend both mother and baby to health, then I'll do it. Just tell me what to do.'

Mrs Dawson clicked her tongue and shook her head. 'I tell you you're wasting your time, but if you don't then nobody else will. She's not capable.' She cocked her head towards the bed. 'Nice lady she were, but all the labours have scattered her wits. Why, I were telling you about that knife, weren't I, when Mr Lumb came out this morning.'

'You were,' replied Cecily cautiously. She was unsure whether she should encourage the woman to gossip but then she felt she ought to know all she could about this family she had come to work for. After all, if the mother was mentally incapacitated then all the more responsiblity was going to fall on her shoulders.

'I must have fallen asleep over my knitting, I reckon,' Mrs Dawson went on. 'I can't think how she did it without waking me. All I know is I woke up sudden-like and my ball of wool had fallen on the floor and rolled under the bed. I bent down to pick it up, and there was this knife. She must have crept down to the kitchen while I were asleep. Then she woke up too and saw me with this knife and she started ranting about murder and said the knife was hers and I shouldn't ought to have it. She were in quite a way, she were. Ranting rubbish and crying. Poor lady. I reckon the pain she's had all these last few days has been too much for her.'

Mrs Lumb lay with closed eyes, obviously unaware of what was being said. Perhaps she was sleeping now after all her efforts, thought Cecily. However, the knife incident was disturbing. A mistress who was absent-minded, even eccentric, she could cope with, but one who gave way to violent thoughts was quite another. But had Mrs Lumb contemplated violence when she took the knife? There was no reason to believe so, except her own reaction to seeing the knife again, when she cried out about murder.

Mrs Dawson voiced the thought that came into Cecily's mind. 'Do you think we ought to tell Mr Lumb about it? Happen he ought to be warned in case she does summat like that again.'

'I think not, Mrs Dawson,' Cecily replied crisply. For some reason she felt irritated by the midwife. 'I don't think it's necessary to alarm him unduly. He is not to be expected to understand that women sometimes do extreme and silly things when they're in pain.'

'True,' the older woman agreed. 'Men know nowt about

childbirth. Women do some funny things and seem like they're crazy. Why, I wish I had a shilling for every time I've heard a wife yell that it was her husband as brought all this on her and she wished she could inflict the same pain on him. Some of them could murder their husbands at that moment but the minute the baby's born they're all lovey and cooing again. Funny creatures, women in labour.'

'Yes, I'm sure you've had many experiences Mrs Dawson,' the nurse said politely. 'I think one of us should go down and see about sending word to Mr Lumb. Would you like me to do it?'

'Nay, I'll announce it,' the other said quickly. 'It's my place, seeing as I delivered it — alive, too.'

She bustled away, leaving Cecily to look down on the tiny creature in the cot. She lay there unmoving, but there was no placidity in her motionlessness. She was staring unseeingly with wan eyes, mucus dribbling from her nose. She looked ugly, almost repellent, like some goblin presaging ill, so devoid of any grace that Cecily felt guilty that she stirred no feeling of tenderness in her. A thing so frail and helpless should move one to compassion, particularly since she was not expected to live. Poor little soul, she thought, to come into the world with such difficulty, unlovable and unloved, only to quit it again so soon.

A sudden determination filled her. It was not fair for a child to be born with such enormous disadvantages, to a mother who would be incapable of doing anything to help her. She must not come and depart again as if she had never been, a tiny spark of humanity never registered by the rest of mankind. It was too cruel and unbearable. She, Cecily Platt, would fight to give the little thing a chance, even if it proved to be for only a short spell on earth, a chance to let that microscopic glimmer of a soul grow. She moved aside the blanket and lifted the child to her breast. The pallid little eyes seemed to swivel round to rest on her face.

A tiny arm, no thicker than Cecily's thumb, broke free from the blanket. Cecily touched the hand, marvelling at its translucent perfection. The tiny fingers closed tightly about her thumb.

It was as though the child was calling out to her, grasping the only link it had with life. Cecily's wonder crystallised into fierce determination. The child must live.

Mrs Lumb was murmuring, gazing around her in bewilderment. 'Where am I? Where's Mr Lumb?'

Cecily approached her, the child in her arms. 'You're in your own bed, Mrs Lumb, and you have a new baby daughter. Word is being sent to Mr Lumb. Here, take your little daughter and perhaps you can persuade her to feed.'

The woman's eyes focussed on the baby Cecily put in her arms, and for a moment she just stared. 'She's very small,' she murmured. 'Will she live?'

'If you feed her she'll soon grow,' Cecily reassured her. 'Here, let me help you unfasten your bodice.'

The baby seemed baffled and reluctant to feed, but at last its little mouth fastened on the nipple. Cecily breathed a sigh of relief. Its sucking was not vigorous and it soon gave up the effort, but it was a start. Mrs Dawson, just returned from the kitchen, watched its feeble efforts, her plump face betraying her evident lack of faith in the child's ability to live.

'What shall you name your little daughter, Mrs Lumb?' She addressed her patient brightly. Mrs Lumb smiled at the child's wizened face in a bemused fashion.

'Dear little thing. If she lives till my lying-in is over, I'll have her christened Constance, I think. That is, if Mr Lumb approves.'

'Constance. That's a pretty name,' Cecily remarked. 'Why not Constance Adeline, after you?'

'No, just Constance,' Mrs Lumb replied with unusual conviction. The midwife glanced across at Cecily, who read the meaning of her look. It warned that Mrs Lumb was evidently back in the land of the sane, for a time at least, and audible comment between midwife and nurse must no longer be frank and unrestrained.

'By the way, did you get up in the night, Mrs Lumb?' Cecily asked casually. The midwife's look showed alarm.

'Me, get up? Why, no,' the mistress replied in amazement. 'You don't get up in labour.'

'I thought I heard footsteps, that's all.' But that knife,

thought Cecily. It was no table-knife which could have fallen from Mrs Lumb's supper tray, but a finely sharpened one that Mrs Roebuck used specially for meat. Someone had brought it up to the bedroom, and no servant would have occasion to do so. Nor would Mr Lumb. That only left the crazed, bewildered Mrs Lumb, her aberration aggravated by labour pains. The laudanum must have only befuddled her without keeping her unconscious all night. Still, no harm had been done. An observant eye would have to be kept on the mistress but there was no need for the master to know.

Especially no need for him to be worried, she resolved later that night when she passed the parlour door, since the doctor had hard words for him. Mr Lumb had kissed his wife warmly when he came home and surveyed his newest child with evident distrust. Cecily could see he did not expect the pathetic little thing to live.

'Mr Lumb,' Dr Ramsden's deep voice intoned inside the parlour, 'you know your wife has had a gruelling time of it again. She is far from strong, as I have told you before, and I freely believe in the circumstances that it would be wiser not to subject her to the rigours of childbirth again.'

Cecily moved on, embarrassed not only for herself but for her master, too. Samuel Lumb, however, was not so fortunate. He was obliged to sit and listen to the doctor's acerbic words. He sat stiffly, hands clenched in his lap, mildly irratated at being thus admonished in his own parlour.

'Not only is your wife physically frail but from recent events it would appear that her mental state is not all that it should be. Again I must remind you, I would strongly advise no further pregnancies for her. After all, you have a son and two, no three, daughters now.'

Samuel endeavoured to change the subject. 'From what you tell me, the baby is not likely to survive the winter.'

The doctor cut in: 'That's very possible in view of its small size and weak condition after such a protracted delivery, but even so you have children already, including a son who is a fine, healthy boy. How old is he now?'

'Edward is nine, rising ten. The girls are twelve and thirteen.'

17

'And all healthy. You should count your blessings, Mr Lumb, and think of your wife. I know it is not easy but I strongly recommend adopting some preventive measures to ensure she does not become pregnant again, or great self-restraint on your part. I cannot answer for the consequences otherwise.'

Samuel Lumb grunted, the nearest he could bring himself to answering, and changed the subject. 'Let me offer you a glass of port, doctor, or madeira if you prefer, before you go. It's a foul night. The snow was drifting up the hillside as I came home.'

'Thank you, no.' Dr Ramsden rose. 'I'd best be on my way. But remember my advice, Mr Lumb. Think it over carefully.'

Samuel Lumb was still thinking about what the doctor had said when he made his heavy-hearted way upstairs to the spare room. A new child soon destined to die, a wife who was going insane and now this final blow: the warning to live celibate — for that was what it amounted to. It was un-thinkable, unnatural. A man had his desires, his conjugal rights too. And a man in his social position, churchwarden and member of the parish council, could not contemplate any woman other than his lawful wife. It was bad enough being deprived her warm closeness for the two weeks of her lying-in, but to sleep apart thereafter he could not contemplate. Nor would Adeline be able to understand it; in her simple mind the belief would grow that he had rejected her. She would doubtless cry and plead, so sharing the same bed was essential. But could he lie by her and remain chaste? That was asking too much of any man. No, he would just have to try to be more careful, to ensure she did not conceive again.

He sighed heavily as he undressed. Life was going to be very difficult, but of one thing he was sure. He was not going to acquaint himself too closely with that tiny, repulsive creature in the cot upstairs who was soon going to break Adeline's heart by dying just as the others had done. She could not protect herself against heartbreak, but Samuel could.

On the landing he paused. It was late but perhaps he should go in and see if Adeline was awake before he went to bed. The prospect of the spare room depressed him. It was small and cold and the bed far from comfortable. He turned the knob of Adeline's door quietly and peeped in. She was alone, sitting up in bed and wide awake, the pool of light from the oil lamp giving her fair head an enchanting golden aura.

'Awake, my love?' he queried. 'You should be fast asleep by now.'

'Something happened today, Samuel, but I can't remember what it was I had to tell you.'

He sighed. 'You had a baby, my dear, remember? A little girl. Have you thought of a name for her?'

'It was something odd, Samuel, so odd I remember thinking I must tell you about it. It was something unpleasant.'

'The baby was born, Adeline.' It was evidently so unpleasant that her poor mind refused to remember it, he thought. 'The baby was born, but it's all over now. You must sleep, my dear.'

'Something to do with blood,' she murmured, her pale eyes misting with the effort to remember. Samuel shuddered. He did not want to hear the grisly details of the birth.

'And a knife,' Adeline added, a glimmer of excitement beginning to spread across her drawn face. 'Yes, that's it, blood and a knife! I remember that much.'

Samuel sighed. 'I told you, my dear, it's all over and you must sleep. I'll see you in the morning. Goodnight, Adeline.'

As he closed the door behind him Samuel caught sight of Miss Platt emerging from the room next door, the nursery. She was carrying a stone hot-water jug. Evidently she had not expected to see anyone about at this hour, because she was wearing a dressing gown and her dark hair fell loose about her shoulders. Samuel could not help noting her slender waist and finely-curved bosom. She looked uncommonly pretty and girlish, far removed from the serenely capable nurse in cap and apron he was accustomed to. He reproached himself mentally for the unbidden sensation that leapt in him. She blushed.

'I was just going down to boil water to refill the bottle,' she offered by way of explanation. 'The nursery is bitterly cold although I've made up the fire.'

'That's right, keep yourself warm, Miss Platt,' he said with a degree of gruffness he had not intended.

'Oh, not for me, sir. For the baby. It's essential to keep her constantly warm if she is to live.'

'Oh yes, of course, quite. Goodnight, Miss Platt.'

It was as he turned away that Samuel heard Adeline's voice cry out, shrieking like a thing possessed, a creature out of Bedlam, and his blood turned cold at the sound.

'Blood and a knife, Samuel! Blood and a knife! Oh, God have pity on me! There's blood on the knife!'

2 : 1845

The deep snows that accompanied Constance Lumb's birth had receded and given way to a burgeoning spring and humid summer, then snows which buried the stolid outline of Thwaite Lodge once again. To Samuel Lumb's amazement the sickly baby not only still lived but was beginning to thrive.

It was all due to the constant care and vigilance of Cecily Platt, he was well aware. Day and night she had devoted herself tirelessly to the child's needs, going without sleep for nights on end when the occasion demanded and coaxing patiently when the baby was reluctant to take food.

'You must take care not to overtire yourself, Miss Platt,' Samuel admonished her when the situation was brought to his attention. 'We cannot afford to have you, too, ill in bed. How would we all fare if you were laid low?'

'Don't worry, sir,' Cecily Platt reassured him. 'I have

sufficient sense not to over-tax my strength. Besides, it gives me great pleasure and satisfaction.'

Samuel beamed. She was certainly achieving miracles. The child was actually beginning to look normal: flesh now covered the little bones, the face was fuller and less repugnant, and wisps of dark hair were starting to soften the bony skull. Even its eyes, once pallid and vacant, had now darkened to almost black and had a brightness about them which might even indicate incipient intelligence. Samuel was hugely relieved. Not only had they been spared another infant funeral due to Miss Platt's tenacity, but with luck they had been spared a cretin child too. He had tried in his gruff, laconic way to express his gratitude for her conscientiousness but Cecily Platt had simply bowed her head in acknowledgement of his tribute and bustled away on her next errand for the child. She was a marvellous young woman, so capable and so fresh-faced and attractive despite lost sleep. She would make some man a magnificent wife, Samuel mused. Luckily her opportunities to meet with gentlemen were few, so he was not likely to lose her yet. That was fortunate, especially in view of Adeline's deteriorating condition.

Dr Ramsden had given Samuel a reproachful look after he had examined her. 'Yes, I can confirm that Mrs Lumb is indeed pregnant,' he had said. 'I fear that it will not be easy for her, especially in view of the condition of her lungs. I suspect consumption.'

Adeline spent the spring mostly in bed in the spare room, where she was now more or less permanently installed. She had a nurse, whose duties were more those of guardian, because Adeline's behaviour was becoming completely irrational and unpredictable. Samuel had even deemed it necessary to have locks fitted to all the bedroom doors since Adeline had wandered into Mary Jane's room one night and terrified the poor fourteen-year-old by her wild manner, singing and shouting and not recognising her own daughter.

As spring wore on into summer Adeline's manner quietened and she appeared subdued, almost normal, as though even in her addled state she recognised that the birth ahead was going to be a terrible ordeal for her. Occasionally she even had brief periods of lucidity when she remembered the last birth.

'I had a little girl,' she told Samuel one evening after dinner as he sat by her bed. 'Where is she? Did she die?'

'That was Constance, my dear,' Samuel replied soothingly. 'No, she did not die, thanks to Miss Platt. She's a fine child now, and Miss Platt says she'll soon start to walk. She's almost fifteen months old and trying to take her first tottering steps.'

'I'm so glad,' Adeline murmured contentedly. 'I did not fail you altogether, then, Samuel.'

'No, of course not, my dear. Mary Jane is very pretty now and Elizabeth, though younger, is far cleverer in the school-room, the governess assures me. And Edward is a sturdy boy. I think I should be considering a good school for him. He needs the company of boys his own age.'

'And Constance? There is a big gap between Edward and Constance, isn't there? Still, the new baby should be company for her.'

Adeline's thoughts evidently drifted off to more ethereal planes and she forgot the baby Constance. Samuel saw the child when Miss Platt brought her down from the nursery before dinner but he found the solemn-eyed little mite hard to comprehend. Thin-featured, with those huge dark eyes, she looked at him with a solemnity that made him feel uncomfortable: an unprepossessing elfin creature with a penetrating look of untold wisdom. It was as though she could read his soul.

Adeline's time was near. Dr Ramsden said that it would be wisest for him to be present at the birth this time, not just Mrs Dawson.

'Of course,' agreed Samuel. 'Expense is no object, as you know, doctor. I'm very comfortably placed and Adeline must have the best.'

He knew the day had arrived when he returned from Balmforth's mill and was greeted by cries from upstairs. Adeline was in labour and the doctor had been sent for. Samuel retreated to the parlour until Miss Platt came to tell him dinner was ready. He looked up at her calm face and thought what a comfort her presence was. On an impulse he spoke as she turned to go.

'Miss Platt, would you dine with me in the dining room this evening instead of down in the kitchen? I have no wish to be alone at the moment.'

'Of course, sir.' She evinced no surprise or discomposure. He could not help admiring her perpetual poise. Miss Platt was already seated at the table when he entered the dining room.

Over soup and then haddock, no word passed between the two. Over the apple duff and custard, Miss Platt took it upon herself to intrude on her employer's thoughts.

'You will no doubt be pleased to learn, Mr Lumb, that little Constance has at last taken her first steps unaided today,' she ventured.

'Really?' Samuel replied abstractedly. 'Very good.'

'Yes. It must have been six or seven steps before she stumbled. Even then she didn't fall. She clutched at the handle of the nursery door and steadied herself, as though waiting for me to open it. One could almost think she was heading there to await the new baby.'

'Indeed,' said Samuel. She was an uncommonly pretty girl when her eyes lit up like that.

'It should be here quite shortly, I understand,' Miss Platt went on. 'Mrs Dawson says Mrs Lumb seems to be progressing far better than last time.'

'I'm mightily relieved to hear it. Would you like some more custard, Miss Platt?'

'Thank you, no, sir. It is high time I went back upstairs.'

She was right. By midnight Adeline's shrieks grew to a crescendo and then a silence. A thin wail from the upper regions announced the baby's arrival. Samuel held his breath until the doctor came downstairs.

'All's well, Mr Lumb. Your wife co-operated well despite her infirmity, and she and the child are well. You have a son, Mr Lumb.'

Samuel could not believe his luck. 'A son? Will he live, doctor?'

'There's no reason why not. He's small but healthy, and now the fine summer weather is here he has an excellent chance. I've handed him over to that splendid nanny of yours. She's done wonders for the little girl.'

'Yes, it's all credit to Miss Platt's devoted care that Constance is thriving. I have every faith in her, doctor.'

'Splendid. Well, I'll look in again in the morning to see how Mrs Lumb is faring. We must make certain fever does not set in.'

Samuel paid a quick visit to his wife first before inspecting his new son. She was lying in bed looking pale and ethereal, even pretty with her fair hair loose about her shoulders. She smiled at him weakly.

'Have you seen him, Samuel? He's beautiful,' she murmured.

'Not yet, my love. You must sleep and grow strong.'

'What shall we name him? Samuel, after you? Or Francis, your second name? I rather like Henry.'

'William,' her husband replied, 'after my father.'

'Very well, dear. William Lumb.' Adeline turned a happy face into the pillow, evidently content that the problem was resolved. By next morning her brief interval of clarity had relapsed into a cloud of confusion again. She had forgotten all about having just given birth to a son.

Samuel accounted himself reasonably lucky in the circumstances. At least Adeline had not raved as she had the night Constance was born, ranting about blood and knives and the like. The birth had been uneventful enough for the good doctor not to take him to task again. And the redoubtable Miss Platt had carried his new son off to the nursery where Samuel could be certain she would give him every care. Bless that girl — she was indispensable, especially since it was now abundantly clear Adeline would never again be capable of running the house.

The morning after the birth the family and servants assembled as always in the parlour at eight for prayers. Samuel read the lesson and offered up a prayer of sincere thanks for the safe delivery. Over his spectacles he caught the movement when Mary Jane nudged Elizabeth. Miss Platt,

24

standing close to Mrs Roebuck, saw it too and frowned. He must have a word privately with Miss Platt about taking the conduct of those two girls in hand, he decided. She would know how to cope with it more smoothly and unobtrusively than the governess.

Before the servants were dismissed Samuel gave them a brief lecture on the virtues of industrious behaviour and the sinfulness of waste in the kitchen. When he gave a nod they all filed out, and he raised a finger for Miss Platt to remain.

She stood listening to him dutifully, hands clasped before her. He could not help admiring the gleam of her smoothly-coiled dark head where the sunlight fell upon it.

'I shall speak to them, sir. I'll do what I can,' she said when he had done.

He smiled. 'I knew I could rely upon you, Miss Platt. You are a truly loyal and devoted servant, a prize above jewels.'

He was surprised at his own involuntary flight of poetic praise but she only bowed her head and withdrew, completely unflustered. She took compliments almost as though they were her due, he noted, like a queen accepting treasures from a would-be suitor.

He pushed the mildly wicked thought from his mind. That was no way for the churchwarden to think. Perhaps it was well that Miss Platt's duties with her two young charges kept her so fully occupied upstairs that she rarely appeared at Mr Lumb's dining table. Nevertheless, with Adeline more or less permanently confined to her room, he would have welcomed Miss Platt's feminine company.

Adeline was becoming an embarrassment. One Monday morning he was about to set off for Holroyd's Mill when suddenly there was uproar. Kitty, one of the maids, came running downstairs into the hallway where Samuel was pulling on his greatcoat. From above he could hear Adeline screeching.

'It wasn't me, sir, honest it wasn't,' Kitty cried, and he could see how red-faced she was.

'What wasn't, Kitty? Have you upset your mistress?' he demanded.

'No, sir, not me. She says someone has stolen her diamond necklace, but it wasn't me! I didn't even know she had one.'

'Get on with your work, girl.' Samuel too, knew that Adeline possessed no diamond necklace.

By nightfall when he came home Adeline had no recollection of the morning's incident. It was Miss Platt who explained.

'It was her Whitby jet, sir. She put it away herself and forgot where she had put it. I found it for her in her bedside drawer.'

Samuel sighed. Adeline accused the servants often these days of stealing from her, and in her dazed state the sparkle of jet probably differed little from diamonds. The furore did not die down so easily, however, when she took a sudden dislike to roast veal and accused cook of trying to poison her. It took hours and the promise of a day off to visit her mother to pacify the indignant Mrs Roebuck.

The realisation that Adeline's illness was rapidly becoming a stigma was borne home to Samuel when Frederick Holroyd, the owner of Holroyd's Mill, referred to her condition in tones of obviously patronising pity for Samuel.

'Such a pity to have your wife *hors de combat* for so long, Lumb,' said the millowner, fondling his walrus moustache. 'Must be damnably disappointing not to be able to entertain or even to go calling socially. Can't be very helpful to you. Such a shame.'

Until that moment Samuel had not been aware that social invitations to members of the Lumb family had become markedly infrequent. It was then too that he began to register the pitying looks of the other members of the parish council. His self-esteem began to dwindle. Something would have to be done to save face, or the high regard in which he had always been held in the district would vanish for ever.

It was a situation which called for careful thought and tactful action. Samuel Lumb was not a man to act precipitately, for that was not how his reputation for judicious opinion had been created. Careful, deliberate thought was essential, preferably tempered by the judgement of others whose opinion he valued. Alone in the parlour at night,

Samuel sat at the rosewood escritoire and dipped his pen in the inkstand, then wiped the pen tip clean again with the embroidered pen-wiper Mary Jane had worked so lovingly for him last Christmas. Another dip, and then he was ready.

'*My dear brother,*' he wrote to Reginald Lumb, a highly-respected draper in Harrogate. Reginald, his elder by three years, was, if anything, more cautious than his brother. He would give a considered opinion.

Samuel scratched out an opening paragraph greeting his brother, enquiring as to his and his family's welfare, and conveying the news that his own family prospered. Then he plunged into the question of Adeline without preamble, incapable as he was of hedging or hinting. Recognising that he wrote with bluntness, he consoled himself that Reginald would recognise it for his characteristic honesty.

'To be frank,' he wrote, to confirm the impression, '*I fear she becomes daily more and more of a problem. I have resolved, therefore, that the solution must lie in one of two paths — either to send Adeline away or to remove the entire family to a place where we are not known.*'

There, now it was out. Once he had written the words, the thought no longer seemed such a betrayal of Adeline. He could hardly discuss the matter with her; it would be disloyal to turn to a local friend; of the servants only Miss Platt could be counted upon for objective comment, and somehow to speak to her was unthinkable. But Reginald, good old reliable brother Reginald, he would help clear the mist of doubt and confusion.

Reginald's reply took over two weeks but when it at last arrived Samuel was content. Reginald made no bones about the solution. To disrupt the whole family and weaken Samuel's chances of promotion by moving away was unrealistic and impractical in the extreme, he said. The simplest answer by far was to find a place in the country for Adeline — a congenial place, of course, where she would be well cared for with all the comforts of home. Far enough away for privacy, he advocated, but not too far for the occasional visit.

'*This, my dear brother,*' wrote Reginald in his ponderous hand, '*would seem by far the most sensible solution. I fully appreciate your dilemma and recommend this course of action to spare yourself and the family any further discomfort.*'

Samuel was satisfied. The matter was settled and all that remained now was to find a home where Adeline would be well cared for. If the thought flickered into his mind that her departure might well throw him into closer contact with Miss Platt, he instantly thrust it out again. All he allowed himself to contemplate was the thought that he would have to make the nanny's position in the household official by appointing her as housekeeper cum nanny. It afforded him a secret pleasure to know that she would accept the new responsibility with her customary dedication, and that she would be even more tied to the Lumb household.

Down in the kitchen Mrs Roebuck called her retinue together to sit down at the long table for supper. Smiling with pride so that her plump face creased into many wrinkles, she served up the boiled potatoes and the cold remains of the beef.

'That's the last of my boiled beef Mrs Lumb'll eat for a while,' she remarked as she passed a plate to Joe, the boot-boy. 'Have you got all her packing done ready for the morning, Kitty?'

'Aye, I think, unless Miss Platt finds owt else,' the girl replied, then casting a quick glance over her shoulder to ensure the lady was not there she added, 'she's fussier nor ever now the master's made her housekeeper. Sharp as a needle before, she were, but now there's no pleasing her.'

'Come now, Kitty,' the cook admonished her, conscious that it was not a maid's place to criticise her superiors or the staff. 'No speaking out of turn in my kitchen, if you don't mind.' She spoke the words kindly because she shared Kitty's view.

'Pity the poor lady has to be sent away,' Kitty opined, 'though she can be a handful at times.'

'Best thing the master could do if he's to hold his head up

in Hawksmoor,' replied the bootboy gruffly.

'And who called for your opinion, my lad?' demanded Mrs Roebuck. 'You'd be better thinking about fetching more coal up from the cellar after supper before it's needed upstairs. And while you're down there you can fetch me up another cheese.'

'That's Kitty's job!' he protested.

'In my kitchen I give the orders, and I say you fetch it. And that's the end of it.'

Kitty was smirking when Miss Platt came in and took her place at table.

'I'm sorry I'm late, Mrs Roebuck,' she said quietly. 'Mr Lumb wanted me to go over some accounts with him.'

Mrs Roebuck grunted, aware that the ceremonies were being observed. Miss Platt was tacitly admitting that Mrs Roebuck, as cook, was in charge of the nether regions of Thwaite Lodge, and therefore apologies were due for being late to a meal. Until now, Mrs Roebuck in turn had recognised Miss Platt as reigning supreme on the second floor, the region of the nursery, but now she was unsure where she stood. Miss Platt was housekeeper, superior to them all despite having been there only two years compared to Mrs Roebuck's fourteen. And Miss Platt's reference to the accounts was undoubtedly her oblique way of pointing out her newly-acquired superiority. Mrs Roebuck gritted her teeth and passed a plate to her with a forced smile.

'No matter, Miss Platt. It's cold beef anyway. Would you like some of my pickles with it?'

If the rest of the assembled staff hoped to hear the housekeeper's verdict about Mrs Lumb's departure the following day, they were doomed to disappointment. They made side-long references to it themselves — Kitty admiring the new nightdresses purchased for her mistress and Joe the bootboy complaining about the number of valises already waiting in the hallway for him to carry out — but Miss Platt maintained a discreet silence throughout. Mrs Roebuck admired her reserve, but at the same time she was irritated by her reticence. She was well aware that until Miss Platt revealed her position she trod dangerous ground, a veritable battlefield in the tacit war that must inevitably ensue until one or other woman had gained the advantage. Mrs Roebuck, at least twenty years the elder, knew she had a better advantage by virtue of her age and far longer experience, but Miss Platt was a shrewd and poised opponent. Moreover, the master smiled upon her.

'How will the babies take it when their mother leaves?' Mrs Roebuck ventured to ask casually as she poured tea from the huge earthenware pot. 'Master William is too young to notice, of course, but what of Miss Constance?'

Miss Platt spooned sugar into her cup with quick, neat movements. 'No more than Master William, I fancy, for she has spent little time with her mother. It is the older ones, Miss Mary Jane and Miss Elizabeth and Master Edward, who are more likely to miss her.'

Kitty giggled and Mrs Roebuck darted her a fierce look though she read what the giggle meant. The eldest three, at fifteen, fourteen and twelve, had barely recognised their sickly mother's existence for years. They might be aware of the absence of sudden screams and pandemonium over the latest incident once she was gone, but they would mourn no motherly hugs and kisses.

Early next morning, directly after family prayers, the carriage was brought to the front door of the lodge and Joe loaded the valises. A slight drizzle of rain was falling as Samuel Lumb helped his wife totter weakly down the steps and into the carriage. Of the children there was no sign. Only the housekeeper, Miss Platt, was standing on the doorstep to watch the carriage pull away, while Kitty and Mrs Roebuck were peering up through the railings from the basement kitchen. The cook could not help a wayward tear, which she quickly wiped away with the corner of her huge apron.

'Poor lady, I do hope the family where she's going'll be kind to her. I wonder if she'll ever come back to Thwaite Lodge?'

'Shouldn't think so,' said Kitty with youthful callousness. 'She's old, isn't she, and quite batty.'

'She's only forty,' the cook protested, but inwardly she

agreed with the kitchenmaid. Mrs Lumb was old and decidedly mad. 'Now off upstairs with you, lass, and strip her bed.'

For Cecily Platt the next three years slipped by almost imperceptibly. She was kept so busy running the Lumb household and caring devotedly for the two little ones that she had little time to notice or regret the passage of time. She was contented enough. Her work afforded her satisfaction, and so did the enhanced salary Mr Lumb had insisted on paying her when her promoted her to housekeeper.

There were other perks, too, When Mr Lumb's brother, Mr Reginald Lumb, and his plump, amiable wife Bertha came to stay at Christmas, Mr Lumb had asked his sister-in-law to dispose of many of Mrs Lumb's clothes.

'She has little need of dresses now,' he had remarked, 'and she has a plentiful supply of nightdresses and dressing gowns.'

Mrs Bertha Lumb had enlisted Miss Platt's help in the selection of the dresses to be disposed of – only a few she had insisted, in case Mrs Lumb were to become well enough to return home – and in the course of examining the gowns she had noticed how close they were to Miss Platt's size.

'It would be folly to throw them out if they would fit you, Miss Platt. Please take them. You can always dispose of them if they are not to your taste or do not fit.'

Cecily had not thrown them away. They not only fitted her to perfection but they were also of a quality she herself could never have afforded. Mr Lumb always provided his family with the best. And if Mrs Roebuck recognised the gowns, she had the wit to hold her tongue. Cecily Platt revelled in the silent superiority she gained over the cook in her new plumes.

Mrs Lumb had been brought home from time to time, but only for a few days on each visit. Her presence threw the whole household into chaos on account of her bizarre behaviour, and uneasy peace settled again over the lodge only when she had gone.

The older children only shrugged their shoulders and

forgot her again, although Samuel Lumb insisted that they pray for their sick mama daily at morning prayers. The little ones, however, Cecily noted, surveyed the shrieking woman with evident alarm and consternation, the five-year-old Constance with dark-eyed fear and little William with all the terror of a child confronted by the bogey-man of his nightmares.

'Is that really our mother?' Constance asked quietly after the creature had gone. 'Are mothers like that?'

William's fair head lifted from the lead soldiers he was playing with on the nursery floor. Cecily could see he feared the answer.

'She is very sick, my dears. Mothers are usually kind and loving people who look after you, dry your tears and hug you. It is sad that your mama is sick and cannot do that.'

'You do that,' said William. 'You kiss me better when I fall and you love me, don't you, Nanny?'

'To be sure I do.' And in William's case Cecily was sincere. He was small and fair and lovable, his firm little body rounded and cuddly, but Constance was another matter. Fifteen months older, she was thin-boned and angular, sparse black hair framing a solemn, rather sallow little face. Her black eyes watched everything and revealed little. With a long, thin nose and sombre lips she had little to endear her to anyone. Certainly the grown children had no time for her and precious little for William.

Mr Lumb sought their company rarely either, so the two young ones were isolated in Cecily's care most of the time. Since she herself had often to be absent downstairs to fulfil her duties, the two were left much in each other's company. It was plain to Cecily that the little boy adored his big sister and she in turn kept a maternal eye on him. Constance was unnaturally mature for a child of five.

But that was no reason to fret, thought Cecily. At least it made life easier than having a harum-scarum child in the nursery leading the smaller one into mischief. Constance could so easily have been like her elder brother, Edward, who now, at the age of fifteen, was proving rather more than a handful for his father. Mr Lumb's patience was wearing out.

'Now look here, young man,' she had heard Mr Lumb's stern voice in the parlour last night, 'I intend to deal severely with your insolence and rebellion. According to the reports from your tutor he finds you difficult, stubborn and unco-operative, and that is a reputation I will not permit in a son of mine. I intend, therefore, to send you away to a military college where you will be taught the meaning of discipline.'

'Just as you sent Mama away when she proved difficult,' the boy retorted, and Cecily held her breath. Mr Lumb was a just man but this insolent accusation might tempt him to strike his son, though she had never known him to raise a hand against one of his children while she had been there.

'Enough, sir. Go to bed. I shall write to the college and ask Miss Platt to prepare your clothes for packing. Goodnight.'

Samuel Lumb's self-control was impressive, Cecily thought. She turned to find Constance half-way down the stairs, her black eyes wide as Edward emerged from the parlour and ran past them.

'What are you doing here, Constance? Back upstairs with you this instant!' Cecily said reprovingly.

The child gazed up at her. 'Is Papa really sending Edward away, too? He can't, oh! he won't, will he, Miss Platt?'

'That's for your papa to decide, Constance. Now come along, upstairs with you. It's almost time for your bath.'

But for the next two weeks, while battle raged between father and son, Cecily repeatedly found the little solemn-eyed girl crouched on the stairs, listening to the heated debate. Scolding her gently, Cecily led her back to the nursery but she could not stem the child's evident and ardent admiration of the big brother who dared to argue with authority.

'Edward said to Papa he would not go to a school for soldiers, whatever Papa says,' she said, her black eyes bright with wondering acclaim. 'He said he loved ships and the sea and would only go to a school like that!'

'Then he's a very forward young man,' Miss Platt replied. 'He should be glad to do what your papa proposes. Your papa only wants what is best for all of you. He's a very concerned and kind papa.'

'I suppose so,' the little one admitted, 'but sometimes he frightens me when he snorts and shouts.'

'That's not fear, Constance, but respect. Children should both love and respect their parents.'

Constance put her dark head to one side and considered. 'Then Edward doesn't respect Papa. He's not frightened when he shouts at all.'

'He's very rude. I hope you will never be rude and answer back. I'm sure little William won't,' the nanny remarked. Constance looked across at her small brother in the cot.

'No, William won't. He's very sweet and gentle.' She laid a finger on his forehead to smooth back a wayward blond curl. 'He always does as I tell him because he loves me.'

Cecily Platt smiled. It was pleasant to see the girl betraying affection for someone, because she was normally so quiet and undemonstrative. Never once could Cecily remember her winding her little arms about her nanny's neck the way William did. He was by far the more lovable and cuddlesome of the two.

Next day Mr Lumb announced to the assembled servants and family at morning prayers that young Master Edward was to leave in three days to go to naval college. Cecily saw little Constance's expression grow starry-eyed.

'He's won, Miss Platt!' she enthused after Mr Lumb had left the parlour. 'Edward has won! Papa is not so strong and terrible after all!'

'Sshh, Constance! Of course he's not. He has made that decision, that is all.'

'No, Miss Platt. Edward has beaten him.' With a proud look of quiet triumph the little girl preceded her up the stairs to the nursery. That black-eyed expression haunted Miss Platt for the rest of the day.

3 : 1853

Cecily Platt's face was glowing from the effort of briskly towelling down her two little charges and from the proximity of the nursery fire. She knelt beside the zinc bathtub rubbing Constance's thin back.

'Hurry up now, William, into your nightshirt before you get cold,' she admonished the other child, who was crouching by the fireguard. 'And you too, Constance. See who can be ready first.'

The fair little boy rushed to grab his nightshirt from the bed where it lay ready, but Constance moved slowly and deliberately. It was typical of her, thought Cecily. She never demonstrated the usual exuberance of a child, unlike William. He was tractable, easy to lead and control, but his older sister always maintained a distant aloofness, as though obedience was a matter of necessity but not to be carried out with enthusiasm or alacrity.

'Shall I brush your hair for you, Constance?' Cecily offered. It was a permanent battle, trying to penetrate the child's reserve.

'Thank you, no. I'll do it myself.'

No one could come near the child, not Cecily nor the maid nor her father. Not that Mr Lumb tried very often — he was far too occupied with other matters to concern himself with nursery affairs. No one could touch Constance — she seemed to have an aversion to physical contact, and her shivering while Cecily was towelling her dry was not entirely due to the chill in the air.

Both children at last brushed and clean, they knelt at their respective bedsides. Cecily surveyed the two little heads, the dark one of the nine-year old and the blond one of her brother over a year younger. By candlelight they looked angelic, she mused, as pious and amenable as cherubs should be. Cecily could never quite place what it was about the solemn-eyed Constance that troubled her, but of one thing she was sure — she could not feel the same warm affection for her that she did for William.

Even the governess, Miss Fairclough, who came in daily to tutor the children had hinted the same. Not openly, in so many words, for Dora Fairclough had all the prim preciseness and attention to decorum of a well-trained governess of fifty.

'So anxious to please, little William, even if he is dreadfully careless at times,' she had remarked. 'Unlike Constance. I don't think she always listens attentively but she hands over an exercise with the same assurance as if she knew it all. And she doesn't. A daydreamer, that one, but it's hard to catch her out.'

Cecily knew just what the governess meant. The child was on the surface dutiful, rarely disobeying, but she sensed a latent defiance in her attitude. Constance's black eyes would rest on her in a most disconcerting way, as though she could read her very soul. She was deep and dark, that one, a stark contrast to her sunny, transparent brother.

And the difference between the children troubled Cecily. William, so malleable and obviously adoring of his sister, was vulnerable. Sunny by nature, he could easily be upset by anyone's displeasure, and especially Constance's. He was emotionally a prey to anyone who was unscrupulous enough to work on him, and at times Cecily feared that Constance, young though she was, was aware of it. She could only hope that the deep affection which obviously existed between the two children would serve to counteract it.

'Amen,' said William with satisfaction when prayers were finished. His sister murmured a quieter *amen*.

'Into bed with you,' said Cecily. She tucked them up, then gave Constance a swift peck on an averted cheek and another, accompanied by a hug, to William. 'Now I'll blow out the candle and I want you both to go straight to sleep, no talking.

Good night, children, and God bless.'

'Good night, Nanny,' William answered sleepily. From Constance there was no sound. Cecily Platt snuffed out the candle then went out, closing the nursery door behind her.

A lingering scent of wax drifted through the nursery, mingling with the smell of carbolic soap. William wriggled and made wincing noises, reluctant to defy Nanny's command of silence and yet anxious to attract his sister's attention.

Constance broke the rule for him. 'Whatever's the matter, William?'

'It's this new woolly nightshirt – it makes me itch. I like my old one better,' he confided in a whisper. 'I'll never be able to sleep in this.'

'Nor shall I tonight.'

'Why? Is yours scratchy too, Constance?'

'No,' Constance murmured, her voice charged with that air of mystery that always enthralled him. 'But I shan't sleep.'

'Why then?'

'Because I can feel something is strange. You know how I can feel things, William.'

The boy sat up in bed, wide-eyed and full of admiration for his sister's mystical sensitivity. 'Can you? What is it, Constance? Not the spirit of Aunt Sarah again, is it? I can't bear that.'

'No, silly. It's something to do with Mama.'

'Oh.' The boy fell silent, reluctant to talk of a subject which always induced a sudden hush when it was mentioned downstairs. He hardly remembered Mama, no more than a chillingly odd character who used to visit years ago and shrieked. Sometimes the common children of the town would waylay him in Royal Lane and call out jeering comments about him having a crazy mother in the loony-bin, and it hurt. He wished Constance would not feel things about Mama. It was vaguely disquieting, especially in the darkness of the nursery with Nanny's reassuring voice gone.

'Do you hear me, William?' Constance's distant voice persisted. 'There's something strange about Mama.'

'Yes, but we've always known that.'

'No, this is different. Do you know what the date is?'

William thought for a moment. 'The twenty-second.'

'Yes, and that's Mama's birthday. I was looking at my old diary today, that's how I know. And you remember Papa always used to ask Miss Fairclough to make us write a letter to Mama on her birthday.'

'Oh, yes, I remember.' Indeed, he could remember still how he had chewed the tip of his pen in the effort to think up pleasant and congratulatory messages to a stranger. It had been very difficult – was it really a year ago? Yes, it was, for he recalled he was wearing his first pair of breeches, bought for him at Easter in Hawksmoor by Papa. Nanny had scolded him soundly for dripping a blob of ink on them while he laboured over that letter.

'No one has mentioned Mama or her birthday this year,' Constance said with emphasis 'There must be a reason.'

William shivered at the ominous tone in her voice. 'Don't talk about it any more, Connie,' he pleaded. 'Tell me a story about ships and pirates instead.'

'Very well, but mark what I say, William. There is something strange about Mama.' And she plunged obligingly into a tale of freebooting adventure that soon captivated her little brother and made him forget about Mama. Tales of ships and the sea were the children's secret delight once Nanny had left them, stirring tales of adventure in which big brother Edward always played a heroic part.

'Is Edward really very tall and broad-shouldered?' William would ask. 'I hardly remember.'

'Oh yes, and strong as an ox.' Constance, too, had only a hazy memory of Edward's appearance, but a vivid recollection of the way he had stood up to Papa four years ago. Fifteen then, he must be a handsome hero by now.

William fell asleep before the tale was ended, and next day, once lessons were over, he begged Constance to tell him again what happened. 'I must know Connie – did Edward outwit the wicked pirate-captain and get safely past the giant crocodile? Oh, do tell me!'

'All right, but not here. Let's slip out through the rhododendron bushes into the fields. We could go up to the tower and I'll tell you there. No telling Miss Platt, though, that we're going out, remember.'

William scarcely needed the warning, for he knew full well that Miss Platt would forbid them to go. The boundary of the gardens of Thwaite Lodge were the limits of their freedom, but long ago the children had learnt the secret gap in the bushes that led to the expanse of grey, heather-swept fields. And on occasion they had escaped further, to the wild, bleak moor where the squat old watch tower stood sentinel on the ridge.

After lunch they sneaked away, when Miss Fairclough had finished eating in the schoolroom and gone, and Miss Platt was down in the kitchen with Mrs Roebuck, having ascertained that the children preferred to play out in the garden and were suitably wrapped up in mufflers and gloves. Constance led the way through the boundary bushes, William following with a heart pounding in excitement.

Constance raced ahead across the fields, her thin legs carrying her swift as a racehorse. William, panting, cried out: 'Wait for me, Connie! You're going too fast!'

At last, where the dry-stone wall marked the edge of the field and the beginning of the steep rise to the tower, she stopped to wait. William came up puffing and blowing.

'Hurry up, slowcoach,' Constance exhorted, 'otherwise we won't have much time before we have to go back.'

Stoically he trudged up the slippery incline behind her, tripping over the rocky projections and slithering on their wet surface. When they finally arrived at the summit of the ridge William collapsed on the wiry grass.

'Not here, William! Let's go to the tower.'

Obediently he rose and followed her. He knew the ritual. If sightseers were on the tower they would linger until the strangers had gone and then climb the narrow flight of stone steps that circled it to the top. There, sheltered by the low stone parapet, they would sit and talk, exchange secrets too private for the nursery, and perhaps eat a forbidden biscuit or two if Constance had managed to smuggle them out. It was a precious time, the two of them alone with no prying adults, and the more to be treasured because it was forbidden escape. It added an element of danger which made his blood tingle. Constance looked so calm and self-possessed he could only gaze at her in admiration. Nothing ever frightened Connie.

There was not a soul about. The grey spring skies were beginning to blow droplets of rain in their faces as they climbed the tower. William sat down but Constance remained standing, staring out over the parapet into the distance.

'Tell me the rest of the story, Connie,' William pleaded.

'Shush. I'm looking.'

She stood immobile for so long that William scrambled to his feet. Looking out to see what she was watching, he could see nothing. Only the grey slate roofs of the houses below, and beyond them the mist-shrouded outlines of mill chimneys in the valley. Apart from a coal barge with its weary grey horse moving slowly along a leaden canal, there was nothing of interest.

'What are you looking at, Connie? What do you see?'

Her dark eyes were veiled in thought. 'I see the moors, the great wide spaces where one is free, not the smoky town down there. Up there, the other way, the air is clean and beautiful, the heather springs under your feet and the wind whistles round the rocks. We'll go there soon, William, you and I.'

He did not care for her in this mood, her gaze abstracted and far-away. She was still his adored Connie, of course, but something in her manner inspired awe in him, fear even, for he could not understand. He tugged at her sleeve fretfully. 'You promised to tell me the story,' he complained.

'So I will. Sit down by me.' And suddenly she was her beloved self again, warm, maternal and loving.

So for the next hour the children sat close together, unaware of the drizzle, with their arms about each other. There, on the exposed roof of the tower they squatted alone, cut off from the rest of an alien world, absorbed in each other. When at last they stretched stiff limbs and rose to go home, William took Constance's hand in his.

'I'm so glad I have you, Connie. You're the only friend I

have in the world.'

'And you mine. We'll always be best friends, William.'

The little boy trotted home content. Even Nanny's scolding about their damp overcoats left him unmoved for once. He regarded Miss Platt with a feeling of compassion. *She* didn't have a best friend to share an illicit outing or an exciting story, poor thing.

The next day in the schoolroom William sneezed. Miss Fairclough looked over her pince-nez reprovingly. 'Caught a chill, William? Playing outside in the rain, perhaps?'

The boy coloured, but Constance's expression remained imperturbable.

'No, Miss Fairclough,' he stammered, terrified lest their secret be discovered. Luckily the governess found other faults to pursue.

'For heaven's sake sit up straight, boy! I shall have to put my ruler down inside your jacket again if you can't remember. Now, conjugate the verb *amo*, present indicative, and don't look at Constance for the answer.'

Over lunch in the nursery William sneezed again. He saw Constance scowl at him as Miss Platt looked up from her plate in concern.

'Oh dear!' she commented. 'I think perhaps you had better stay indoors this afternoon, William. And Constance, too, since you seem to have lost your appetite. We can't have you fading away.'

'It's only because I don't like liver,' the girl replied coolly.

'Don't like? Good heavens, my dear, there are hundreds of poor children far worse off than you, literally starving in fact, who would give a great deal to have your lovely liver and onions.'

'Then let them eat it,' Constance murmured. William stared at her, open-mouthed, aghast at her words. Such defiance would surely provoke terrible wrath and a possible report to Papa.

'You're certainly not well, Constance,' Nanny said smoothly. 'A couple of days indoors and a dose of brimstone and treacle will soon put you right. Finished, William?

41

You'll eat prunes and custard now even if Constance doesn't, won't you?'

Connie was admirable, thought William, the way she stoically endured the indignity of the revolting decoction of brimstone and treacle for the next three days, but what with an intervening weekend and then Miss Platt's preparations to go on holiday to visit her mother, a week had passed before the prospect of that adventurous trip up to the moor became possible. Lizzie, who had taken over Miss Platt's responsibilities as nanny, was a far more indulgent and kindly supervisor. Truth to tell, she had a mid-afternoon assignation with an admirer in the village, and the children's request to stray out into the fields on a sunny afternoon fitted in with her plans admirably.

'Mind now,' she warned as she tied on her bonnet, 'don't let any of the others know, specially that Miss Fairclough. She's a sharp tongue, that one, when she's a mind to it and she might tell your Papa. He looks fair bothered today, so I shouldn't vex him if I were you.'

The children needed no further admonition, for they had noted their father's furrowed brow at prayers that morning. They scampered away across the fields, up the cliff face and along the ridge towards the open moors.

Constance ran headlong across the wiry heather, pulling off her bonnet so that her long black hair streamed in the wind. Her black eyes glowed with a fire William had never seen before.

'Don't you feel it, Willy, a kind of freedom and space we never feel at home? It's wild and beautiful, and oh! so free!'

He ran and leapt after her, gradually rousing to the same fever-pitch of excitement in the wild abandon of leaping and running unchecked. He revelled in the gusts of wind flapping his breeches and stinging his cheeks, and he adored Constance because she was the only creature in the world who could produce such delirious exuberance in him.

Suddenly she stopped by an outcrop of gaunt grey rock and, turning to him, she flung thin arms about him, hugging him close. 'Oh, Willy! Swear to me that we shall always be as close as we are now. No one else matters, only us, and we'll love each other till death. Swear it, Willy.'

He gazed up into her fiery black eyes, nonplussed by her vehemence but trusting and adoring. 'I swear, Connie,' he said.

'And I swear too!' She gripped his hands so tightly that it hurt, her eyes blazing. Then she broke away suddenly and, laughing shrilly, ran away over the moor. Her laughter, borne on the wind, floated back to the boy and he shivered. It was cold up on the exposed moor despite the spring sunshine.

Miss Fairclough was standing at the kitchen door when they returned, her expression so troubled that the children knew at once that something was wrong.

'I've been looking for you everywhere,' she muttered seizing both by the shoulder. She neither explained why she was still at the lodge at this time of day nor enquired where they had been. Something was evidently very wrong. 'Your father wishes to see you both in his study immediately.'

Papa was standing by the window, gazing out over the shrubbery. At their entrance he turned, grim-faced. Fear clutched at William's heart. Retribution, swift and terrible, was about to descend on them for their misdeeds.

'Ah, Constance and William, I'm afraid I have sad news to impart to you,' he began soberly. 'I have already informed your sisters and they are bearing it with composure. Now I must ask you both to be strong and bear in mind that God's will must be accepted with fortitude.'

William stared, uncomprehending. It was Constance who spoke. 'Is it Mama?'

'Yes, my dear. I regret to have to tell you she died yesterday. I have sent word to Edward and I expect his superior officer will give him leave to return for the funeral. I have also sent word to Miss Platt.'

He looked hard at his son and daughter, and William felt uncomfortable. He did not know exactly how he was expected to react to the news. He took his cue from Connie, who stood erect and dry-eyed. Papa had not looked so closely at them in years.

'I am glad to see you take the sad news so well, children,'

he said quietly. 'Do not be ashamed if you must weep in private for your poor mama. We are all human. Go now.'

In the nursery, William again looked to Connie for a lead in this novel situation. Lizze had not yet returned from her rendezvous so they were alone for a few minutes.

'Shall you weep, Connie? Did you love Mama?' he asked.

The girl shook her head gravely. 'We did not know her, so how can we mourn her? Other children love their mother dearly, but all we knew of Mama was that she was mad. We are different from other children, Willie. They don't like us because they knew about her. She made us different.'

William nodded. He remembered with hurt the times the village children had pursued them, cat-calling and jeering: *'Thy mother's in the loony-bin! Thou art crazy too! Willy Lumb and Connie Lumb, mad as hatters!'*

That had set them apart from other children, as well as the fact that Mr Lumb considered it unsuitable for his children to associate with those of mill-workers. Unfitting to his position as an inspector, he had said, so all his family had been reared away from the contagion of working-class children.

Secretly William could feel no grief, only a growing sense of excitement as the lodge began to bustle with preparations for Mama's burial. A funeral was a new and exciting experience – Papa's black-edged cards to be sent out in black-edged envelopes; the postman returning bearing many letters of condolence; new black clothes to be measured and tailored within days; and then the arrival of big brother Edward, gloriously resplendent in naval uniform. Although Constance said little, William could see how her black eyes rounded in admiration as she gazed upon her elder brother, and for a moment William experienced a twinge of jealousy. Connie was *his*, and he was not prepared to share her with Edward, but then Edward would soon be gone again, and besides they had sworn to remain best friends for ever.

It was the day before the funeral that unmanned William. Miss Platt, hurriedly returned from her mother's home, stood at the nursery door looking taller and more remote than ever in severe black moiré.

'Come downstairs, children. Your papa wishes you to say goodbye to your mother.'

William had seen the men from the window carrying in a long black box, but it was only when he entered the parlour with Constance that he realised its significance. The box lay along the table, its brass handles gleaming in the lamplight, and Papa was standing looking down into it.

'Your mama looks very serene, Constance. Come close and kiss her goodbye as she goes on her journey to the angels.'

William stood terrified as Constance approached the table and stepped on the low footstool. He could not bear to visualise what lay inside the box, and he felt sick. Constance bent her dark head over it and slowly straightened, then stepped down.

'Now you, William.'

Longing for flight, the boy nerved himself for the ordeal. After all, Connie had done it. He moved forward and stepped up, hardly daring to look.

A woman, grey-haired and drawn, lay there. She was a stranger, not the pale-haired vision he remembered but an old woman draped in white and cradled in white satin. Her skin was grey, and his whole being rebelled at the thought of touching his lips to that grey, lifeless thing in there. He looked up at his father helplessly.

'Go on, William.' Papa's voice was stern and there was no way out. Summoning up all his courage the boy closed his eyes, gritted his teeth and bent down. For a fraction of a second his lips touched on substance that felt like ice-cold marble, and his stomach heaved.

'God rest her soul in eternal peace,' Papa murmured.

'Amen,' he heard Connie say.

'God grant you will see your mama again one day in a happier world,' Papa went on. 'Work and pray hard, my children, to be worthy of heaven when your time comes. Go now.'

Relief flooded William as they turned to go, and he was glad of Connie's firm grip on his hand. Outside the parlour door he stood shaking.

'We won't have to see her again, will we?' he whispered.

She smiled. 'No. Tomorrow they'll put her in the ground, bury her like we buried the kitten, remember?'

That had been fun, he recollected, for it was a strange kitten they had found dead under the shrubbery and Connie had enacted an elaborate ritual for its burial in a cardboard box, complete with candles and water she'd sprinkled, saying it was holy water she herself had blessed and sanctified. If a proper funeral was at all like that then tomorrow held no fears. The nasty part was over. William felt considerably happier.

Next morning the whole family and staff assembled as usual in the parlour for prayers, and William was relieved to see that the coffin now had a lid on it. Papa did not read a text from the Holy Book today, since the family and servants were to re-assemble later when the cortège would make its way down to the churchyard.

At eleven o'clock, William stood silently behind Mary Jane, Elizabeth, Connie and Uncle Reginald and his family while Papa and Edward stood by the window watching.

'I fear it's beginning to rain,' Edward remarked. William heard Aunt Bertha start to sob quietly.

'Here they come now,' said Papa. The family began to leave the room, and William found Connie's hand again sneaking into his.

In the vestibule the servants were waiting, Mrs Roebuck sniffing into her handkerchief and Lizzie staring at Aunt Bertha's crape-veiled bonnet. Miss Platt stood unobtrusively by the door to the kitchens, her eyes downcast. She did not look up as four men in black frock coats and tall draped black hats entered the house and went out again solemnly bearing the coffin. William could just see through the open doorway when they slid the box slowly into the big black hearse and covered it with spring flowers.

It was exciting riding in the carriage behind four horses as shiny and black as Aunt Bertha's jet necklace, their tall black plumes dancing as they moved. The service in church was not so entertaining as Connie's kitten-burial had been, and the last part, standing in the drizzling rain while the big black box was lowered into a muddy hole was no fun at all. Connie evidently thought so too, for she looked very solemn and pale. It wasn't so bad that Aunt Bertha needed to weep so noisily, however. Trust a woman to make a fuss — Aunt Bertha was prone to do things like that, and the worst part was yet to come, he discovered, when they returned home. A meal of veal and ham sandwiches and sultana cake lay waiting on the table where the black box had so recently resided.

Aunt Bertha had thrown back her black veil to sip tea, revealing reddened, bloodshot eyes, which lingered on William. 'How old is the baby now?' she asked Samuel Lumb.

'No baby, Bertha, my dear. He's nearly eight.'

She put down her cup suddenly and rushed over to William, flinging her arms about him so that he was almost smothered in her ample breasts. 'Poor little mite!' she cried. 'To be orphaned so young, it's tragic!'

Uncle Reginald prised his wife away. 'Come now, Bertha. He's not an orphan at all.'

'You know what I mean, Reginald. To have no mother and him so young, and Constance too. It's so sad.'

'I'm sure we can rely upon Samuel to see they want for nothing, nonetheless. Isn't that so, Samuel?'

Reassured, Aunt Bertha stopped her sobbing and nibbled a sandwich. William, rescued from her embrace, tucked into the sultana cake and wished fervently that he and Connie could be invited to eat downstairs more often.

4

Samuel Lumb sat in his parlour on a pleasant summer evening, watching contentedly as Miss Platt rearranged in a pewter vase the sweet-smelling roses she had just brought in from the garden.

'Evening is the best time to cut roses,' she explained, as she moved a delicate pink one to nestle alongside a crimson beauty. He could not help admiring her graceful movements.

'They smell wonderful,' he remarked. And so did she, he thought. There was always a delicate aroma of something vaguely floral when she came close. She was as alluring and seductive as any rose, with her slender grace and slow, warm smile. He longed to pluck her but he must hold his peace. Only three months had passed since Adeline was laid to rest.

'It is comforting to have you here to run my home so capably,' he murmured, and was encouraged by her smile. 'Let's see, it's how long now I have depended on you? Over nine years, it must be, for you came when Constance was born.'

'That's right, sir. Nine years last February.'

'And in all that time you have never failed me. So dependable, always calm and cheerful. A man needs a woman like you.'

'I am honoured, Mr Lumb, that you see me so. It is a great pleasure for me to see to all your needs.'

Was it his imagination that she seemed to stress the words oddly, he wondered, or wishful thinking? He pursued his point. 'A helpmeet in my need, that's what you are and always have been, my dear, and my gratitude knows no bounds.'

'You've always been very kind to me, sir, and if I can be your handmaiden, as it were, I am at your disposal.'

Her eyes were meekly downcast but Samuel Lumb could not resist the leap of hope in his heart at her encouraging manner. He ventured on. 'A mother to my children, for the young ones have known no other mother but you.'

'That's true, sir; indeed I dare to claim that little Constance would not have survived had I not been here. She's like my own child to me.'

'How very true! And little William adores you, too, that's plain to see. Here, sit with me a while and I'll ring for some tea.'

She lowered herself so gracefully into the chair that Samuel ached to seize her, to span his hands around that slender waist and feel again the touch of soft, yielding flesh. He had had to stifle his own natural desires for so long, that it came to him in a joyous flash that now he was free to recognise them again. Miss Platt never looked more demure and enticing.

When the maid had brought the tea tray and left, Miss Platt poured out from the china teapot into the two china cups and passed one to her master. Samuel took hold of the saucer and leaned towards her. She did not let go but looked at him, her wide grey eyes inches from his own.

'Miss Platt — or may I call you Cecily?'

'By all means, sir. We have known each other long enough.'

'Cecily, what do you say to a man of turned fifty proposing to a young lady some twenty years his junior?'

'Why not, sir? That the husband is older brings a great deal of maturity and wisdom to the marriage. A young lady would be wise to consider those advantages.'

His heart swelled in hope. She was a shrewd young woman and must know what he was driving at. The children, though — would they present a problem? Five of them, and of such disparate ages too.

'And if the gentleman has been married before and has a family?' he suggested.

'Ah, then that presents a problem.'

His hopes sank. If she saw his five children as an impediment, then there was no hope for him.

'If the children love the lady and are prepared to accept her as their new mama, all is well: but if they do not accept her, then the marriage could well be doomed,' Cecily Platt pronounced. 'The children would always be a barrier between husband and wife.'

He seized on it. 'My children love you dearly, Cecily.'

She inclined her dark head. 'The young ones, to be sure, but what of Elizabeth and Mary Jane — and Edward?'

He was hardly listening, enraptured by the thought that she had recognised they were speaking of themselves. She was, however obliquely, discussing the possibility of marrying him! He was forced to exercise again the self-discipline of years to resist the impulse to seize her. He spoke in a matter-of-fact tone that belied the agitation within.

'Elizabeth, once I have planned it, will soon leave Thwaite Lodge to be married herself. After all, she is twenty-two years old and it's high time she was wed. Likewise Mary Jane who also has an admirer. Edward we can discount — he's never at home anyway, and it's likely he'll be sent overseas soon. Which leaves the little ones, and I know they'll be delighted to have you officially as their mama after all these years. I see no problem, Cecily.'

'Are you sure? They know me as Nanny and as your housekeeper. Can you be sure?'

'Quite certain. And as for marrying my housekeeper, well I know you're not penniless, so no one could believe you had ulterior motives, my dear.'

'No, I have my own private income which, together with my salary, keeps me comfortably,' she agreed. The curve of her fingers around the handle of the teacup was driving him insane. He leaned forward again and laid his hand on hers. She did not flutter or grow agitated as other women would, and Samuel Lumb loved her for it.

'Cecily, my dear, would you do me the honour of consenting to be my wife?'

Her grey eyes met his directly. 'Yes, sir, I will, and I too am honoured that you should ask me.'

'Capital!' He slapped his thigh exuberantly, still fighting

the impulse to grab hold of her. 'Let us seal the bargain with a kiss then, my love, and we'll tell the family after dinner.'

She turned her face up to his, her eyes closed, and with a murmur of satisfaction Samuel felt her cool lips under his. A coolness he would warm to heat before many weeks were out, he promised himself, and the prospect afforded him great pleasure. Another gratifying thought followed fast upon it — not only would he savour the joys of the connubial bed once again, but his thrifty move would save him a housekeeper's salary too.

It was Mary Jane who broke the news to the two youngest Lumb children as she sat sewing in the conservatory.

'Have you heard, Constance, that Elizabeth and I are not the only ones sewing for our marriage chests?' she said, and winced as she pricked her finger. Constance looked at her enquiringly but made no answer. She knew how big sister Mary Jane, with the superiority of years, liked to tease.

'Well, have you heard or not?' Mary Jane demanded. 'I'm sure you must have heard something from the servants because they see it as the juiciest bit of gossip in years.'

'I've heard nothing, Mary Jane. I don't know what gossip you mean.'

Mary Jane sighed. 'I suppose you're far too young to be interested in such things and I suppose Papa will tell you in his own good time.'

She peered closely at her needlework to see if the prick had caused a bloodstain. By rights she should wear the spectacles Papa had had specially made by the spectacle-maker for her, but vanity prevented her from wearing them and obscuring her fair, fluffy prettiness.

Constance, her curiosity aroused, came to stand by her chair. 'What gossip? Do tell me, Mary Jane.'

Her sister frowned at her before recollecting that frowns made ugly wrinkles. 'Curiosity killed the cat, Constance,' she scolded.

'But you spoke of it first. Do tell, please.'

Mary Jane considered for a moment. 'Well, all right, but don't tell that you know. Promise.'

'I promise. What is it?'

'Papa told Elizabeth and me this morning that he is to marry Miss Platt very soon. There, what do you think of that?'

Constance's jaw sagged. 'Marry Miss Platt? Oh, you're teasing me again, Mary Jane, I know you are.'

The older girl laid her sewing aside. 'I'm not, I swear! Elizabeth and I could hardly believe it, but there it is. In a few weeks Miss Platt will be the new Mrs Lumb, mistress of Thwaite Lodge. Things have turned out rather well for her, I'd say.'

'Don't you mind? So soon after Mama's death?' The child's voice was charged with scandalised incredulity.

Her sister shrugged. 'Three months, three years, what's the difference. Papa probably feels he needs a mother for you and William, and it's a convenient arrangement since Miss Platt brought you both up anyway.' She giggled as another thought crossed her mind. 'I know who won't be pleased, however, and that's Miss Fairclough. She always regarded Miss Platt as a rival, and it won't please her one little bit to have to call Miss Platt ma'am and acknowledge her as mistress. I'm longing to see her face when she finds out. Where are you going Constance?'

'To the nursery. I must find William.'

'Well, remember what I said and don't let on I told you. Papa probably wants to announce it to you himself.'

'I won't. I promise.'

In the nursery William watched his sister's face, clouded and angry, and wondered why the news upset her so.

'How could he! How dare he!' Constance fumed. 'He can't marry Nanny!'

'Why is that so bad, Connie? She's quite nice.'

His sister turned and glared at him. 'You don't understand, Willy. She's a *servant*, that's what she is, and she has no right to marry Papa! And he . . .' There was a catch in her voice and William, not understanding but knowing she was miserable, put his hand on hers.

Constance managed a faint smile, though he could see

unshed tears glittering in her eyes. 'If Papa needed comfort, why didn't he turn to us, Willy?' she murmured.

He shrugged. 'Because we're children, I suppose. After all, what difference will it make? She lives here in any case.'

'But as a servant, don't you see? Soon we'll have to call her *Mama*!'

William sat stunned. 'Mama? But she isn't our Mama. She's dead.'

'Yes. And I for one will never call Miss Platt *Mama*, whatever Papa says,' Constance muttered fiercely.

William, loyal as ever and still overwhelmed at the thought of Nanny becoming mistress of Thwaite Lodge agreed heartily. 'Nor shall I, Connie. I like her but I'll never love her as I love you. What are you doing with your doll's house?'

She did not answer for she could not. Turbulent emotions were tumbling in her, filling her with fury and hate. She took the front wall off the large wooden house and began moving the peg-dolls inside. The one dressed as a man she removed from the bedroom to the study and the black-gowned female figure in the nursery she tossed out on to the floor.

'She'll never be our mother, never, never!'

Samuel Lumb reckoned he had reason to feel content. The older girls seemed quite to welcome the idea of his re-marriage, and he guessed that was probably because he would then start to entertain again in a way he had not been able to for ten years and more. Cecily would make a delightful hostess at his table, he thought with pleasure, so charming and gracious that he would be the envy of his colleagues.

Edward's reaction he did not yet know, for there had been no reply to his letter, but there was no reason to believe that he would be any less pleased than Elizabeth and Mary Jane. The little ones, Constance and William, had shown no feeling one way or the other, probably because they were too young to understand. Cecily, however, seemed a little dubious about their silence.

'I'm not very happy about it, Samuel,' she said as they sat alone together in the parlour. 'Constance was never one to show her feelings but William is different. I think he takes a

53

lead from her.'

'Then all you need to do is to ask Constance to be your bridesmaid and you've won her over,' said Samuel. Problems were easily resolved if one took decisive action. 'After all, no little girl can resist dressing up in a fine new dress. She'll be enchanted.'

'What a splendid idea! Samuel, you are so clever!'

It was only later that evening, after she had tucked the children into bed, that Cecily Platt found the peg doll on the nursery floor. She picked it up and regarded it curiously. A clothes-peg from the kitchen swathed in a scrap of black moiré, it was evidently a female doll. But the unpleasant fact that gave Cecily a shiver was that transfixed through the belly of the doll was Lizzie's hatpin.

A week later Constance stood in the parlour while the dress-maker fussed about her, pinning and tacking lengths of cornflower blue silk. Miss Platt stood by watching critically.

'Higher at the neck, I think, Mrs Parkin. Constance is far too young for décolleté. Not too tight at the waist either.'

Constance stood still, fuming internally. It was terrible enough to be forced to attend the wedding without having to submit to being dressed like a peg doll at Miss Platt's will. The housekeeper's keen grey eyes were watching closely and Constance tried hard not to betray her feelings.

'For goodness sake, keep still, Constance,' Miss Platt said firmly. 'It's hard enough for Mrs Parkin without you wriggling like an eel.'

'You'd wriggle if you had pins stuck in you,' the girl muttered.

'What's this? Are you being insolent, Constance?'

'It's the truth!' Constance exploded. 'She stuck a pin in my arm!'

'An accident, I'm sure,' replied Miss Platt calmly while Mrs Parkin began to cluck apologies. 'A little patience is all that is needed and in a few days Mrs Parkin will bring your lovely new dress. You'll look beautiful at church.'

'No I won't! Blue doesn't suit me and it was you who chose it, not me,' Constance snapped.

Miss Platt smiled at the dressmaker. 'The excitement has quite over-tired the child,' she explained. 'She'll adore the dress, I know, but I think perhaps that's enough for today. How is my gown coming along?'

Constance escaped gladly from the layers of silk while the women talked happily of cream brocade and lace trimming and pearl buttons. They were so engrossed that out in the vestibule she hesitated. What she needed more than anything at this moment, even more than William's company, was space and solitude and fresh air to think. No need of a coat since the sun was warm. No one about, since Papa was at work and the servants occupied elsewhere — it was all too easy to slip out into the garden undetected, and from there through the shrubbery and away.

The air was so pure and clean up on the moors! It was as though she could shrug off all her pent-up resentment and fury along with the smoke and grime below in the valley. She looked down over its roofs, grey and lifeless despite the sunlight, and felt a flicker of compassion for all the poor souls locked down there, William and Papa included. But she could feel no compassion for Miss Platt in her cool dignity and her composure which no one could ruffle. Only a smouldering, hate-filled resentment which she knew would burn in her forever.

For over an hour she walked over the purple heather, stopping to caress the sun-warmed rocks and filling her lungs with cool, clean air. This was where she belonged, alone and free and close to some great force she could not name. It was not God, was it? Whatever it was she could sense its nearness and its power, and in its rays she felt her soul restored and made whole again. At last she made her way downhill.

The day of the wedding dawned as bright and clear as any bride could wish, and Cecily Platt was highly content as Mrs Parkin helped her to dress and put the final stitches into the bridal gown.

'Oh, Miss Platt! You look truly regal!' the dressmaker enthused, and as Cecily surveyed her reflection in the long pier glass she silently agreed. Her dark hair, smoothly coiled, gleamed from the vigorous brushing she had given it and looked magnificent crowned with its tiny cap of Honiton lace spattered with pearls. And the rich ivory gown with its train enhanced her slenderness and made her seem taller and more graceful than ever. The low satin slippers would ensure she did not appear taller than her bridegroom.

She picked up from the dressing table the strand of pearls Samuel had given her as a wedding gift. They, and the spray of thornless roses lying on the bed, would complete the picture and she knew her husband-to-be would be more than gratified when she took her place at his side before the altar within the next hour. Everything was as perfect as it could be.

Mrs Parkin was looking out of the window. 'Mr Lumb is ready to leave,' she said excitedly. 'He looks magnificent, and Master Edward too in his uniform! Oh, what a lovely wedding it's going to be!'

Satisfied that her preparations were complete, the dressmaker bustled away to join the servants waiting below. Cecily Platt looked around her small, sparse bedroom for the last time and smiled to herself. When she returned to Thwaite Lodge this afternoon it would be as Mrs Lumb, mistress of the house, to a beautifully refurbished double bedroom on the first floor whose redecoration she herself had supervised. Lizzie could take over this room on the second floor next to the nursery.

That the servants assembled in the vestibule to watch her leave for the church had assembled there only weeks ago to watch the first Mrs Lumb leave in her coffin did not occur to Cecily's matter-of-fact mind. Yesterday was yesterday; it was today and tomorrow that mattered.

The wedding, she reflected afterwards, had gone off without a hitch. Mrs Platt, her mother, had looked as dignified and regal as her daughter when she left the church on the arm of Frederick Balton, Cecily's banker uncle. No one could deny that the new Mrs Lumb was not her husband's equal even if she had once been his housekeeper.

'Constance, you performed your duties beautifully,' she commended the child afterwards, but the girl had simply looked at her with those inscrutable black eyes. It was impossible to tell what she felt, but there was plenty of time ahead to win her trust and confidence. Edward had to return to his college immediately after the wedding. His surliness was a clear indication of his distaste and it was a great relief that he was shortly to set sail for the Indies.

Elizabeth and Mary Jane presented no problem – they would soon marry and leave the nest. Only Constance and William would remain. The thought occurred to Cecily that Thwaite Lodge, remote and somewhat neglected, would be far too large for the family and it might be possible to persuade Samuel to move to a smaller, better-quality house in Hawksmoor where there would be more activity and entertainment. At an opportune moment, soon after Samuel had extinguished the bedside candle, she broached the subject.

'Don't you think it's an idea to consider, my dear?' she coaxed.

To her pleasure and surprise Samuel was more than responsive. 'An excellent idea, my love, and very worthy of your sensible and practical nature.' He began to untie the strings at the neck of her nightgown.

She stayed his hand. 'Just outside the town, I thought. Edgerton is becoming a very popular area for a gentleman of distinction.'

'Not Edgerton,' he murmured into her hair.

'No? Well, Gledholt then. It's very pretty there overlooking all those lovely parklands.'

'Nor Gledholt,' he muttered as the nightdress proved intractable. Cecily realised she must move swiftly.

'Very well then, dear. You tell me where you prefer, please, dear.'

He sighed and lay back on his pillow. 'I was going to tell you later. However, have you noticed how events often seem to happen in a run?'

'How do you mean, Samuel?'

'Well, life seems to go on for years in the same old pattern, day in, day out, unchanging, and then suddenly everything seems to start happening all at once.'

His wife's death. The wedding. Edward being sent

abroad. But there was evidently something else. By his air of suppressed excitement she guessed it was pleasurable.

'Yes, dear. It is often so.'

'And now at last, I've got my promotion today,' he breathed happily. 'I'm to be Chief Inspector.'

'Samuel, how splendid! And how well you deserve it!' she enthused. His arms slid round her again.

'There's just one thing, Cecily. It will mean moving, near the coast. Not yet, but in the spring. Shall you mind?'

'Mind? I shall be delighted, my dear, and think how good it will be for the children, sea air instead of smoke. Oh, Samuel! They will be so excited!'

'Dear Cecily, to think of the children first. I am a lucky man indeed.' And Samuel Lumb went on to prove the depth of his love and appreciation of his wife.

Some weeks later, Constance and William were bidden to join the grown-ups for dinner in the dining room as a special treat. The occasion was in celebration of Edward's having passed out as an officer, and he was home on leave.

'Doesn't he look splendid!' Constance whispered to William as she gazed up at her elder brother's tall breadth, resplendent in shiny-buttoned uniform and braid. With his laughing, handsome face and fair hair close-cropped beneath his cap, he appeared to her like some kind of demi-god. 'You too will grow up to look like him, William, one day soon.'

William stared, entranced at the prospect of turning overnight into an Adonis, and inwardly resolved to be as deserving of Connie's admiration as Edward was. The two children watched and listened eagerly to his every word.

Samuel Lumb, too, was highly pleased with his son. 'You've done well, Edward,' he said across the table as the maid poured soup, 'and I hope you will continue to reflect glory on the name of Lumb.'

'I'm sure he will, dear,' murmured his wife. Edward cast her a swift dismissive glance.

'I shall do my best, Papa. I'm looking forward no end to seeing all those exotic, far-away places. What an adventure it will be!'

'Do you know anything of the Indies?' asked Cecily.

'Of course, ma'am. I have been reading books about them.'

Samuel dipped his spoon in the soup. 'Ah, Edward, I don't think you can go on calling Mrs Lumb ma'am. Why not call her Mama?'

Constance looked up from her plate quickly and saw Edward redden. Cecily Lumb smiled at him. 'It's not so difficult once you get used to it. Elizabeth and Mary Jane do and I think the little ones are learning to get their tongues around it. Isn't that so, William?'

'Yes, Mama,' said William dutifully, and felt Connie's quick nudge with her toe.

'I'm sorry, ma'am,' Edward muttered. Constance felt inwardly angered. Why could he not say aloud what they both felt? Papa's new wife she might be, but their mother, never!

Samuel Lumb must have been aware of the air of tension around his family dinner table, for he at once changed the subject and asked Edward whether young Ormerod, the mill-owner's son, newly commissioned, was also Indies-bound. By the end of the meal the moment of embarrassment was forgotten, and when Cecily rose to see the children up to bed while the gentlemen drank their port, only Constance regretted that more had not been said.

Bathed and brushed and nightgowned, Constance was permitted to go down to say goodnight.

'Don't forget now, say goodnight to the master and mistress separate and remember to call Mrs Lumb Mama,' Lizzie reminded her firmly. At the bottom of the stairs Constance saw the parlourmaid hovering outside the dining room door. As Constance approached she laid a finger to her lips.

'I wouldn't go in if I were thee, Miss Constance. I were going in to make up the fire but I dursn't. Master's very angry.'

Constance hesitated. Her father's voice came clearly through the mahogany door, controlled but clearly angry: 'So let's have done with your insolence, Edward. Remember that she is mistress of Thwaite Lodge and my wife, and she shall have the respect due to her.'

'Which is not a great deal, Papa.' Edward's voice too was controlled but Constance could detect the bitterness in his tone.

'What do you mean by that, young man?' Papa demanded.

'What I say. She commands little respect from me, whatever you may think of her, and precious little in the neighbourhood, I'll be bound. The servants and everyone who knows you must see her for what she is – a shrewd, conniving opportunist! You're a laughing stock, Papa. Take her to wife if you must, but do not submit us to the indignity of calling that woman Mama!'

Constance clasped her hands together, her eyes shining in admiration, but she was fearful of Papa's explosive reaction.

Again his voice ran clearly through the door. 'You forget, Edward, as my wife she is also your stepmother. Call her Stepmama, if you will, but you must spare her embarrassment. I insist.'

'Embarrassment for her? And what of us? We have always known her as Miss Platt, the nanny. How can you expect the little ones, especially, suddenly to see her no longer as a servant but instead as our mother? So soon after Mama's death too. It's not only embarrassing, it's shameful!'

Samuel Lumb's voice was ice-cold with fury. 'Leave this house, Edward. Leave first thing in the morning and tell no one why. In her present delicate condition the knowledge of what you have said could have serious consequences for – for Mrs Lumb. Go quickly and quietly, and do not return until you have apologised to me. God speed you on your voyage, but do not return to Thwaite Lodge.'

The parlourmaid clapped a hand to her mouth. 'Ooh! Delicate condition!' she exclaimed, and fled towards the kitchen. Constance too ran upstairs before the dining room door should open.

William was already asleep, and Constance lay awake a long time re-living what she had overheard. Edward was a hero. The way he had stood up to Papa and spoken his mind was magnificent; if only she had more years to her advantage so she could emulate him.

And what did Papa mean about Miss Platt being in a delicate condition? She had not appeared at all ill at dinner but just as flowing and healthy as always. Perhaps he was pretending, to persuade Edward to be kinder to her and call her Mama, but if so, Edward had not been stupid enough to be deceived. He had stuck to his opinion bravely — what a gallant officer he would be when faced with the enemy at sea!

Next morning Edward was gone and the lodge was a gloomy, oppressive place without his bright, brave presence. Constance hid her sadness even from William. It was a relief, almost, when Miss Fairclough made her unpick the stitches of her sampler for the third time and she was able to make an excuse of having pricked her thumb badly to shed a few tears.

'Come along now, Miss Constance. Stop feeling so sorry for yourself,' the governess said primly. 'Make your stitches neat and fine and there will be no need to keep unpicking. Slipshod ways do not pay, as you must learn.'

That night more tears slid from under Constance's eyelids as she lay in her bed. Life seemed so dismal, with Edward gone in disgrace and Papa so engrossed in Miss Platt. William heard her sniff and, scrambling out of his own bed, he slid in beside her, cuddling close. His warm, sturdy little body was reassuring.

'What's wrong, Connie? Why are you crying?'

She told him about Edward. 'One day we will break free of this place like him, William. We can only pray that we too will be as strong and brave as our brother,' she murmured into his fair curls. 'We must strive hard to be like him and in the meantime, to trust no one but each other. We must keep faith with each other always, you and I.'

'Of course, Connie.' He was not quite sure what keeping faith meant, but if it meant being loyal to Connie and following her even to the ends of the earth, then he would willingly keep faith. With his chubby arms about her neck and her salt tears on his cheek, he fell asleep.

5: 1854

Gloom and discontent seemed to Constance to settle over Thwaite Lodge as relentlessly as the winter snows that enveloped it and obscured the distant moors from sight. By spring there was a feverish air of activity and the place sprang to life again.

Elizabeth was soon to be married, Lizzie revealed, to that weak-chinned James Ormerod, who had been a constant afternoon caller ever since he came on a visit with his father at Christmas.

'Your papa is very pleased,' Lizzie confided, 'so perhaps you will be a bridesmaid again soon.'

'I don't want to be a bridesmaid,' Constance said scornfully. 'I hate weddings!'

'Go on with you! You'll be a bride yourself one day, I've no doubt,' smiled Lizzie.

'Not me. I'll never marry!'

Lizzie was not to be deterred. 'And just think, if Miss Elizabeth has babies when she's married, you'll be an aunt. And little William will be Uncle William.'

Constance thought. 'And Papa will be a grandpapa.'

Lizzie chuckled. 'I doubt the mistress will welcome being a grandmama, though.'

'But she won't be. Miss Platt is not Elizabeth's mother,' Constance said, so sharply that William looked up.

'And she's not Miss Platt — she's Mrs Lumb,' said Lizzie. 'You must never let her hear you say that.'

'She's Miss Platt and always will be,' said Constance, with a conviction that indicated the matter was closed. Lizzie sighed and continued laying the nursery table for tea.

It was not only the forthcoming wedding that gave rise to so much activity. Samuel and Cecily kept making frequent trips away from home for a few days at a time and the vestibule seemed to be constantly littered with their luggage on its way out or back into the lodge. One day Constance and William stood on the doorstep to watch their departure. Samuel Lumb offered his hand to his wife as she climbed into the carriage. Constance noted her cumbersome movements.

'Miss Platt is getting very fat,' she commented in a whisper to William. 'I think she eats too much.'

'Shush,' said Lizzie.

'Gingerbread and seed cake,' said William with envy. 'They have lots of cake downstairs. Chocolate cake, and jelly too, I expect.'

'Nonsense!' said Lizzie. 'Now wave nicely to your papa and mama.'

'Why do they keep going away?' William asked as they all trooped back upstairs.

Lizzie's normally open, cheerful face developed a veiled look. 'They'll tell you when they're ready, I'm sure.'

Constance felt resentful. Whatever the secret, Papa had no business to share it with that woman and not them. Miss Platt was diverting Papa's loyalty further and further from his children.

'I think she's horrible!' she muttered to William when they were alone in bed. 'And she's fat and ugly!'

'Oh, she's not so bad,' William protested gently. 'She's really quite kind — she asked Mr Ormerod to mend my train for me.'

'To win your confidence. Oh, she's cunning, can't you see? She's not really our friend, or Edward wouldn't have argued with Papa about her. Edward was right — she's shrewd and clever.'

William murmured agreement. He could not really understand why kindness was cunning, but if Constance said so then she must be right. Connie was always right.

As the wedding approached, Constance had reason to fume again — not only was she obliged to act as bridesmaid for her sister but she was obliged also to wear again the hated blue gown made for Papa's wedding to Miss Platt. It was adding insult to injury, but for Elizabeth's sake she held her tongue.

Mrs Roebuck presided over her table, pouring tea for the assembled staff from the big brown teapot.

'She must be getting near her time now,' she pronounced with the air of one who knows. 'I wonder she still keeps gallivanting off with him like that. Do the children know yet that they're to have a new baby?'

'Not yet,' said Lizzie. 'It's not my place to tell them.'

Joe sniggered. 'They must have guessed from the size of her. By heck, she's as big as a house-end!'

'Enough of that!' snapped Mrs Roebuck. Comments verging on ribaldry were forbidden in her kitchen and, in any event, portentous matters such as childbirth were women's domain, not for the likes of Joe Sugden to be allowed to proffer an opinion on. Still, as he said, it would be surprising if Miss Constance and Master William were still unaware of the coming birth.

'No one's dropped a hint to them, even?' she asked Lizzie.

The girl shook her head. 'Not as I know of. And of course they still think babies are found under gooseberry bushes, so Mrs Lumb's size would mean nowt to them. Fact, I heard them say they thought she'd been guzzling too much cake!'

Laughter broke out round the table. It was Kitty, the parlourmaid who came up with a new thought: 'I say, if Miss Elizabeth has a baby soon as she's wed, that'll make Mrs Lumb a mother and a grandmother for the first time both at once!'

Mrs Roebuck considered that speculation about Miss Elizabeth's fertility was not quite nice and changed the subject quickly. 'Those young ones are going to have a surprise when they find out about the baby and moving to a new house as well. Which reminds me, will you be going with them to Whitby, Lizzie?'

The girl's face fell. 'Nay, I fear not. My Jack wants us to be wed this autumn. I shall miss those kids, young William especially. But you'll be going, Mrs Roebuck?'

'Oh aye, I've nowt to keep me in Hawksmoor 'cepting my sister, but she's got her husband and family. Me being a widow there's nowt to stop me going. I fancy the sea air will do my chest good. How about you, Miss Fairclough? You've your old mother to consider, haven't you?'

The governess gave a nervous little laugh. 'Oh no! I won't be going with the family, I fear. Not only because of Mother, but because Mr Lumb indicated he might send young Master William away to school soon.'

Mrs Roebuck was startled. This was a piece of information which had not hitherto reached her ears but she was not going to confess it. She covered her ignorance ably.

'No, well, there'd be no sense, would there? Still, I reckon your mother will be pleased. You won't be going either, Joe, so there'll only be Kitty I'll know on my staff. There'll be new ones Mrs Lumb will engage when we get there, but strangers is not the same.'

She shook her head sadly, then brightened instantly. 'Still, we've the new baby to come yet before all that happens. Another cup of tea, Miss Fairclough?

'May I have another cup of tea, Mrs Sidebotham?' said William in the nursery, holding out the tiny doll's cup to Constance.

'To be sure, Mr Harper, and perhaps you would care to taste a piece of my seed cake with it,' replied Constance, offering a piece of chalk on a microscopic plate. William took it delicately and pretended to nibble. Suddenly Constance tired of the game.

'Oh, William, I'm so weary,' she moaned, leaning back in her chair. It was more than weariness; it was an unbearable sadness. Whispers had reached the nursery of the family's move to another house far away. Thwaite Lodge, despite being her home all her life, held no special appeal for her, but the prospect of leaving behind forever the beauty of those great, sprawling moors just beyond the garden wall filled her with aching misery.

William abandoned the game gladly. 'Let's play soldiers instead.' he suggested.

Constance sighed deeply. 'I feel so weak, so tired, Willie. I almost feel as if I were fading away.' The thought gave her an idea. 'That's it, Willie, I know it now. I'm dying, I'm fading away.' She whispered the words in a voice so weak that the boy looked up in alarm. He knelt beside her.

'No you're not! You're not, are you, Connie?'

'Yes, little brother,' she murmured. 'I can feel my strength trickling away out of my fingers and toes. I'm dying, dying for want of love.'

The boy's eyes grew wide in terror. 'No, you can't, Connie! You can't die and leave me alone! Oh, Connie, Connie, don't die!'

Tears gushed from his eyes and poured down his cheeks, his hands gripping hers in abject terror. Constance rolled her head slowly to look at him with half-closed, compassionate eyes. 'Dear Willie, who will care for you when I am gone?' she murmured. 'My precious beloved brother. It is so tragic we must be parted so young.' She was secretly pleased at her own acting ability; her words sounded exactly like those in one of the novelettes Lizzie sometimes read aloud to them. William sobbed noisily.

'I die for lack of love,' she uttered tragically.

William flung his arms about her neck. 'But I love you, Connie! I love you better than anyone else in the whole world!' he protested between sobs.

She turned black, piteous eyes on him. 'Then only you can save me, Willie. Only you have the power. Pray to God for me, beg Him to be merciful, to spare me to care for you. Perhaps He will listen to you because you love me so much.'

'I do, I do!' William was almost screaming.

'Then kneel by me, and pray.'

He released his tight hold and knelt, clasping his hands together. 'Dear Jesus,' he prayed aloud, 'please don't let Connie die! I love her very much because she's the kindest, nicest person in the whole world and I need her. Don't let her die, Jesus! Please let her stay alive with me!' A sob choked him.

'Amen,' said Connie weakly.

'Amen.'

He raised huge, tear-filled eyes to look at her fearfully. She knew he was waiting anxiously to see if the magic had worked. After a moment a faint smile curved the corners of her lips.

'It's working, I can feel it! There's a warmth spreading slowly through me – see, I can move my hands! And my feet – oh, Willie! Your love has restored me!'

She sat up slowly, revelling in the beatific smile on William's face. He flung himself upon her, weeping this time from sheer happiness. 'You see what love and faith in God's goodness can do – it can achieve miracles,' she whispered contentedly into his ear. He looked at her with great blood-shot eyes. 'Our love is so great we can do anything we set our hearts to, Willie.'

'Yes, oh yes!' he cried, utterly convinced.

'But we'll tell no one about our power, will we?'

'Oh, no, Connie! It's our secret.'

And she knew it was, and that she could count on him to keep it until death; even ordeal by fire would not extract the secret from him if Constance forbade it. She knew the full extent of her influence over William and was glad, for she too adored him better than anyone else in the whole world. Nothing and no one would ever come between them to spoil that love.

Two weeks later Constance stared at Lizzie in horror. 'A baby?' she gasped. 'Miss Platt is to have a baby?'

'That's why everyone's running about and why you two must stay quiet in the nursery today,' Lizzie explained. 'With luck, happen you'll have your new baby brother or sister by nightfall.'

William looked puzzled. 'But where will the baby come from, Lizzie?'

The young woman turned pink. 'I've told you before. Babies are found under gooseberry bushes. Now be good, the pair of you, because I'll be busy all day. Don't play with the coal bucket, Master William,' she pleaded. 'You'll get dirty marks all over your clean smock. Do be good, and I'll see if I've time to tell you a story tonight.'

So promising, she dashed to join the seeming multitude of people processing back and forth to the master's bedroom. William stared out of the window at the frost-spangled bushes below.

'The gooseberry bushes aren't even in leaf yet,' he remarked. 'A baby will get very cold under there.'

'I don't care,' his sister replied coldly. 'We don't want Miss Platt's baby here.'

'No,' William admitted. 'But won't it be Papa's baby too?'

'Yes, but not our brother or sister.'

'Oh.' He did not understand; Lizzie said it would be and yet Connie said not.

All day there was bustle and hustle in the house. The doctor's trap arrived and then Papa came home from work unusually early. And from the first floor bedroom where all the activity centred there were periodic cries and screams. William stayed very close to Connie and wished it would all end.

It was while Kitty, in Lizzie's absence, was serving up nursery tea of boiled eggs and cress that Papa suddenly appeared in the doorway. Kitty, flustered, bobbed a curtsey and wiped her hands apologetically on her apron.

'Oh, sorry, sir. I'm afraid you caught us unawares,' she babbled.

Mr Lumb waved beneficently. 'No matter, Kitty. I came to fetch Miss Constance and Master William to come and visit their Mama and new baby brother,' he said proudly.

Kitty gaped. 'It's over, sir? Is the mistress well?'

'Very well, Kitty, and baby Francis too. Come, children, you may see him and Mama before they go to sleep. You can finish your tea afterwards.'

Both children rose from the table and followed him obediently. In the big bed the new mother, pale but serene even now, watched with a gentle smile as they approached the crib.

'Isn't he a fine baby, Constance?' she murmured. 'William, don't you think he has your father's handsome features? I know you'll soon come to love him as dearly as you do Constance.'

The boy stared at the red, wizened creature squirming in the cot and thought privately that it resembled nothing more than a skinned rabbit. Connie was looking down at it dispassionately.

'Now kiss your mama, children, and then leave her to sleep,' Papa said brightly. William leaned over first to kiss her cheek, and watched Connie do likewise. Then, bidding the adults goodnight, they left.

Back in the nursery William re-attacked his boiled egg with energy. Connie sat, uneating, and he could see she was shaking.

'Are you crying, Connie? There's nothing to cry about, is there?'

She shook her head fiercely. 'She said you would love it as much as me,' she muttered.

William stared. 'Love the new baby? I couldn't, Connie. He's ugly, and anyway we love each other best, you and I.'

'And he's not really our brother anyway – he's *hers*!' Connie said with venom. 'She's not going to use him against us.'

'How could she? Nothing can change us, Connie, surely you know that?'

Without a word Constance pushed her plate aside and sprang up from the table. William watched while she flung open the cupboard door and ransacked the shelves. She came back with Lizzie's sewing basket. From it she took a long, sharp darning-needle.

'What are you doing?' William enquired.

Connie's face was pale and her mouth firmly set. 'We must swear a pact, William. A pact in blood.'

It was the boy's turn to blanch. 'Blood?' he echoed.

'Yes. I read about it somewhere. If we mingle our blood, you and I, we'll be inseparable in life and in death. We'll be blood-brothers, Willie, and then no one can ever come between us. Don't be afraid, I won't hurt you. Just hold out your finger and look the other way.'

Unquestioning, he held out his hand. He could not see the reason for the action since they were brother and sister already, but Connie's rituals held their own kind of magic.

Whatever it was she thought might threaten them, her magic would hold its terrors at bay. He felt a sudden jab and then saw the fierce red blob of blood that swelled on his fingertip.

Connie seated herself in Lizzie's deep armchair and he saw her stab her own forefinger. There was no change of expression on her white face.

'Come here, Willie.'

He crossed to her and she moved aside in the armchair to leave room for him to sit beside her. She smiled at him, a gentle, loving smile.

'Now lay your finger on mine and let the blood mingle. Then we'll be pledged, utterly, one to the other throughout our lives. We'll be one, Willie, like one person. We'll share all our hopes and fears and sins as one person, and no one can come between us, ever, ever . . .'

With complete trust and belief he laid his fingertip to hers and watched her closely, certain that some magical feeling would come over him to indicate the ritual's success. Connie's smile became angelic, beatific, but William felt nothing and was ashamed.

At last Connie stood up, her small face glowing in triumph. 'We've done it, Willie! We're pledged to each other for life! You are mine and I am yours, for always!'

He was pleased she was so happy, for her smile had become a rare event lately. He stood up on the chair and leaned over the back to watch her. 'My finger is still bleeding,' he told her.

'Pinch it with your thumb. It will stop in a moment.' She put the needle away and restored the basket to the cupboard.

A minute later Lizzie reappeared to clear away the tea things. She was quick to note the girl's smile. 'Glad to see you looking so much more cheerful, Miss Constance,' she remarked. 'You've been a right little Miss Mope lately. A new baby brother seems to have cheered you up, I'm glad to say.'

Constance smiled across at her brother behind the nanny's back, a slow, secret smile that filled him with pleasure. 'Oh yes, Lizzie, I feel far happier today than I have for a long time,' she agreed. Willie understood and winked at her.

'That's good, I'm right glad to hear it,' said Lizzie contentedly as she stacked up the tray and left. It was only late that night when both the children were tucked up in bed, fast asleep, that she discovered the bloodstain. She picked up the antimacassar off the armchair and scrutinised it under the light of the candle.

'Dear me, what's this? Blood? Now how on earth can that have got there?' she murmured, then with a sigh she carried it downstairs. Mrs Lumb had embroidered it herself when she was still Miss Platt, so she would be displeased about the stain. It would have to be washed at once, and questions could wait until tomorrow.

6

The new baby was transferred to the nursery a few days later. Constance and William watched the small intruder with curiosity as Lizzie fed and bathed him and put him to bed.

'He's not very interesting, is he?' William confided in his sister. 'All he seems to do is to eat or cry or sleep.'

'And makes unpleasant noises and smells,' Constance added. 'You're quite right, he's of no interest at all. I can't think why the grown-ups make such a fuss of him.'

Lizzie came back with a bucket of damp napkins. Constance wrinkled her nose in distaste, and Lizzie smiled. 'You'll get used to it, Miss Constance,' she said.

'No, I won't. It's horrid.'

'Well, I believe you're to have your own room once you get to the new house, so nursery smells won't bother you then.'

'Am I to have my own room too?' William asked.

'I'm sure you will. You're getting too big to share with Miss Constance now,' she assured him. William's face fell. The advent of this baby was upsetting the way life had always been. It would not be the same without Connie there to share secrets and to comfort him in the dark.

Constance did not seem to be as troubled as he was by the news. 'After all, don't forget we're blood-brothers, Willie, and nothing can really separate us. I'll know when you need me and I'll always be there.'

Pacified, William went on with the normal routine of life and as the weeks went by he almost forgot the baby. Except for its distant cries from its nursery bedroom he was hardly aware of it, except when he watched its bathtime ritual. Constance never watched; she preferred to withdraw to a quiet place to read – to avoid the smells, she said.

Then suddenly came disorder and confusion. The servants stripped cupboards and drawers and the house became barren and strange, then he and Constance were sitting in a coach opposite Papa and Miss Platt, who was carrying the baby in a shawl. It was a long, bumpy ride and William was half-asleep when they finally climbed out, stiff and aching, and were led away by strange people to strange rooms. It was not the new house yet, but a hotel in Scarborough, where they were to stay a few days, said Papa, until the new servants at Weatherhead had prepared the house for their arrival.

At the very first sight of Weatherhead, a grey stone house shrouded in trees, William took a dislike to it. Constance too; he could tell by her expression as they were taken inside that she did not care for it. More strange people led them to strange rooms, and that night as William lay, alone for the first time, between tight, hard sheets in an unfamiliar room that was to be his, he could not help the few tears that trickled on to his pillow.

Constance could not bear the thought of William's loneliness a moment longer. She swung her feet out of bed and crossed the cold floor, lit a taper from the embers of the fire and re-lit the candle. Then, making sure there was no loitering maid, she crept along to William's room, let herself in quietly and whispered to him: 'William, it's only me. Don't be afraid. Move over and let me in.'

She heard his sigh of pleasure as he moved aside and she slithered into the warm place. His arms folded about her neck. 'Oh, Connie! I'm so glad you've come. It's horrid here, with all those squeaks and noises. I don't like Weatherhead, do you?'

'It feels wrong,' she murmured thoughtfully. 'I don't know why, but it feels wrong.'

'Papa said it would be a lovely house and we'd be so happy here,' William complained.

'Perhaps it's better by daylight. We'll explore it in the morning.'

'I don't like it. I don't want to stay here.'

'Shush, or someone will hear you. Listen, I'll come every night, as long as no one finds out. I'll stay until you're asleep, so there's nothing to fear, Willie. Say your prayers now, and then sleep.'

Together they whispered their prayers and William was content. Before long he was fast asleep, but his sister lay wide awake and troubled. William was right. There was something cold and eerie about Weatherhead, something unwelcoming and at the same time unnatural. There was no happiness in the house, only a strange, brooding sadness, and she felt afraid. She looked down at the fair head cradling on her shoulder and felt a rush of warmth. Poor Willie. He was sensitive to atmosphere too and knew that Weatherhead boded no good for either of them. But whatever lay ahead, she promised herself fiercely, she would watch over and protect William if it should cost her very life.

Satisfied that he was sleeping peacefully, she crept quietly back to her own cold bed.

Weatherhead, the children soon discovered, was quite an attractive house by daylight, with large rooms and tall bay windows and lots of new, solid furniture. It was in fact no smaller than Thwaite Lodge and far more impressive in its large grounds situated near the hill top. The sea was not actually visible from Weatherhead, but on a still day they could hear the distant breakers and smell the salt tang.

Below the house a dusty road led down to the village, and alongside the grounds a lane led up to a row of cottages. Samuel Lumb, seeing the faces of curious village children peering in to watch his family in the gardens, grew irritable. 'Privacy is what we sought and what we shall have,' he barked at his wife. 'I'll have a solid fence put along that side at once.'

And he did, much to the locals' disappointment. But they were even more dismayed when he fenced in a length of the stream that ran downhill near his house. 'I'll fish in private without them gawping at me,' he remarked to Cecily. She held her tongue, for she had heard the servants' comments by chance as she entered the kitchen to give orders for the day.

'No more trout for tea,' the new kitchen maid was saying. 'Me dad's fair vexed about that. We've had trout from the stream since I were a baby.'

'Be quiet, girl,' snapped Mrs Roebuck. 'You've no call to criticise your betters.'

Her entrance had quelled whatever argument might have ensued, but Cecily had heard enough to know her husband's actions were not making him popular in the district any more than his severe factory discipline had endeared him to mill-owners and workers. She could only hope that befriending the village rector and the doctor, both highly esteemed by the locals, and inviting them to their dinner table would render the Lumb household more acceptable.

Her hopes were shattered when Constance and William dashed into the hallway one day, scarves flying and faces red with anger.

'What on earth is the matter, children?' she demanded crisply. 'Something must be very wrong for you to be throwing yourself headlong like a hoyden, Constance.'

'We were being chased,' William gasped. Constance stood glowering.

'Chased? By whom, and why?'

'By some children up the lane,' William explained breathlessly. 'They called us names and said we were stuck-up.'

'William! I won't have you using such common expressions!' she scolded. 'You must have angered them in some way.'

'No, really! That's what they called us,' William insisted

74

hotly. 'They said Papa had no right to steal their trout stream and we were snobs because really we're no better than they are.'

'And in any case we're only newcomers here,' Constance added in a mutter. 'They said they'd never play with us.'

'Indeed they won't,' agreed their stepmother. 'They're evidently not fit company for you. Off upstairs with you and wash your hands before tea.'

'And their parents won't accept you and Papa either,' Constance flared before she turned away. Cecily bit her lip in vexation. The girl was being surly yet again, but perhaps it would be best not to scold her. Too often lately Constance's attitude had seemed provocative, almost insolent. If only there were more time in the day to approach the child, but what with the new house, a new set of servants to train and the baby starting to teethe, there was so much to do. And she really must go into Whitby again to try to find the right curtaining to match the parlour decor. The child's tantrums would have to wait. If only she did not feel so tired always these days . . .

William watched as Connie stood by the cradle looking down at baby Francis. She was actually smiling, the insults of the children in the lane forgotten. The baby had one tiny fist tightly clutched about her forefinger.

'Look, Willie,' she said softly. 'He's smiling at me.'

William looked down at the baby. Its face was contorted in a funny way, exposing toothless gums, but it hardly resembled a smile.

'Are you sure?' he said. 'Ellen says he does that when he's got wind.'

Connie stood back and folded her thin arms. 'He's not really so bad after all, is he? He's beginning to get more interesting. As he gets older and sits up and then walks, he might be quite fun.'

William felt a pang of jealousy. 'We have more fun together, Connie, because we're nearly the same age. I'm almost as big as you now.'

She turned and hugged him quickly. 'Yes, I know, and

you'll always be my dearest, most loved brother, Willie. I only meant that baby Francis is not quite so horrid as we thought. But he's only a half-brother, not a blood-brother like you.'

Content, William washed his hands for tea. Connie's smile was for him, and the world was rosy again. Ellen, the new young nanny, came in at that moment.

'How's my little man, then?' she asked, looking into the cot. 'Been a good boy, has he?'

'Yes,' said Connie.

'Connie thought he smiled, but I said it was wind,' said William.

Ellen laughed. 'Perhaps it was, but he is starting to take notice now. He knows who he likes, don't you, my little pet?'

'Ellen,' Connie said seriously. 'There was a boy in the lane with his legs all bent. What was wrong with him?'

'Rickets, most like. Poor children don't get such good food as you, so make sure you eat up all your liver next time or you'll get bowed legs too. Come on now, up to the table. Tea's ready.'

'I don't think the baby smiled,' William asserted as he took the chair next to Connie. 'It was wind.'

'No, he smiled at me. I know he did. He likes me.'

'How can you be sure?'

'I know, that's all. He's quite a nice little thing.'

'Are you sure?' Samuel Lumb asked his wife some weeks later. 'Are you quite sure, my dear?'

'Well, almost,' Cecily admitted with a shy smile. 'Will you be pleased?'

'To be sure I will, my love! After all, you gave me such a fine son in Francis. We must ask the doctor to call tomorrow.'

'He'll be here for dinner tonight,' Cecily reminded him.

'So he will, but it would not be seemly to ask him to examine you then. But I can have a quiet word with him and ask him to pay you a visit tomorrow. Will that suit you, my dear?'

As he dressed for dinner, Samuel Lumb considered his

wife's news. Of course, it would account for her unaccustomed lethargy of late, her apparent loss of interest in the other children and her frequent giddy attacks. He felt quite rejuvenated at the prospect of another fine healthy child like Francis. What a fertile wife he had chosen! With the older girls now married and Edward far away on the other side of the world, it was pleasant having another family of young children again. Constance and William were now ten and almost nine, and baby Francis would be about fifteen months old when the new baby came. What a stroke of luck that he had been appointed Chief Inspector and had no financial worries over increasing his family, even though the appointment did mean frequent stays away from home. A fine house, a good position, a flourishing family and soon a new carriage in the stables – what more could a man wish? Luck had certainly turned in his favour since his re-marriage. He had Cecily to thank for that. He had never made a wiser decision in his life than resolving to propose to her.

Dr Lockwood raised his bushy eyebrows only momentarily when Samuel Lumb murmured his request that evening. There was only a fraction of a pause as he handed on the port decanter to the vicar.

'To be sure, Lumb. I'll call in the morning,' he replied, and privately wondered. The Lumb children were all well. The baby's teeth, probably.

So when he called at Weatherhead next day and caught sight of the nanny in the hallway, he asked her cheerfully how her charges fared.

'Fine, doctor,' she replied. 'Here's Miss Constance and Master William coming down now.'

The two children hesitated at the foot of the stairs. Dr Lockwood smiled at them. 'Put out your tongues,' he commanded.

They did so. Nothing wrong there. He glanced quickly at their hands. No sign of the itch, common hereabouts. They looked well enough, though the girl was slight for her age and lacked the brightness of eye of her brother. She looked withdrawn, almost suspicious, but his concern was health and she looked fit enough.

'The baby?' he asked the nanny.

'He's splendid, sir, eating enough for a lad twice his age,' Ellen replied with pride. 'No troubles with him.'

'I see. Well, Mr Lumb asked me to call – ' the doctor began.

'Oh yes, sir. To see the mistress. She's in her room – I'll take you up.'

Twenty minutes later Dr Lockwood left Weatherhead. Mrs Lumb was pregnant again. That accounted for Samuel Lumb's glow of anticipation last night. Mrs Lumb was still young, early thirties he guessed, and her pregnancy should prove as straightforward as the last. Lumb was a lucky fellow indeed – fine family, charming wife, splendid home – and he served an excellent port at table. Not quite in the doctor's class, as the vicar was, but a man who had made his way in the world and worth cultivating on that account. He must remember to ask Emily about inviting the Lumbs to dinner before Mrs Lumb's pregnancy became too advanced.

Several months passed but Constance Lumb still felt restless and discontented. Weatherhead was a nice enough house, but for her it still seemed to have something oddly unnatural about it. Perhaps it was only because it was not close to purple moors and distant mountains, but surrounded by fields and cottages and the far-off sound of the sea. She longed for the moors, their space and wildness and freedom. Here in Weatherhead she felt constrained, out of her element and with a continual sense of oppression.

Not that anyone oppressed her; quite the contrary. Papa, though stern, was often away from home these days. Ellen, the nanny, and the new governess, Miss Broadbent, were far less exacting than their counterparts at Thwaite Lodge had been. And Miss Platt, usually the most critical of all, seemed to have lost all interest in her.

'Miss Broadbent sent you down to show me what?' Miss Platt had asked wearily yesterday.

'My sewing. She wanted you to see how much improved my fine seams are,' replied Constance.

Her stepmother took the piece of rather grubby linen from

her carelessly. 'Oh, yes. Constance, on your way back ask Mrs Roebuck to make me a pot of tea, would you? And a cucumber sandwich with some of her delicious tomato chutney.'

Chutney, thought Constance irritably. That was all Miss Platt wanted nowadays. Once she would have remarked upon the grubby state of Constance's needlework, suggesting she washed her hands more often, but now she showed total unconcern. It was because she had her own baby now, Constance thought resentfully. Before he came, Miss Platt had had much more time for her and William.

'We're different from other children,' she remarked to her brother over tea.

Ellen looked up sharply. 'Different? How do you mean?'

'We're just different, that's all.' Constance's tone was airy. She was not prepared to explain herself to someone who would not understand. But in private she elucidated to William.

'Unlike other children, we had a strange mother we hardly knew. We're kept away from other children, and we don't have rickets or the itch like they do. We're sensitive and refined, as though we had a special purpose in life. I wonder what it could be, Willie?'

'And we're blood-brothers, and they aren't,' concluded William proudly.

'Don't you wish you could play with other children, Willie?'

The boy shrugged. 'It would be nice,' he replied. Then, seeing her expression, he added quickly, 'but as long as I have you, I don't need anyone else.'

She hugged thin arms about thin knees. 'Yes, that's how I feel. Deep inside us there is some great power. I feel it, a power which is exclusive to us and only works so long as we only share it with each other. We'll use it one day when we're older and when we know what it's for. We only have to wait and be patient, Willie.'

He felt proud and important at her words. Whatever it was he possessed, it must be some kind of magic, and even if he could not feel it himself, it was undoubtedly there if Connie said so. He was content to await his destiny.

Samuel Lumb waited contentedly for the arrival of his seventh living child, complacent with his world and his possessions. It came as a rude shock to the even tenor of his life when a messenger arrived one day at Nelson's factory just as the bell was clanging for the lunch break. Mr Nelson had already invited him to take lunch at the White Horse, and Samuel was looking forward to a tasty helping of sirloin and roast potatoes when the mud-grimed coachman came into the office.

'Mr Lumb, sir, sorry to trouble you but Dr Lockwood sent me to find you and bid you come home at once.'

'What is it, man?' Lumb exclaimed testily. 'One of the children sick?' He was loth to relinquish his lunch for a fevered, spotty child.

'No, sir. It's Mrs Lumb.' The coachman glanced at Nelson as though undecided whether he could speak in confidence. 'She's been taken bad, sir.'

Samuel Lumb paled. 'An accident? Did she fall or something?' It was unlike Cecily to be ill. Her vigour and health had always been reliable — but she had been a shade off-colour lately.

'No accident, sir. She just collapsed and the doctor were sent for. He fears she may lose the baby.'

Lumb stood up. 'I'll come at once.' He turned to Nelson. 'I'll be back in a day or two, but in the meantime take heed what I said about those machines. I'll expect to see them right when I come.'

The carriage clattered over the cobblestones out of town and over the rutted lanes to Weatherhead. But Samuel was too late. The doctor, pale and tense, met him in the vestibule.

'I'm sorry, Lumb. I did what I could. But she's young and fit enough to bear you more sons yet, never fear. A disappointment, I know, but not a tragedy.'

He was allowed to see Cecily only briefly because, the doctor said, she had lost a great deal of blood and was very weak. Samuel was shocked to see how pallid and fragile she looked, and his world was shaken. He had come to rely so

80

much on her serene strength and capability that it made him feel oddly vulnerable to see her laid low. A ripple of presentiment ran through him – please God she was not going to turn into a feeble invalid like Adeline.

He ate dinner alone and then sat morosely in his favourite armchair, resenting the emptiness of the chair opposite. Cecily ought to be sitting there sewing and telling him in her gentle, modulated voice about the days doings at Weatherhead.

There was a tap at the door and Ellen entered, ushering two shining, scrubbed children in their nightgowns. 'Miss Constance and Master William want to say goodnight to you, sir,' she said brightly, and the harshness of her country voice irritated him.

'Oh, for goodness' sake, take them to bed, Ellen,' he snapped, and then remembering his duty he added less harshly, 'Goodnight, children.'

'Goodnight, Papa,' two small voices answered. If it crossed his mind, fleetingly, that he should have offered his cheek for a kiss, it certainly did not cross his mind the following night. Cecily had a high fever.

'Puerperal fever,' Dr Lockwood pronounced.

'I thought women only had that after childbirth?' Samuel queried, mystified.

'A miscarriage can have the same effect, unfortunately, but Mrs Lumb is young and strong. She'll throw it off soon.'

But two weeks dragged by before the doctor could declare his patient free of the fever, and Samuel was horrified to see how ravaged Cecily had been by the ordeal. Dr Lockwood was insistent that she should have a long, quiet rest from all household chores and preferably a holiday.

Cecily, however, refused to go away. 'What better place to rest than here with the sea air and all?' She smiled gently. 'I'll be best here.'

'Then at least you must do as the doctor says and have a complete rest,' Samuel said firmly. 'You shall not even be troubled for orders – the staff can manage perfectly well.'

'Very well, dear.' The fact that she complied so readily was a clear indication of her weak state, thought Samuel. Everything should be done to spare her effort and worry. The sooner she was back downstairs in the parlour with him again, the sooner life would resume something approaching normality.

Constance slipped into William's bed and he smiled sleepily.

'Did you see Miss Platt, Connie? She came down at last tonight, to have dinner with Papa.'

'I know. I saw her,' Constance snorted. 'I swear she was putting it on, pretending to be weak. She had Ellen and Hetty on either side of her to help her downstairs.'

'Why should she put it on?' asked William. 'Papa told us she's been very ill. I don't know what was wrong with her, do you?'

'Nothing, probably. It was just a way to get Papa's attention and make him worried.'

'But why, Connie?'

'I don't know, but I'm certain she's not really ill like Mama was. I think she's up to something and I wish I knew what it was.'

'Oh well,' sighed William sleepily, 'you'll find out. You're so clever, Connie. You'll find out soon.'

To Connie it seemed clear that her suspicions were correct. In the succeeding days Miss Platt queened it from the parlour, giving orders with such gentle feebleness that the servants seemed to redouble their efforts to serve her with alacrity. And Papa sternly forbade the children ever to set foot downstairs while she was there in case their noise and chatter should disturb her. Even the gardens were forbidden them in case she should wish to sit outside in the sun for a while.

So the two children were obliged to stay in the nursery with baby Francis, able only to gaze out at the passing summer days disconsolately. On the whole William suffered in stoic silence, but Constance's frustration found outlet on occasion by snapping at the governess. Miss Broadbent rapped her knuckles with a ruler and threatened to report such insolence to the master.

'I don't care!' flared Constance, while William sat fearful.

'Tell him, and perhaps he'll notice us! He never notices us now!'

Whether Miss Broadbent carried out her threat to report the incident to Papa Constance did not discover, because another incident that night caused an explosion. After Ellen had extinguished the candle and bidden Connie goodnight, the girl crept as usual along to William's room. It was just as she was climbing into bed beside him that the door opened.

'Excuse me, Master William,' Ellen whispered from the doorway, 'don't be frightened, it's only me. I came back to collect your things for the wash in the morning.'

In the gloom she came to the foot of the bed and then stiffened. 'Who's that? Who's with you, Master William?'

Connie slid out of bed. 'It's me, Ellen.' She stood, small and defenceless in her nightgown. The nanny stared, shocked and scandalised, for several seconds before she found voice.

'Back to your room, miss. I shall speak to your father about this.'

Constance walked past her, head erect and features set. They could do and say as they liked, but they could not defile the perfect love and trust between her and William. They could rage and protest, forbid and punish, but she and he were one, and that was all that mattered.

In the morning she waited apprehensively with a white-faced William for the summons to Papa's study. It was Saturday and he was not going to work. At last there came a tap at the nursery door and Hetty, the parlourmaid, came in.

'The master wishes to see Master William in the study immediately,' she announced. Constance stared.

'William? Not me, Hetty?'

'He asked for Master William on his own, miss.'

Connie watched as William trotted out after the maid, and she raged inwardly. Papa, no doubt abetted by Miss Platt, had picked on William knowing him to be the weaker and less able to defend himself. Her fury and frustration boiled so helplessly that she felt another of her headaches coming on.

In the study Samuel Lumb looked at his wife in concern.

'This is really the last straw, Cecily! I cannot expect you to recover your full health with a house and staff to manage as well as children to control who behave as appallingly as this!'

Cecily, from under the blanket in the depths of her armchair, nodded weakly. 'I must confess they are getting a little beyond me. There just isn't time to do everything as efficiently as I would like.'

'It is not the spirit but the flesh that is weak, my dear. You must be given the chance to recover completely, and such problems as the children present are hardly conducive to that.'

'Are you sure this is the answer though, Samuel? I would not have you do anything you might regret later. They have always been so close, Constance and William, lacking their own mother.'

'They had an excellent mother in you, Cecily, caring for them both from the moment of their birth, and what gratitude do they show to worry you so? Close, you say? Too close, according to what Ellen tells us. I tell you, it's unhealthy, unnatural! A boy of ten and a girl of eleven in the same bed! It's monstrous, and must be put a stop to at once.'

He stopped pacing the room and turned to his wife. 'My mind is made up, Cecily,' he said soberly. 'Plead no more for them. It must be done.'

A timid knock came at the door. 'Come in, William,' said Mr Lumb sternly. 'Close the door behind you and sit down.'

Connie stood aghast, her life shattered into smithereens around her. William stood helpless before her and wondered how, in a few brief moments, the world could sheer so wildly off-course.

'Papa says it is best for all of us,' he said in a small voice. 'He says it will be good for me to have the company of boys my own age.'

Connie seized him, her heart swelling with compassion. He could not face the taunts of the local children, let alone the teasing and even bullying he might now have to face. Her black eyes probed his tenderly. 'Is it what you want, Willie? Do you secretly wish you had other boys to play with?'

He clung to her, fighting back the tears that scorched his eyelids. 'No, Connie, no! I don't want to go away to school. I want to stay with you, for ever and always!'

Constance fought a silent battle inside herself. Despite her rage and resentment she must allay William's terrors about the ordeal ahead of him. Raining mute curses on the woman she was convinced had persuaded Papa to this, she cradled her brother close.

'Never mind, Willie. Before you know it, it will be time to come home for the Christmas holidays. I'll write to you every week and you can write and tell me your adventures. It will be fun, Willie, with new playmates, and you'll have something the others won't have.'

'I will?' He brushed the tears aside to look at her with trust.

'You'll have me, Willie, and our secret pledge. No matter how many miles separate us we will still be one. If you come across problems, remember that, Willie. I'm there with you all the time.'

'Yes,' he murmured shakily. 'If you are with me, I can be strong.'

That night as Constance lay alone in her high, narrow bed she stared at the bedpost and visualised in its sharp mahogany shape the features of Miss Platt.

'I hate you! I hate you!' she sobbed bitterly. 'For you I have lost my mother, my father's love, my home, my lovely moors, and now you steal William from me! I'll never forgive you, never!'

In his little bed William sobbed alone. The shadows of the darkened room held all the terrors of the universe, and Connie was not there to hold them at bay. And what was worse, soon he would be uprooted and thrust into a world where he would have to combat the demons totally alone. His tears were of pure terror, unmixed with hatred as Constance's were.

7

Watching William's forlorn figure waving goodbye and climbing into the coach, Constance had to fight hard to keep back the tears. It was so cruel, so senselessly destructive to send him away from all he knew and loved! Never, never would she forgive Miss Platt for causing him such unnecessary misery.

The days without William dragged by in a meaningless jumble of confused thoughts. She felt bereft and aimless, and even the daily regime of lessons and meals brought no order to her disordered world.

'Come along now, Miss Constance,' the governess would say sharply to regain the girl's wandering attention. 'You should be able to concentrate far more easily now Master William is not here to distract you.'

Ellen, between ministrations to the baby, tried more gently to engage her in useful pursuits. 'It won't be long before Christmas is upon us, Miss Constance. Happen it's time you started knitting and sewing your presents for your family. How about a nice warm muffler for your papa? He'd be glad to that of a cold winter morning.'

'I don't want to knit or sew anything,' Constance muttered.

'Now, now, where's your Christmas spirit — goodwill to all men and that? I'm sure you want to give your loved ones a nice gift.'

'No, I don't. I haven't any loved ones.'

'Nonsense,' said Ellen cheerfully. 'You're a very lucky girl with brothers and sisters and a kind mama and papa. What would you like to give your mama?'

'She's dead. Do you mean Miss Platt?'

'Of course. She's your stepmama, anyway.'

Constance pointed to the baby in Ellen's arms. 'She's *his* mama, and nothing to me. I'll think of gifts later, but there's really only William I love, and she sent him away from me.'

'Nay, that were the master, so she could rest. You mustn't blame her. Anyway, Master William will be home for Christmas.'

Constance shrugged and turned away. The gullible could think as they pleased, but she knew better. It was a calculated, malicious move on Miss Platt's part to strengthen her power in the household, dividing them and alienating Papa yet further. He seemed to think her infallible, and he evidently doted on baby Francis because he frequently popped into the nursery with his wife in the evening to play with the child before it was put to bed.

'Isn't he a fine baby, Constance? It won't be long before he's running around now. Aren't you proud of your little brother?' he asked. She did not reply; it was a rhetorical question to which Papa did not expect an answer, and it would be unwisely contentious of her to say what she really thought – that the baby was not her brother, and that she loved and was proud of her real brother far more.

Still, baby Francis was rather sweet for all that. He had a sunny nature and always gurgled and laughed when she came near. He could sit up and crawl about now and was becoming quite interesting. On occasions he even clambered with difficulty on to his sturdy little legs, teetered precariously for a moment and then flopped on to his fat little backside, grinning in triumph. At moments like that she could not resist giving him an affectionate hug.

In fact, if it were not for the aching void in her heart caused by William's absence, she knew she could have become quite fond of baby Francis.

'But I won't, I won't,' she vowed, lying stiffly in her bed, 'it would be a betrayal. He's hers, not ours! I love William best of all.'

Confused by the conflict and bitterness that raged in her, Constance was sleeping badly. Letters from William, though restrained and stiff, showed he was far from happy in his new school, although he did not complain. When she did sleep, fitful dreams and even nightmares caused her to waken still tired and unrefreshed. Dark circles under her eyes made Ellen reach for the brimstone and treacle, and Constance ached for her beloved brother and freedom from stupidity and misunderstanding. Still the miasmic dreams of rolling wide moors returned to her, punctuated by looming demons and ogres.

One morning Ellen roused Constance. 'My goodness, you've overslept! Up with you and get washed while I feed the baby.'

As Constance rose sleepily, Ellen seized her hand. 'What's this? The hem of your nightdress is all muddy! And look at your slippers too — coated in mud! Have you been out in the garden dressed like that?' She stared, horrified.

'No, Ellen, truly I haven't.'

But even as Constance denied it she could still hazily recall the dream in which she fled, free and untrammelled, across the heather moors above Thwaite Lodge, William at her side, laughing and happy. She looked down at her nightdress, mud-stained and still damp. Could she actually have risen from bed in her sleep and gone outside on a cold October night?

Ellen evidently thought the matter serious enough to report to the mistress. Cecily, in turn, felt it essential to report the matter to her husband.

'So she walked in her sleep, did she?' said Samuel with a yawn. 'Children often do that. Didn't you tell me William did it once? It's nothing to worry about.'

'I think she misses William more that she will admit,' said Cecily thoughtfully. 'She may be unhappy.'

'Unhappy?' snapped Samuel. 'What right has she to be unhappy, the ungrateful child! She's well fed and dressed and cared for, educated and given every advantage! She doesn't know she's born, that young Constance. She should go out and see how some children have to live. Unhappy, indeed!'

So the matter was forgotten. Only Cecily retained an unspoken thought that troubled her — that Constance's disturbed state of mind was unpleasantly reminiscent of the late Adeline Lumb. Cecily could remember still the gleaming knife that had appeared under the bed where Adeline lay in labour, and Adeline's demented shrieks.

'Blood and a knife!'

The mystery of how the knife came there had never been satisfactorily resolved, though Cecily and the midwife were both sure in their own minds that Adeline herself, conscious or laudanum-soaked, had fetched it in the night. If the child was doomed to inherit her mother's unbalanced mind, it would be as well not to alarm Samuel, not yet, at least . . .

Autumn's golden days had yielded to the damp mists of November. Constance still roamed the gardens of Weatherhead in the afternoon because that was the only place she felt she could breathe and think. Moreover, the falling of the leaves had revealed a hidey-hole where, for a brief hour, she could be mistress of herself. It was a thick shrubbery of yew in a far corner of the garden, away from the neatly-laid vegetable plots and the formal lawns and rose-beds. Poking around it gloomily one afternoon she had caught a glimpse of stonework, and by vigorously pulling the branches aside she had made a tunnel through.

Within the dense shrubbery stood a small stone building with a door swinging awkwardly on rusty hinges. Its flaking green paint indicated that it had long been overlooked. Forcing the door open she found it was a privy, its wooden bench seat mildewed and running alive with beetles. There was still water in the privy, fusty and stagnant. It was not a pleasant place but it was secluded, private from the hostile world outside.

On brighter days she would sit on the flagged path outside the privy and read or think. When the rain fell she would creep inside and listen to the raindrops pelting on the tin roof, revelling in the feeling of being safe from the elements and from prying eyes. It was *her* domain, her castle, a place where only she could rule. William would share and enjoy her secret retreat, but no one else.

The time for William's return was approaching. Constance had already been invited down to the kitchen by Mrs Roebuck to have a stir of the great plum puddings she was making in preparation for Christmas.

'Make a wish as you stir, Miss Constance,' the cook told her. 'It's bound to come true.' And then she had let Constance scrape out the big bowl and lick the mixture until she felt quite sick.

Now the maids were out in the grounds with the gardener, laughing and giggling as they collected branches of holly for the holly-boughs to decorate the front door and the parlour. William was due home tomorrow. Constance could barely sleep for excitement.

Suddenly he was there on the doorstep, his face aglow and his fair head gleaming in the pale December sun. Constance stared up at him, shocked to see how tall he had grown in three months. Ellen noticed too.

'Come, let me measure you against the nursery door again,' she laughed. 'I swear you've put on inches! Yes, see, a clear two inches above your last mark, two inches taller than Miss Constance now! They must be feeding you well at that school of yours!'

'Oh yes, Ellen, the food's not half bad,' replied William airily, and Constance noted how manly he sounded, so distant and different from the William who had gone away. It filled her with a strange, sad sense of dismay. No, she tried to tell herself, he was growing up, growing more like Edward and she should be proud.

For the Christmas festivities Mrs Lumb relaxed the nursery routine and allowed Constance and William to dine downstairs regularly. Constance listened with quiet pride to William's answers when Papa questioned him about school.

'I am progressing well with arithmetic and Latin, sir. I think you will be satisfied with the head's report on your desk,' the boy said confidently.

Papa nodded. 'Indeed, I have read it and Mr Duke seems to think you have settled in satisfactorily. Work hard, my boy, for diligence brings its own reward. Diligence and thrift, that is what a man needs to learn.'

Soon after dinner the carol-singers called and Mrs Lumb insisted upon inviting them in. Six bright young voices chorused 'The Holly and the Ivy', while Papa stood beaming, his back to the fire, and when the singing was ended he evidently forgot his maxim about thrift because he gave the singers a shining silver florin and ushered them out with a cheery 'Happy Christmas to you all.'

William was undoubtedly glad to be home but Constance sensed a certain distance between them at first. However, it was almost entirely bridged before the New Year came in. Then, towards the end of his holiday, William let his manly poise slip, betraying the still-vulnerable boy beneath.

'You do not seem anxious to return to school,' Connie remarked. 'You told Papa you liked it and were doing well.'

'I know,' William admitted.

'Then what is it? Do you get on with the other boys?'

'They're not bad chaps. They like their fun, of course, and they do tease rather.'

'Tease? How?'

'Oh, you know, playing pranks. It's traditional, I understand, but sometimes I find it a bit — well . . .'

His voice tailed away and he averted his face to avoid her searching eyes. She knew at once that he was troubled. She grabbed his arm. 'Come with me, Willie. There's a place I want to show you.'

And it was in the privacy of her secret little domain that she at last persuaded him to talk. It all came out: the frog in his bed, the spattering of ink over his copy books and, most humiliating of all, the ritual baptism. He was reluctant to talk about this.

'Baptism? How, Willie? In a bath?'

'No,' he said shamefacedly. 'They wrapped the new boys up tightly in a blanket so we couldn't move a muscle, then turned us upside down and dipped our heads in the water closet. It was horrible!'

She could see the tear glistening in his eye and understood then why his letters had been so stiff and formal. He would not complain, like a baby howling to its big sister. She patted his arm reassuringly. 'You were very brave, Willie, and I'm proud of you. Never once did you hint at this when you wrote.'

'I wasn't brave!' he cried. 'They read what I wrote so I couldn't tell you! And I cried myself to sleep every night for weeks. The more they saw how miserable I was, the more they bullied me!'

'Oh, Willie!' She folded her arms about him and felt his shoulders heave with the effort to repress his tears. 'Do you hate it very much?'

'I hate it so much I thought of running away over and over again! Oh, Connie, what shall I do? Papa will make me go back!'

She stood speechless for a moment. It was unthinkable that he should have to go back to all that misery but, as he said, Papa would insist. What escape was there from the inevitable?

Unaccountably the words of the carol flitted through her mind:

> 'The holly and the ivy
> When they are both full grown . . .'

Full grown. She looked up at her brother and the sudden idea was born. 'William — let's run away! Remember Edward and how he escaped to sea? We could do that — run away to Hull and board a ship there! Just think, Willie, we could travel the world and no one will be able to find us — you'd never have to go back to that horrible school and we'll be together for always!'

He stared at her, bereft of words for a moment, but then, by the dawning gleam in his blue eyes, she could see the idea appealed to him despite its enormity.

'But you're a girl — girls can't work on ships,' he protested.

'That's easy. I can cut off my long hair and put on some of your outgrown clothes. I know Ellen darned and mended everything and put them away in the linen cupboard.' Her black eyes glowed like coals with excitement. 'Listen, let's plan it all carefully! We'll need food and stout shoes . . .'

'Shoes?' echoed William. 'Why stout shoes?'

'Because we'll have to walk there. People would notice two children on a coach alone.'

'Walk? All the way to Hull?'

'It's not terribly far — thirty-five or forty miles at a guess. We can get there in two days, three at most.'

William's enthusiasm waned visibly. Born into a comfortably-off family they were not accustomed to walking further than the half-mile or so to church on a Sunday.

'Where shall we sleep, Connie?'

'Anywhere — in a barn, under a hedge — what does it matter? We can cuddle close to keep warm. Just think, Willie, it's the biggest adventure of our lives and we mustn't be deterred by trifling problems. Oh, Willie! We'll be free and happy and together!'

Gradually, carried along by her enthusiasm, William became fired with her idea. By the time they parted at bedtime it was all arranged. Constance would raid the little gilt casket Papa had brought for her from the Great Exhibition in which she stored her fortune: the pennies given her from time to time and the gleaming sovereign which had been her Christmas gift from Uncle Reginald. In the casket also lay the seed pearl necklace Papa had given her last year for her birthday and a silver ring with a curl of Mama's hair embedded in it.

'I'll take them in case we need money for food and perhaps even for a coach part of the way, once we've passed Bridlington,' she told William. Reassured by her foresight and mind for detail, William slept soundly until she came, just before dawn, to wake him.

Weatherhead was in a state of uproar and confusion. Constance and William were missing, and although the house had been searched from attic to cellars and the grounds thoroughly combed, there was no sign of them anywhere.

Cecily's serenity deserted her when, after midday, the servants who had been sent to scour the surrounding fields and woods returned to report nothing. The gardener, however, had made one important find. In a disused privy in the shrubbery, he said, he had found a mass of long, black hair.

He held it out to his mistress.

Cecily recognised Constance's hair and she paled. 'Why was this not found before? I thought the grounds had been thoroughly searched?'

'The shrubbery is dense, ma'am, and the privy has not been used for years. It was only just now that I noticed someone had cut a hole through the bushes.'

There was nothing for it but to send the footman to fetch Samuel home, for he had gone to work before their disappearance was known.

'Oh, Samuel! Where can they be?' Cecily moaned. 'They have no friends hereabouts. Can they have been abducted?'

'Nonsense!' snapped Samuel. 'I am not rich enough to make ransom worthwhile. And it would take several men to overpower those two — William is a sturdy young chap. In any event, the house was not broken into and kidnappers don't cut off their victim's hair. No, it's clear to me that they've run away, the little devils. I'll take a strap to the pair of them when we lay hands on them.'

'Oh no, my dear! If they are safe and well that is all that matters,' his wife protested.

'You were always too soft with them,' muttered Samuel. 'I'll take the carriage to go and look for them. Perhaps the police have picked them up by now.'

But the police simply stared at him when he enquired. Until long after nightfall he drove around Flamborough and the neighbouring villages of Bempton and Sewerby but there was no sign of them.

Cecily was distraught when he returned at last, exhausted and empty-handed. 'Oh, the poor children! It's so cold and frosty out there! They'll freeze to death, Samuel, if they haven't come to harm already!'

'They'll not come to harm,' he said fiercely, and she knew he was willing it rather than stating a fact. In the first grey light of dawn Samuel was out in the carriage again. Cecily could concentrate on nothing and when near midday she heard the carriage wheels on the gravel she could hardly contain her joy when she saw Samuel step out with the two children.

'Thank God! Oh, thank God!' she cried, and hurried downstairs to meet them. William looked pale and shame-faced but Constance, her shaggy short hair jutting out in black spikes from under her cap, simply stared at her with an insolent expression which hurt Cecily. Though not of her flesh, she did feel affection and concern for these motherless mites, but Constance would not let her near. Standing there, legs defiantly spread in threadbare trousers and a tweed jacket long past its youth, she looked more like an urchin from the backstreets of grimy Hawksmoor than a prosperous gentleman's daughter. Cecily held out her arms to them but Samuel pushed them past her.

Once they had been banished upstairs to Ellen's care with orders for a thorough scrubbing, Samuel Lumb beckoned his wife to the parlour.

'I shall have to take those two severely in hand,' he said quietly. 'Do you know what they were doing? Running away to Hull to take ship and leave England, would you believe it!'

'Leave England?' echoed Cecily, incredulous. 'Did Constance tell you that?'

'She?' snorted Samuel. 'She'll tell me nothing! No, it was William who broke down and told me. It seems they had walked ten miles or more and then at night, when it was so cold, they had tried to book a room at an inn. The pro-prietress became suspicious of two young boys out alone and questioned them. Constance was cheeky, said she'd only just met William and did not know him and was cagey about where she came from. The woman, very rightly, took them to the police station. Lucky I called there again, or Constance might never have told them where she came from.'

Cecily digested the information. 'I thought she was un-happy. Why else should she run away?'

'Unhappy? She'll be a damn sight more unhappy before I've done with her!' snapped Samuel. 'Children of mine, parading like ragamuffins and trying to take ship! What disgrace! What will the millowners think?'

She could understand his concern for his reputation, but plead as she might, Cecily could not dissuade him from taking strong action. 'A spanking is no use,' he concluded,

95

'because she would simply grit her teeth and then become moodier than ever. I reckon she's been too leniently treated, Cecily, by you and by Ellen and that governess. She doesn't know what discipline is and it's high time she learnt.'

'How will you discipline her, Samuel, without making her more morose and difficult than ever?'

'By delegating the responsibility to others, my dear. A good school, one with a name for firmness, that's what she needs. William will return to his school and I'll see about finding one for her. Mr Nelson has a girl at school somewhere near Scarborough — I'll ask his advice.'

William was escorted firmly back to school. Constance felt not only bereft and miserable without him but apprehensive too. Papa had punished neither of them, nor had he scolded them. Sometimes she caught him looking at her with an oddly set expression about his lips, and she was filled with fear.

Even Miss Platt forbore from scolding her. Despite the jagged, unkempt appearance of Constance's once long and glossy black hair, Miss Platt made no comment, only regarded her with an air of pity. Constance fumed. It was bad enough that that woman had alienated Papa's affections; she need not add insult to injury by patronising Constance too. If only they would scold her, beat her even, she could endure it — but this oppressive silence was ominous.

Constance stood at her bedroom window and looked out at the leafless garden bathed in the light of the low, lambent moon, which hung like a watchful eye. She shivered. Not only was it cold but desperately lonely with no loving arms to cling to, no one to love. *Oh God*, she prayed, *I have so much love burning inside me, aching to be lavished on someone, but William is far away*. There was no one else. Edward a thousand miles away, Papa engrossed in Miss Platt, baby Francis — well, he was sweet and engaging but never in a million years could she love him like William.

'Oh God, help me! So much love burns in me with no release! I'll die, I'll shrivel, caged up here alone!'

By day too she moped about the house, listless and constantly reproached by Miss Broadbent for her lack of concentration. To Miss Platt's kindly-meant enquiries she could only snap monosyllabic answers, and thus she was surprised when Ellen came into the nursery, beaming, and offered an invitation.

'I've to go down to the jetty and fetch some cockles and the mistress says you can come with me. Would you like that, Miss Constance?'

Constance leapt at the opportunity to quit the oppressive house and go down to the sea. As they took the path across the fields the smell of salt sea grew stronger and a chilly wind whipped their cheeks. The grass ended suddenly and Constance saw that the ground fell away in a sheer, steep cliff to tumbled rocks below where the sea waves crashed. She breathed deeply. How William would love this place!

'Take care now, not too near the edge,' Ellen warned. 'Here's the cliff path down to the village.'

Constance, entranced, did not want to move. Ellen waited patiently. Behind them came a clanking, creaking sound and Constance glanced back. Two carts laiden with poles and planks were pulling to a halt. A blonde youth leapt down from one of the carts and began to unload.

'Oh!' cried Ellen. 'I do believe it's the fair! They're starting to set up some of the stalls!'

A fair! Constance grew excited. Fairs were events she had only ever read about and they sounded magical with their toffee apples and sideshows and gipsy fortune-tellers. The boy was still busy unloading but she could see that he was casting her sidelong glances.

'My legs are aching, Ellen. I don't think I can walk down that very rocky path and then climb it again. You go on.'

'Oh dear, I'd better take you home,' sighed Ellen.

'No, go, or it will be dark before you get the cockles. You go on down and I'll wait quietly here and admire the view. It's so lovely here, Ellen.'

'Well,' said Ellen reluctantly. 'If you're sure you'll be all right and promise not to move from here . . . I won't be many minutes.'

'I won't, I promise. I'll be perfectly all right,' Constance reassured her. After a moment's hesitation, Ellen went.

Constance sat on the wiry grass, drawing her woollen shawl warmly about her but letting the hood fall back so that her black hair, now beginning to grow again, blew about in the gusty wind. She could feel the boy's eyes on her back and knew that before long he would leave the men and the carts and come to her. She knew it as surely as if she had willed it. There was something about him that she recognised, some affinity that was more than his passing resemblance to William.

'Hullo.'

She did not turn at first. The sound of his voice right behind her did not alarm her because she was expecting it. At length she turned to him slowly but did not smile. He knew she welcomed his coming.

'My name's Tom. Tom Lawson. What's your name?'

'Constance Lumb.'

He stood awkwardly, cap in hand, watching her expression. 'Constance. Can I call you Connie?'

She could not help her lips curving into a smile. *Connie.* Yes, he was like William, though some years older. About seventeen, she guessed. She nodded towards the men now busy erecting a scaffolding of poles.

'Are you with the fair?'

'Aye. I'm travelling about with them.'

'A vagabond?' she murmured. It was a romantic-sounding name she had read about. She envied him − the freedom of the road, constantly moving, never tied . . .

'Nay, I'm not!' he protested, but there was no anger in his tone. 'I'm no vagabond, nor a gipsy either. They're true romanies, but I've a home and family in Bridlington. I just travel with them up and down the coast while they're here.'

She closed her eyes and felt the wind, whipping her cheeks. 'How wonderful!' she murmured. 'I wish I too could be free like you.'

He smiled. 'Nay, not so free as you think. I've to work same as anyone else when me mam and me dad have five younger children to see to. Me dad wants me to settle down to a proper job but I'm not ready yet. Some day I'll have to. Do you have brothers and sisters?'

She rose to her feet, pulling her cloak about her. The grass was damp and chilly. He towered several inches above her. 'Four, two sisters much older than me and married, a brother away at sea and another away at boarding school.' Intentionally she made no reference to baby Francis.

'That must make life lonely for you,' Tom commented.

Without answer she began to move slowly along the cliff top towards the headland. Unquestioningly Tom followed. At the furthermost point of the headland she paused. The cliff edge fell away in a perilously steep drop and the rocks below jutted from the water like a thousand shark's teeth. Huge white breakers rolling in from the sea cast themselves wildly on the rocks, throwing up great mountains of grey-green water and spitting spume which the wind snatched and carried aloft. For a time she stared at the wild seascape, conscious of Tom's quiet, undemanding presence at her elbow, and felt a measure of peace. It was like being alone with William.

For a time there was no word between them, then at last Constance spoke. 'See the way the waves crash on the rocks? Those great white breakers? And see the white foam that floats off the top of the waves?' she murmured.

'Aye. They call it spindrift.'

'Spindrift,' she repeated slowly. 'That's me, Tom. I'm spindrift, belonging neither to the water nor to the air, having no element of its own. Just drifting and floating, tossed about by turbulences, pushed back and forth till I don't know where I am. I belong nowhere in this mad world, Tom, nor ever shall.' She looked at him with a slow, sad smile. 'If I disappeared now, like that wisp of foam on your collar, no one would miss me.'

He looked away quickly, obviously embarrassed and only half-understanding. 'Isn't there no one you care about and who cares about you?' he muttered.

'Yes, my brother, the one at school.'

'Well, he'd miss you, wouldn't he?'

'You're right, yes, he would. Let's walk back. Ellen will be looking for me.'

As they walked side by side he glanced at her. 'How old are you, Connie?'

'Thirteen.' Twelve sounded so childish, she thought inwardly. 'When does the fair open?'

'Monday. Will you come? I'll look for you.'

Her heart leapt at the idea. Of course Papa and Miss Platt would forbid it, but perhaps somehow she could contrive it. Perhaps with Ellen — the maids would want to go — or perhaps even secretly. After all, she and William had managed to sneak out of Weatherhead unobserved not so long ago . . .

'I'll come, somehow, I'll come,' she promised.

His hard, work-roughened and reddened hand touched her gloved hand for a brief second and a smile irradiated his young face. 'I'll look for you, lass,' he said. 'I'll be waiting.'

They reached the top of the cliff path only moments before Ellen staggered, rosy and panting, to the top. Tom melted away to rejoin the men.

'There now, I wasn't too long, was I?' said Ellen. 'How do your legs feel now?'

'Much better for the rest, thanks.'

Constance nursed a warm glow as they retraced their steps across the fields. Now there was a tiny ray of hope and excitement to lighten her dark world and it was her secret to hug possessively and share with no one.

Two days later the blow fell, a blow so swift and sudden that it took Constance's breath away. In fact, as it turned out, it was to be a double bitter blow.

Papa had sent for her and she stood now before his desk, her hands dutifully clasped. Papa's face was ashen. Miss Platt sat by the window, her back towards them.

'Constance,' Papa said in a shaking voice, 'I fear I have sad news I must tell you.' Constance had a sense of premonition. Her mind instantly raced back to the day she and William stood before Papa while he announced their mother's death, and her heart turned to a lump of apprehensive lead.

'Yes, Papa?'

'Your brother . . .' She felt giddy. William! 'Your brother

Edward — there was a letter today. It seems he took ill of the yellow fever in Havana. I regret to say, he is dead.'

There was a catch in his voice and he turned away. Constance saw Miss Platt's shoulders heaving silently. She herself could feel nothing, only a stunned sense of shock.

'Go back upstairs, Constance.' she heard her father's muffled voice. 'I shall write to the others.'

Upstairs again, Constance sat alone in the empty schoolroom waiting for grief to overwhelm her, and felt guilty that she could feel nothing, only an empty sense of desolation. Dear Edward, so tall and handsome and brave to defy Papa, so adventurous and full of life. It was impossible that he was dead, never more to burst in the door bringing sunshine and vitality. It was unbelievable. It was a betrayal of what ought to be, of what one had the right to expect.

There would be no funeral, Ellen told her later, for he had died some weeks ago and been buried at sea. The news made his death even more unbelievable for Constance. Her mother's coffin had been lowered into the earth in a ritual which had made the finality plain, but Edward had just vanished, faded from her life like — like spindrift. She felt strangely confused and disorientated, and wept that she could feel pity only for herself. She was wicked, she felt sure, not to be weeping and grieving for Edward, and God would surely punish her for it.

Retaliation was swift. Next day she was summoned again to the study. Papa looked more composed and Miss Platt was absent. 'Constance, I have good news for you today. On Monday you are to start school.'

She looked up, startled. 'School, Papa? In the village, with the other children?'

'No, at Miss Scott's school for young ladies near Scarborough. You will be a boarder there. Your stepmama agrees that in the circumstances it would be wisest for us all.'

She stared, stunned. To lose William, then Edward, and then to be banished from the family because Miss Platt wanted her out of the way — that was too much insult and indignity for any human being to bear!

'She wants me to go?' she said quietly.

'Yes, and I too. Your stepmama has had to undergo a great deal lately and it will make life easier for her. Now go upstairs and help Ellen to sort and pack your things.'

Constance left the study, limp with rage and hatred. That woman had succeeded in getting rid of her as she had of William, and she had won Papa over to the idea too. With a pang she realised too that if she was to be banished on Monday, she would not be able to keep her assignation with Tom, who might have become her friend. A cold, arid feeling settled like ice over what had been Constance's heart.

8 : 1859

In the kitchen at Weatherhead Mrs Roebuck put away the last burnished pan and set the new kitchen maid, Doris, to scrub down the deal table. As the thirteen-year-old worked vigorously the cook watched approvingly. With luck this one would turn out better than the last one, Esther.

Esther had been amiable enough and eager to please but the way she kept scratching her head had alerted Mrs Roebuck to the child's lice. Lice, fleas and the itch were anathema to Mrs Lumb and a disgrace to Mrs Roebuck's kitchen. Many a girl had lice but Esther's were intractable. No sooner had Mrs Roebuck scoured them with carbolic soap, fine-combed them out and cracked them between finger and thumb than Esther would go on leave and return from her family home, where she shared a bed with her two younger sisters, and again she would be 'running alive', as the cook put it. There was no choice. The girl had had to go and be replaced by Doris.

'Soon as you've done I'll write a letter to me sister,' Mrs Roebuck told Doris. 'You can write home too if you like, if you're careful not to get ink spots on my table.'

The girl shook her head. 'Thanks all the same, Mrs Roebuck, but I can't write. I'll see 'em on me day off.'

The cook sniffed. Not able to write, indeed. Standards of staff were getting worse these days. It hadn't been the same quality since Miss Broadbent was dismissed, the family having no further need of a governess once Miss Constance went away three years ago. The little fellow, Master Francis, was not yet out of the nursery and would not need a governess for a year or two. Pity, she thought. It elevated the tone of her kitchen to have an educated lady present at her table from time to time.

Hetty came into the kitchen and fetched a hot-water bottle from the pantry. 'Is the water boiled, Mrs Roebuck? I've one more bottle to put in Master William's bed and then I've done for the night.'

'It's ready.' The cook watched as Hetty filled the stone bottle. 'Did you remember to take coals up to his room and Miss Constance's? You know how Mrs Lumb fusses about them being properly aired before they come home.'

'Aye, I've done all that. It's not Mrs Lumb I worry about but Miss Constance. There's no pleasing her sometimes,' the maid sighed.

'Nay, she's changed now. She's fifteen and turning into a right young lady. She's not as awkward as she used to be,' the cook reassured her.

Hetty screwed the stopper in. 'I hope you're right, for a right little madam she was once.'

'She was upset, her brother dying and her being sent away. I heard the master telling Mrs Lumb she were a handful at that school at first, but she's settled down and has good reports now. The master's quite pleased with her.'

'That's what the school says, but Mrs Lumb says different. I heard her say she just couldn't get through to Miss Constance, that she had no patience with her stubborn ways,' Hetty remarked.

'Ah, well, it's only Mrs Lumb who has trouble with her,' said Mrs Roebuck, with the air of one who knows. 'She's fine with everyone else, specially Master William. And she seems fond of the little fellow too.'

'I'd better take this bottle up before it gets cold,' said Hetty.

'Aye. Doris, scrub the way of the grain, will you, not across it!' said the cook, suddenly mindful of her duty to train the newcomer. 'Scrub the way the wood runs, girl, up and down and never across!'

Hector, the huge tom cat, the only animal Mrs Roebuck ever allowed to enter her kitchen because of his superb mousing skills, strolled in and curled his enormous body in front of the fire. The cook smiled. His sleek grey body bore the scars of battle with other toms that roamed the neighbourhood, a ragged half ear bearing testimony to his valour. He was lordly for all that, and never a mouse showed its whisker in the Lumb kitchen. Majestic, expansive, self-assured despite his lowly origins, Mrs Roebuck often thought to herself (though she would never dream of saying so to her staff) that Hector bore more than a passing resemblance to the master upstairs.

'When you've done, Doris, you can give Hector a saucer of milk.'

Constance lay awake in the darkness of the dormitory, tense and restless. Around her she could hear the regular breathing of the other girls, already asleep, and Miss Savage, beyond the curtain that screened off her cubicle, murmuring prayers.

Constance could not pray. It troubled her deeply that ever since she came here, three years ago, she had been unable to pray. Once it had been a habit so easy that it had been taken for granted, but since the day she had been turned out of Weatherhead, just as William had been, the familiar phrases had deserted her. She could not even talk privately to the Saviour now. It left a terrible, cold darkness within her, a fearful desert she could not talk about, not even to Sophie.

But what made her anxious tonight was Sophie's astounding revelation that afternoon as they sat under the sycamore tree, painting a water colour for Miss Scott. What she had said had taken Constance's breath away, and then made her feel sick with revulsion.

'You're lying, Sophie! You think I'm gullible and will believe anything, like that time you told me you'd seen Miss Savage down by the pond eating tadpoles! I don't believe a word of it! It's too disgusting!'

'It's true, I tell you,' Sophie had insisted. 'Sybil told me. She's getting married and my mother told her. She said it wasn't nice, but ladies have to submit to it with good grace, otherwise there'd be no babies.'

Constance compressed her lips and argued no more. She remembered Sophie's sister Sybil, the pretty, pouting girl who had come with her parents on visitors' day. Papa and Miss Platt had been too busy to come. Sybil had a lisp, and for some minutes Constance had believed her name to be Thibble.

There was a wriggle in the next bed and Sophie whispered softly: 'We'll be home in our own beds tomorrow, Constance. Aren't you excited?'

'No,' said Constance.

'Ah, yes. I forgot. Your parents prefer your baby brother. Never mind, you'll see William again.'

That was the one glorious consolation, thought Constance. Dear William, unfailingly loving and loyal. On him she could rely for unswerving, unquestioning devotion till the end of her days. She sighed. She could almost feel at peace, but for that revolting thing Sophie had said.

'Sophie,' she whispered. 'Are you sure Sybil told you the truth?'

'Who's that? Who's talking?' Miss Savage's voice demanded angrily. 'If I have to come out there, the culprit will have to write me an essay on obedience before she goes home tomorrow, do you hear?'

For a moment there was silence. Constance held her breath.

'Yes,' Sophie whispered very softly. 'It's no tease. It's true, honestly.'

Constance lay stunned, trying to visualise the vile scene Sophie had described so graphically, visualising Papa and Miss Platt in their bedroom, and she felt her stomach heave. Until now she had felt shut out, unwanted and unloved, but in the light of this new knowledge she felt ashamed and guilty. It was *they* who should feel guilty, she thought fiercely, ashamed of their sinful complicity, but in that vile conspiracy they were shutting her out in the cold even more firmly.

When at last she slept Constance had confused, disturbing dreams of serpents surrounding her in a pit from which there was no escape. She awoke sweating and could see Sophie, bathed in a shaft of moonlight, sleeping peacefully with a serene smile on her face.

Samuel Lumb was sitting contentedly by the fire, amusing himself by reading the advertisements on the front page of *The Times* now that he had digested all the financial news. It was curious how genteel young ladies, anxious to secure a post as governess or companion to a family of substance, would declare to the world their passionate devotion to butterfly-hunting, bee-keeping or fossil-collection, wearing their hearts on their sleeves to offer their service to the highest bidder.

Cecily sat opposite, flicking through the pages of the *Pall Mall Gazette*. Between them lay the cups containing the dregs of their bedtime hot chocolate. The clock on the mantelshelf began whirring as a prelude to striking eleven. Cecily yawned, laid aside her magazine and stretched her arms gracefully above her head.

'Time for bed, my dear,' she murmured. 'I've been thinking, looking at those fashion plates . . .'

Samuel smiled. 'Ah, yes. You need a new gown for when the Durrants come to dinner, is that it?'

'No, no, my love. You are generous to a fault and I have gowns enough. No, I was thinking about Constance. She's fifteen now, and perhaps it is time she wore her hair up, don't you think?'

Samuel's smile faded. Constance. She would be home from school again tomorrow, bringing with her that air of tension and the silent, reproachful looks in her dark eyes which always disturbed him. Girls were a dratted nuisance; he never could understand them. Sons, now, presented no problem. William, newly arrived home today, had as usual made himself inconspicuous, reading or whatever he did in his own room.

He ignored Cecily's question, knowing it to be a purely rhetorical one. She would make the decision, as she always did in matters relating to the children, and her judgment was always faultless.

'How was my son today?' he enquired.

Her eyes twinkled. 'Which one, my dear? Francis was beautifully behaved as always. He's so clever at things with his hands for all he's so young — you should see the little boat he carved today!'

Samuel felt reproved. He had not been enquiring about Francis, and he had not been up to see the baby at bath-time. He endeavoured to put matters right. 'And how is William?'

'Well, my dear, and I swear he's still growing fast. Why, he's almost as tall as you now.'

'Did he bring a report from Dr Wallace?'

'It is on your desk, my dear, unopened.'

Samuel grunted. 'Well, we shall see what his headmaster has to say about him in the morning.'

Cecily replaced the cups on the tray. 'There's just one thing, Samuel . . .'

'What's that?' He looked up sharply, aware of the hesitation in her voice. She was trying to cover some misdeed.

'Oh, nothing serious, my dear. It's just that when William came in this afternoon his boots were all muddy and he didn't wipe his feet properly on the doormat. I could see Hetty was quite cross about having to clean all the muddy footmarks all the way up the stairs. Could you have a word with him about it, Samuel?'

Samuel thrust his newspaper aside irritably. 'Thoughtless young oaf,' he muttered. He disliked being bothered with such trivial domestic matters. 'Come to think of it, I heard him clattering up the stairs while I was in my study. Well, that matter is soon settled — from now on he can use the back stairs. I'll tell him in the morning.'

'And Constance . . .' Cecily began as she rose from her chair.

'You may put up her hair and do with her as you wish,' Samuel snapped.

'I was going to suggest that as she is a young lady now, perhaps we might invite her to join us at dinner occasionally, when we entertain,' Cecily said mildly. 'Perhaps when Mr and Mrs Durrant come next week?'

'If that's what you want,' muttered Samuel, rising wearily. 'I'm tired. I hope that wretched girl has heated the bed properly tonight.' Suddenly he sneezed. 'There! I'm catching a chill!' he said triumphantly.

'It's all this damp weather, very unusual for June,' Cecily said reassuringly. 'There's a new physic advertised in the *Gazette* which claims to be very efficacious – Doctor Isicek's Balsam. I'll drive into town in the morning to the pharmacy and get some for you.'

Mollified, Samuel headed for bed. Cecily was an admirable wife and mother and an excellent nurse to boot. He climbed into his nightshirt and congratulated himself inwardly once again on his unerring judgment in choosing her.

The next afternoon Samuel Lumb's carriage rolled into the drive of Weatherhead and Constance stepped out. Even in the pale sunlight which had at last penetrated the rainclouds, the house still looked gaunt and unwelcoming, and a shudder ran up her spine. To her relief and delight, when Hetty opened the front door it was William's handsome face which waited to welcome her, not Miss Platt's. Constance flung herself upon him rapturously.

'William! Oh, William! I'm so happy to see you again! Oh, my dear William, are you well?'

She held him at arm's length to savour his handsomeness, and noted at once how pale he looked. The happy glow in her dark eyes faded. 'What is it, Willie? What's wrong?' she asked in concern.

Servants were moving about them, the coachmen carrying in Constance's trunk and heaving it up the stairs, Hetty waiting patiently to take her jacket and straw bonnet. 'Nothing,' said William shortly.

Constance handed over her jacket to the maid. 'I'll see my

father after I've been upstairs to refresh myself,' she told her. Hetty nodded and left. Constance stood on the bottom step of the stairs. 'Come on up to my room, Willie. We can talk there.'

She turned to go. William coughed. 'I'll see you up there. I'm only allowed to use the back stairs,' he said, and was gone. Constance was mystified. Sitting on her bed a few minutes later, William explained. She stood stiffly by the window, seeing but not seeing the myriad daisies and buttercups that spattered the lawns. That familiar cold, hard feeling was rising inside her again.

'*She's* put Papa up to this,' she muttered bitterly. 'It is she who has made him treat you like a servant, using the back stairs, indeed! She was always jealous of you, so handsome and all. She wants him to prefer the little one.'

'He does anyway,' murmured William. 'They both do.'

'How could Papa be so cruel?' Constance cried. 'It's unforgivable! He should be so proud of you, especially since Edward . . .' Her voice tailed away, but the bitterness grew. 'I hate that boy,' she muttered.

'Oh, Connie! He's a nice little fellow really,' William remonstrated.

'I know, but he'll grow up knowing he's the favoured one. And he's not really one of us – he's *hers!*' Those hideous pictures Sophie had conjured up flitted into her inner vision. 'Oh, it's foul, it's loathsome and unnatural!' she cried hotly. William sat hunched, gratified by her anger on his behalf but not fully understanding her vehemence. Girls could be embarrassingly emotional.

'It's not the back stairs I mind so much,' he said begrudgingly. 'I'm much more annoyed that Stepmama – Miss Platt, I mean – says I've got to take Francis out for an airing if the weather is fine tomorrow. I mean, I shall feel such a fool. Suppose any of the chaps at school should come to hear of it? I'd never live that down. They'll nickname me Nanny or even worse. Really, Connie, that's women's work, not a man's.' He frowned in irritation.

Constance was staring at him, horrified. The glow had returned to her black eyes but this time it was not happiness but raging anger. 'How could she!' she hissed, and William did not care for the venom in her tone. 'Dear heaven! Is there no humiliation she would spare you? Oh, William, she must hate you as deeply as she hates me!'

'Oh, really, Connie . . .'

'She does! She hates us! She wants Papa to love only her child and not us!' The anger was gone from her voice, and now there was only fathomless, piteous despair. William laid his arm about her shoulders.

'Oh, don't take on like that, Connie. We'll survive,' he said roughly. He was out of his depth in such emotional upheaval. At school feelings were hidden if one did not want to be vulnerable. He had almost forgotten how emotional Connie could be. If only she too would grow out of it.

She clung to him now. 'You're right, Willie,' she murmured into his chest. 'We'll survive just as long as we remain true to each other. Remember our pact?'

He let go of her. 'I remember,' he said, turning away. She caught hold of his arm, looking up at him with her earnest black eyes.

'Willie? You do still feel the same, don't you?'

Embarrassed, he tried not to meet her gaze but those black eyes were commanding, penetrating. 'Of course I do. Come on now, you've got to go down and greet them.'

'They can wait. It's you I love, you I came home to see. Oh, do tell me you still love me best in the world, Willie, as I do you.'

Her voice was pleading, pathetic. He patted her arm reassuringly. 'You know I do, Connie. I'd do anything for you.'

The tense frightened look faded. 'I just needed to hear you say it. There is nothing in life for me but your love.' There was such sweet sadness in the black depths of her eyes that he bent suddenly and kissed her forehead.

'Don't be such a goose, Connie. You need never doubt me.'

A gentle smile curved the corners of her lips. 'I'm so glad, Willie, for you're all I have. Only I want you to know this – if ever there comes a day when you no longer feel the same, when you come to care for someone else more than me . . . '

'Don't say that, Connie! How could I?' he protested.

She laid a finger to his lips. 'No, listen. Perhaps you will fall in love with a girl you want to marry. I want you to know that if that happens you must feel free of our pact, for I would not chain you, Willie. I know what imprisonment feels like, and I would not do that to you. When that time comes, all you have to do is to prick your finger again, let that mingled blood of ours run out, and you will be free of me. Is that understood?'

He frowned. All this mumbo-jumbo was very childish and he did not like to be reminded of it. 'Very well. That holds for both of us. Now let's go downstairs.'

'I'll follow in a moment.'

She watched him go and felt a tinge of sadness. He was loyal and loving still, but he was growing away from her. It was this house, that woman, and that child that were the cause of it all. But for them she and William would still be roaming free on the moors above Thwaite Lodge, isolated but happy and secure in each other's love . . . But as long as they clung together and remained steadfast to their pact, they had a power that no one could undermine, a power so potent that even she could not understand it.

Dinner with the Durrants was disastrous. To begin with, Constance was infuriated by the calm, managing way in which Miss Platt had supervised the coiling up and pinning of Constance's hair in a style which felt unnatural to her, leaving her neck and ears all bare. Then the woman had added insult to injury by producing an elegant gown she had had specially made for the occasion in a dull mud colour which Constance felt only exaggerated her pallor. Papa seemed to approve Miss Platt's execrable taste, which made the humiliation all the worse.

'You look quite the young lady, my dear,' he remarked just before the guests arrived. 'You should be very grateful to your stepmama.'

Constance took her seat at table opposite Mrs Durrant and was so conscious of that lady's critical stare that she dropped her soup spoon and then accidentally trailed her napkin in the soup. Miss Platt noticed and frowned.

'Your daughter is older than I expected,' Mrs Durrant remarked to Papa. 'How old is she?'

'Fifteen already. She'll be leaving school next year.'

'And married soon after, I'll be bound,' the lady commented. 'She's really quite pretty.'

Miss Platt smiled sweetly. 'I'm afraid Constance has little to say for herself as yet. She is unused to company and has yet to learn the social graces.'

Constance busied herself trying to pick up the green peas delicately, wishing they would not talk across her and about her so rudely. It was not Papa who encouraged the comments but Miss Platt. She glared at her stepmother, who looked away with composure.

'She's really quite intelligent, though her silence would not lead one to think so. I believe she'll learn fast.'

'I'm sure she will,' said Papa. 'Now William, on the other hand, is as great an oaf as one could come across. Do you know what the scoundrel did the other day?'

Constance felt the heat rise dizzyingly to her head but Miss Platt's cool voice cut in. 'The little fellow, on the other hand, is as good as gold. One couldn't wish for a better child.'

There it was again, thought Constance savagely, the constant comparison between William and Francis in which William always lost. She longed to fling a forkful of peas in Miss Platt's cool, contemptuous face.

'That's true,' agreed Papa, and then he smiled across at Constance. 'But then, you too were a good baby, my dear. Never heard a sound from you.'

Mrs Durrant's laughter tinkled like ice in a glass. 'Nor do we hear much from her now, it seems. Don't be shy, my dear, we won't bite you.'

'I'm not shy. I just have nothing to say,' Constance growled.

'Don't be snappish, dear. It's not ladylike.' Miss Platt's tone was cold. Constance felt her cheeks redden, but she could not hold back the words.

'Nor is it ladylike to discuss me as if I weren't here,' she said hotly.

'Constance!' Papa's voice thundered. 'Leave the table at once!'

Without a word Constance rose and left the room, the cold bitterness inside her vying with raging anger. From beyond the door she heard them speak of her.

'Pity,' said Mrs Durrant. 'Such a pretty girl too.'

'And a defiant one. I shall deal with her in the morning,' she heard Papa growl. Miss Platt started talking animatedly about the fashion plates she had seen in a magazine. Constance, hurt and angry, rushed upstairs to her room.

Later, when the guests had gone, Samuel Lumb reverted to the subject of his unmannerly daughter. 'It was your idea, Cecily, to introduce her to adult company. It was a mistake. She's obviously not yet acquired any of the social graces despite what that school costs me.'

Cecily sighed. 'I'm afraid you're right, my dear, and I was wrong. We really cannot risk having more embarrassing moments like that. I fear we'll have to ban her from the parlour whenever we have guests.'

'Ban her from our company downstairs altogether until she grows up and learns some manners, that's what I'll do,' Samuel growled. 'I'll tell her that in the morning. She and William are little better than savages.'

A pall of grey smoke belched out from the fireplace. 'Oh dear,' said Cecily. 'I'm afraid it's time we had the chimneys swept again. How fortunate that did not happen while the Durrants were here. I'll arrange for the sweep to come in later this week.'

Samuel ignored the domestic crisis and left the room, still pondering irritably why Miss Scott's Academy for Young Ladies had failed so long in civilising his youngest daughter. It was unfortunate, because as Mrs Durrant had remarked, she was becoming an uncommonly attractive girl these days despite her solemn manner. Just a little charm, a little more feminine warmth and she might readily make a good catch on the marriage market in a year or so. He'd write a letter couched in strong terms to Miss Scott before the autumn term began.

To her surprise Constance found that, at last divested of the hateful gown and her hair let down again, she climbed into her bed and began to pray. Not the orthodox prayers she had been accustomed to in childhood but a series of jerky, angry phrases and questions directed at her Maker, but at least she was in communication with her God once again, and her fury began to soften.

But her fierce antagonism towards Miss Platt did not fade and Constance felt guilty even as she prayed. One had no business to commune with the divine spirit while one's heart was filled with hate.

'Lord, show me what I must do,' she begged, eyes tightly shut and hands clasped in pleading. 'Show me the way, Lord. Give me a sign.'

Over and over she repeated her plea but no illuminating flash of perception or guidance came blindingly to light her way. Morose, disenchanted, she lay for hours in the darkness and thought of Sophie. That worldly-wise young lady, accustomed to the sophistication of her father's gay social life in a London villa, would have no hesitation in finding a solution. Sophie seemed to get to know everything, from Signor Leotard's newest act at the Alhambra music hall to the horrendous details of how babies were really created. Constance shuddered again at the thought and shied away from it. Sophie would know how to put a supercilious ex-nanny like Miss Platt in her place and how to reinstate William. Treating him like a servant, indeed – the woman was insufferable!

There was only one defence against her – that Constance and William clung together in united opposition. Together they held a power even *she* could not overcome, and now that Constance could pray again, that power was invincible. Constance, Willie and God – a triumvirate proof against all.

Constance awoke with a start, droplets of sweat clammy on her face. It had been a confused dream, which left her shaken and afraid. Lying in the dark she could see images from the dream still, graphic and clear in her mind but disjointed. Clifftops, dark and jagged against the skyline and great white breakers crashing on the rocks below. William's tall, fair slenderness beside her, and then William's face melting and changing to that of another young man and he, too, had penetrating blue eyes which probed relentlessly into hers. William was far away, and appeared as a lone, tiny figure on the moor.

Her father's bedroom, large and imposing with its huge empty bed and its mahogany wardrobes and oyster-shaded lamps. Yes, she had dreamt she was in his bedroom, floating in the air like a disembodied wraith looking down on the deep turkey rug and the long cheval mirror draped by a dust sheet. Constance remembered pulling off the sheet and recoiling in horror. Reflected in the mirror was Miss Platt, naked and smiling that cool, imperial smile of hers. In the adjoining dressing room, Constance could see the gleam of the flower-patterned ewer and bowl on the dressing chest, and alongside lay Papa's leather strap next to his razor. The steel razor glowed brightly; the other objects in the room faded and vanished until only the razor remained, glowing with a radiance that seemed ethereal. Constance, drawn to it, picked it up cautiously and put a tentative finger to its sharpened edge. Behind her Miss Platt's quiet, musical laugh reached her from the bedroom. A strange, powerful sensation of mingled fear and determination that seemed to come from some outer source filled Constance and she stood there, razor in hand, transfixed and in some odd way elevated by the sensation.

And that was when she had awakened. Constance shivered. The dream was so clear, so real, and yet seemed meaningless. The one part that remained most vividly with her was that hauntingly uncanny sensation of being at once afraid and yet somehow exalted, sanctified. Like an Arthurian knight in search of the Holy Grail, she mused. What could it all signify? If only she could unravel it, she might even discover it held the sign she longed for.

From the next room the sound of a thin wail trembled on the night air. Young Francis was awake and fretful. Constance listened for the footsteps which would confirm that his nanny had come to comfort him. In a moment she heard

Ellen's voice crooning softly to the child.

'Poor little man, it's that nasty tummy-ache again, isn't it? Nanny will give you a nice warm drink and then it will all go away.'

No more tears disturbed the night and at last Constance fell asleep again. In the morning when she awoke sunlight was already shafting across the room through a gap in the curtains and her eyes were dazzled by something bright which caught and reflected the sun's brilliance. Shielding her eyes she sat up and reached across to her bedside cupboard to discover what it was.

She stared, aghast and disbelieving. It was Papa's razor, its steely blade glowing and significant, and she felt that sensation of exaltation creeping back into her body.

9

Ellen was extremely irritable next day. 'I'm sorry, Miss Constance,' she muttered apologetically at last. 'I didn't mean to snap. It's just that I'm that tired, not getting any sleep these last few nights. Of course you can come down to the village with me if Mrs Lumb agrees.'

'Perhaps you should tell her about your sleeplessness and about little Francis's pain,' Constance remarked. 'She'll want to prescribe a dose of something for him.'

Ellen glanced at the girl, unable to tell whether her remark was intended to be concerned or scornful. The mistress did indeed tend to fuss over the little one, even insisting he take his airing in a perambulator lest he should fall.

'Aye, you're right. I'll tell her now and ask at the same time if you can walk out with me.'

'Of course,' said Cecily. 'But I don't like the sound of this persistent pain of Francis's. I'll speak to Dr Lockwood today about it.'

Constance took her turn at pushing the perambulator down to the village. Ellen yawned frequently and noted that the girl, always quiet, seemed unusually preoccupied today. She did not even respond to the little one's prattling. Along the cliff path the fresh, salt-laden air helped to clear the mist from Ellen's sleepy head and she could not resist speaking mischievously to the girl.

'Are you thinking about that young man, Miss Constance? It was here you met him, wasn't it?'

The girl coloured up. 'I don't know what you mean, Ellen, I'm sure.'

'Ah, but you do. It must be more than three years ago now but you remember, same as I do. I saw you standing close by him and looking up at him when I came up that path. I never said nowt, but I saw the way you looked at him, and him at you.'

The girl did not meet her gaze. 'You didn't tell, did you, Ellen? I never saw him again.'

'Of course I didn't tell. What was there to tell, and you away to school the very next week? No, I never said owt.'

As they descended the path to the village Ellen let the matter drop and did not refer to it again while she completed her errands. Constance bought only some water-paints for William and a small coloured picture of a railway engine for Francis. The child's face glowed in pleasure but it was left to Ellen to articulate his gratitude.

'Oh, you can see he's right pleased, Miss Constance! He loves railway engines! His papa took him to York to see a railway engine in the spring and he's never stopped talking about it! Say thank you to your sister, Master Francis.'

'Thank you,' the little one lisped. Constance smiled, a fleeting, far-away smile.

'He's been busy threading a string of beads for you, Miss Constance,' Ellen confided. 'You'll finish them beads now, won't you, Master Francis?'

The child nodded. Constance made no reply, only handed over the perambulator for Ellen to push. When they reached the clifftop path again Constance lingered, staring out to sea and down at the rocks below for so long that Ellen became impatient.

'Come on now, Miss Constance, or you'll have the mistress scolding me again for bringing the baby back late for his lunch. You know how punctual she always is.'

Constance joined her alongside the perambulator and walked the rest of the way in silence.

'You're very preoccupied today,' William remarked as he lunched alone with Constance in the schoolroom. They usually ate in the nursery since Constance's disgrace had banished her from the family table, but today Dr Lockwood was in the nursery, examining Francis.

'I'm sorry,' said Constance. 'I was thinking about the sea and the breakers. Do you know what they call that fine spray that the wind blows off the top of the breakers?'

'Spray? Spume?' ventured William.

'Spindrift, blown about willy-nilly in the wind. I was watching it this morning.'

'Why should that make you so quiet?'

She shrugged and pushed her plate of prunes away. 'I don't know. It's just that the sea is so impressive, so powerful, that's all. The way it directs those huge breakers against the rocks, so majestically and brooking no refusal, it fascinates me. Don't you ever feel that you too are controlled by a force so immense that you must obey it, without question?'

William shrugged apologetically. Much as he loved his sister he found her feminine philosophy incomprehensible.

Suddenly Constance leaned forward, 'But there is something I want to tell you, William.'

She told him about the dream. 'And when I awoke, Papa's razor was at my bedside. Tell me, Willie, what do you think it all means?'

The boy was embarrassed. Interpretation of dreams was as fanciful as reading the tea-leaves. Female triviality, he thought irritably. What did dreams matter, anyway?

'Tell me, Willie, what you think?' Constance persisted.

He shrugged. 'Well, the razor didn't walk there by itself

118

and I'm sure the maid didn't put it there. Stupid as Hetty is, even she couldn't mistake you for Papa.'

He sniggered but Constance did not smile. 'Then who put it there, Willie, and why? Do you think it could be some other power?' Her black eyes were staring hard into her brother's, and he shivered.

'You've been sleepwalking again, Connie. After all, you used to quite a lot.'

'But not for years now.'

'Then you must have started again. All I can say is, you'd best put Papa's razor back before he gets angry.'

'It's not the one he uses every day but his second best one, the one he keeps in the cupboard,' Constance murmured. That was odd. In the dream it was the best one, the one lying by the leather strop. It lay now in her Great Exhibition box.

'All the same,' muttered William. 'You'd best get it back. You know how he hates anything out of place.'

'Yes,' said Constance. 'You're right.'

Not even the master was free of the irritability which seemed prevalent among his household. Samuel returned home from work that summer evening only to have to endure Cecily's list of complaints about the domestic minutiae of her day. He listened balefully, wondering why her normal serenity seemed to have deserted her so suddenly.

'The parlour isn't yet ready to use because the maids are still cleaning up after the chimney sweeps,' she said. 'The dining room is more or less ready but supper will be somewhat delayed.'

That was enough to cast gloom over him. All he wanted on his return was a quiet, leisurely supper followed by quiet conversation and an unhurried read of *The Times* accompanied by a glass or two of brandy. A late supper was a bad start.

'And I had to call Dr Lockwood in to have a look at Francis.'

'Francis? What's wrong?'

'Nothing serious, fortunately. The doctor says its only constipation, so he has prescribed a strong purgative I shall administer tonight. But the poor little thing had wretched pain again today so he missed his afternoon nap and has been fretful all day.'

Samuel looked around, desperate for consolation. 'Where's my newspaper? It should be here on the hall table.'

'Oh dear! Having the sweeps in has upset routine dreadfully! I'll ring for Hetty and enquire.'

And even when they sat at last to supper, Samuel was further annoyed. Ellen apologised for disturbing them but said Master Francis was ready for his medicine and bed. Cecily had to leave the table to see to the child. She seemed edgy and nervous today, unlike her usual self, and he wondered idly if she could be pregnant again.

As the clock struck ten the dog in the yard began to bark. Samuel looked at his wife accusingly. 'Hasn't that dog been fed yet, Cecily?'

With a sigh he put aside his paper, rose from his chair and went outside. It was a clear night, still twilight, and the dog seemed nervous rather than hungry. In its bowl Samuel could see vestiges of food.

'Must have been someone passing in the lane,' he told Cecily. 'Are the children all asleep?'

'Yes, dear. I've just been up to them. Even Francis is fast asleep, I'm glad to say. Deeply asleep — he didn't even move when I dropped my keys.'

Within an hour Samuel too was deep in slumber. He would have slept soundly throughout the night if he had not suddenly been wrenched out of his dreams by his wife nudging him sharply with her elbow. He turned over slowly.

'For heaven's sake, Cecily!' he mumbled angrily. 'What the devil is the matter?'

'Listen! Didn't you hear it? It sounded like someone opening or closing a window downstairs!' Cecily's voice trembled.

'Probably one of the maids closing the window,' he muttered. 'Go back to sleep.'

'No, Samuel. They all went to bed ages ago. I heard them. Oh Samuel! It could be a burglar! Do go down and see, but take care to arm yourself first!'

It was not like Cecily to become so agitated. Muttering

imprecations he climbed out of bed, struck a lucifer to light the candle and lumbered sleepily down the stairs. The house seemed quiet and he did not believe for one second that any intruder had broken in. Into the house of Samuel Lumb, and with a fierce guard dog in the yard? It was impossible.

Near the bottom of the stairs he halted. The arc of candle-light had suddenly encircled a white figure in the hallway, and he caught his breath. 'Who's that?' he demanded.

It was Constance. She came towards him slowly but she did not speak. There was something strange about her manner, her dark eyes wide and her black hair spilling down over the white of her nightdress. She was gliding up the stairs but looking straight ahead and past him, as though unaware of his presence.

Samuel drew back to let her pass, a trifle uneasy. It looked as if the girl was sleepwalking again just as she used to. He heard her return to her room and close the door.

Breathing a deep sigh he went back upstairs. No need to investigate further now. Cecily's keen ears must have detected Constance's barefoot wanderings, that was all. Should he tell Cecily about the recurrence of the girl's sleepwalking, he wondered? It might worry her unnecessarily if indeed she was pregnant again. Samuel's decision did not have to be made until the morning, for when he returned to his bed his wife, he discovered, was already soundly asleep again.

Ellen opened her eyes slowly, yawned and stretched. Daylight glowed between the curtains, and from force of habit over the years she found herself already up and crossing to the door. Still rubbing her sleep-filled eyes, she looked into Francis' nursery.

The cot was empty, and the sheets neatly refolded into place. Puzzled, Ellen came close and looked down. It was only five o'clock, but the mistress must have been up in the night and taken the child to her room as she sometimes did when he was fretful.

Her limbs still heavy with sleep, Ellen made for the mistress's bedroom and tapped lightly on the door. No reply met her ears beyond the master's heavy snores. Mrs Lumb would be angry if she were awakened, especially if she had had to see to the child in the night. Gratefully, Ellen returned to her narrow bed and the unfinished dream of a golden day in the countryside spent alone with young Arnold from the bakery.

Cecily Lumb rolled over and stretched leisurely. Samuel's place in the bed was empty and already cold. She looked across at the mantel clock. Past eight. He must have risen quietly so as not to disturb her. How thoughtful he could be on occasions!

There was a tap at the door, agitatedly repeated. Cecily frowned. 'Come in.'

Ellen's pink face appeared round the door. 'The older children are washed and dressed, madam. Shall I . . .?' she stopped suddenly.

'Shall you what, Ellen?' her mistress demanded.

The girl's face was red, her jaw agape. Cecily Lumb felt irritated.

'Master Francis – he's not with you,' Ellen stumbled.

'Of course he's not! Why on earth should you think he was?'

'But I thought – he's not in his cot – he hasn't been since five o'clock – I thought you'd taken him!' The colour was draining from the girl's face.

Cecily sat up. 'What are you talking about? Of course I didn't get up in the night, and he was sleeping deeply in any case.'

'But he's not there, madam!' Ellen's voice was rising.

'Then he's with Constance, or Hetty, perhaps.'

'No, madam, he isn't. I've seen them both and they thought he must be with you too! Oh Lord! Where can he be?'

Cecily paled and swung her legs out of bed. 'Pass me my robe, then go down to the kitchen and ask Mrs Roebuck and Doris and the bootboy if they've seen him.'

Ellen's lip trembled. 'Cook hasn't, for I've asked.'

Her mistress seized her by the shoulders. 'Don't panic, girl. Has the master been gone long? Send the boy after him to fetch him back.'

Ellen scuttled away. The mistress hurried to the nursery. The cot was empty and its sheets neatly tucked in place. She rushed into the schoolroom, where Constance sat, hands folded in her lap and eyes downcast, opposite William.

'Have you seen Francis at all, anywhere, today?' their stepmother demanded.

'No, Mama,' said William. Constance shook her head slowly without looking up. Cecily withdrew quickly to continue her quest elsewhere.

William came up close to his sister. 'You're very quiet this morning, Connie. Are you worried about Francis? Surely nothing can have happened to him. He's hiding, probably. He can be very mischievous at times.'

Constance looked at him, her black eyes clouded. 'Willie, have you opened my box — you know, the one Papa brought for me from the Great Exhibition?'

'Box? What box? I was talking about Francis.'

'Willie. Answer me! I have a reason for asking. Tell me, *did* you open my box?'

'No, of course not. What would I want with your trinkets? Chaps don't go snooping in girls' trinket boxes!' His injured tone conveyed his innocence. Constance sighed. 'Why do you ask, anyway?'

'No matter. It makes no difference.' Her voice was small, defeated.

William sat down opposite her. 'What is it, Connie? What makes no difference?'

She shrugged and turned away, avoiding his gaze. 'As I said once, we are one and what one of us does the other is responsible for too.'

The words she used at the blood-pact, he recalled. 'Oh, that, yes,' he murmured. He could not undestand its significance now; it was a childish incident he preferred to forget.

His sister rose suddenly and hugged him. 'It holds true still, Willie, I swear. Whatever you do I share in it, and vice versa. Do not fear. I am with you always.'

'I know.' Her words had given him courage once when life was hard at the hands of bullies at school. But they no longer seemed appropriate. 'Shall we go down, Connie?'

She seated herself again and folded her hands in her lap. 'We'll wait. They'll send for us soon enough.'

Weatherhead was in a state of frenzy. The master had been overtaken as he rode to work, had returned and ordered a thorough search of the house. It was scoured in vain. There was no sign of Francis or of what could have happened to him. All that was unusual was that the parlour window was open and, according to Hetty, she had found it open when she went in first thing in the morning.

'I thought maybe Mrs Lumb left it open to air the room, sir,' she told her master. He scowled, for he knew the womenfolk did not care for the aroma of his cigar.

Cecily Lumb paled. 'There, I thought I heard a window being opened in the night,' she said agitatedly. 'You went down, Samuel. Didn't you see it was open?'

'No,' he replied shortly, and some inner caution prevented him from adding that he had encountered Constance on the stairs. 'We'll waste no more time. Send the boy to fetch the police. In the meantime tell the coachman to round up some of the locals to start searching the neighbourhood.'

Hetty scuttled away. Samuel, his normally ruddy face pale and taut, strode out to lead the search. Within minutes men from the lane came eagerly to help, their anger over the fence and the fishing rights forgotten.

When he returned an hour later, even paler and more tense from his fruitless search, he found two men closeted in the parlour with his red-eyed wife. He recognised the older man.

'Oh, Inspector Garlick, I'm so glad you're here!' he cried. 'Someone has stolen my son!'

'So I understand, sir. Now if you would be so good . . .'

For the next few minutes the police inspector questioned and Samuel protested. 'While you're keeping us here those gipsies are making off with my son!' he cried out. 'By now they'll be miles away and we'll never find their trail!'

'What makes you think it's gipsies, sir?' the inspector asked mildly.

'Who else could it be? They're well-known for kidnapping, especially the children of — of gentlemen known to be comfortably placed,' he roared.

'But there are no gipsies in the neighbourhood at the moment, sir. If you would permit, it would be better to investigate my way, sir. We are accustomed to these things. Diligent questioning of your family and servants may reveal the boy's whereabouts.'

Samuel cast a helpless look at his silent wife. 'Well, I think we'd be better employed searching,' he rumbled.

'Just what I was about to say, sir,' rejoined the inspector. 'The constable here will go with your manservants to search the grounds while I ask Mrs Lumb more questions.'

'The grounds have been searched, man! The child is far away by now!'

'Nevertheless, sir, we shall observe the customary routine. Constable.'

The younger man stepped forward. 'Sir?'

'Do as I say. Search the grounds, thoroughly.'

Samuel slumped in a chair, momentarily defeated. The inspector was asking questions again about just what Mrs Lumb heard in the night, whether she had in fact left the parlour window open, and whether she believed all her servants to be entirely trustworthy. Samuel fulminated inwardly.

There was a rap at the door. Cecily called, 'Come in.'

The constable entered. 'Well?' demanded the inspector.

'Sir, could I have a word with you?'

The inspector rose quickly and went outside, closing the door. Samuel looked across at his wife expectantly, but neither spoke. In a few moments the inspector returned, alone. He stood by the door, eyes downcast.

'Mr and Mrs Lumb, I'm afraid I have bad news to impart to you. I hope you can bear it with fortitude.' He spoke quietly, so quietly that Mrs Lumb's answering gasp filled the air with the shot-crack of a pistol. Samuel, standing, reached for the chairback.

'Tell us, Inspector.'

'Your son has been found. I regret to tell you that he is dead.'

For a moment there was a silence so tangible it cloaked the air of the parlour like a shroud. Samuel turned away. 'Where?' His voice was minute, trembling.

'In the garden, sir, in the privy amongst the shrubbery. He had been stabbed.'

Cecily's screams slashed through the air, piercing, knife-like. From upstairs Constance could hear the sound and understood. Clasping her hands together she stood by the bedroom window.

'Dear Lord, if it was Your will, then so be it.'

Inspector Garlick fingered his chin while the constable stood awaiting further orders. 'Odd business this, Tom,' he murmured. 'Despite that open window there's something makes me feel it was an inside job. But who on earth would want to kill a small child?'

The constable made no answer. The two officers were alone together in the stone-flagged laundry room of Weatherhead where the small corpse lay, covered by a sheet, on the table. The scullery next door had been designated for Garlick to interview the household staff and now, preliminary questions completed, Garlick was mulling over what he had learnt.

'The child was put to bed with a dose of some medicine — we must enquire of Dr Lockwood about that — and both the mistress and the child's nurse say that he was deeply asleep at midnight. About that time the yard dog was heard to bark but no one was about in the grounds. Some time after that Mrs Lumb thinks she heard a window being opened, but Mr Lumb says when he went down he noticed no window open.

'The nurse tells us that at five o'clock she found the child gone from his cot and the sheets folded. Believing her mistress to have taken him, she tried to enquire but did not wish to disturb her. At eight it was confirmed the child was missing and then the open window was discovered. What do you deduce from that, then, Tom?'

The young constable shrugged. 'Only that it appears likely the child was taken between midnight and three or four o'clock.'

'The same conclusion as I have reached. The window?'

'That may have been left open last night.'

'But Mr Lumb did not notice it when he went down. Odd, that. I had the feeling he was telling us less than he knew.'

'My feeling too, sir. His eyes never once met yours.'

'You noticed that too? Glad to see you're developing the right powers of observation, young Lawson. Still, it is our duty to work from facts, not intuition.'

'Nor does it make sense that a man should have any part in the murder of his own child,' Lawson murmured.

'Perhaps not, though stranger things have happened. Remind me to tell you about the Agnes Dawson affair some time. No, it was more likely one of the servants. That boot boy, it seems, is under notice to leave and so he has a motive. Moreover, he came early to work today to clean the knives.'

He glanced meaningfully at the sheet-covered corpse. Tom Lawson shook his head. 'All the knives have been accounted for, sir. I've watched the cook count them, and there's no bloodstains. Mrs Roebuck was quite offended; she said she always keeps her knives gleaming.'

'It could have been another knife, a gardening tool, perhaps,' the inspector ventured. 'After all, the child was put down the privy after being stabbed. He could have been killed outside.'

'The wound is clean, sir, no sign of dirt or mud. And it seems narrow and deep, not like a scythe or secateurs would make.'

Inspector Garlick sighed. The motive for the boot boy was too flimsy, anyway. But who could possibly have any motive that would direct a keen knife at a five-year-old child? Mother and nurse were clearly distraught, though the inspector was experienced enough to know that apparent grief could be a cloak for secret guilt. The father was in turns numbed and angry. The remaining family, the boy of fourteen and girl of fifteen, were both said by the nurse to be devoted to the child whenever they were home from school. Still, they had better be interviewed too, although it was unlikely they would add any further light to the mystery.

Inspector Garlick rose and left the laundry. The children

would have to be interviewed upstairs, not down here in the servants' area. As he trudged up the stairs, followed by Lawson, he wondered what sixth sense it was that kept telling him, again and again, most insistently, that this was an inside job.

'You know,' he said to his constable as he seated himself at Mr Lumb's desk in the study, 'there will have to be an inquest about this. Prepare a report for the coroner after we've interviewed the children.'

'Yes, sir.'

'And by the way, if you carry on as well as you have, I think I'll be recommending you to be made up before long to sergeant,' Garlick added casually. 'You've been with us long enough now and you've proved yourself.'

'That's very good of you, sir.'

'Now send for the boy. What's his name? Ah yes, Master William.'

Constance hovered at the door of her bedroom feeling lost and afraid. Everyone else in the house seemed to be intent on other business and forgetful of her presence. She felt bewildered, frightened, and once more very lonely.

William had locked himself in his room all morning and refused to open the door until Papa ordered him downstairs to answer questions. He was down there now, alone in the study with the police officers, and she feared what he might say. If only she could have talked to him. But for the first time in his life William had shut her out.

There was a strange silence over Weatherhead. The servants had vanished, no doubt to congregate and speculate in whispers in some remote region of the house. Miss Platt's screams had ended after Dr Lockwood was summoned to give her a sedative. She was in her room now, probably sleeping, and Papa was in the parlour alone. Constance shivered. She had felt lonely many times before, but never so desolate as now.

The study door opened and closed and she heard William's footsteps coming upstairs. She went forward eagerly to meet him. 'William, what did they ask? What did you tell them?'

She gazed up anxiously into his clouded eyes.

William brushed her hands away. 'Nothing. There was nothing I could tell them. I didn't hear or see anything until this morning, just like you.'

'You didn't tell them you used to sleepwalk?'

'Sleepwalk? Of course not! For heaven's sake, Connie, that was only once years ago, when I was a child. I'd forgotten.' He pushed past her and went into his room closing the door.

She bit her lip She had frightened him by reminding him of what he would rather forget, like the difficulties in his early days at school. Another footstep, firmer and more resolute, sounded on the stairs, and she knew it was that of a stranger. She hurried back into her room and shut the door.

There was a tap. 'Miss Constance?' A male voice, muffled by the thick wood.

'Yes?'

'Inspector Garlick would like a word with you, Miss.'

'Very well. I'll be down in a moment.'

The footsteps receded. Constance stood before the mirror and surveyed her reflection. The smooth dark hair and composed features betrayed no sign of the turmoil within. All she need do was to stand before her interrogators, hands clasped and eyes downcast, and answer their questions truthfully, and they would never guess the turbulent suspicions that eddied in her brain.

Inspector Garlick leaned on the desk, making a steeple of his fingertips. 'Well, Lawson? What did you make of Master William?'

'Very little, sir. He could tell us nothing since he himself knew nothing until he heard the panic this morning.'

'Didn't you think it odd that, like his father, he could not bring himself to meet my gaze?'

Young Lawson spread his hands. 'Embarrassment, sir. I'm sure he had nothing to hide.'

'You may be right,' the inspector admitted. 'Boys of that age are inclined to be gauche. Let's see if the girl can tell us any more.'

A tap came at the door. 'Enter,' called the inspector. He watched her entrance carefully from under his bushy eye-brows; he was trained to observe and deduce. The girl was tall for her age, slender and fine-boned. With her dark eyes and raven hair she showed signs of becoming a very hand-some woman. She moved well too, with grace and gentleness.

'Come in, my dear. Lawson, a chair for the young lady.'

Her dark eyes moved towards the young constable stand-ing unobtrusively in the corner, and Garlick saw the slight movement as she saw him, a silent intake of breath. Lawson stood immobile for a second, staring at her.

'Do you know Miss Lumb, Constable?' Garlick enquired.

Galvanised, Lawson moved to fetch a straight-backed chair. 'For a moment I thought it was a young lady I met once, long ago, sir,' Garlick heard him murmur, 'but it seems I was mistaken. Will you please to be seated, Miss Lumb?'

The girl sat. It did not escape Inspector Garlick's notice that throughout his questions to her, which revealed nothing, her eyes did not stray from the young constable who stood behind them. Garlick sighed as he took notes. It was always difficult examining young ladies when there was a presentable young officer to divert their attention.

When at last she was gone, Garlick turned in his chair. 'Well. No further light from that quarter, it seems.'

'No, sir.

Garlick sighed. 'We have a dead child, stabbed and pushed down a privy in the garden and no apparent reason, no motive. Everyone seems to have been fond of the little boy. There are suspects, but with no strong motive.'

'Suspects, sir?'

'The nurse, the father and the older boy who behaved suspiciously, the villagers who, we know, resented Mr Lumb, not to mention the boot boy, who was under notice. But there's no case we could present, not unless we've over-looked something. Get cracking on that report at once, Lawson, for there will have to be an inquest.

10

On the day of the inquest grey drizzle-laden skies lowered over the village. The little corpse had been transferred from the laundry of Weatherhead to the saloon bar of the Black Lion. Samuel Lumb, grief-stricken as he was, was stupefied by the vast numbers of local folk who thronged the bar and pressed eagerly at the doorway of the inn. A mass of moon-faces stared at him and his family.

Whether it was out of sympathy or morbid curiosity Samuel hardly cared. It was pure anguish for him that the enormity of his son's death was to be compounded by the public interrogation of his family and servants. With bowed head he sat at Cecily's side, not daring to look at her pale, expressionless face lest his manhood should desert him. William and Constance sat beyond her.

The jury was sworn in and the coroner began. Hetty and Ellen's evidence was straightforward and soon concluded. The nurse testified that the child, always a heavy sleeper, slept unusually soundly that night after having missed his afternoon nap. She also swore that no one had entered her room and that she had heard no sound from the child's room. The police inspector, who followed, gave evidence of how the body was discovered and how there was remarkably little blood on the corpse and its clothing. Dr Lockwood also averred that he would have expected more bloodstains, since the child's death was due to stabbing and not to drowning after immersion in the privy.

The coroner was calling Constance's name. Samuel looked up as his daughter, pale but dry-eyed, rose from her seat beside Cecily and stood erect before the coroner, her eyes downcast. The brim of her bonnet, he could see, was still damp from the fine rain.

'Now, my dear,' said the coroner, looking at Constance kindly over the top of his pince-nez, 'tell us briefly, in your own words, what you recall of that night, and how everyone felt towards your little brother.'

Constance did not look up. 'I knew nothing until he was found,' she said, in a voice so low Samuel had to strain to hear. 'I went to bed at half-past ten and fell asleep quickly. I slept soundly, as usual, and did not get up during the night. I heard no noise nor anything unusual. In the morning as I was getting up I heard he was missing.'

'And how did people feel about him?' prompted the coroner.

'I am not aware of anyone having a grudge against him. Ellen has always been kind and attentive.'

The coroner, satisfied, dismissed Constance and called William. He stood erect but, unlike his sister, looked his inquisitor full in the face. His evidence varied little from Constance's; having once gone to bed he slept soundly, did not get out of bed until seven next morning, and heard nothing.

'Did everyone in the house get on well with your little brother?' the coroner asked.

'Indeed,' asserted William. 'He was a great favourite with everyone.'

'Then you know of no reason why anyone should have a grudge against him?'

'None at all.'

Ridiculous questions, thought Samuel. Why on earth should anyone dislike a child of only five years? It was clear to him, at least, that the motive for an otherwise pointless act must be revenge – against himself, not poor little Francis. He looked at the sea of faces. He knew the villagers hated him for his fence and his private stretch of the river, but surely that was a feeble reason to rob him of his beloved son. Any one of those whispering, speculating locals could have done it – must have done it, for it surely could not be one of his own. Not the children, decidedly not Cecily, and hardly any of the servants; even if he was an exacting master he was no more so than any gentleman of his standing. He was so immersed in his thoughts that he barely noticed when the jury retired to the tap room.

Cecily would not look at him; her gaze fixed on her black-gloved hands folded in her lap. Constance was exchanging looks with William. Samuel leaned across to her. 'They already have my deposition and your Mama's,' he said softly, to explain why they had not been called. As he spoke he remembered with a twinge of guilt that there was one fact he had omitted to put down in that deposition — but why, he argued with himself, should he cast unwarranted suspicion on his daughter by mentioning his midnight encounter with her on the stairs? The girl was clearly sleepwalking, as she had done so often before. She was up to no mischief. A handful she might be at times, for Cecily anyway, but a vicious creature, never!

He looked at her from the corner of his eye. She sat composed, as if unaware of the plebeian scrutiny. He was fond of her, proud of her quick brain and well-read opinions on the rare occasions he enjoyed her company alone. It was a great pity she and Cecily had never understood each other.

And William. Samuel transferred his gaze to his son. He was the sole heir to all Samuel Lumb's wealth and acquisitions now Edward and Francis were gone. Samuel sighed deeply. William was a pleasant enough boy but weak and not too bright, hardly the shrewd and ruthless man needed to succeed to the Lumb estate. At fourteen he still showed no sign of toughening up into a man despite that school. The army, perhaps, would rub the effeminate edges off him and do the trick.

Cecily nudged him. 'They're coming back,' she whispered. Instantly the murmuring and whisperings ceased and the sea of faces turned as one toward the foreman of the jury. The coroner spoke gravely. 'Have you reached your verdict?'

'We have,' replied the foreman. 'Wilful murder by some person or persons unknown.'

Lumb snorted. The verdict was self-evident. The silence

in the saloon bar was broken by murmurs and comments as one of the jurymen added audibly, 'Aye, but there's a suspicion which don't easily settle on my stomach.'

Samuel sat still, shocked by the implication, and the murmur grew to a sudden buzz and a few 'Ayes' and 'Hear, hears.' He saw Cecily waver and reach out, as though she were going to faint.

'Come,' said Samuel abruptly. 'Let's leave,' and quickly he led his family through the crowd and out into the rain. Ellen, Mrs Roebuck and the other servants stumbled out after them, and from the carriage Samuel watched them lower their heads against the drizzle to follow their master on foot. A trickle of villagers emerged from the inn to watch, and amongst them Samuel recognised a young man. It was the constable who had come to Weatherhead with Inspector Garlick.

Late that evening Samuel could bear the oppressive silence in the parlour no longer. Cecily refused to speak or to cry, and the servants crept in and out with lowered gaze and made him feel as though speech would be sacrilege. He made up his mind to go and talk to William. Perhaps with male company he would feel more at ease.

He tapped at the boy's door and turned the knob, but the door would not yield. It was locked. From inside he heard William's tremulous voice.

'Go away, Connie! I don't want to talk to anyone, not even you!'

Surprised, Samuel knocked harder. 'William, it's me. Open this door.'

A moment later he heard the grate of the key in the lock and William's face appeared, level with his own but drawn and white. 'I'm sorry, Papa, I thought it was Constance but I truly don't want to talk to anyone. Please forgive me.'

Samuel cleared his throat. 'Well, that's understandable in the circumstances. We all grieve in our different ways. I did want to have a talk with you, my boy, but it can wait if you prefer to meditate and pray.'

'Thank you, sir.'

'Ah, well, goodnight then, William.'

'Goodnight, Papa.' The door closed again, and once more the key grated in the lock. Samuel turned away, walking straight past Constance's room.

Mrs Roebuck stood, hands on hips, watching critically as Doris applied Zebo to the black lead grate. The world might be going topsy-turvy but the one sure way to try and bring it back under control was to cling rigidly to routine, to carry on as normal as though madness had never attacked Weatherhead.

'Not too thick, then polish it up with the brush,' Mrs Roebuck admonished. 'And just what are they saying in the village? You said there was gossip about Weatherhead.'

'Aye, well, there would be, wouldn't there, when the inquest said it was murder. Everyone thinks different about who did it,' the girl replied, her already rosy cheeks reddening more with effort as she rubbed.

'Oh, yes? And who do you think did it? No one in this house, I hope.'

Doris cast her a wary glance and shrugged. 'Nay, I said nowt.'

'I should hope not. It must have been gipsies or vagabonds who broke in. It's certainly no one here,' said the cook, folding her arms in defiance of argument. 'I reckon they'll never find him.'

'Well, I heard as the magistrates aren't satisfied,' Doris muttered. 'The newspapers are still full of it so they want more enquiries made.'

'Dear heaven!' exploded Mrs Roebuck. 'Don't they think as Mr and Mrs Lumb has had enough?'

'That's as may be, but I hear they're calling Scotland Yard in,' said Doris through clenched teeth. 'Is that shiny enough?'

Mrs Roebuck sensed an air of triumph in Doris's tone, proud of disclosing news to her superior. 'No, it's not,' she snapped. 'In my kitchen it's not good enough till you can see your face in it so get a bit of elbow grease to it, my girl. You'll not go home till it's right.'

Doris sighed. 'Here,' she said after a moment, 'did you see that handsome young policeman at the Black Lion today? Constable Lawson, I think he were called.'

'You keep your mind on your work and never mind young men, my girl. You're far too young for followers yet.'

'No, I'm not. But it weren't me he kept looking at,' Doris said mischievously. Mrs Roebuck scented more gossip but determined to set a good example.

'I'm quite sure it wasn't. Where's Hetty?' she demanded.

'Gone to bed. Miss Constance wanted her to sleep in her room with her.'

'Poor little thing. She must be very frightened to ask that. Now you finish the grate while I go down to the larder. By the time I get back that grate will be gleaming like a new pin or you'll not be home this side of midnight. Do I make myself clear?'

'Yes, Mrs Roebuck,' sighed Doris, but she wished with all her heart that Constable Lawson had kept his eyes fixed on her instead of on Miss Constance, who neither saw nor cared.

Constance lay in the feather depths of her bed listening to the snuffles of Hetty in the low bed in the corner. A night candle still burned on the washstand, Hetty's tacit admission that she too was nervous and afraid.

The girl's muffled snores, though unpleasant, were reassuring. It was less frightening than being alone. William was alone, but by choice. Locked into his room, he would not even allow Constance to come in, and the thought distressed her. Always so close in times of trouble in the past, he chose to shut her out now when the worst trouble of all overtook them.

But she would not think of that for the deed was so ghastly, so horrifying that it did not bear further contemplation. She must find some way to shut it out of her mind forever. Constance clenched her eyes tightly and tried to visualise a beautiful scene.

The cliffs, and the spinning sea below. And a handsome, grave-faced youth who gazed deeply into her eyes. She had recognised him at once when Inspector Garlick called her to the study, though he had given no sign of recognition, not then. But at the inquest today she knew that Tom Lawson remembered her just as vividly as she remembered him. But would he ever speak of it, she wondered. A policeman now, upholder of law and authority, perhaps he might not, dare not, as long as she lay under the dark shadow of suspicion. The thought saddened her almost as much as William's rejection and, sighing deeply, she turned her face to the wall to try and sleep. Attempts at prayer were useless and she felt even more desperately alone, isolated with a terrible dark secret she could share with no one, not even God.

Ironically, the sun shone with all the heat and brilliance of July the day the tiny body of Francis Lumb was lowered into its grave in the little parish churchyard. The whole scene seemed strangely unreal to the brother and sister who stood at the graveside, solemnly casting down a handful of earth to ring hollowly on the little coffin, just as the mourning parents had done.

'It wasn't at all like Mama's funeral,' William commented later when they were alone together. 'Do you remember, Connie?'

'Yes.' She removed her black-veiled bonnet and laid it aside.

'It poured with rain and there were horses with black plumes and everything. Lots of people were there, too. I wonder why Uncle Reginald and Aunt Bertha didn't come today, or Elizabeth and Mary Jane.'

'Funerals for little children never are as ceremonious as for grown-ups. Too many children die young,' his sister replied.

'Perhaps they didn't want to come, considering the way Francis died,' William remarked. Constance looked at him curiously, but his face betrayed nothing. 'Still, it's not over yet. Papa told me an inspector from Scotland Yard is coming on Monday. There'll be more questions yet.'

'I fear so,' said Constance. 'We must just pray for strength, Willie.'

'I'm just glad about one thing: they didn't ask us to go and kiss him in his coffin,' the boy murmured, and she could see

137

the slight ripple of a shudder that passed across his broad shoulders. Poor William. She could remember still how sick he was after being obliged to kiss poor dead Mama.

'I wonder what the man from Scotland Yard will find when Inspector Garlick failed to find anything,' Constance mused.

She did not have long to wait. On Monday morning Ellen announced, pink with embarrassment, that the master had already received the gentleman, Inspector Wheeler, and that the police officer was to come up to Miss Constance's room to talk to her.

'In a young lady's bedroom, really, I never heard the like!' Ellen exclaimed, bustling around to remove items of Constance's clothing and Hetty's nightgown from the little bed. 'Surely he could have used Master William's room?'

'He probably thinks to put me at my ease in my own territory,' Constance said smoothly. 'Don't worry, for I'm not embarrassed, Ellen.'

Her composure vanished as soon as she saw him – a short, portly man with a pock-marked skin and a formidable air. She acknowledged Ellen's introduction with an inclination of her head.

'Pray be seated, sir,' Constance said, indicating the one high-backed chair the bedroom boasted. He ignored her invitation, producing instead a slip of paper from his pocket. 'Is this your handwriting, Miss Constance?'

She took the paper and inspected it. 'Indeed it is. It's my laundry list.'

'For last week. Three nightdresses, it says. Can you show them to me?'

She opened the dresser drawer and took out two neatly folded nightdresses. 'The third is currently in use, under my pillow.'

Inspector Wheeler shook out and inspected all three. She knew what he sought: bloodstains. The murder had taken place during the night, so he would expect to find bloodstains on someone's nightgown – if it was a member of the household.

Disappointed, he threw them on the bed. 'Thank you. A matter of routine, you understand. Were you fond of your brother, Miss Constance?' The inspector was regarding her thoughtfully.

Constance drew herself upright. 'Are you referring to my brother William, or my half-brother?'

'Ah yes, forgive me, I forgot. I referred to young Master Francis.'

'Yes, I was fond of him.'

'I was led to believe you resented him,' the inspector said coolly.

'Who told you that?'

'A school friend of yours. A Miss Sophie Haversham. I took the precaution of speaking to her after your head teacher told me you were friends. I spoke to Master William's friends too.'

'Sophie evidently misunderstood. I was genuinely fond of Francis — ask Ellen.'

'Ellen?' His eyebrows rose in question.

'The nanny. She'll tell you how well I got on with Francis. I bought him a gift the day he died and he was making a string of beads for me. I played with him for a while in the nursery before he went to bed.'

'I see. I understand Master William was not so eager to play with him as you were.' She saw the inspector's abstracted gaze but knew his shrewd ears were waiting for any inflection which could betray more than words. She spoke with careful control, despite the clamour in her head.

'I believe he was just as fond of him but you must ask William for yourself, sir.'

'I shall, in due course. But I had heard something about your brother being obliged to push the perambulator and resenting it.'

'And what boy of fourteen would not?' Constance countered.

'And that he had to use the back stairs.'

Constance turned away to the window to hide the flush that leapt to her cheeks. 'That had nothing to do with Francis, only that William once came in with muddy boots.'

'And Mrs Lumb ordered him to go in and out by the back stairs?'

'Yes, but that did not anger William,' Constance said crossly. If the man was trying to make her reveal motives to point to William being the murderer, he would fail.

'Perhaps not,' said Inspector Wheeler smoothly, 'but it does seem likely that the murderer could have used the back stairs. Someone would surely have seen or heard him — or her — on the main staircase.'

Constance bit her lip. This man was clearly far more alert and cunning than Inspector Garlick — and far more suspicious. He took his leave of her as abruptly as he had come.

By the end of the day an ominous, oppressive air of silent suspense lay over Weatherhead, for it became clear that Inspector Wheeler had behaved towards everyone, from the master down to the boot-boy, as if he believed each one in turn to be the villain. Only Cecily Platt had been spared his probing tongue, Constance discovered. Everyone else went about his or her duties furtively or clung to the privacy of his room.

She waited tensely, fearful of the outcome. For a whole week it seemed as if all the house was prepared for the inspector's accusation, but none came. The air was filled with a sense of brooding and mutual distrust. Doors remained locked and the occupants of the house morose. Daily routine changed little except that none of the family was allowed out of the house because the locals were loitering inquisitively around the lane and boundary fences. And Constance and William now dined with their parents instead of in the deserted nursery.

The following Monday, the air shimmering in a heat-haze, Constance was walking alone in the gardens, savouring the heady scent of the roses, when she saw a blue-uniformed figure walk up the drive to the front door.

She knew at once it was Tom Lawson and that despite his unwavering step he had seen her. She resolved to sit in the little arbour and await his exit. He would come, he would speak to her this time, she knew, whatever his errand to Weatherhead. It did not take many minutes for soon she heard the front door open again and then steady footsteps crunching over the gravel towards her.

She did not look up as his tall shadow fell across her lap.

'Miss Constance?' His tone was politely curious.

'Ah, Constable Lawson! Do you bring news?' She allowed her gaze to travel up to the handsome, sober face and felt again the same sense of kinship as she met his blue eyes.

'I have just reported to your father that Inspector Wheeler has returned to London. He is to prefer no charge.' If he felt anything, he did not allow emotion to enter his voice.

'So we are all cleared of suspicion? That is wonderful. I can't tell you how happy that makes me, and you, as the bearer of good news, are doubly welcome. Will you stay and talk a while?'

Removing his helmet he accepted the seat beside her on the bench. His sober eyes grew more solemn. 'I cannot, unfortunately, say that all suspicion is lifted, Miss Constance, only that the inspector could not find sufficient evidence to substantiate a case. He was very angry about it. I fancy he felt defeated. He said the local police were far from co-operative.'

'Is that true?' Constance enquired.

'To a certain extent. Inspector Garlick was hurt that the Yard was called in and the matter taken out of his hands. And Inspector Wheeler's attitude with us was high-handed, to say the least.'

Constance felt warmed by his manner, the confidential comments one would only entrust to a friend. She knew he felt just as at ease with her as she with him.

'You say Inspector Wheeler was angry over not being able to bring a charge – did he suspect someone?'

There was a moment's pause. She glanced up and saw his troubled gaze before he answered. 'I must be honest with you, Miss Constance. He was convinced it was you.'

She drew in her breath sharply. 'Me? Oh, Tom! Do you believe it too, that I killed Francis?'

His hand reached out and his fingertips touched hers, only for a fleeting second, but she felt a surge of emotion that wavered between fear and yearning. He was shaking his fair head slowly.

'I remember you and the spindrift and the strange things

141

you said. I looked forward so much to that Monday and the fair and seeing you again. You never came. I could not understand it.'

'They sent me away, Tom. I could not tell you.'

The cloud lifted from his expression. 'So that was it! I was so sure there was something – something special – between us, though we had barely met. Some kind of understanding that did not need words. I thought you sensed it too.'

Withdrawing her gaze from his Constance nodded dumbly. Now that he spoke of it she could feel it growing again, that warm sense of trust and hope that once she had been able to share only with William. Was it possible one could experience that wonderful closeness twice in a lifetime? It was almost too much to hope.

Suddenly he rose and picked up his helmet. 'I must be on my way, Constance, but I shall see you again soon. You have no further need to fear – the police will not trouble you again over this dreadful business, but I shall return as a friend, if you'll have me.'

She looked up at his tall breadth, so much more muscular and filled out now than when she had first met him. He was a man now, no longer a stripling youth.

'Oh yes,' she said softly. 'I recognised you at once when you came with Inspector Garlick, and you did not give me away. I looked for your face at the inquest to give me strength.'

'I was at the graveyard too, at the funeral, though you did not see me. Now that I've found you again I shall always be close.'

She watched him stride away along the path to the drive, her heart warming to the sight of him.

'Miss Constance! Where are you? The master wants you!' Hetty called out from the house.

Constance stole several more seconds alone in the arbour before she emerged to acknowledge the summons. If not with a light heart, then at least with a warmth at having established human contact at last, she made her way up to the house.

Papa was in the parlour, the greyness gone from his face.

'Constance my dear, your mama and I are going out into the town. The constable has just called to inform us that the inspector has returned to London and the whole matter has been dropped. That being so, we are no longer confined to the house. Is there anything you would like us to bring you?'

'Thank you, no, Papa. I am relieved.'

'So are we all, my dear. Pray tell William for me.'

But William was nowhere to be seen. After the carriage had rattled away down the drive Constance went upstairs. William's room was empty. Closing the door behind her Constance opened each of the drawers in the chest in turn, scoured the cupboard and looked under the mattress and the bed. Then, leaving the room as she had found it, she made for her father's bedroom and passed through it into the dressing room.

Papa's best razor lay gleaming on the washstand just as it always did. The second-best one lay in its cupboard, and this one Constance recognised. It was the one which had appeared so miraculously beside her bed after that awful dream, and then disappeared again just as mysteriously from her little box. She inspected it closely. No trace of blood stained its smooth blade. Either it was innocent or it had been carefully cleaned.

Replacing it as she had found it, Constance was about to leave when she glimpsed herself in the mirror. A flush suffused her normally pale cheeks and there was a lustre in her dark eyes she had not seen before. Catching sight of herself unexpectedly gave her a start; she looked attractive, pretty even, and she recalled with a prick of irritation how Mrs Durrant had spoken of her prettiness across her.

Was she really pretty? Had Tom Lawson thought so, she wondered as she returned downstairs. She rebuked herself. Why should she care what he thought? He was nice, but only a policeman, not worthy of the special affection she felt for William.

William. Where could he be? Clearly he was not in the house and he never ventured down to the kitchen area. He must be out in the grounds. In the old days she would have known where to find him: in their secret hidey-hole at the privy. But not now. Since the murder William had cut himself off completely from everything to do with Francis. He would surely not go near the place where his little body had been found.

William was not at the privy, nor anywhere else in the grounds. She walked around the whole garden, along all the walks between the herbaceous borders glowing with delphiniums and lupins, around the rose garden and the white-blossomed shrubs of viburnum and azalea. When at last she returned to the house she met him coming down the stairs from the attic.

'I've been looking for you everywhere,' she said in a tone of reproachful tenderness, then noticed how pale and tense he looked. She went to take his hand but, accidentally or intentionally, he turned so that she could not reach it.

'Nothing's the same, Connie,' he muttered. 'Everything is different. Those policemen even turned the attics upside down and my toy soldiers were scattered.'

'You have no need of them now,' his sister remarked.

'I know, but I hate the upset. Nothing's the same. At school I used to think of home and how things never changed there.'

She pondered over his words. Strange that thoughts of Weatherhead which they had both agreed they hated after Thwaite Lodge, should bring him comfort in his solitude. It had never done so for her.

'I feel afraid, Connie,' the boy murmured, his back to her. Instantly she moved around him and reached up to take his face in her hands.

'There is nothing to fear, Willie, nothing. I am here, remember, and while we are together nothing can harm us.'

Her words, soft and low-spoken, did not have the soothing effect she intended. He broke away from her touch.

'You don't understand. There's something odd, something mysterious in the air, something I can't understand, and it frightens me. How can you stay so serene and confident? Aren't you able to feel it too?'

'It's nothing that wasn't here when we came to Weatherhead, Willie. We'll cope as we always have. What's happened recently hasn't changed that.'

He turned slowly and looked down at her long and hard, as though seeing her for the first time. 'I don't understand you any more, Connie. You're so cool, so distant at times you're like a stranger. I don't know you any more.'

He turned away so quickly that he did not hear her gasp of startled hurt. She stood facing the blankness of his closed door and felt the tears prick her eyelids. They were both alone, desperately alone, and it was stupid that a rift should yawn between two isolated souls who shared a secret so terrible that neither could speak of it. Out of her own private wilderness she could sense the aridity in William's heart, but she could do nothing to succour him, and the helplessness hurt bitterly. Saddened and disconsolate, she went to her own room.

Cecily Lumb sat in the carriage opposite her husband as they rolled homewards from the town. He had done his best to enliven and entertain her, but now his attempts had given way to silent moroseness. He was staring out of the window at the expanse of fields and farms spread out under the hot summer sun, but he saw nothing.

She knew what was on his mind but dared not venture her views because his thought centred on his children, flesh of his flesh and not hers. Of course his heart bled for Francis just as hers did, but his concern now was for his living children.

And which one of them had killed the little one. Cecily knew that was what obsessed him, and she guessed his suspicions. For herself, robbed of her child, she no longer cared. Vengeance and hate were useless. She could feel only total lack of interest in Constance and William, both so far removed from her despite her efforts over the years. Especially Constance; that girl could be aloof, remote and unreachable even in moments of supreme passion, but she was dear to her father's heart. That was why Cecily must hold her tongue. If either child could raise a hand against a small child it was Constance, not William, and ever since that night, over fifteen years ago, when Adeline Lumb gave birth, Cecily had been haunted by her prophetic words.

'Blood and a knife!' she had cried out in an hysterical state brought on by pain and dementia, 'I see blood and a knife!' That was the night Constance had been born.

Samuel stared out of the window, reluctant to meet Cecily's gaze. He did not want to repeat his earlier attempt to divert her from her melancholy, for his own thoughts were unpleasant in the extreme. It was clear to all but a fool that someone in the house had killed Francis — even the police believed that — and to him it was plain that it must have been William. Not Constance — she was never given to outbursts of any kind, always composed and mature for her years, unlike William. He was a pale shadow of the irrepressible Edward, God rest his soul, reacting with unpremeditated violence to any provocation.

And Cecily had provoked him though she might not admit it. A boy his age, to be obliged to use the back stairs like a servant and push a perambulator like some snivel-nosed chit of a girl. He must have resented such treatment bitterly, but to take a knife to a toddler — that was a thought too horrific to contemplate. Shades of Adeline, thought Samuel miserably. Her madness must have tainted William's blood, but what gentleman could lose face by admitting to an insane son?

He could not be sent away secretly to an asylum, for sooner or later tongues would wag and the secret emerge. Better to hand over responsibility for the poor weak boy to some other authority who perhaps could control and discipline his blood. That would solve half the problem. Then he'd send Constance away to a remote school for a time while he cast around for a suitable husband for her. He and Cecily could then start to pick up the pieces of their lives together, unhampered by the past.

A few days later, without warning, he broke the news at dinner. Three white faces looked up from their plates in astonishment.

'William, my boy, I've decided to send you away to military college. That will make a man of you. No more school. Pack and prepare to be off next week.'

146

11

Constance found the ensuing weeks extremely hard to bear. William was gone; Papa and Miss Platt spent all their time closeted together in the parlour or the bedroom, making it plain that her company was unwanted; and Ellen, her services as nanny no longer required, was under notice. Short of talking to Hetty or cook there was no one to whom Constance could turn. Only on Sundays did she sense a faint warmth, in church, sitting alongside Papa in the family pew, when she caught sight of Tom Lawson. His eyes were intent on her throughout the sermon, and when her gaze chanced to meet his she saw the corners of his blue eyes crease into a smile which she dared not acknowledge. But it was reassuring to know that at least one person cared.

The summer holidays were drawing to a close. Constance began to prepare herself for the return to school and the ordeal of facing her schoolfriends and their prying questions. They would be sure to have read of the tragedy in the newspapers and would all be eager, morbidly eager, to know what it was like to be in a home where such a horrifying event had taken place. Most of them she could ignore, but Sophie was different. She longed to be with her friend again but she dreaded the inevitable curiosity.

Then came the thunderclap which made even William's dismissal slight by contrast. Miss Platt came unexpectedly one night as Constance knelt by her bed in her nightgown, trying to pray for guidance.

Miss Platt smiled, making no apology for entering without knocking. 'Ah, my dear, it is good to see you at prayer. Please do not let me disturb you.'

She made no move to leave, simply stood there with hands clasped across her black moiré gown.

Constance scrambled to her feet. 'No matter. I have finished,' she murmured.

Miss Platt sat on the edge of the bed. 'Then let me tell you some good news which will send you to sleep happy.'

'Happy?' Constance regarded her hopefully. 'Is William to come home?'

'No, you little goose! It is a fine plan your father and I have devised. Next week you are to go away.'

'Back to school.'

'But not to Miss Scott's, my dear. To save you embarrassment and because of your piety your papa has decided that you should go to a convent school. You will like that, won't you?'

'A convent school,' repeated Constance thoughtfully.

'It will mean a new uniform, of course, and other new clothes but your father is happy to accept the expense of it if it will benefit you. He is a very charitable and honourable gentleman and you're a lucky girl.'

'Indeed,' assented Constance.

'Tomorrow is Sunday, but we'll go into town on Monday to order all you need. There, doesn't that make you happy?'

'It is thoughtful of Papa, but I shall miss Sophie.'

'You'll soon make new friends. Now into bed with you, and after church tomorrow we'll make a list of everything you'll need — shoes, stockings, chemises, nightgowns, chest-warmers . . .'

Constance started. 'What need have I of all those? I shall be home again for Christmas.'

Miss Platt's eyes slid away from hers, examining the ceiling in detail instead. 'Well, not necessarily, my dear. You see the school is rather a long way away . . .'

Constance felt a leap of apprehension. 'How far away?'

'In Ireland, actually. Near Cork. It's very lovely there, I believe.'

Something snapped in Constance and she leapt to her feet, eyes flashing black fire. 'You've planned this! You wanted to get Papa all to yourself so you've had William sent away and now me! It's all your doing!'

Miss Platt rose, majestic and cold. 'Control yourself, Constance. You are quite wrong and I will not have you speak to me thus. Your father would be very angry if he knew, and is that how you repay him for his thoughtful concern for you?'

'But I know you put the idea in his head! Oh, I'll never forgive you!'

The fire in Miss Platt's eyes matched her own. 'You have threatened me thus before, Miss Constance. I do not forget. I know your temper, and I think it wisest for all of us if you leave.'

'Wise?' repeated Constance angrily.

'Yes,' her stepmother snapped. 'Your moods and your unnatural influence over others have to be stopped, whatever the cost. That is why you and William had to be separated.'

'Are you saying I had unnatural influence over him?' Constance challenged.

'Do you deny it? I saw the embarrassment on his face. You made him hold his tongue when he could have spoken.'

'Spoken about what?'

'About that night. You know. You swore him to secrecy, didn't you?'

A scarlet inferno of fury blazed in Constance's brain. 'What are you saying, Miss Platt?' she hissed. 'Are you hinting that I – that I . . .?'

The older woman looked at her scornfully. 'I know what my instincts tell me, and what your conscience torments you with incessantly. Why else do you pray so often? I am no fool, Constance, but I fear you inherit your mother's blood.'

She turned and left abruptly, leaving only a whiff of eau de cologne behind her. Constance clenched her fists, threw herself across the bed and pummelled the pillows, weeping hysterically. She was not mad like her mother, she sobbed over and over again, it was only that vile Platt woman's wishful thinking. It was *she* who was evil, breaking up a family and separating brother from sister and father from children!

At dinner Constance could not bring herself to speak. She

sat with downcast eyes and angry resentment in her heart. Miss Platt and Papa carried on a desultory conversation across her, apparently oblivious to the scalding tension. Papa looked distinctly pleased with himself and Miss Platt wore an air of quiet triumph.

A week later, on Sunday morning, all was ready. A large tin trunk crammed with Constance's new clothes stood in the hallway ready to be loaded into the carriage next morning. Papa was to accompany her to the coast to see her safely aboard ship knowing she would be met as soon as she disembarked.

Tom Lawson was in church again. Constance could see him over the tall-backed pew, but he kept his eyes averted throughout the service. It was only when they came home that Ellen, pink-faced and smiling, thrust the note into her hand.

'Mr Lawson asked me to give you this,' she whispered conspiratorially, 'and I'm to take your reply.'

Constance flushed with pleasure as she read it, then immediately panicked. 'Oh Ellen! I can't! I'm leaving tomorrow! Oh dear! What am I to do?'

'What does he say, Miss Constance?'

'He wants us to meet. Oh Ellen! I dare not write – you must tell him what has happened, but say I'm grateful for his friendship, for I have much need of friendship. Perhaps one day . . .'

'I'll tell him, miss, don't you worry,' Ellen reassured her.

That night Constance paced her room by candlelight, her eyes blurred with unshed tears, and wondered why she should feel so angered and unhappy to leave a house she had always hated.

'I must pray,' she told herself fiercely. 'I must pray!'

It took some time before she could bring her anger sufficiently under control to be able to commune with her Creator. At last she felt a measure of peace begin to suffuse her and she knew the future must be faced. The tie with the past must be broken and everything pertaining to it put behind her – except her love for William. That would never change or be diminished, whatever they did to her.

All her childhood possessions had been thrown or locked away, but one thing remained to be done. Constance took the school notebook from the bedside drawer and stood holding it, close to her breast. It had been her diary these past four years, enfolding within its pages a minutely-written record of her hopes and fears and, above all, her passionate love of William. It had remained hidden during her days at Miss Scott's Academy but now, leaving as she was for a foreign land, the journal of her secret, inmost thoughts must go.

The fire grate was empty. The night candle burned on the bedside table. Constance hesitated, clutching the notebook closed as though to relive the love it contained, reluctant to let it pass out of her life. Then, with sudden resolve, she took up the candle and carried it to the grate. Within moments the diary was no more than a charred heap of black ash. Constance drew a deep breath. Now let tomorrow and the unknown future begin.

Constance stood in the bow of the ship watching the great white wash behind and the receding coastline of England fading into the mist.

Papa had been full of last-minute exhortations on the pier head in Liverpool: 'Do as the nuns tell you, Constance, no argument or sulks, remember. They are kindly, Christian creatures who can do much to help you.'

She knew what he hoped: that she would prove more tractable to their gentle discipline than to Miss Platt's imperious command. He need have no fear. She was naturally reticent with strangers, and it was only Miss Platt who called out sullen moroseness — and sometimes even heated rebellion — in her. She would be a dutiful pupil, she assured her father.

He was all smiles as he waved goodbye, a slowly-receding plump figure in a mulberry velvet-collared greatcoat and well-brushed hat. She was saddened that he should smile so, when she would be away for at least a year. He had noticeably avoided answering his daughter's question as to whether she would be allowed home for Christmas. No Christmas at home, no William — Constance steeled herself to face a solitary, unknown future among strangers.

In the wake of the ship, gulls swooped and dived over the eddying white rush of water. Spray rose and drifted in the wind. Constance recalled the breakers on the rocks below the cliffs, and her fingers tightened on the note concealed inside her muff.

'Meet me tomorrow, Monday, on the cliff path where we should have met that Monday long ago,' Tom had written. *'I shall wait for you at three o'clock, watching the spindrift till you come.'*

So he had not forgotten, any more than she had. The turmoil in her heart that day when she had compared herself to that helpless, wind-tossed spume had not been lessened by the intervening years and it was heart-warming to know that one man still remembered and cared. But he would soon forget her, far away in another land. She sighed deeply, tasting the salt on her lips. Would there ever be such a friend again, with whom she could feel at one despite the differences between them? Such an affinity must be rare, if not unique.

Her musing was cut short by a coarse but not unkindly voice at her elbow. 'Excuse me, miss. Your father asked me to keep an eye on you.'

She looked round to see a sailor, middle-aged and wizened and weather-beaten as an apple out of the hayloft. Twisting his woollen cap between his hands, he explained: 'He said to make sure you had a good berth below and didn't stay on deck too long,' he muttered. 'He gave me a shilling.'

She smiled at his conscientiousness. 'Don't worry. I'll go below soon. I just want to stay and watch the water for a while.'

He grunted. 'Wind's blowing up. It'll get a mite choppy before long.'

'I'll bear it in mind. Thank you.'

He left her with a curt nod. Constance was in no mood to go down to the dark, airless berth, which reminded her of her enclosed feeling at Weatherhead. She lingered on deck as the wind gathered strength, drawing her warm woollen mantle closely about her and holding on to her bonnet, which was in danger of being whipped off and blown away.

A faint moon showed even before the sun had set, and the air was bitterly cold for September. Reluctantly Constance turned from the rail and made her way down the companionway to her berth. As she began untying the strings of her bonnet she was taken unawares by a huge sneeze, and by morning her eyes were sore and streaming and her throat burning. By the time the ship docked in Queenstown she was at the same time shivering and burning with fever.

With aching head and unsteady step, Constance disembarked. She was relieved when a messenger from the harbour master's office informed her that a trap was waiting for her at the dock gates.

'You'll not mistake it, miss, for 'tis a nun in a habit who sits holding the reins, so it is,' he added with a cheery smile.

Through a haze Constance saw her, small and erect, a neat white figure with a pink face encircled by her wimple.

As Constance approached the nun stepped down and greeted her warmly. 'Miss Lumb, is it? God be praised you've arrived safely. Porter, put the lady's trunk up here, will you? Do climb up, Miss Lumb — or Constance, if you will permit me.'

'To be sure,' said Constance wearily. She was glad to be driven anywhere, so long as she could soon lay down her aching head on a cool pillow.

'I'm Sister Teresa. I'll not tire you with talking now, my dear, for you look right jaded and no wonder after your journey. You'll feel better after a wash and a meal.'

The trap clattered off at a brisk pace over the cobbled streets, away from the bustling quayside alive with passengers searching for luggage and anxious porters and officials, between tall buildings in narrow streets where stray dogs loped and urchins with pleading eyes ran after the trap crying for pennies. Sister Teresa drove purposefully and Constance fell into a half-doze, her head nodding on to her chest.

At length she became aware that the trap had stopped moving and hands were lifting down her trunk and helping her out. She took a hand gratefully, dizzy with fatigue and fever, and saw dimly that it belonged to a tall, thin-faced nun. The nun's eyes widened.

'Your hand is very hot,' she murmured, and raised a finger to Constance's brow. 'Heavens, you have a fever, child. Sister Josephine!' Another nun hurried forward. 'Take the girl upstairs at once, help her undress and put her to bed. She has a high fever.'

Sister Josephine nodded and took hold of Constance's arm. Up steps, into a hallway, up a flight of wide stairs – the whole surroundings passed by Constance's vision hazily, as if in a dream. A room, a bed, sitting while someone unbuttoned and pulled off her boots and then eased her jacket and dress off her back. When she was reduced to her chemise Constance closed her hand over the hand on her body.

'Don't worry, my dear,' a gentle voice said. 'In a moment I shall give you a cool wash and you will feel better, so you will.'

Constance resisted no more. The clothes melted away and a deliciously cool sponge eased the aching heat of her body. Then someone put a cup to her lips.

' 'Tis Sister Marie Louise's special potion for the fever – never known to fail. Drink it up, my dear.'

Constance drank gratefully. The mellow liquid soothed her burning throat and the next thing she knew was a cool pillow under her fevered cheek, and then darkness.

Time and space lost meaning for Constance. She seemed to hover in a limbo of eddying dark vortices where faces appeared and faded again, voices drifting through the haze as though from a vast distance. Papa's face, stern but kindly, then a stranger's framed in a white coif, followed out of the mists by a pock-marked face which glared at her. Inspector Wheeler, fierce-browed and accusing, filled her vision. Behind the inspector's shoulder, Tom's gentle face came softly into focus and then faded.

'*Guilty!*' The word came to her ears with the sound of a rushing torrent, and she tried to close her ears to its clamour. '*Guilty!*'

Constance writhed and tossed, trying to blot out all the faces that stared in accusation. '*Guilty! Guilty!*' The roar deafened her and she cried out: *'Oh God! Where are you? Please, God, don't desert me!'*

A cool hand touched her brow, easing the pain momentarily. 'Hush my child, rest and lie still.'

Gradually the pain and the nightmares began to recede. At last Constance opened her eyes and looked around. A distant bell was chiming. She lay in a narrow bed in a large, airy room filled with sunlight. Three other little beds, virginal with their white coverlets, ranged the far walls of the room, and a large wooden crucifix dominated the wall at the opposite end to the door, through which a figure in white habit and wimple was entering. Constance lay bemused. After her recent agony and delirium such brilliance was like a vision of Heaven.

The figure crossed to the window opposite Constance's bed and raised the blind. More sunlight streamed in to swell the pool of yellow on the bare floorboards.

'Ah, you're awake,' the nun remarked with pleasure. 'It is not too bright for you, is it, my dear? 'Tis a shame to shut out our Lord's wonderful sunshine. Before we know where we are winter will be upon us again.'

Constance watched her as she moved about the room, vaguely recalling her face. The nun came closer and smiled.

'Remember me? I'm Sister Josephine. I brought you in the night you arrived, so tired and sick.'

'I remember,' Constance replied weakly. 'You put me to bed. Have I been ill for long?'

'Above a week, I fear, but you're well on the mend now, thanks be to God. Sister Marie Louise's medicines never fail. The hand of our Lord is in her potions.'

She patted Constance's hand, looking at her with deep concern. 'You had a dreadful fever, I fear, a dreadful delirium. I know you were having awful nightmares. You kept crying out about terrible things.'

'Did I?'

'Things like dead babies and blood and knives. I was really quite alarmed.' She smiled indulgently.

'I'm so sorry.'

'Oh, you couldn't help it, my dear! It's the fever, you know — we can't control our nightmares or delirium. No, no, don't fret. The girls were concerned for you — they're very nice girls, you know. They kept asking after you. You'll like them. Now, are you hungry? Could you eat some broth?'

She bustled away to fetch food. Constance wondered if other girls slept in those neat beds, girls who had listened avidly to those delirious dreams. She asked Sister Josephine on her return.

'No, to be sure, child. This is the sick bay. You'll go to join the others in the dormitory in a day or two. Now sit up while I give you your broth.'

She spooned the liquid into Constance's mouth with all care and tenderness of a mother. Constance accepted her ministrations shyly, embarrassed by the unaccustomed attention.

Days of mellow autumn sunlight passed to the accompaniment of melodious bells which rang out at intervals throughout the day. From time to time Constance could hear the hum of voices in the distance and sometimes the singing of treble voices.

'That's Benediction,' Sister Josephine told her one evening. 'Tomorrow, God willing, you'll be in the chapel with them.'

So the day came when Constance, tremulous and apprehensive, was moved out of the infirmary to the dormitory. She was deeply conscious of the sidelong looks of curiosity from the other girls already there.

'Siobhan, Deirdre, Carmel, come here and meet your new schoolmate, Constance Lumb. She's been very sick but I know you'll be good girls and take care of her,' Sister Josephine said brightly. Two pairs of blue eyes and one pair of green inspected Constance. Determined to hide her apprehension, she held out a hand to the tallest girl.

'How do you do?' murmured Constance.

The girl took her hand slowly then pressed it in a firm, easy grip. 'Hello, Constance. I'm Carmel Mulcahy.'

Green eyes challenged black with an open, honest gaze and Constance could not help liking her. Here, she sensed, was a girl of spirit, either a good friend or a fierce opponent.

'You're from England, aren't you?' Carmel asked. Her voice was low and liquid, tinged with a lilting accent pleasant to the ear. Constance nodded. 'Can I call you Connie?'

No one had ever called her by that name except William and Tom. She was about to refuse, and then changed her mind. 'If you wish,' she said quietly.

Sister Josephine swept the two of them away. 'Come along now, girls, or you'll be late for chapel,' she admonished them. 'Can't you hear the bell?'

In the days to come the sound of the convent chapel bells was sweet music to Constance, peaceful and soothing, balm to her wounded soul. The hurts and slights she had left behind in England began to recede and only the longing for William still pained her. By night she lay awake in the dormitory and thought of him, aching with love, and wishing she could pray. Occasionally she thought of Tom Lawson, but it was William who filled her dreams. Now, with the expanse of the Irish Channel between them, she felt even more isolated and lonely.

The mother superior went to great pains to make her new pupil feel at one with her new surroundings. 'I know you are not a Catholic like most of the other girls, Constance, but nevertheless you will attend classes in the scriptures with them and go to chapel with them. We shall not leave you out of our devotions but, of course, you will not be able to receive the sacraments of Confession and Communion since you are not a baptised and confirmed Catholic. In all other essentials, however, your daily routine will be as for everyone else.'

'Thank you, Reverend Mother.' Constance felt the mother superior's approving gaze over the pince-nez as she turned to go. Every day, every action and every face in this new milieu was unfamiliar. She felt not fear, but apprehension — could she meet it all with the fortitude and composure Papa would expect of her? Accustomed to remote surroundings and much privacy she was unhappy at being thrown into the hurly-burly of communal living. If only William were within reach, it would ease the strangeness.

Even the prayers they spoke here were new, lacking the comfort of the old familiar phrases.

Carmel, sunny and anxious to be of help, reassured her. 'You'll soon learn them. Heavens, we say them often enough! Bt the time Sister Marie Louise has made us say three rosaries I'll guarantee you'll know the Hail Mary by heart!'

She was right. Constance soon discovered that the daily regime in the school was built around a regular pattern of rising early for Mass in the chapel, lengthy lessons of doctrine and catechism, more prayers in the chapel, school lessons and back to the chapel after tea for Benediction. Within weeks the catechismal questions and answers became as familiar as food. Sister Bridget's thin, cadaverous face flushed as she flung the questions at them.

'Who made you?'

'God made me.'

'Why did God make you?'

'God made me to know Him, love Him, and serve Him in this world and to be happy with Him for ever in the next.'

The contrast repetition, not only of familiar phrases but of daily movements and preoccupations, brought with it in time a reassuring feeling, a sense of rightness and solidity that Constance had not experienced before, and she began to feel more at ease. Only Sister Bridget's continual, vehement reminders that sin was terrible and unconfessed sins would lead a soul to eternal damnation disturbed Constance. How could her soul find eternal peace with this secret oppressive weight of guilt about which she could not speak?

Constance's inability to pray, except in chorus with the other girls, troubled her deeply. But there was no one in whom to confide.

In the haven of the convent school, time passed. At Christmas, Papa wrote to say she was to stay at school for the holiday because he and her stepmama were going away to visit friends in Hampshire. Again at Easter it was not convenient for Constance to come home. The only bright spots in her life were William's letters, never long but full of news about his new way of life. Gradually they became more intermittent and even briefer.

One summer afternoon Sister Teresa took a group of girls

out into the fields for a sketching lesson. Constance and Carmel sat, sketch-pad in hand, under a hawthorn hedge while Sister Teresa was instructing another pupil on the far side of the field, near the stream.

Puffballs of white cloud floated across an azure sky and the air was warm and rich with the smell of the hayfield. Here and there an isolated poppy glowed scarlet amid the gold and Constance, frowning in concentration as her pencil outlined the clump of trees, reflected how the lonely red flower was like herself, a stranger amongst strangers. What was it Mr Keats had written?

> '. . . the sad heart of Ruth, when, sick for home,
> She stood in tears amid the alien corn.'

Constance sighed. Loneliness was sad; loneliness with a secret unshared was worse. William knew, but he never made mention of it, not even in the letter which had come by the morning post. Not that he would be foolish enough to commit careless words to paper, but it was hard that the secret lay unspoken between them, heavy and oppressive at the back of her mind from the moment she awoke until sleep came again.

William's letter was cool, matter-of-fact and concerned only with telling her about his life as a cadet. He had been posted to another camp, where the other chaps were good sorts, the food tolerable, and the régime harsh — but no more so than school had been, he assured her. Of his feelings he wrote nothing. He had signed it simply 'Your loving brother, William.'

She tried hard to read between the lines, to visualise William in uniform in the mess and on parade, to guess how he was feeling. At the new camp he would be bewildered and uncertain, she felt sure, but he would do his very best to hide it under a façade of hearty camaraderie. Dear William. If only she could be near him to give him strength. Instead Constance closed her eyes tightly and sent forceful volumes of love out into the air around her. He would sense and absorb them.

Carmel laid aside her sketch-pad and leaned back on the

grass. 'You had a letter today,' she remarked. 'Was it from your brother?'

'Yes.'

'You don't talk much about him. Is he your only brother?'

'Yes. My sisters are both married.'

Carmel waved away a bee buzzing round her head. 'What is William like? Is he handsome?'

'Oh yes, tall and fair and broad-shouldered, not dark like me. He'll make a very handsome officer.'

Carmel wrinkled her snub nose. 'He sounds intriguing. Perhaps you will introduce him to me one day if he comes visiting.'

Constance felt an angry lump of resentment in her throat. 'Don't be silly!' she exploded. 'He's too young for you. Anyway, he's not at all interested in girls.'

Carmel sighed. 'He'll change. My brother used to say all girls were silly and flighty, but he got married just like everyone else. Why don't you ever talk about your family, Connie? You're very reserved about them; come to that you're reserved about everything. The girls find you deep and quiet and they don't understand why you don't chatter and share secrets like everyone else. Have you always been so quiet?'

Constance made a show of holding up her pencil to compare the height of the oak with its neighbouring elm. 'I suppose so. God didn't make us all alike.'

'True. It would be a dull world if He did. But you intrigue me, Connie. I fancy some dark, mysterious secret in your past.'

Constance snapped her sketch-book shut. 'You have a wild and fanciful imagination, Carmel. What secrets could a well-brought-up girl of sixteen have to hide?'

Carmel folded her hands behind her head and lay staring up at the sky. 'Oh, I don't know, a brutal father, a secret lover, a mad mother . . .'

Constance paled and the breath caught in her throat. 'What on earth makes you say that?' she murmured.

Carmel sighed. 'As you say, a fanciful imagination and the sheer bliss of lying in the sun, nothing more. But something

160

is troubling you. Connie, I feel sure. If you don't want to talk I won't pry, but I can be the soul of discretion if you feel you want to talk.'

The tension in Constance eased. Carmel was doing her best to hold out the hand of friendship and God knew, she had need of comfort. 'Oh, it's nothing really. It's just that I find all your Catholic ways of life a little different from what I'm accustomed to.'

'Catechism and saying the rosary and all that? But you've fallen into the way of it without any problem,' Carmel countered.

'On the surface, yes. But all that about examining one's conscience regularly and praying for forgiveness for sins — Sister Bridget keeps saying we are doomed if we don't do it and I don't find it easy. You were brought up to it from childhood.' Constance kept her head bent lest Carmel's shrewd gaze should read and interpret her expression.

'Well, yes, we were, but examination of conscience is a duty to prepare for going to confession, you know, and you don't have to do that.'

'We should all examine our consciences,' Constance demurred.

'To discover if we have committed a mortal sin, one which would otherwise condemn us to hell,' Carmel pointed out. 'Lesser sins, the ones the catechism calls venial sins, will not condemn our souls and it's usually venial sins we all confess to the priest because we haven't any mortal ones.'

'It must give you comfort, nevertheless, to know they are absolved and forgiven,' remarked Constance.

Carmel sat up and retrieved her pencil with a smile. 'Yes, I admit I feel better after I've confessed I've been unkind about Siobhan behind her back! But surely you can tell God your sins in your prayers too and be forgiven?'

'That's just it, Carmel. I can't pray.'

Constance could not bring herself to look Carmel in the face, unwilling to see the shock and horror registered there. A moment passed before Carmel spoke. 'I'm sorry, Connie,' she said quietly. 'I wish I could help. Perhaps you could talk to one of the sisters about it.'

'No, I can't.'

'Or the priest, then. I know he's a rather frightening man, but who else is there?' Carmel spread her hands in helplessness.

'He wouldn't help me, a non-Catholic.' Constance's voice was barely audible.

Carmel thought a moment and sat upright. 'I have it! Why don't you go into the confessional along with the rest of us? The priest can't see you through the grille — he'll never know! Tell him your problem then.'

Constance stared at her, aghast. 'But I don't know what to do or say in there! He'll soon find out!'

She visualised the confessional, the tall black box at the side of the chapel where girls vanished inside for three or four minutes, emerging with chastened looks and hurrying to kneel in a pew to pray busily. There was some secret ritual within that box which no one ever mentioned.

'Listen,' said Carmel eagerly, 'there's nothing difficult about it. It's the same pattern every time and I can coach you in the words. All we have to do is rehearse it, think up some venial sins for you to confess, and you can go with us on Saturday night. Don't you see, it's easy! The priest will be able to give you good advice and then, with your soul in a nice, clean state of grace, you'll be in the best possible position to start praying again. Oh, do say you will, Connie, please!'

Please, Connie. Carmel's voice held the same eager pathos that William's used to do. Constance felt her heart soften at the girl's concern. Besides, the prospect of confessing and being absolved from sin, of emerging from the confessional with a pure soul, appealed to her. She was a little apprehensive, but the potential benefit to be reaped from Carmel's suggestion was too glorious to be denied. She would do it, even if discovery led to Sister Bridget's wrathful vengeance.

Sister Teresa's slim white-robed figure came gliding across the hayfield towards them and Carmel began sketching again feverishly.

Sister Teresa examined their work critically. 'Too slow, Carmel, you should have finished by now. That's better,

Constance. Your sense of perspective is far better than in your last piece.'

'Yes, Sister,' Constance murmured. 'I'm beginning to get things in perspective now, I feel.'

12 : 1860

That evening, Thursday, it was too unbearably hot and stuffy in the dormitory for sleep. The air held that torpid, airless stillness that presages a thunderstorm and the other girls were evidently just as restless as she. Sister Teresa, having forbidden talking, wished them goodnight and bade God bless them, had retired to her cell. Constance could hear forbidden whispers and giggles at the far end of the room. That would be Fanny and Edith, always in trouble for their unbridled tongues.

Fanny called out in a loud whisper: 'You have a handsome brother, Constance, don't you? Or so Carmel tells us.'

Constance buried her head in the pillow. Carmel, obviously embarrassed, called back softly: 'Hush now, Fanny! You and Edith should be ashamed of yourselves, always talking about boys!'

'It's natural enough at eighteen,' Fanny retorted. 'We're not children now — why, Deirdre is to be married next Christmas.'

'That's not what Sister Bridget thinks,' muttered Carmel. 'She says we'll burn in hell for thinking about fleshly things.'

'Who said we were talking of fleshly things?' Edith countered. 'We were only talking about the handsome young men we know, that's all. It's your suspicious mind, Carmel Goody-goody.'

'I've heard the way you talk before — and I heard you

reading aloud from that novelette you brought back in your valise: "His strong arms encircled her slender waist," and all that. What's that if not fleshly?'

The logic of Carmel's argument was lost in the chorus of shrieks and giggles. Carmel turned away crossly. 'I hope you remember that when you come to Confession on Saturday,' she said, loud enough to be heard. At once the merriment died and a subdued quiet settled over the heat-saturated air of the dormitory.

By Saturday teatime the long-threatened storm still had not broken and the humid air lay heavy as a steam bath in the empty classroom where Constance sat listening attentively to her friend.

'There, you know the whole thing by heart now,' Carmel was saying. 'Don't forget, the priest can't see you, and if you go into the confessional last, after all the other girls, they'll never know either.'

Constance hesitated. 'Thank you, Carmel. Are you sure he won't say anything else, though, which I can't answer.'

'I doubt it. If he does, just say "Yes, Father," to everything.'

Constance touched the other girl's hand lightly. 'I'm grateful to you, Carmel. You don't know how much this means to me.'

Carmel rose from the desk. 'You're so keen, perhaps you should think of becoming a convert. Come on, let's go down by the stream for a walk before tea. It might be cooler there.'

Constance followed her out. 'We'd best go out by the back — Sister Josephine will have me mending torn sheets with her again if she spots me. She said while the others were at Confession I, too, could do some good for my soul.'

Later that evening Father Murphy eased his ample girth trying to make himself more comfortable within the restricted confines of the narrow confessional. A cushion on his hard little bench would improve matters slightly. Suffering was good for the soul but intolerably hard on one's posterior after nearly two hours of listening to the confession of multitudinous sins by adolescent girls. Lord bless us and save us, he thought, but there was barely a venial sin between the lot of them.

As a rule, that was. Tonight had been something of a revelation to him. There had been the usual crop of sins, of course, the catalogue which by now was almost as familiar to him as the litany, of petty grudges and spiteful comments spoken in haste; of lapses of duty in the performance of schoolwork; of laziness and preoccupation with the looking glass. Sloth, pride, envy — they were all there to a greater or lesser degree, but what troubled the good priest's mind was that the early signs of a far more terrible sin were there — and not only in one poor misguided sinner.

Lust, that was where the signs pointed. Lust, the most debasing sin that rendered man no better than an animal, far removed from the spiritual creature close to God which the mother superior aimed to make of her girls. Poor lady — she would be shocked if she knew.

He reckoned he knew who was at the back of all this sudden contamination. As priest to the convent, he visited often and discussed matters of the school with the mother superior sometimes meeting the parents of new girls too. The girls themselves he met only in the confessional, hidden from his view. At Mass they were a sea of faces gazing up at him in the pulpit.

Some girls he came to know by voices in the darkness, and he was convinced it was the thin-voiced child, the one he knew was called Edith Fanshaw because she had come to the mother superior's office on an errand during one of his visits, and the mother superior had pointed to her name on a list: a silly English name which began Feather-something-or other but was pronounced Fanshaw. Edith Fanshaw. She had not been the first girl to confess to impure thoughts tonight, but she had gone into greater detail than the others. She knew too much, and it was undoubtedly she who was the instigator of this new threat. Reverend Mother ought to be warned of the danger, though how that could be achieved without infringing the secrecy of the confessional, Father Murphy could not fathom.

The latch on the far side of the grille clicked as the door

closed. The priest sighed. Yet another confession still to be heard; he could swear there were more girls than usual tonight. He waited patiently, ear close to the curtained grille, while young knees settled on the hassock and a deep breath was drawn.

'Bless me, Father, for I have sinned,' came the whisper.

'How long is it since you were last at Confession?'

A pause. She was evidently debating this one. 'A week, Father.'

'And what sins have you committed in that time?'

Another deep breath, a pause, and then the whispered litany he had heard so often. Spite, envy, laziness. Sister Bridget's fierce teaching in defence of the true faith evidently trained these girls to examine their conscience closely before offering themselves for the sacrament of Confession. The litany ended.

'Are there any other sins you should confess to God before I grant you absolution, my child?' he prompted gently. Often they held back the one that troubled them most deeply to the last.

'Yes, Father. Impure thoughts.' The whisper was barely audible.

Father Murphy's tongue clicked in disappointment. Yet another! 'And did you enjoy these thoughts, my child?'

A long pause followed. 'I'm not sure what impure thoughts are,' the small voice said tentatively.

'Were these thoughts centred on young men?' he offered.

'Yes, Father — well, one young man.'

'And thoughts of him gave you pleasure?'

'Oh yes, Father.'

She was not offering much in the way of explanation. He must probe, but delicately. 'Did you think of yourself and him doing something together?'

'Yes, Father,' came the timid admission.

'And was that thought pleasing to you — what you visualised you were doing with him?'

'No, Father.' The voice was emphatic this time. 'It has made me unable to pray.'

Father Murphy breathed a sigh. There was hope for this

one. 'God bless you, my child. The road to Heaven is still open to you if you are sincerely contrite and are firmly resolved never again to commit this sin. Are you ashamed, my child, of the way you have offended God?'

'Oh yes, Father.' There was no doubting the girl's sincerity. Father Murphy smiled in the darkness.

'Then pray to God for forgiveness and for penance you must say three Hail Marys and one Our Father. And remember if you would like to say a Novena to Our Lady you can gain thirty days indulgence of your time in Purgatory. Do you think you can pray now? Say the *Confiteor* with me.'

While he spoke the words in Latin he heard the youthful voice murmuring beyond the grille. 'Oh my God, I am sorry and beg pardon for all my sins and detest them above all things because they offend Thine infinite goodness . . . I firmly resolve, by the help of Thy grace, never to offend Thee again and carefully to avoid the occasions of sin.'

'*Te absolvo . . . in nomine Patris et Filii et Spiritu Sancti, Amen,*' he said softly, making the sign of the Cross with outstretched hand towards the invisible head of the penitent. 'Go in peace, my child.'

'Thank you, father.'

The latch rose and clicked into place and the confessional felt silent. Father Murphy sat for a time, head bowed in prayer as he besought God's mercy for these misguided children. Secrecy of the confessional or not, he must find some way to alert Reverend Mother to the poisonous influence of the Fanshaw girl and make some attempt to rescue her from perdition before it was too late.

As Constance emerged from the chapel to cross the courtyard to the main building, rain was beginning to fall in huge drops. The air was still humid and heavy as she paused to lean against the cool stone wall, and she turned her face upwards gratefully to feel the raindrops on her cheeks.

They were coming down heavily now, spangling her black hair with diamonds and running down her face. Cool, refreshing. Constance felt elated — it was God's balm for her soul, His sign that He was now listening again. The guilt still lay heavy, but she could now pray again and know she would be heard.

'Constance Lumb! Is that you out there in the rain?' It was Sister Bridget in the open doorway. 'For pity's sake, child, come in or you'll have a fever again!'

She pushed the girl before her along the corridor, but no word of admonishment could dampen the elation in Constance's heart. However gross the sin yet unconfessed, God was smiling upon her again, welcoming her back, and the avenue of communication with Him was open once more. The air seemed to vibrate with love and understanding. Alone in the dormitory she stood stock-still to savour it, feeling her soul re-charging from its current.

'Is that you, William, sending out your love to me?' she asked the unanswering air. 'Or is it you, God?'

It did not matter. It was all one. The atmosphere of the convent was filled with peace.

Next evening after high tea the girls sat down to write the weekly letter home. Constance wrote to William:

'I hope you are happy at your new barracks — you do not tell me how you feel and I want so much for you to be happy. For myself, I am at peace. The air of the convent and of the surrounding countryside is so soothing. You should see the fields here — so lush and green, much greener than at home on the moors. It is because there is always much rain in Ireland, I am told. I hope some day you will be able to come and visit here, for I am sure you too would find it a blissful place.

'Papa has written to say it would not be wise for me to go home this summer because Miss Platt is not well. This does not trouble me unduly for the sisters are kind and make every effort to entertain me when I am here alone. The place seems strangely silent when all the girls have gone, but I do not mind the solitude.'

She made no mention of that which had lain unspoken for so long. He must know as well as she that the secret joined them together even more tightly and irrevocably than their childhood blood-pact. When he was ready, William would speak of it himself.

It was some weeks before William found time in his busy life to answer his sister's letter. When it came the convent was deserted. Carmel and Siobhan and Fanny and everyone else having vanished to the bosoms of their families for the summer holiday. Constance came downstairs into the vestibule one morning and caught sight of the solitary white envelope tucked into the tapes on the green baize notice board. She reached for it eagerly.

Sister Teresa glided by. 'Ah, a letter from home, Constance?' she said with a gentle smile.

'No, from my brother,' Constance replied as she recognised the careless scrawl.

'The young man in the army? You must be very proud of him,' the nun remarked.

'Indeed. May I take it into the garden to read?'

'Of course, my dear. Breakfast is not for ten minutes yet.'

Ten minutes to savour William and the thoughts of his heart. Constance could barely wait until she had reached the privacy of a secluded walk. Breathlessly she tore the letter open, feeling her heart thud as if she were meeting a lover.

'Dear Constance. It was pleasant to receive your letter,' William wrote. Constance smiled to herself. He always under-stated his feelings. *'Life has been so busy lately with drills and parades and mock forays as well as all the social obligations of army life that I have had little time for letter-writing. It's all becoming a bit of a bore, really, and I wish at times I could get away from it and enjoy the peace you are evidently enjoying.'*

Poor William. He was clearly having a rather stressful time and her heart ached to be with him. She read on.

'You shouldn't grumble about being alone in the hols,' he wrote. Constance frowned. She hadn't complained, had she? *'I would give anything at times to have the chance to be alone and think for a while. Here, all the thinking is done for one and one simply carries out orders, so many and*

169

*so rapid that one becomes bewildered and could wish it
would all slow down. At the end of the day's activities one
still has to show the flag with the best of them in the mess —
but then, I think I can boast that I keep up as manfully as
Papa would expect of me.'*

Constance smiled sadly. Poor William. He was still mindful of Papa's expectations and doing his best to earn Papa's
approval. Not an easy feat, she recalled, and her mind refused to dwell on what that had led to. Her heart bled for
William, not only because he was still so anxious to please but
also because she could sense the tone of desperation in his
words.

*'However, I too have heard from Papa that I may not
spend my next leave at Weatherhead,'* William said, and
Constance felt a lunge of pity for him. *'As you say,
Mama is not well. She is expecting a baby at Christmas
and Papa is anxious to keep her rested and quiet.'*

So that was it. Papa's preoccupation with his wife and
prospective child left no room for his older children.
Constance sighed. No wonder there was that hopelessness in
William's tone. That wretched Platt woman left no room in
Papa's thoughts for others.

*'I shall probably spend my leave in London, go to the
theatre and that sort of thing,'* William concluded. *'Have
a happy holiday. Your loving brother, William.'*

Constance folded the letter slowly. He had made no mention of coming to visit her, as she had suggested. It was
unlikely now that she would see him until Christmas —
always provided, of course, that Miss Platt's state of health
permitted visitors, for that was how Constance and William
seemed to be regarded.

The mellow tone of the breakfast gong sounded across the
sunlit lawn. Slowly Constance retraced her steps towards the
dining hall, mustering a smile for Sister Teresa as she
entered. Not even to her, the youngest and most approach-
able of the nuns, could she voice the vague unease that stirred
in her.

It was well before Christmas that news came of Miss Platt's baby. It arrived some weeks before it was due, and was stillborn. Papa wrote that Miss Platt was very distressed and still in a delicate state of health, and for that reason the doctors had advised that he should not yet remove his household back to Hawksmoor, as he had promised his wife.

Constance's presence over Christmas would present unnecessary strain, he opined, and so he was obliged to suggest once again that she would stay at the convent over the holiday. As soon as spring came he would have Thwaite Lodge prepared in readiness for the family's return, and perhaps Constance would come for Easter.

> '*Of course it saddens me not to have seen you for some time,*' he wrote. '*No doubt you have grown taller and I shall scarcely recognise you. William has grown enormously; he is taller than I by some inches now.*'

So William must have paid a visit home, or Papa been south to see him, but William had not mentioned it in his letters. True, his letters had become far fewer and more scant of content over the past year, so he might simply have forgotten.

Carmel's young face registered concern when she said goodbye to her friend at the end of the autumn term. 'It seems terrible that you can't share all the fun of presents and garlands and carol-singing, Connie. Are you dreadfully unhappy?'

Constance squeezed her hand. 'No, truly I'm not, I am content, Carmel, and grateful to you for enabling me to pray again. Now I can face anything. I'm not alone, you know. William and I will be thinking of each other even though we are far apart. Nothing can take that from me.'

She watched them all leave, a laughing, happy bunch surrounded by valises and carefully-wrapped gifts. The convent rang hollow without them, and on Christmas Day in the little chapel the nuns' responses in the Mass, denuded of the usual backing of young voices, rang thinly through the air.

'Christe Eleison.'

'*Christe Eleison.*'

'Kyrie Eleison.'
'Kyrie Eleison.'

Constance sat apart from the nuns, her heart filled with all-encompassing love. She prayed to God, begging His forgiveness and love, and she thought of William, alone and miserable, and felt her soul exuding voluminous emanations of love to him.

'I am thinking of you, William, my dearest love,' she murmured between prayers. 'I know you think of me and of the bond we share. Have no fear, William, for I shall keep faith, as I have always done, and I know that you too keep faith with me. I love you, William, as no one else has ever done or ever can. Trust me, William. We are indivisible.'

Mass over, Constance rose from her knees and followed the sisters out into the frosty air of the courtyard. Sister Bridget was waiting by the school door. She nodded without smiling.

'I have been watching you, Constance,' she said sternly, and for a second Constance's heart quailed. What was it she had done wrong or overlooked? 'You have been exhibiting recently a pleasing air of conscientiousness and devoutness,' the nun remarked. 'It would seem our teaching has had a rewarding effect upon you. Have you considered becoming a convert to the faith? I think you would do well to think upon it. You might even have a vocation.'

So saying she turned and left abruptly. Constance stood speechless, watching her breath rise like clouds of steam in the air. Something inside her trembled and stirred with excitement. A vocation? She, a nun, a servant of God? It was a thought too daring to grasp at once.

Over the remainder of the Christmas holiday Constance found ample time and solitude to return to the idea often. By the time Carmel and the others made their noisy irruption in early January, Constance had firmly made up her mind on the first step: she would, Papa permitting, become a Catholic.

Papa's reply to Constance's letter was thoughtful:

'As you know our family has always been a staunch up-holder of the established Church of England, but it would be shortsighted of me not to recognise that convent schooling would undoubtedly influence your young and impression-able mind.

'No matter. The fact appears to be that you have achieved a degree of contentment and poise under that influence. Even you would not deny that you were hitherto a restless and moody child, with whom it was not always easy to communicate. Reverend mother writes to me that you are earnest and sincere in your desire. If, as you tell me, you have found peace in your present way of life, then far be it for me to stand between you and your conscience.

'I trust you remain in good health and continue to concen-trate on your studies. I remain, your loving Papa.'

Constance sat with the letter on her lap, wondering why she felt disappointed. Was it that he made no mention of looking forward to seeing her at Easter? Or was it that she sensed that his apparent magnanimity in allowing her to follow her own conscience amounted to no more than a tacit abandoning of his daughter so that life remained uncom-plicated? Whatever it was, she told herself firmly, she was going ahead with her plan. Reverend Mother had suggested that, with Father Murphy's agreement, Constance could be made ready for the sacrament of First Communion in time for Easter Day. Even Sister Bridget permitted her pleasure and triumph to show through in a glimmer of a smile.

'That's another soul saved from the devil's hands to the eternal glory of God,' she said with satisfaction. 'Our Lord moves in mysterious ways, but it was always plain to me that He had a purpose in sending you here to be educated.'

Constance mused over this thought. It did indeed appear that her life so far had been pre-ordained to reach this point. Salvation was at hand. If only she could find some way to save William, too.

William's response was terse:

*'Why the devil should you think of turning Catholic just
because you have some bee in your bonnet?'* he demanded.
*'Still, if you must, you must, but don't ask me to follow you.
Since I left Weatherhead I haven't been to church at all,
nor do I intend to. A lot of stuffy hypocrisy, that's what it is.
Donations to impress others, status-seeking as a churchwarden or parish councillor to exert a little power. That's
not for me.'*

Like Papa, he meant, thought Constance. A respected
pillar of society, fighting desperately to maintain his prestige
after the tragedy occurred. That was why he wanted to move
away from Weatherhead, where all the local people now eyed
him with suspicion, back to the comparative safety of
Hawksmoor. There he would be viewed with compassion as
an unfortunate man who had lost one son at sea, an infant in
an accident, and suffered the blow of having a dead prema-
ture son. Constance glanced down again at William's letter.

*'Let others do as they wish so long as they leave me to
please myself, that's my motto,'* William said. *'My philosophy is pleasure — to find all that I can in a hard world. I
enjoy riding and going to the theatre and a flutter on the
cards now and again when finances permit. You seek refuge
in religion if you wish, but do not ask me to run away from
life with you.'*

Running away? Was that how he saw it? Constance could
not help feeling sad and disappointed in him. Where was the
closeness between them now, the ability to understand without need of words? Could he not read her unspoken meaning
— that she was seeking salvation for them both? It seemed he
could not, and she felt a lonely sense of isolation. If William
were growing away from her, how could she hold him and
make him see her purpose when they never met face to face?
Once, when he was at school, the miles between had formed
no barrier. If only she could help him recapture that precious
feeling of oneness. He was drifting like a boat without a
rudder towards perilous rocks, and she felt afraid.

At least the way was clear: Papa and William might neither

commend nor approve her course of action, still less understand it, but they raised no voice of protest so long as she walked that path alone. So be it.

It was some weeks later, when Constance's course of instruction was well advanced, that the letter she least expected turned up on the green baize board. Carmel, her eyes agleam with curiosity, reached it down and scanned it before handing it to Constance.

'A letter from England, and not your papa's or your brother's handwriting,' she commented mischievously, 'but definitely a masculine hand. What have you been up to, Connie? You're always a dark horse, you are.'

Constance blushed as the other girls, overhearing, crowded around. 'I've been up to nothing, Carmel, as well you know. Why, I haven't even been back to England in over a year.'

A year and a half. It hardly seemed credible. No wonder the old life seemed so remote and unreal, except her unquenchable love for William. She pushed the letter into the pocket of her smock to read later when giggling curiosity should not disturb her.

When at last she found a private moment she broke the seal curiously. The handwriting, firm and bold and, as Carmel had commented, clearly masculine, was totally unfamiliar. Yet the writer knew her for it began, *'Dear Constance.'*

Curiosity could not wait. Her eyes sped to the signature at the foot of the single sheet of paper: *Tom Lawson.* Amazed, she returned to the first paragraph:

'Dear Constance, Forgive me writing to you uninvited, but it is not without long and careful thought. Ellen told me why you could not come that day, and I pressed her to give me your address. She did so reluctantly and I have held my impatience until now.

'Your black eyes and gleaming dark hair haunt my dreams, for I know in my heart you were innocent of what others believed you had done. I knew you only briefly, but long enough to know without a shadow of doubt that you

*are a creature of conscience and purity. I believe in you now
as I did then, and the thought dogs me that I must find some
way to clear your name. Many have forgotten by now, but
some still remember and it pains me to think that your
honour is blackened.*

'*Forgive me, Constance, a mere policeman, for taking
the liberty of writing to you without your father's per-
mission, but I must. I think of you constantly and I beg you
to allow me to try to find the evidence to clear you.*

'*Twice on a Monday I hoped to meet you and continue a
friendship which I prized. In your absence let me prove that
friendship I feel. With luck perhaps there will be a third
Monday.*'

Despite her alarm, Constance smiled at his touch of
humour. He seemed such a kind and thoughtful person, and
she wished they had had the opportunity to come to know
each other better. As it was, she had other plans to pursue,
and Tom must be prevented at all costs from reviving the
past. Only more pain could follow from that.

Her reply to Tom was civil but firm:

'*Under no circumstances can I allow you to start all over
again questioning which would only cause more suffering to
my family. My stepmother has recently undergone much
illness and distress and nothing could be worse than what
you propose.*

'*I appreciate your concern and your trust and, believe
me, I am grateful. Perhaps, as you say, we may become
friends one day. At the present time I have much on my
mind as I am being converted to the Catholic faith.*'

His response was quick:

'*I am saddened by your refusal, though I recognise it is
your concern for others which prompts it. You are ever the
soul of purity. I shall always continue to respect and cherish
you. Ever yours, Tom.*'

Constance's smile of pleasure faded. He believed in her too
deeply, too trustingly, and without basis. But she could not

disillusion him, for there was comfort in knowing that, in the whole world, there was one human being who had faith in her, and cared, as hitherto only William had cared. He, too, used to believe in her unquestioningly, but now, he seemed to be taking off on a path of his own.

Constance folded Tom's letter carefully and put it away in her little casket, locking it with a sigh. If only those words of affection and trust had been written by William.

13

As Holy Week came, Constance grew more and more tense. For on Good Friday, Father Murphy had agreed, she was to receive First Communion.

She should be happy, but instead Constance felt apprehensive. In January, exhilarated by the wonderful sense of release which that first confession had given her, the prospect of conversion had seemed marvellous. Now she feared that what she was about to do would damn her for ever.

'It is most important — indeed, essential,' Sister Bridget had said sternly in the course of Constance's special instruction, 'that one's soul is in a state of perfect grace before going to Communion. When you are about to consume the Body and Blood of Our Lord himself, your soul must be as pure as snow, absolved from all sin.'

It did not matter too much, apparently, if one had forgotten to confess a venial sin, a lesser one which could be expiated at the next confession, but to receive the sacrament with a mortal sin still unconfessed was sacriligious to the point of damnation.

'If anyone should be so sinful as to do that, he would burn in the fires of Hell for ever,' proclaimed Sister Bridget, scowling fiercely over her spectacles. 'No Purgatory, even, for him, no chance of redemption after thousands of years of penance. Straight to Hell, there to stay for eternity.'

Constance repeated her words to Carmel, wondering if the warning would be confirmed. It was. 'Didn't Sister tell you about the man who went to Mass to receive Communion the morning after he'd killed his best friend in a fight?' Carmel asked. 'Do you know what happened to him? As he knelt at the altar rail, awaiting his turn, there was a terrible flash of lightning and the man was struck dead where he knelt. God's vengeance, Sister Bridget says, for daring to try to eat God's body while he wasn't in a state of grace with that mortal sin on his soul.'

Her eyes were wide and her voice sepulchral as she told the tale. Constance looked away quickly lest the guilt should show in her eyes. It was now Maundy Thursday, and in a day's time she was to present herself at the altar rails in the chapel. She and William, had both shared that terrible responsibility, but it was she who now dared too much.

The parcel had already arrived from England containing the white gown she had asked Papa to provide for Communion day. Papa had evidently considered the request to belong more to a woman's domain than his, for the note inside the parcel was from Miss Platt — signed '*Your loving Stepmama.*' It was the first letter Constance had ever received from her.

> '*I hope the gown will fit, as I had to ask the dressmaker to decide for herself your approximate height. I told her you were tall for your age and slim.*'

A matter-of-fact tone, Constance noted, neither complaining nor affectionate. Crisp, calm, capable as the woman herself. She lifted out the cream folds of the dress, while Carmel cooed appreciatively. It was pretty enough, silk and finely sewn, simple and plain but for a single band of lace across the bodice. The dressmaker had estimated well, for it fitted beautifully. Beneath another layer of paper lay a lace cap with a short veil.

'You look like a bride!' Carmel exclaimed in admiration.

178

'The ensemble sets off your dark hair and eyes to perfection! How sweet and pure you look!'

Constance felt a flush redden her cheeks, and she pulled off the cap and laid it aside. Carmel picked it up, placed it on her own head and pirouetted in front of the mirror.

'I wish I were taking my First Communion now instead of when I was seven,' she sighed. 'We only appreciated the pretty clothes then. Come on, or we'll be late for Mass.'

In the chapel Father Murphy conducted the ceremony and placed a mark of ash on the foreheads of all the penitents preparing for Easter Communion. Constance knelt, her heart thudding, and felt the symbol burn on her forehead like the mark of Cain but she knew she could not turn back.

On the night of Maundy Thursday she barely slept at all, debating whether to feign illness in the morning or plead some other excuse to save her soul from eternal perdition. Better, perhaps, to be truthful and tell the sisters her unfitness to receive the sacrament, but that would only result in their insisting that she confessed the mortal sin that held her back. And how could she? Her soul was her own to save, but she had no dominion over William's soul, united in all else though they were.

Good Friday morning dawned clear and bright with the promise of a fine day ahead. Carmel glanced out of the dormitory window as she pulled her smock over her gown.

'Seems set fair enough now,' she commented, 'but just you watch. Have you ever noticed on Good Friday how the sky always clouds over at three in the afternoon?'

Fanny pricked up her ears. 'You're making that up, Carmel. Isn't she, Edith?'

'No, I'm not!' Carmel protested. 'I've noticed it for several years, ever since my nanny told me when I was little. You just watch when we go to Mass this afternoon.'

For once Mass was to be said at three o'clock instead of early morning, to coincide with the traditional hour of Christ's death. As the day drew on Constance watched the sky through the tall window, trying to read a significance in its aspect. The sun did not actually appear, but the sky was cloudless.

Constance struck an arrangement with God. The sky should represent the state of her soul. If it remained unbesmirched by cloud, her soul was in a pure enough state to receive Him. If not, then she must find some way to delay.

Fortune played tricks. Throughout most of the day the sky remained blue and clear but after noon a stray puff or two began to flit across the square of window frame. Constance watched, trying to convince herself that such minuscule blots must represent only venial sins, no barrier to the great event ahead. But nearing mid-afternoon, as the girls put away their embroidery to prepare for chapel, the sky was decidedly greying. Constance kept her eyes averted.

The crocodile of girls, led by Sister Bridget and followed by Sister Josephine, filed across the courtyard as the first heavy drops of rain began to fall. Carmel nudged her pointedly. 'You see! Always at three on Good Friday!'

'Quiet there, girls. Compose yourselves for the sacrament,' Sister Bridget admonished, and she watched them with her eagle-like gaze as they filed into the pews. Constance knelt, her heart trembling as she thought of what she was daring to do.

The Mass took longer than usual, it seemed to her, but all too soon Father Murphy was elevating the Host, praying for its miraculous transformation to the true body of Christ. Constance could not raise her head, conscious of the slashing sound of rain outside and the distant rumble of thunder.

'*Ecce, Agnus Dei.*' Behold, the Lamb of God. The girls moved slowly forward to the altar rails, Constance among them. She knelt, feeling weak and dizzy. In a moment Father Murphy would work his way along the line, administering the Host to each open mouth until he reached hers. Her clasped hands trembled in fear. Suddenly the priest's white robe was there, just before her eyes. She closed them, tilted back her head and opened her mouth.

'*Agnus Dei, qui tollis peccata mundi, sed tantum dic verbo et sanabitur anima mea,*' the priest intoned. A flat disc of some substance clung tenaciously to Constance's tongue just as a great peal of thunder reverberated through the tiny chapel, and Constance felt herself sway in terror.

But no damning thunderbolt came. Carmel, kneeling next to her, accepted the Host next and bent her head in prayer. The girl before Constance was rising to go back to her seat. When Carmel too rose to leave Constance stumbled after her.

She was alive! God had not exacted retribution! In a haze of exhilaration, deeply conscious of the precious sacrament adhering to her tongue, Constance resumed her seat next to Carmel and prayed fervently. Her gratitude knew no bounds: God had accepted her, and she was His servant.

The next two minutes were ones of extreme embarrassment as she tried to remove the gluey sacrament from her tongue to her throat to swallow it. Sister Bridget's orders had made it plain that never, but never, must one's teeth come into contact with Our Lord's precious body. Two whole minutes of agonising effort, persuading the now glutinous object to move, seemed like hours but at last it was gone. *'Ite, missa est.'* Mass was over and already the girls were leaving the pews.

'You looked lovely,' said Carmel with a sigh. 'So fresh and pure in your white, while we all wore our dark Sunday-best worsted. Just like a bride, as I'm sure you will be, one day soon.'

Not I, thought Constance privately. No man will influence my life but William. I shall be bride to no one — unless a bride of Christ.

A week later a still-radiant Constance wrote to William about her happiness. Weeks passed and he made no comment. Constance wrote to Tom Lawson instead. He replied with heartfelt congratulations and hoped her happiness would be lasting, after all the sadness she had endured. She put his letter away with a warm glow of satisfaction. At least one friend understood and appreciated her need. Her letters to Tom were few, but they always elicited just the response she hoped. If only William were as reliable a correspondent, she sighed. It had been months now since she had heard from him.

News of him came through Papa's regular but distant

letters. He seemed proud that his son had now achieved the rank of lieutenant but his comments about William's recent activities gradually became fewer and briefer. Constance guessed that Papa had learnt of his gambling and theatre-going and did not entirely approve of such a hedonistic way of life.

Papa had, it seemed, accepted her conversion to an alien faith philosophically enough. Privately he probably despaired that his two children had taken off along paths very divergent from their upbringing, but at least he kept his counsel.

'*Your Mama and I are satisfied if you are doing what you feel is right and what your conscience dictates,*' he wrote solemnly. '*So long as you are content, that is all that matters. As the bard put it, "Unto thine own self be true", and I know you would do no less.*'

Constance sighed. The old year was slipping away and it would soon be Christmas. This time she *was* going home to Thwaite Lodge, home for the first time in over two years. Would Papa still remain so philosophical, she wondered, when he heard of the plan that now occupied her thoughts night and day? A far-away daughter with odd ideas was one thing, but a daughter close to home and wearing the veil of a nun was quite another.

Constance could not quite understand why Thwaite Lodge seemed to have shrunk in size over the seven years since she had last been there. The rooms, the corridors, even the gardens seemed far smaller than she remembered. Only Papa and Miss Platt appeared the same.

'Lovely to have you home again,' murmured Miss Platt, sweeping forward smoothly to place a dutiful kiss on Constance's cheek. The thought that crossed Constance's mind she dismissed at once as uncharitable and unworthy. Of course they were truly glad to see her, secure in the knowledge that by New Year she would be ready to leave again.

'Not much longer to go at the convent now, eh?' said Papa with a cheery smile. 'We must give some thought to what you must do after the summer. Time enough for that, though, after the festivities are over.'

'Is William coming home?' Constance asked eagerly. 'I haven't had a letter from him for some time.'

Papa's smile faded and Miss Platt turned away to busy herself rearranging the bowl of chrysanthemums on the table. 'Ah well, perhaps,' said Papa slowly. 'We don't receive many letters from him either, but I gather he's rather occupied. With luck he may get leave for a day or two.'

The festivities rang hollow without him. Miss Platt had seen to it that all the necessary ingredients were there · the holly boughs and candles, the turkey and plum pudding, the sherry and madeira and even the annual serenade by the local carol-singers. But the one ingredient that made the festival a holiday for Constance was missing, and her heart ached for William. He did not even send a message of seasonal greetings to her.

A distinct sign of disturbance crept into the atmosphere of Thwaite Lodge when Constance announced that on Christmas morning she would go, not to the village church with Papa, but to the Catholic church in Bridlington. Papa frowned and Miss Platt lowered her head.

'Really Constance!' Papa said with a touch of irritation. 'Could you not go to church with us just this once? I should be obliged if you would observe the proprieties of a good Anglican family for the occasion.'

'I do not wish to embarrass you, Papa,' Constance replied meekly, 'but it is not *my* church. You said I should follow my conscience, and so I must. Would you oblige me by letting the coachman drive me to Bridlington?'

He clicked his tongue testily and no more was said, but Constance knew he was grieved. She had no wish to hurt anyone, least of all Papa, but she must do what was right.

On her return to the lodge the tension had miraculously vanished. 'William has come home!' Papa announced with delight. 'He was here when we returned from church. He's in the kitchen now, talking to cook.'

William emerged minutes later, a broad smile on his handsome face and a fistful of sugared almonds in his hand.

Constance flung herself upon him eagerly. 'William, oh William! What a wonderful Christmas surprise!'

'Hey, hold on! You're making me spill my almonds all over the floor!' he protested laughingly. 'I thought you'd be a sober lady by now, not a young hoyden flinging herself about wildly!'

Reluctantly Constance let go with a smile. 'It's just that I'm so happy to see you, Willie. It's made my Christmas complete.'

'Not for long, I fear. I only have two days' leave so I must go back to the grindstone tomorrow,' he said ruefully. 'Never mind, let's live while we can and to hell with tomorrow. Let's go and join the parents in the parlour and I'll see if I can persuade Papa to open the port before lunch.'

'If anyone can, you can, Willie.' She gazed up at him, awash with admiration. He was so tall and broad, so muscular and handsome, and so endearingly charming. No one could deny him anything.

It was only that night, over dinner by candlelight, that she noticed the hollows under his eyes. His bonhomie seemed to fade too as the wine decanter passed back and forth. Over dessert he actually became irritable.

'I know I don't write often, Papa, but to be truthful I don't care much for letter-writing. I had enough of the weekly letter when I was at school, and it was an awful bore. I'll write soon enough if there's anything to tell you.'

'Or to ask,' said Papa. Constance could see the stern light in his eye. 'You write quickly enough when you've overspent your pay and you want a loan.'

'Ah, so that's what's troubling you,' replied William. 'Well, you needn't fret. I have every intention of repaying you.'

'But how, if you cannot live within your means?' Papa demanded.

'Excuse me,' Miss Platt interrupted, 'but I think Constance and I will leave you to your port. Coming, my dear?'

A diplomatic exit, thought Constance as she followed her stepmother to the drawing room. Whatever the lady's faults, she knew the value of discretion.

184

Constance yielded to a sudden impulse. 'There is something I would like to tell you and Papa,' she said quietly. 'I have decided to become a nun.'

Miss Platt's eyelids did not flicker. 'Indeed? Well, that is your affair, my dear, but I would be obliged if you did not trouble your papa at the moment with your news. He has enough on his mind as it is without adding to his problems with an announcement which would surely disturb him.'

Constance's eyes widened. 'Why should it disturb him? He already knows that I am an ardent convert to Catholicism. Why should he be horrified that I am to take the veil?'

'But so soon, my dear? You could at least be considerate enough to delay the matter for some time.'

Constance frowned. 'Does it matter when it is? I see no reason to delay.'

Miss Platt sighed. 'Ah, one is so impatient with life at seventeen! I entreat you, wait at least until Papa's anxiety over William is ended before telling him.'

For a moment there was silence, Constance felt disappointed that her news was brushed aside so quickly and resentful that her stepmother set herself up as a barricade between Papa and herself. But perhaps she was being selfish. William's troubles were more important.

'I didn't know William was in debt,' Constance commented. 'Has he borrowed from Papa often?'

'Once or twice, but I'm sure they'll sort it out. Would you care for a glass of madeira, or would you prefer tea?'

The matter was closed. Neither Willie nor Papa referred to it again in her hearing that night or next morning, but as Willie prepared to leave there was still a coolness in the air. Constance hastened to try to bridge the gap. In the vestibule she came close to him. 'Willie, you will write to me sometimes, won't you?' she pleaded. 'I long so much for news of you.'

'As I said, I'll write when there's anything to tell,' he replied carelessly. His tone cut her deeply.

'We're still special to each other, aren't we? You could write to me of how you feel sometimes.'

He shrugged. 'That's for girls, not men. The army teaches

one not to have feelings.'

She was shocked. 'But you must still have feelings, Willie! As I have, strong and deep but not to be talked about except to someone very special and close. And we are close, Willie. Remember?'

She held up the index finger of her left hand. He glanced at it and looked away quickly. 'Children's games, Connie, that's what that was,' he muttered.

'But symbolic of a special bond. We have a secret that unites us closer than any brother and sister, Willie. You'll always be very special to me.'

'I know.'

He did not add that it was reciprocal and the omission hurt her. Impulsively she took his arm.

'But remember, too, that I said either of us could break that bond when the need arose. You have only to find a needle.' She looked up at him, imploring him silently to say he would never do such a thing, but he deliberately avoided her gaze.

'Come on, Connie,' he said peevishly. 'If you delay me any longer I'm not going to get down into Hawksmoor in time for the coach. Behave yourself now, old girl, and if you're good perhaps I'll write to you for your birthday. Come on outside and wave me off.'

'I'll do more — I'll ride into town with you!' said Constance eagerly. 'Let me just fetch my coat.'

William did not answer. Perhaps he had not heard, for he was already on his way out. Constance, fearful that he would vanish without a farewell kiss if she lingered for her coat, ran out of the open doorway after him. Icy December air struck cold through her dress.

William was mounting the carriage step. Constance ran to him. 'Willie! You forgot to kiss me goodbye!'

He turned on the step and, without dismounting, bent to kiss her. 'Goodbye, Connie. Take care of yourself.'

And then he was shut inside, waving and smiling, and the carriage moved off. Constance watched the horses' breath making clouds of steam in the crisp air until the carriage rounded the stone pillar and vanished completely behind the high wall. Shivering a little, she turned to re-enter the house.

Thwaite Lodge was lonely and silent without his presence, and in the days that remained she could not bring herself to tell Papa about her plan. He seemed older now, greyer at the temples and more drawn than when she came home, and she could only think that it was the strained relationship between himself and William which had caused it. She could not add to his anxiety now by revealing to him a plan she knew he would contemplate with horror. It must wait until the moment was more opportune.

It was curious, but without William even the appeal of the moors seemed to have gone. Alone, unchaperoned and un-questioned, Constance walked on the heights on a grey, drizzling day, looking down on the huddled houses below, and could capture none of that magical sense of freedom the moors had once yielded to her. Only once, briefly, standing against the parapet of the old watch tower and feeling the rain on her cheek, did she feel a fleeting sensation of oneness with William. It was here they had first sworn eternal loyalty to each other. Then the recollection of his careless leave-taking banished her contentment.

'I did mean to discuss with you your future mode of employment,' Papa said in an air of abstraction when she went to his study one January morning to bid him farewell. 'Time passes so quickly. Perhaps you could give some thought to the matter and let me know what you think – governess, perhaps, or companion to a lady of standing. Something of that kind.'

Something which would keep her away from Thwaite Lodge, she mused sadly on the long, cold journey back to the convent. Papa would not oppose her taking the veil. She belonged to nobody's world now, not Papa's and Miss Platt's, nor William's. Only God was willing to offer her a home despite her transgressions, and her heart swelled with love and gratitude.

Soon after the new term at school began, a reminder came that she was not entirely friendless. It was a letter from Tom.

187

'*I could have sworn I caught a glimpse of you in Hawksmoor at Christmas,*' he wrote. '*I was visiting friends there and was riding in a tram one day and thought I saw your face in the crowd, but it could not have been for I am sure you would have let me know if you were coming home to England. It must have been fancy on my part because I see your face in my mind so often.*'

Tom Lawson. She recalled his open, honest face with pleasure and felt ashamed that she had given him no thought in weeks. Contritely she wrote him a note, apologising for not letting him know: '*After all, one would hardly have expected a policeman in the east of Yorkshire to be so far away from home.*' And so near to me, she thought. Perhaps your nearness could have helped to fill the cold, empty space left by William, just a little.

Constance's eighteenth birthday came before the snows melted away, but not the promised letter from William. Not long afterwards came a letter from Papa telling of his wife's new-found interest in voluntary work for the poor of Hawksmoor.

'*She is actively involved in organising some kind of soup-kitchen for the destitute,*' he wrote, '*and is also busily making plans for a seaside holiday for a number of poor urchins at Easter. I do so hope she does not over-tax her strength, for I fear she forgets her limitations when she is carried away by enthusiasm.*'

Although he did not say it, it was implicit that his daughter's return home at Easter was not envisaged, and Constance fancied she recognised Miss Platt's hand in this. Perhaps the prospect of her fulfilling her Easter duties at the Catholic church was too embarrassing to be faced again, but Constance resigned herself to celebrating God's supreme sacrifice here amongst the pious nuns. It would be more fitting somehow than amidst the bustle and industry of a Yorkshire factory town.

But as the end of the spring term approached, Constance

felt restless and unhappy. Her dreams by night were pervaded by Miss Platt's calm presence, shaking her head always and holding Constance firmly back, while Papa's distant figure seemed unaware. Frequently the girl awoke with a burning, angry resentment towards her stepmother which bordered on hate.

'Forgive me, Father,' she prayed contritely, 'and teach me the virtue of patience.'

But again and again the dream returned. Sometimes Miss Platt's black-gowned figure melted and transmuted to a fat black spider sitting possessively at the centre of her web, waiting silently for unwary prey to venture too close. On those occasions Constance awoke sweating.

Sister Bridget was in militant mood one Monday morning. Her shrill voice rippled around the classroom: 'I saw you all at Mass, fidgetting and not paying attention,' she cried. 'How can you expect your Creator to pay attention to you if you pay none to Him? There will be no more of this, do you hear, you sinful girls? You do not deserve His mercy and a place in Heaven with Him.'

Her baleful gaze turned on Constance, who was gazing out of the window. 'Constance Lumb! Do you hear what I say?'

Constance, startled, withdrew her gaze from the budding green leaves beyond the window to meet the nun's fierce eyes. 'Sister?'

Sister Bridget threw up her hands. 'Dear Lord. I am wasting my time with wretched creatures like you! Hours, days, months of my life I spend trying to teach you the ways of goodness so that you too can enter the Kingdom of God; hours, days, months on my knees on a cold cell floor praying for your redemption, and what do you do? You turn deaf ears and idle your time away in sinful laziness! Dear Heaven! Is this how You test my piety, oh Lord?'

Constance stared, anger thundering in her veins. It was not the sharp features of a nun encircled by a wimple she saw before her, standing between herself and God, but Miss Platt, serene and triumphant as she held Constance back from Papa. Constance felt blood suffusing her cheeks and fury clamping like icy steel around her heart. Before she could think she was on her feet.

'You beast!' she cried out, raising her fist to shake it angrily at the stupefied nun. A gasp of horror broke from thirty throats, but Constance raved on, unheeding. 'What right have you to make yourself his self-appointed guardian? You shall not stand between me and him! I won't have it! You seem to think that no one but you is good enough or matters enough to him – but what about us?'

William and me, she raged inside. 'We are his children and you keep him from us as if he were your own private property, to be rationed out to us only now and again when you feel like it. I won't have it, I tell you! He's my father, and I have some right to his love!'

She sat down abruptly, tears rolling down her cheeks in rage, and buried her face in her hands. There was a murmuring around her, a few quiet words, a scraping of chairs, and then silence. When at last, fury subsided, she looked up and realised with alarm where she was, she found the classroom deserted.

For a time she sat numbly, appalled at what she had done. She must be going crazy, to mistake Sister Bridget for Miss Platt and let her tongue run away with her. Sister Teresa appeared at the door, beckoned, and then led Constance out.

The mother superior's manner was remarkably mild in the circumstances. 'Sister Bridget told me of what occurred, Constance, and is very concerned for you. I would welcome your assurance that such unseemly behaviour will not be repeated.'

Chastened, Constance expressed contrition and apology, omitting to explain her momentary hallucination. Reverend Mother, mollified by her humility, patted Constance's shoulder as she was leaving. 'We know the strain you are under, my dear, but do not mistake Sister Bridget's fierce concern for you for severity. She is the last person on earth to stand between you and Our Lord, believe me.'

Sister Bridget did not appear in the classroom next day. Sister Josephine told the class she was unwell and was to spend a few days in bed.

The convent held an air of sadness for Constance, despite the laughter and chatter of the other girls preparing to go home. Next day Reverend Mother broke the terrible news: Sister Bridget had died suddenly. There was a subdued hush in the dormitory that night as the chapel bell tolled. Every girl was remembering the sister's fierce and frequent onslaughts on them, her admonitions to avoid the devil's temptations in order to attain the glory of Heaven.

'Do you think Sister Bridget has gone to Heaven?' Carmel asked in hushed tones.

'Sure to,' replied Constance. 'She was a very holy lady.'

'But she was always angry, and that's a sin. Maybe she'll only spend some time in Purgatory.'

'No, she'll go straight to Heaven,' said Constance firmly. 'Her anger was always against the devil, not us. She fought hard to save all our souls for Our Lord, and He will recognise her battle.'

'Perhaps you're right,' murmured Carmel. 'She used to frighten me terribly but in some odd way I shall miss her.'

Edith and Fanny and the others murmured agreement. The school would not be the same without her militant evangelism.

Father Murphy conducted a simple funeral service and the girls stood silently in the little churchyard adjoining the cloisters while the good nun's body was laid to rest. Constance stood, her hands tightly in silent prayer, as the coffin was lowered. *God forgive me*, she prayed. *I hastened her death*.

'In the midst of life we are in death.'

She heard a muffled sob from Carmel, and Fanny's shoulders were shaking slightly. The other girls stood whitefaced, a bewildered look about them. For most of them, children of the middle-classes who came less often into contact with death than the poor, this was a new and bewildering experience.

But not for Constance. She remembered vividly still the dead marble face of her mother which she and William had been obliged to kiss, standing on tiptoe in the darkened parlour. And the dead child at Weatherhead. Mercifully, she had not been obliged to view his little corpse when it lay in the laundry, but the harrowing memory of the circumstances of his death and the terrible air of suspicion and distrust that enveloped the house would remain with her for ever. She pushed the memory fiercely from her mind. The pain of guilt was too great to bear: the guilt over Sister Bridget, and the guilt of responsibility for which she could never make amends until William agreed. And his silence on the subject over the years, and now his failure to keep in touch with her at all, made it impossible for her to act. She must continue to be silent and to suffer.

Early in the summer term, Constance received a summons to the mother superior's office. She tapped at the door nervously, racking her conscience in an effort to discover what error she might have committed to warrant this unusual request.

Reverend Mother's warm manner soon dispelled her fears. 'Ah, Constance, come in and sit down, my dear,' she said, indicating the chair across her desk. 'Let me come straight to the point. I have today received a letter from your father.'

'From Papa?' Constance repeated. He had not written to her for some weeks.

'He writes that he is concerned as to your future and, not having been in the best of health lately —'

'Papa is ill?' Constance interrupted, agitated by the news.

'He simply says he hasn't been in the best of health, my dear, so do not alarm yourself unduly. No, his real concern is for your future, and he has asked me to ascertain your aptitudes and perhaps help with finding suitable employment for you. Now I know your qualities, Constance, but I know nothing of your preferences. Do you know what you would like to do?'

Constance hesitated. She could not confess to this pious, gentle lady that her dearest wish was to become a nun like herself. The wish was too audacious, especially after that scene with poor Sister Bridget. 'I should like to work for others, Reverend Mother.'

'But of course, to be employed means working for someone else.'

'I mean, to be of service to others in some way, to help others less fortunate than I.'

'A laudable ambition. Now, would that be with children, perhaps? As a nanny or governess? Or with older people as a companion or nurse? We have a sister order of nuns in England who nurse where we teach. Would that perhaps appeal to you?'

Constance stared at her, hope leaping in her heart. 'Oh yes, Reverend Mother! I would love to work with nuns. Would they have me?'

The mother superior smiled. 'They accept girls either just to assist or as postulants who must work hard to prove their dedication to the service of Our Lord, and the work is not easy.'

'I can work hard, Reverend Mother, and I should enjoy it. What is a postulant?'

'A novice, training to become a nun, and I have seen the depth of your devotion, Constance. I would be happy to recommend you to the mother superior there.'

She evidently saw the girl's hesitation. 'What is it, Constance? Are you not sure that you want to devote your life to God's service? Have no fear, you are not irrevocably committed until you take your final vows, and the mother superior will not allow that until she is convinced you are truly ready. You can always turn back to the world.'

'Oh no, Reverend Mother, the world holds nothing for me! I willingly give my life to God!' Constance said breathlessly. 'But if I fail, can I still stay there and continue to nurse?'

'I'm sure you can, for there are always too few people willing to serve the poor. And the people you will nurse will be very pitiful creatures, Constance — babies and women who have fallen so low that all your prayers will be needed as well as a strong back to save them.'

'Oh please, Reverend Mother, will you recommend me there?' Constance pleaded. To serve God in a humble way beside noble women who had taken the veil seemed perfection.

'Very well,' she said, laying aside Mr Lumb's letter and taking a fresh sheet of paper, 'I shall write to tell your papa of our plan, and then write directly to the mother superior to ask if you may come to work in the summer in her hospice for fallen women.'

14 : 1862

As the early summer days passed, Constance expected daily to hear word from her father about how he reacted to the idea of her nursing the poor. She felt a little apprehensive that he might demur, particularly when she learnt just what the term 'fallen women' denoted.

He might well be shocked, outraged at the thought of his well-bred daughter coming into contact with such contamination, she suspected, and she dreaded the arrival of a letter from him sternly forbidding her even to contemplate such a notion. But the letter did not come and Constance waited anxiously.

Reverend Mother had news before her. 'I have heard from the mother superior that she is happy to accept you on my recommendation, Constance, and your father has sent a message to say he has no objection. So that's settled, my dear. You may enter the hospice as soon as you like after term ends.'

That was a great relief, but Constance still had some misgivings about Papa's approval. He had written to Reverend Mother, not to her. A brief message, not enthusiastic pleasure, evidently. Laconic comments from Papa had always meant quite the contrary in the past. Still, he had not forbidden the venture, and for that Constance was grateful. She wrote a letter to William and to Tom and another home, and confidently awaited a reply giving instructions about her return at the end of term. Papa would surely expect her to spend a little time at home before going south to start work.

William Lumb sat on the edge of his bed and re-read the letter in his hand in amazement. It needed to be read twice, partly because his head was still muzzy and ached like fury, and partly because what Constance wrote seemed too incredible to be true.

'What's up, Willie? Another letter dunning you for debt?'

William scowled at the tall russet-haired young man pulling on his uniform jacket who stood, the jacket only half pulled up his arms, regarding William with teasing amusement.

'No, thank God, it isn't.' William muttered, 'but it's damn funny news from my sister.'

'The pious one, the one who got religion and became a Papist? What's funny, then? Has she run off with an organ-grinder after all?'

'Oh, you're very amusing at this damnable hour of the morning, Locke-Whitley. Still, it's damn near as odd. She's going to work in a home for fallen women, would you believe, and she the most innocent and ignorant creature I know.'

Locke-Whitley threw back his head and laughed uproariously. 'Oh, I say, Jardine, did you hear that? Willie Lumb's sister is going to work in a home for fallen women! Do you think she'll get us all introductions?'

William screwed up the letter and tossed it aside, angered by their ribald laughter and by the pain in his head. He strode outside into the yard to cool his throbbing temples under the water spilling from the pump. Even thus refreshed he felt reluctant to face the day. To hear Connie was letting her religious mania demean her to such an extent was just too much, when his debts were mounting up and Papa was remaining deaf to his letters of entreaty; the Colonel wanted to see him in his office today for an explanation about a prank in the mess; and last night Dolly had refused to grant him her favours yet again without a shilling. The result was he had drowned his disappointments in drink, but now the warning had been given that there would be no more tick at the mess until his dues were paid. Did ever a fellow have such a tough time at a stage of life when he ought to be free to enjoy himself?

A subaltern's pay went nowhere. Papa's meagre allowance did not afford luxury and one had to keep up with the other fellows. If only there were some other way to augment his income, on a regular basis. . .

There was one possible solution, he reflected moodily as he returned indoors to dress. Cynthia Baverstock. Major Lionel Baverstock's plain but amiable daughter had made it pretty evident, simpering behind her fan at the military ball and over the teacups when the senior officers' ladies entertained, that she found young William agreeable and interesting. In fact Jardine and the others had teased him about whether or not he would pick the fruit that was ripe to fall into his lap and had jokingly reminded him that not only was she the major's daughter, but heiress to the Baverstock shipping line too. His first instincts had been those of revulsion because Cynthia Baverstock, thin and gawky, held none of the pneumatic attraction of Dolly Larkin, the little seamstress who obliged gentlemen discreetly in her basement apartment. But on second thoughts William was beginning to see some little appeal in Cynthia. Her amiability would ensure his life continued along the lines he chose, and Papa would be certain to smile benevolently on such a match.

And it would take care of all those wretched bills, from the tailor, the bootmaker, the wine merchant and those other officers pressing for payment of card-playing debts. Not to mention Dolly Larkin, who was now shrilly threatening to come to the barracks and speak to the major.

He would have to do something drastic, William thought moodily, as he sat on the edge of the bed to pull on his boots. And now Connie, always emotional and intense, going round the bend altogether by going to work amongst whores — it was all too much for a fellow of sensitivity to bear.

Fortunately his allowance arrived and he decided he would forget it all with the help of a magnum of champagne and one of those delectable little chorus girls from the music hall. Cynthia Baverstock could wait until he was really desperate.

Tom Lawson sat at the chenille-covered table in the fading evening light and chewed the tip of his pen thoughtfully.

'Who are you writing to, lad?' demanded his father from the depths of the chair before the fire. 'Is it that Lumb lass again?'

'Yes, father. She's leaving for London soon.'

'Oh, aye? Going to join the fashionable lot like her brother?'

'No, father. She's going to work, work hard.'

'Is she, then?' A rumbling noise indicated that Mr Lawson, senior, found that difficult to believe. Tom dipped the pen in the inkwell and scratched on the paper.

> *'You are the dearest, kindest creature to offer yourself for such laborious work, and my love and respect for you deepen all the more. But take care of yourself, little Constance, and I beg you not to over-exert yourself. I wish I could take care of you. . .'*

He broke off, reluctant to commit to paper the depth of his devotion in a manner so rash it could frighten her away. How could he, so far beneath her, confess his adoration, his longing to undertake any feat which could spare her pain and bring her peace?

He contented himself with penning only words of eternal friendship and concern, begging her to keep in touch with him. That must suffice for now, and who knew? Perhaps some day he would find a way to help the beleaguered soul who so much needed love and devotion.

The summer term still had a few days left to run when Constance, already organising her packing to leave the convent school for the last time, received Miss Platt's letter.

> *'My dear Constance, I am loth to alarm you, but I really feel you should come home at once and not wait until the school closes. You see Papa, who has been in a rather delicate state of health for some months, has now taken a turn for the worse.*
>
> *'He had a nasty spell a few days ago and the doctor thinks it was an attack of apoplexy. Papa is now rather ill,*

confined to bed, and I feel it best his family be near him.

'The girls are making arrangements to leave their families to come at once. William too has been sent for. I am writing separately to reverend mother to ask her to arrange your passage home. You will be met when you disembark at Liverpool.'

Constance's heart thudded with anxiety. Papa sounded very ill but he could not be dying, surely. Miss Platt's letter, cool, calm and practical as herself, did not betray any anxiety for Papa, only concern that his family should be near him in his time of need. *His* family, Miss Platt had written, Constance noted, and not *our* family.

The mother superior rose with speedy efficiency to the situation and before Constance could draw breath, she was on her way home. The long and tearful farewells she had been anticipating for weeks with Carmel and the nuns had not happened, for there had been no time. Constance watched the dark waters tumbling in the wake of the ship and realised sadly that the haven of peace in the convent for the last three years was now part of the past. Uncertainly she wondered what the immediate future would bring. *Please God, do not let Papa die.*

There was one ray of light in the hurried, anxious home-coming. William would be there at Thwaite Lodge, together with her in their childhood home again, and with luck he would be there for longer this time.

Constance's heart plummeted the moment the front door of Thwaite Lodge was opened that night. In the lamp-lit vestibule Miss Platt advanced on her slowly, unsmiling, dressed in black and Mrs Roebuck, passing through the vestibule, wore a black arm band.

'Constance, my dear,' said Miss Platt in a hollow voice. 'Thank you for coming so quickly, but I'm afraid it's too late. Poor Papa passed away this morning, quite peacefully.'

Already exhausted from the journey, Constance felt the last remaining strength drain away from her limbs. Miss Platt took her arm and steered her towards the parlour. A few minutes later as she sipped hot tea, she tried to force her brain to accept that Papa was gone, finally and irrevocably, but her brain refused to acquiesce. It was too unreal, impossible, just part of the turbulent nightmare of a mind confused and exhausted. After a night's sleep she would waken to find it was only a dream.

A book lay open on the low table between Constance and Miss Platt. *'Manners and Rules of Good Society'*, Constance read at the top of the page and below, *'Chapter Seven: The Proprieties To Be Observed on a Death'*. Constance felt sickened. Trust Miss Platt to be coolly efficient even at a moment of family tragedy. By now she had probably already ordered the black-edged cards to inform acquaintances and settled in her mind the details of oak or elm coffin, brass or silver handles, and how many black-plumed horses were to draw the funeral hearse. Constance's mind withdrew from the whole nauseous idea.

'Is William here?' she enquired weakly.

'He arrived yesterday and so he was here at the end. He's gone to bed now because he knew you would be very late. The girls have gone home but will come back for the funeral.'

Constance rose, desperate to brush the talk aside. 'I think I'll go to bed too,' she said lamely.

'Do, my dear. You can see Papa tomorrow.'

But in the morning, having slept fitfully, tormented by dreams, Constance still could not face the fact of Papa's death, and she refused Miss Platt's offer to take her to see Papa.

'But he looks so peaceful, you would be glad to see him so,' Miss Platt urged. 'There is no sign of the suffering he endured. He looks a little thinner, that's all.'

'No, no, I won't see him!' Constance cried out. 'I don't want to! I want to remember him as he was!'

Miss Platt sighed. 'Very well. You're an odd pair, William and you. The girls wept to see how placid Papa looked. You really ought to, you know. It's your duty.'

Constance, near to tears, had to bite her tongue not to cry out. Her heart ached to protest that Papa had never done his duty by her or William, shutting them both out of his life long ago, but she could not bring herself to say it. Once, in her wild and wilful youth, she would have argued with Miss Platt, but not now. Now it was more important to try to find again that peace and solace she had discovered in the convent.

Her joy at seeing William was short-lived. 'Damn bad luck about Papa,' he muttered. 'I'm in a devil of a hole so I can only hope his will may help matters. But I'm damned if I'm going to kiss his corpse whatever Stepmama says.'

Suddenly Constance was mentally transported back through the years. It was Mama's body on the table, and she was standing aside as William climbed on a box and bent over the coffin, then straightened again and revealed the expression of horror and disgust on his young face. His expression today was very different – moody, sullen, resentful. Constance was horrifyingly aware of the gulf that was growing between them, and she felt afraid. It was like walking on treacherous quicksand, wondering whether the next step would bring one back to firm earth and familiarity, or to disaster.

The next few days passed in a haze of activity conducted in low-toned reverence until the day of the funeral. Constance climbed aboard one of the two black carriages with William and Miss Platt and Elizabeth, while Mary Jane rode with her husband and Uncle Reginald and Aunt Bertha in the other. The black-plumed horses, well-schooled to their duties, stood passive and unmoving until the moment came for the cortège to move off at the customary three miles an hour to Hawksmoor parish church. The clergyman, in honour of the deceased's standing as churchwarden, was waiting at the church door as the four bearers in their black silk-banded hats carried the coffin with its black silk pall through the lych gate and up the path.

Constance and William followed with Miss Platt. Behind her Constance could hear Elizabeth's little girl, Rebecca, proud of her new white silk dress with black ribbons, complaining to her mama that she was sqeezing her hand too tightly. Elizabeth's only reply was a muffled sob.

200

It was strange, but Constance could feel no desire to weep as the clergyman began to intone the words of the service. Through her veil she glanced up at William. He was dry-eyed, looking a trifle sheepish, as though conscious of all the stares in the family's direction. Miss Platt, too, on the other side of her, seemed to be in control of herself, though her expression remained invisible behind her veil. In her neat black gown, liberally trimmed with black crepe, and her veiled bonnet, she appeared a woman of mystery. As she had always been, thought Constance. One never knew what went on inside her neatly-coiffed head because she always and unfailingly remained cool and poised and gave nothing of her inmost feelings away.

And what of her own feelings? It was frightening that she could feel nothing, no grief, no terror, at the finality of Papa's death, no guilt over things done or undone, only a vague sense of being left behind, abandoned once more and this time irrevocably, unequivocally.

The clergyman was holding forth about 'our dear brother departed', speaking of his high standing and esteem in the parish and how sorely he would be missed by his family and colleagues. Constance wondered if it was true. Elizabeth and Mary Jane had their own lives and families now; William and Miss Platt had shed no tears that she had witnessed. Only she herself, comparative stranger though she was to her father, would feel her life robbed by his going. Thank God she had work to occupy her, to give meaning to life, or she would have felt completely rudderless.

There was William, of course, but then she had always known he was the lode-star of her life. Papa had not seemed so important till this moment. She missed him desperately, but still the tears would not come.

Miss Platt had seen to it that the whole ritual was as admirably executed as the most demanding household guide to etiquette could expect. Two days after the funeral when all the relatives had returned to their respective homes, Miss Platt asked Constance over breakfast to come and talk to her in the study as soon as the meal was over.

*　　*　　*

The room was empty as Constance entered. Papers lay on Papa's desk and she glanced at them curiously.

'*Meakin's Funeral Parlour*', the letterhead declared, and below it an itemised bill: elm coffin with brass handles; cambric headcushion and winding sheet; two coaches each with four horses; ostrich plumes; mourners and bearers, all with silk hatbands; velvet coverings for horses and coaches; silk pall for coffin. . . on and on it went, ending in a total figure of forty-three pounds two and ninepence. Miss Platt had spared no expense. Constance started as the door opened and her stepmother entered. A jet brooch glittered on her black bombazine bosom.

'Ah, Constance, two matters I wanted to tell you,' Miss Platt said crisply. 'I see no reason to prolong the sad atmosphere here for you, and so I have written to the mother superior that you will be travelling down to London on Friday. I'm sure she will arrange for you to be met, and I have already booked your seat on the train.'

She paused, but there was nothing in her manner which invited comment upon her announcement. She was, Constance realised, simply allowing the first point to register before embarking on the second.

'I would like you to have a piece of jewellery as a memento of your papa,' she went on, 'and I thought perhaps a small piece of his hair embedded in a silver brooch. I could order an opal or two to be added if you wish.'

Constance wondered at the angry resentment that rose in her. 'Thank you, no,' she said.

'Good. I'm glad you agree. A touch over-sentimental to add symbolic tears I think,' said Miss Platt. 'Mourning is proper and natural, but I think it can be done to excess. The Queen, despite her many virtues, does seem rather to wallow in sentimentality, but it does not suit my nature. After all, this household has known death before, has it not? A plain silver brooch then?'

'Thank you, yes. Is William to have a memento?'

'A ring with a lock of hair. Well, that settled, you can begin packing for Friday then. William is to leave today – I can manage perfectly well. Now I'd better start replying to some of the many letters of condolence I have received.'

She pulled Papa's chair closer to the desk and reached for the black-edged notepaper, her manner as brisk and efficient as always. Constance turned for a moment at the door and looked at her, seated at Papa's desk, at the helm of the household.

The resentment smouldered into hate. Impulsively Constance took a step back into the room. 'You have no heart, Miss Platt,' she said in a tone that, though quiet, was charged with ice. 'You deal out portions of Papa to William and me now he is dead, but you kept him entirely to yourself when he was alive. I hardly knew my father because of you, Miss Platt, and I shall never forgive you for robbing us of his love.'

Her stepmother heard her out imperturbably. 'Constance, I must remind you that my name is Mrs Lumb, not Miss Platt. It is not true you lacked for love because he and I both cared for you deeply — indeed, you might not have lived but for me. But I recognise that grief has made you speak so irrationally and I make due allowance for it. Like me you must learn to accept the death of one's own flesh and blood with fortitude. See to your packing, my dear, and think on what I have said.'

Constance went out, closing the door behind her sharply. Back in her own room, she sat on the bed feeling choked. There was a tumult within her that she could not quite understand, a mingled sense of anger and outrage — and wonder. What had Miss Platt meant by saying in ice-cold tones that this household had known death before? It had indeed — Mama's death here in Thwaite Lodge so long ago and then Edward's death far away, then little Francis at Weatherhead — that was it, that was the death which made her stepmother speak in such tones. She was blaming someone unnamed for the loss of her child, reminding Constance not to grieve too openly for her father but to show self-control just as Miss Platt had done when robbed of her flesh and blood. But the tinge of venom in her voice — was she indicating that she knew whom to blame? Did she suspect Constance or William? Or, and Constance reddened as the thought came to her, was Miss Platt implying that she believed Papa was the murderer, and hence no tears of grief would fall from her eyes on his account?

Constance's mind refused to contemplate the thought any further. Desperate to communicate her distress to someone she opened a cupboard, took out pen, ink and paper and began a letter. After writing her address and the date she paused. To whom should she write? Not Carmel, nor any of the other girls. Tom Lawson, yes, he always understood and never judged.

'*My dear Tom,*' she wrote, and began by explaining how her father's sudden death had brought her home. She described how grand and impressive the funeral had been and then suddenly her pen ran away unguardedly:

> '*I hate all the panoply of death, the wearing of everything black down even to handkerchieves and walking sticks, the hateful tradition of remaining in black clothes for a year — or for the widow, two years. And making memorial jewellery from dead people's hair seems to me downright obscene — one should remember the dead as they were when living: positive and active, not treasure scraps of the fleshly body which the soul once inhabited!*'

She looked down on the words she had written, surprised at her own vehemence, and deliberated whether to scratch them out, then decided to leave them. Her pen had revealed to her the reason for the tumult inside her at least. It was the hypocrisy of Miss Platt's gesture, offering a memento of Papa without any genuine feeling for him which had offended her — not so much the memento itself, as her stepmother's apparent concern to do the correct thing.

Constance plunged on to talk about going to London to work with the Sisters of Charity and of the nature of her work:

> '*I shall be content being of service to others less fortunate than I,*' she wrote. '*I leave Hawksmoor early on Friday to catch the noon train from Leeds. By Friday night I shall be in my new home, ready to start a new life.*'

Carefully she wrote out the address of the hospice for him:

'Because I should like to hear news from you from time to time,' she added. *'It is so reassuring to have one friend to whom one can confide the thoughts of one's heart in confidence.'*

She smiled wryly. Sister Bridget would not have approved of the repetition of the words 'confide' and 'confidence' but she was not going to alter it. That was part of the pleasure of communicating with Tom — one could speak as the words came and, however clumsy, he always understood.

The letter sealed, Constance felt more composed. The gong, which had been muffled with a cloth while Papa's body still lay in state in the dining room, now rang resonantly through the house. Constance realised with a start that it was lunchtime already and William would soon be leaving. She put away her pen and inkwell and went quickly downstairs. The dining table had now resumed its former function and was laid for two.

Miss Platt entered. 'Where is William?' Constance asked in surprise.

'He's left, my dear. He went about eleven. Didn't you know?'

Constance's heart sank. Gone without saying goodbye? He must be more upset than he showed, but she felt saddened nonetheless. William, of all people the closest to her heart, to leave without a kiss.

'Saddle of mutton today,' said Miss Platt, shaking out her napkin and evidently having decided to forget the recent interview. 'I chose it myself yesterday at the butcher's. Mrs Roebuck's mind doesn't seem to be on her work at the moment. The beef yesterday was quite gristly, I thought.'

'She's upset. She's worked for Papa for years,' Constance pointed out quietly.

'That's no excuse for slapdash work. We could all plead that excuse. Ah, Molly, are you sure the soup is piping hot today, because it wasn't yesterday.'

Constance watched her stepmother as the parlourmaid ladled out the soup. She was so distant, so remote and self-contained that one could never really come close to her.

All those years of my childhood when she cared for me, she never allowed me or anyone else to approach too near, almost as though she feared she might be hurt. Conscientious, kindly even, but never warm and loving. Was that how Papa had found her? He had made every opportunity for intimacy with her, even banishing his own family, but had he succeeded? Constance ate her meal in silence, unable to rid herself of a feeling of deep regret.

On Thursday, the day before Constance's departure, Miss Platt was unusually busy. In the morning she was closeted in the study for a lengthy time with Mr Bartholomew, Papa's solicitor, and after lunch she was in the vestibule supervising the loading of a number of boxes on to a cart. Two muscular young men in corduroy breeches and jerseys strained to lift the heavy boxes outside. Constance passed on quickly, curious but knowing better than to question her stepmother in front of strangers. Later, Miss Platt explained as she poured afternoon tea into two china teacups in the parlour.

'I've been sorting out and disposing of Papa's things,' she said. Constance darted her a look of surprise. So soon? He had not been in his grave a week. 'His clothes would not fit William so I thought it best to give them to charity,' Miss Platt went on.

True, William was taller and slimmer than Papa.

'But I've kept some of his personal things I thought William might like to have. His gold hunter, his silver-headed cane, his tortoise-shell hairbrushes — oh, and his razors. Papa had two very good razors.'

The teacup almost slid from Constance's fingers and she felt the blood rush to her cheeks. 'His razors?' she repeated. 'Oh, I don't think William should have those.'

'Why not? They are very good Sheffield steel. Too good to throw away,' Miss Platt remonstrated.

'William has a very good razor of his own. I think he would be glad to have the watch and hairbrushes and the cane, but I really don't think he would care to have the razors, really I don't!'

Miss Platt sighed deeply. 'Oh very well. I'll give them to

Elizabeth's husband — he always looks as if he could do with a good shave. Now, let me tell you what Mr Bartholomew told me: your papa left a very carefully thought-out will to provide for us all.'

'That was very good of him.'

'Indeed. He left a portion to each of his children, and Elizabeth and Mary Jane will receive theirs almost immediately. You, being under age and as yet unmarried, will receive your portion either when you attain the age of twenty-one or when you marry, whichever should happen first.'

'When I reach twenty-one,' said Constance.

'It is a reasonable sum, enough to be a dowry or to be invested in an annuity, but not large enough to lay you open to the predatory approaches of some adventurer. Your papa was a sensible man and he did not want to render you vulnerable.'

'Very thoughtful,' agreed Constance. The size of the bequest did not concern her. There was no danger of falling prey to a fortune-hunter even if it had been large, for she did not plan to marry.

'And William? Is he to inherit Papa's estate?' she enquired.

Miss Platt put down her cup and Constance noted how her lips set. 'He is not. Evidently Papa considered him too much of a spendthrift, weak and foolish in his ways. He, too, is to inherit a sum of money when he marries.'

'Or comes of age?'

'No. When he marries. Until then he will continue to receive the monthly allowance your papa used to give him to supplement his salary, that is all.'

Constance was bewildered. Surely it was customary for the eldest — and only — son to inherit the estate? She could not stop herself. 'Then who has the bulk of Papa's money and the house and everything?'

Miss Platt rose. 'I do. Your father trusted my judgement and discretion. Now, are you sure you have forgotten nothing for your journey tomorrow? It will have to be an early start in the morning, so nothing must be left to the last moment. Come upstairs and we'll check your trunk.'

Constance followed her out, uneasy in her mind. William had been moody and morose enough lately. The news of Papa's will would surely make him angry.

And why shouldn't he be angry, Constance thought resentfully. After all, he was being cheated of his inheritance by this woman who walked ahead of her, mounting the staircase with the calm self-assurance of the owner of this house. Constance's dark eyes glared at Miss Platt's back.

'You took our father from us,' she shouted inwardly, 'and now you rob William of what is rightfully his. You have won all you wanted, regardless of us. I hate you, for Willie's sake, I hate you!'

But the decorum bred out of years of repression stopped the words leaving her lips. In silence she followed Miss Platt's thin figure to the bedroom.

On Friday morning, as Constance and her stepmother climbed the steps of the impressive entrance to Hawksmoor railway station, it was clear that the older woman's mind was already on future tasks.

'I think I shall have the study repainted and hang dove grey curtains,' she told Constance, 'and dispose of many of those books. They harbour so much dust.'

At the last moment as the train steamed into the platform she expressed the right degree of maternal concern. 'Don't sit too near an open window, my dear, or your gown will be covered in smuts, and we can't have you arriving there like some filthy street-arab. And don't forget to write at once to let me know you've arrived safely. Such a pity William couldn't have escorted you. Now, are you sure you can manage the change in Leeds by yourself?'

'Don't worry,' Constance assured her. 'I'm eighteen you know, a grown woman, not a child.'

The porter placed her trunk aboard the train and Miss Platt dipped in her bag to retrieve a sixpence, which she handed to him. Constance climbed aboard.

'Choose a seat near an older lady, preferably, and don't talk to strangers,' Miss Platt admonished. 'I'll have a word with the guard to keep an eye on you, so I'll say goodbye now.'

She lifted her face and Constance bent to kiss her cheek. At once Miss Platt moved away along the platform in search of the guard. Constance sat down with a sigh. She felt a sense of guilt that she could not, however hard she tried, summon up any affection for her stepmother. The woman did all the right things, correctly and smoothly, yet never once did a glimmer of warmth escape her cool guard. Constance was glad to be leaving, and that added to her sense of guilt.

As the train began to chug its heavy way out of the station she looked out to see if the black-garbed figure of Miss Platt was waiting to wave her off. She did not see her. No doubt she was already on her way to the draper's to order the dove-grey curtains.

Grey factories with their tall belching chimneys receded beyond the window, giving way to summer-bright fields criss-crossed by dry-stone walls and, here and there, a white-washed farmhouse, or cluster of cottages. Constance became so lost in thought that the time went quickly. Then, with a start of surprise, she realised that they had reached the out-skirts of Leeds. The train was passing smoking chimneys, warehouses and mills. In a moment it slowed and entered under the roof of the station. The guard, mindful of Miss Platt's tip, came to tell Constance that he would arrange for a porter to see that her valise was carried to the London train for her.

The train steamed slowly to a halt and Constance stepped out. A hawk-faced porter fetched her trunk and set off to lead the way. Constance followed dutifully, wondering whether she had a sixpence in her purse. Suddenly she caught her breath and stopped. Someone was calling her name.

'Constance! Constance!'

She turned, disbelieving, and then felt her heart leap to her throat as she caught sight of a tall, fair-headed young man pushing his way through the mass of passengers towards her. William? Here, in Leeds? She called out to the porter ahead of her, and he turned.

The blond head was nearly at her side before she recognised him. Tom Lawson smiled down at her, his blue eyes sparkling.

'I found you! I'm so glad I didn't miss you in the crowd.'

Her heart lunged in disappointment, and instantly she felt remorse. He might not be William, but to have sought her out showed affection and friendship of a kind that was all too rare in her life.

15

Constance smiled up at Tom. 'Tom, I'm so glad to see you,' she said. 'How on earth did you find me?'

'You told me you would be on the noon train so I decided to try and catch you. You look well, Connie. I haven't seen you for so long. You look older and wiser and, if possible, even prettier.'

She blushed. 'The porter is waiting with my valise,' she pointed out.

'I'll take it for you. The train doesn't leave for half an hour yet, so we have time to talk.' Without waiting for an answer he gave the porter a coin, took up the trunk in one hand and cupped Constance's elbow with the other. Unresisting, Constance let him guide her to the tea-room. Once they were seated at a wooden table, a steaming cup of tea before each of them, Tom leaned across to touch her hand.

'I'm so glad I caught you, Connie. I would never have forgiven myself if I had missed you. Tell me, my dear, how you have been.'

His blue eyes searched hers deeply and Constance, embarrassed, looked away. There was such penetration in his keen gaze that she felt he could read her inmost soul. She began to talk, slowly and with difficulty at first, about Papa's death. Gradually the words came more easily. Tom listened attentively, nodding from time to time. Constance felt at ease with him, conscious of the grave concern in his eyes.

'So now I'm on my way to start work at the hospice,' she concluded. 'I am looking forward to that.'

'I wonder if you are really ready to face the shock of what you will see,' Tom commented. 'You will be among people far poorer than you have ever known before, brought into contact with all the misery and brutality of their lives. I doubt if you have been prepared for what you will undoubtedly experience.'

'God will guide me,' said Constance confidently. 'He will help me to perform His work.'

Tom shook his head. 'From what you tell me it seems you are running away from your life, but should it be to this?'

Constance withdrew her hand from his. 'Running away? I did not say that,' she frowned.

'No, but that is how it appears. You think you are running to the arms of gentle nuns such as those you left in Ireland. You say you may join the Order of the Sisters of Charity — what is entering a nuns' order if not running away from life? Oh, Constance, are you sure you are doing the right thing?'

'I'm certain of it. My train leaves in five minutes — will you take me to the platform now, please?'

Without demur he took her to the train and stowed her valise aboard. Then turning to her he took her by the shoulders.

'Constance, don't be angry with me. I still remember what you once said about being spindrift, blown about hither and thither by forces you could not understand. I sense you are still in the grip of those unknown forces and don't really know why you do what you do. Aren't I right?'

She looked up into his probing eyes and felt a stab of guilt. Was he referring to Francis' death? He had been there, close by, so soon after.

'All aboard!' the guard called out. Constance turned and felt Tom's grip fall away. From the train window she leaned out to him.

'Don't do anything impetuous,' Tom urged. 'Don't commit your life irrevocably. It could be for the wrong reasons.'

'I listen to my heart, Tom, and to my conscience.'

'And listen to me, I beg you. Will you write to me? Can I come to visit you? Oh, Connie! I care so much. . .'

The last words were drowned by the screech of the guard's whistle and the slamming of doors. Constance waved and smiled. 'Thank you for coming,' she called.

'Take care of yourself, Connie!' The pale oval of his face receded among the crowd as the train pulled away but he waved to the last. Then Constance settled herself in the corner of a carriage and let the warm glow left by his nearness seep through her bones.

Next morning Constance discovered that the hospice of the Sisters of Charity was not what she had expected at all. The previous night, arriving in the dark and feeling very fatigued, she had barely taken it in. A white-robed nun had shown her to a little room, where she had undressed and fallen asleep quickly. But now, by day, after she had washed in the cold water on the wash stand and dressed herself in her mourning gown, she had time to assimilate her new surroundings. She had not really known what to expect, but it was certainly not this gaunt stone-corridored building.

The mother superior, in her unheated office, explained how the sisters had to perform what work they could on the limited amount of money at their disposal. 'We have no regular funds, only donations from benefactors, and their charity varies,' she said, eyeing her new employee over the top of her spectacles. 'Wages, therefore, are of necessity not as high as one might earn elsewhere.'

'I do not mind,' Constance assured her. 'I want only to be of service to God and my fellow-man.'

The mother superior grunted. 'Fellow-women, to be specific. Many of them are here because of the selfishness of men. However, reverend mother tells me you are a conscientious worker, and that is what we need. Hard work and low pay — can you endure that?'

'Oh yes, Reverend Mother,' Constance said fervently. 'I'm sure I can.'

The mother superior's gaze was penetrating. 'Many girls say that, but many fall by the wayside after a time. They are

212

not to be blamed, for the suffering and poverty of our patients is sometimes terrible to behold. I shall not think less of you if you, too, admit one day that it is too much and you wish to leave. You understand?'

'Thank you, Reverend Mother, but I pray God's grace that I shall not fail.' Constance's tone was proud and the older woman nodded.

'I too beg His grace, but remember my words if you change your mind. Now I'll ask Sister Agnes to take you down to the infirmary and give you an apron. You may well feel shocked at what you see. Brought up as you were, you have not yet witnessed the squalor of the lower classes who make up most of our patients. This is a very poverty-stricken part of London. Hold your tongue, make no comment, and pray for them as sincerely as you work for them.'

'Yes, Reverend Mother.'

Constance followed Sister Agnes' short, plump figure along the echoing corridors of the convent, down stone stairs to a basement laundry next to the steamy kitchen. Once Sister Agnes had fitted her new helper out with a starched white overall she led her outside. Alongside the convent, separated from the busy main road only by a high wall and a narrow strip of cobbled yard, ran a long shed-like building which looked to Constance like one of the wool warehouses back home in Yorkshire.

'This is the hospice,' Sister Agnes informed her. 'Take a deep breath.'

It was good advice, for the moment Constance entered her nostrils were assailed by the foulest odour. It was a sickly-sweet, nauseous smell such as she had never before encountered, but the dozens of shabbily-dressed, under-nourished women she saw sitting about or lying in low truckle beds seemed undisturbed. Some had tiny babies in their arms and other mites lay in cribs. She looked at her companion, puzzled. Sister Agnes smiled grimly.

'That is the smell of poverty, my dear, the sign of utter distress and of women who have given up hope. We have to persuade them to wash, but the poor things often have no better clothes to change into. We do what we can.'

213

Constance looked in horror at the gaunt, staring faces. No light gleamed in their dull vacant eyes, only a misty look of utter hopelessness. They looked old, most of them, too old to bear children but, as she was soon to learn, poverty and misery turned even young women prematurely into hags.

A pink-faced young nun approached them carrying a pail of soapy water. As she passed Sister Agnes, the older nun stopped her. 'What is it, Sister Mary? A delivery?'

The younger nun shook her head. 'Not yet, Sister. Mrs Lacey is having a long, hard time of it. We gave her laudanum early this morning and I fear she's been very sick.'

'Constance will help. Show her the way and then you go to breakfast. Constance won't mind scrubbing the floor, will you? Sister Mary has been working all night.'

'Oh no, of course not, I'll be glad to help.' Constance indeed was eager to begin work. She followed the white-robed nun through the door to what was evidently the labour room, a sense of excitement growing in her. Here babies were born, to fallen women it was true, but nonetheless it was the miracle of life vouchsafed by God and soon, perhaps, she would be able to witness and to assist at the miracle. If only she knew more about what to expect.

A single bed stood in the centre of the room and on it lay a young woman, her flaxen hair spread out over the pillow and her eyes closed. A soft moan escaped her lips. Her stomach rose high under the blanket. She was younger than herself, Constance guessed, but she was very pale and sweat beaded her forehead. At the side of the bed a yellow puddle of vomit stained the dark floor.

'Here you are,' said Sister Mary wearily, handing Constance the pail of water and fetching a mop from a corner cupboard. 'And if she's sick again, fetch more water from the kitchen.'

Sister Mary left, clearly relieved to be able to rest at last. Constance fetched the mop and began to work, but as she watched the slimy mess congeal on the mop and smelt its foulness her stomach began to heave. The determination to offer her life to serving the poor was beginning to lose its allure.

The girl on the bed moaned again. Constance looked up. Young Mrs Lacey's eyes were upon her. 'Who are you?' the girl asked weakly.

'Constance. I'm new here.'

'Stay with me, Constance. I feel bad.'

Constance moved to her and took her thin hand. 'Of course I will.'

Mrs Lacey asked feebly: 'Will the baby come today? They said it would yesterday, but it didn't. I wish it would come. I can't stand the pain. Oh, I wish Frank was here!'

'Your husband?'

'I have no husband. The nuns call me Mrs Lacey but I'm not married. I'm Rose Lacey, chambermaid at the Cock Inn or at least I was. I got the sack when the landlord found out, and by then Frank had gone back to sea.'

Constance's heart contracted in pity. This was no fallen woman, just a frightened, desperate girl who had been unfortunate.

When Sister Mary, refreshed by breakfast, returned to the labour room she sent Constance to help bathe the new babies. Constance loved the feel of their tiny bodies and soon lost her fear that she would drop them in the water. Sister Agnes came to watch how she performed.

'I was talking to Mrs Lacey,' Constance remarked. 'Such an unlucky girl.'

'Indeed, to be used and betrayed by a sailor,' the nun agreed. 'We have many such gullible young things pass through here.'

By nightfall Constance took with her to bed an aching back and stiff shoulders, and also many bewildering thoughts. She had encountered so many women during the day, some still swollen with their unborn children and others relieved of their burden, but not one of them was what she had understood to be a fallen woman. Not one, according to Sister Agnes, had been a whore and fallen victim to her own avarice. Most had been, like Rose Lacey, unhappy creatures who had lost their man, either through desertion or death. Thrown out of their homes, they wandered the streets, kept alive by the charity of the parish and often with their other small children too. The hopelessness in their eyes was all too understandable – no work to support themselves and their child, no home to go to. No one would employ a mother of a bastard child, and parents would no longer own them and offer shelter. Constance lay in bed, filled with compassion for their plight and nursing yet a new guilt. Poor things; far from being wicked souls doomed to perdition, they were tragic victims of fate. Her plan to preach to the less fortunate and save their souls had been the height of presumption on her part. Constance prayed long for forgiveness and was filled with a new sensation of humility. Before she fell asleep she thought of William and sent out a wave of love to him, wishing she could tell him about her new experiences. If only she had had a chance to talk to him. He looked so troubled and withdrawn before he left and his manner had been casual almost to the point of abruptness. If only she had had a chance to find out what was troubling him. Filled with concern, Constance fell asleep.

Her dreams were of muddled scenes – the battered, broken-nosed faces of women rejected by overworked husbands for daring to conceive again; blood and filth; puny babies lying still in their cribs anticipating the death which was soon to overtake them; Reverend Mother in her convent study warning of the hard work and exhorting Constance to have faith and persevere; and Papa's stern face.

'Once one has given one's word there is no going back,' he admonished. 'A pledge must be honoured, whatever the cost.'

'I know, Papa! I will not fail!'

Then he was lying in his coffin, his cold, dead face seeming to reprove. Constance was trying to hold back the lid as they nailed it down.

'I won't fail you, Papa! I'll keep my promise, truly I will! I do honour promises, Papa, as I honoured you!'

The scene shifted to the nursery and William's wide-eyed, half-frightened look as they clasped bloody fingertip to fingertip. Constance was murmuring reassurance. 'Forever, Willie, we are one and indivisible. So long as we are united, no one can break our power.' She swore the oath with fierce, unquenchable love, watching the fear in his eyes fade.

She awoke in a sweat. 'Willie,' she breathed in the darkness, 'feel my love coming to surround and protect you, and send me yours in return. Keep close, my Willie, don't let them divide us.'

Her heart yearned in prayer, trying to shut out the clamouring reason in her brain. She would not listen to it reminding her of William's recent coolness and the absence of letters. He would hear and reply. A bell sounded along the corridor to summon the nuns to matins. Trained by habit, Constance rose and prepared to go down to chapel:

Only white-robed figures knelt in prayer before the priest at his small altar. Feeling like an intruder, Constance knelt at the back. God forgive my presumption, laden with sin as I am, to join these holy women at their devotions, she prayed. In her mourning gown of black, a stark contrast to their pure white habits, she could not help comparing herself to a raven somehow inadvertently arrived at a gathering of gentle doves. An outsider still, staring at the inside through a wall of glass, just as she had done all her life.

She regarded the nuns with undisguised envy. They were at peace within themselves, certain of their commitment to God's work and to a place in paradise with Him in the afterlife. They worked hard, it was true — unstinting of their dedication, disciplined to obey and never question — but they were insiders, members of a select society, belonging to each other and to the community and to God. She, however, belonged to no one.

If only. . ., she yearned, if only William would write to confirm his love for her. If only Papa had, just once, said he loved her. If only she had someone's warm arms to turn to for comfort. She should be glad she was not one of those poor rejected creatures in the infirmary, but even they had once possessed someone's love.

God grant me a sign that I shall be acknowledged one day, accepted and loved by someone. Give me a sign William cares, that he may write. But what sign?

Rose, that was it — with a pang Constance realised she had not given a thought to the poor pain-wracked girl, but if, when she reached the infirmary, Rose had at last given birth, a letter from William would arrive speedily. If the girl was still struggling in labour, however. . .

Constance rejected the alternative. As the nuns rose and filed out of the little chapel, she followed. The silent breakfast of hot tea and bread and butter could not end swiftly enough for Constance, and when at last the nuns said grace and dispersed to their various duties, she could hardly don her overall and hasten out to the infirmary fast enough.

In the main dormitory, nuns were already busy doling out hunks of bread and cups of tea, while others mopped the stone floor. Women patients were gobbling greedily or breaking the bread for their older children, and those still waiting to be fed sat expectantly on their beds. Sister Mary opened the door of the labour room as Constance approached.

'Ah, Constance, would you take off the soiled bed linen and fetch clean linen from the kitchen,' she said gently.

Constance's gaze flicked past her to the bed. It was empty. 'Mrs Lacey?' she asked. 'Has she given birth?'

Sister Mary lowered her eyes. 'Pray for her soul, Constance. She has gone.'

'Gone?' Constance half-understood but refused to believe. 'Gone where?'

'She was in labour all night and at dawn we delivered her dead baby. She died shortly afterwards. God rest her soul, for she was a sweet young thing.'

Constance stood bewildered. Dead? It seemed unbelievable. Women often died in childbirth but Rose was so young, hardly more than a child herself.

'Where is she?'

'In the mortuary, along with the baby.' Sister Mary glanced at the further door, then sighed. 'We grow used to suffering here, but it was tragic to see her struggles. A breech birth, you see, feet first. No chance of saving the child and she lost so much blood . . .'

The state of the bed confirmed her words. A huge crimson stain glared on the white sheet. Constance felt tears leap to her eyes.

'Come on, down to work,' Sister Mary said sharply. 'There is much to be done.'

Tears scalded Constance's cheeks as she worked to clear away the last vestiges of Rose Lacey's fight to give birth. It all seemed so terribly cruel and unfair, a young life thrown away almost before it had begun.

Once the bed was refurbished with a clean sheet and blanket to await its next occupant, Constance looked at the far door. Before she put Rose Lacey from her mind she must take one final, farewell glimpse of her. No other mourners would stand by her pauper's grave. One glimpse, one heart-felt prayer to speed her on her journey.

Someone had taken pains to comb the long fair hair, for it lay like a curtain of gold silk around the pale, haggard face. Work-worn hands lay folded across the calico winding sheet, and Constance bowed her head in prayer. When she looked up, the breath caught in her throat. She had not seen the baby as she entered. It lay beside its mother, a wizened little face no larger than her fist. No winding sheet enfolded its tiny body, so Constance could see clearly that there was a space. The head lay separate from the body, only by an inch or two, but it was plain to see what had happened. Delivered feet first, the head must have been pulled off in the struggle of labour.

Constance, nauseated, fled from the room. At least Rose had been spared the knowledge — or had she? Perhaps she had lived on, her life-blood seeping away, aware of the dead, mutilated little thing and knowing before she died that her fight had been all in vain. Tears poured unrestrainedly down Constance's cheeks.

Sister Agnes caught her arm. 'Now look here, my girl, you must harden yourself if you plan to go on working here. We lose many mothers, not all as young as Mrs Lacey, but badly-fed as they are, and often knocked about, they have little chance to give birth easily. And others often have to watch their babies die as soon as they are born. Death is a constant visitor. Now pull yourself together, take that soiled linen down to the laundry and then stay and help in the kitchen for a while. But realise that you cannot run away,

Constance. Tomorrow you'll be back here in the infirmary, perhaps witnessing another death.'

Constance ran to the laundry and wept profusely for some minutes before she could muster sufficient control to report to the kitchen. 'You can't run away from life,' Sister Agnes had said. Tom had said the same thing, that day on Leeds railway station. Running away? Here she was encountering more life in its rawest, cruellest form than ever she had witnessed in eighteen years.

But in a way they were both right, Tom and Sister Agnes. She must find more inward resolve to cope with life if she was to perform her duty and serve God. She must pray for strength.

Tom: such a kindly man, and she had hardly spared him a moment's thought since her arrival in London. As she recalled their meeting, his earnest gaze across the tea-room table, she remembered with a pang of conscience that she had asked him nothing about himself, how he was faring and what his plans were. How selfish he must think her, to spend the whole half-hour talking about herself and her fears. She hoped he did not despise her, for his friendship was invaluable and she would be sorely saddened to lose it.

She resolved to write to him, but in fact it was Tom who wrote first, some three weeks later, enquiring how she was getting on. Constance was glad she had not written hastily to complain because by now she was becoming accustomed to the hard physical work. Her hands were no longer smooth and white, but endless hours of sweeping and scrubbing, carrying heavy cauldrons of soup, bending and lifting had, after the initial exhaustion, toughened up her muscles so that her body felt hard and smooth to the touch. She was just a little proud of her achievement. Papa would surely have approved. In his stead she confided to Tom her quiet pride.

To her surprise, he did not reply for some weeks. Christmas had almost arrived when the letter came.

'Dear Connie, It grieves me to have to tell you that my delay in writing to you is because my mother was taken seriously ill. She died last month. My father has still not

*recovered from the blow and I think I must consider resign-
ing my position as a police officer in order to help with the
children. It is not an easy decision because my pay is sorely
needed. But God will show me the way.*

'*I was proud to hear how well you are coping with a way
of life which is not what you are accustomed to. But then, I
always knew you were a girl of spirit. Suffering does not
beat you, and I know how deeply you care about others.*

'*Keep up your noble work, my dear friend. You are
acting out your Christian principles, whereas others only
talk. I have long admired you even from a distance, and
what you are fearlessly doing now fills me with yet more
admiration. Only, I beg you, do not let your ardent will to
do good lead you into entering the order as you proposed.
God has work enough for you, I feel sure, without calling
upon you to surrender your life to prayer. There are those in
the outside world who have need of you.*

'*God bless and keep you. Your loving friend, Tom.*'

Constance was stricken. Dear Tom, bowed down by
troubles of his own and yet he could spare thought for her.
Others in the outside world? Yes, indeed, Willie needed her,
he was right. That was a thought to be contemplated
seriously before asking the mother superior to accept her as a
postulant. But the time was not yet ripe for that; guilt and sin
lay dark on Constance's soul, and expiation must be effected
first somehow.

It was not easy composing words of consolation for Tom. It
was true that she too had lost a parent recently and shared
that grief, but beyond that their circumstances were so different. Being orphaned had not meant poverty and the
responsibility of feeding younger brothers and sisters for her.
How could she possibly advise or console Tom?'

Christmas brought fewer patients than usual into the hospice
but it did bring the excitement of a visit from Mrs Gray. All
the nuns were in a flutter.

'Who is Mrs Gray?' Constance asked, as she helped the
laundress lift steaming bundles of linen out of the copper.

'Mrs Emmeline Gray is our benefactress,' the perspiring nun replied. 'She only visits at Christmas and if she is satisfied she pays her annual donation to Reverend Mother. That's why it's so important that everything is spotless.'

Everything was always spotless, Constance thought privately, for the nuns worked indefatigably to ensure that it was. On Christmas Eve the infirmary glowed with candles around boughs of crimson-berried holly, and Mrs Gray, small and plump and erect, stood beaming in the centre of the room at the mother superior's side. A jet brooch and necklace glittered on her bombazine bodice — Mrs Gray was evidently a rich widow.

'Excellent, Reverend Mother!' she enthused. 'You and the sisters have worked wonders! All these ladies must be very grateful to you.'

She smiled at the blank-faced occupants of the beds. Constance could see they were puzzled by the entrance of a lady into their ranks. The mother superior explained: 'Mrs Gray is our benefactress, and tomorrow you shall all have roast chicken and plum pudding for dinner, the gracious gift of Mrs Gray.'

Silence met her words. The mother superior turned to her guest. 'They are not given to talking much, Mrs Gray, but I know they are as deeply grateful as I and my sisters. May God bless you for your generosity.'

'Then if we could return to your office, Mother, I shall write the usual cheque for you,' Mrs Gray said graciously. 'Shall we go?'

Constance stood still, watching her leave, and wondered at the irritation that rose inside her. Was it that the woman made such a public display of her charity, absolving her conscience from having to do anything more for these poor creatures? Would Rose Lacey have thanked her for roast chicken?

Instantly Constance felt remorse. It was uncharitable of her to think such thoughts. She must confess that to Father Lawrence.

'And what sins have you committed since last you came to

222

confession, my child?'

'Uncharitable thoughts, Father.'

'About whom?'

'About Mrs Gray. I thought her hypocritical to spend two minutes in the infirmary, dispense her charity and then leave.'

Father Lawrence was clearly shocked. 'Mrs Gray! My dear child, that lady is the soul of compassion, a shining example to us all! Why, without her generous donation the hospice could not continue its work.'

'I know, Father.'

'And are you sorry for your uncharitable thoughts?'

'Yes, Father.'

'Then go and say ten Hail Marys for penance, and ask Our Lord to help you to be more understanding.'

The snows of the new year lay slushy and blackened on the cobbled yard when Constance picked her way carefully back from the infirmary one afternoon. In the hospice corridor she met Sister Agnes with a number of envelopes in her hand.

'Ah, Constance, you lucky girl! Two letters for you today.' She handed her the two gleaming white envelopes and hurried on by. One was addressed in Tom's firm, upright script and the other – her heart leapt. It was William's hand. She glanced up at the hall clock. Still ten minutes until the lunch bell sounded – just enough time to savour them in peace.

In the privacy of her little room she tore open Tom's letter first, hugging for a little longer the joy of opening William's. Her eyes skimmed over Tom's phrases of thanks and came to rest on the main substance of the letter.

'My father wants me to resign from the police and work on a sheep farm with him. It was my uncle's farm until he died and Father is now too old to run it alone. I think perhaps he is right, for the children would be happy there and the moorland air will be good for them. You would like it, Connie, on the moors near Whitby, near the sea-cliffs where first we met.'

223

Her concentration melted into memory for a moment, recalling the serious-eyed youth and the spume on the jagged rocks below. She remembered the eternity of that moment, the strong feeling of affinity with a stranger, as if they had known each other before in some earlier life. Suddenly she remembered William's letter was waiting, and she read on quickly.

> 'We can make a new life there, I know, but Father will miss my mother sorely. He tells me we need a woman about the house and says it's high time I found a wife — at twenty-five, almost, I should be wed and have a son as he did. However, we shall see. In the meantime, take good care, of yourself, beloved friend, and spare a thought in your prayers for
>
> > Your devoted friend, Tom.'

Whatever feelings Constance might have entertained now were thrust aside by her eagerness to read William's words. She took up his letter, gazed at the familiar hand fondly and kissed it before opening the letter.

'I knew you would write in the end, Willie,' she murmured. 'I knew you had not forgotten me.'

The warm glow engendered by the scrawl on the envelope was not increased by the letter's contents. William spoke no word of Constance at all but sprang straight into petulant complaint.

> 'Dear Constance, I can get no help from Stepmama in my present predicament. She obviously does not understand a young man's needs at all and is even less approachable than Papa was. You see, I have these bills which have to be paid, and three times I've written to explain to her and every time she refuses to help. I can have what's due to me when I'm twenty-one. I can't wait another three years!
>
> 'Or I may have it when I marry. Really, the woman is preposterous! All that money she inherited from Papa has gone to her head, I believe, and she enjoys wielding her power. Money which by rights should have come to me, as

his son, not to his housekeeper. She had no real right to it in the first place but having got it, she's as hard as nails. You were right, when you used to say she wasn't nice. Miss Platt, you still called her, and so she is — just a money-grabbing housekeeper.

'I'm really in a hole, Connie. Can you help me out now you're earning? I wouldn't ask but I can't think where else to turn. I've already pawned my watch and can't afford to redeem it. Please write by return and tell me you can help — a loan from a friend perhaps, if you can. Otherwise I might be driven to some drastic action I might later regret.

'Your loving brother, William.'

Constance lay the letter aside sadly, all the warm glow vanished. The whining, pleading tone of his message bore all the petulant anxiety of his boyhood, when he complained to her about the spanking he received for a misdeed, or being obliged to use the back stairs because of his muddy boots. His self-righteous indignation over Miss Platt's stubbornness made it plain Willie was still a boy, still in need of her.

It was Papa's gold hunter that Willie must have pawned, a watch he had inherited only months ago. No wonder Miss Platt would give him no more of his patrimony to squander. But poor Willie, nevertheless. He had always been accustomed to having someone to bail him out of trouble in the past. That was why he now turned to his older sister to solve his problems.

But she could do nothing. Her few shillings a week would hardly keep William in boot polish. She must write to Miss Platt, endeavouring to persuade her to help Willie out, just this once. She *must* help, Constance thought fiercely, for there was no one else. William's last sentence had been ominous — just what drastic action did he have in mind? A flicker of fear trembled in Constance's heart just as the dinner bell sounded.

16 : 1863

Miss Platt's reply was crisp and to the point:

> *'My dear Constance. Despite your eloquent pleas on William's behalf I am determined that he must be made to resolve his own affairs.*
>
> *'It is high time William grew up. At his age he should be capable of balancing his outgoings against his income capably. His older brother, poor dear Edward, never presented your papa with such a problem though he too had mess-bills to meet as a naval officer. William is feckless, I fear, and must not be encouraged to become an utter wastrel.*
>
> *'I was deeply grieved to hear about your papa's watch, but it seems that William is still weak and easily led into foolish ways. I hope you will not encourage him to worsen his position by endeavouring to find the money for him, for he must learn to fend for himself.*
>
> *'Since your birthday is at hand I enclose a cheque so you may choose a gift to your liking. I trust you continue to prosper and enjoy your work.*
>
> *'Your ever-loving Stepmama.'*

Constance looked at the cheque. Ten pounds. It was a generous gift and would enable her to buy the new pair of boots she needed. The old ones leaked and her stockings were still wet from crossing the snow-covered yard. But Willaim's need was greater than hers. It might not be enough to discharge his debts, but it would help. She would post the money on to him at once.

Constance wrote her stepmother a letter of thanks, indicating that she was indeed in need of new boots but taking care not actually to say she would buy them. A few days later she sent the money to William.

Willie Lumb sat on his bed staring disbelievingly at the cheque in his hand. He flung aside carelessly the accompanying letter which began, *'My darling Willie'* and ended, *'Yours in everlasting union, Connie,'* a taste of nausea rising in his throat.

It was not only that Connie was so cloying in her manner towards him, but also the contents of her letters always sickened him, her pious hopes for those stupid whores she tended, her determination to improve herself — which implied unspoken remorse for an episode he preferred to forget.

But the cheque helped to dispel the throbbing cloud in his brain. Ten pounds — no fortune, to be sure, not enough to pay off all he owed, but it held the key to the answer. Astutely invested on the right horse. . . he would write and thank Connie some time, tomorrow perhaps, or next week.

The immediate problem was the investment, and it irritated him that he could not for the life of him recall the name of the horse mentioned in the inn last night. The little weasel-faced man had a brother in the stables, Willie recalled, and on his advice weasel-face was going to place his shirt on the nag. But what the devil did he say it was called? Willie sat, head buried in his hands, endeavouring to remember.

Shakespeare, that was it: the horse's name was a character in a Shakespeare play. Macbeth, Lear, Othello? No, no, what the blazes had it been?

Young Rupert Tancred breezed into the room. Seeing William, his sunny smile faded and a frown rutted his forehead.

'You disgusting creature, Lumb,' he said crossly. 'You vomited all over my bed last night. In future have the decency to foul your own patch, if you don't mind.'

'Stop bleating,' William snarled. 'You fuss like my stepmother. Turning into a woman, you are.'

The other young man coloured up and bit his tongue.

William looked up at him sideways. 'Know what's running in the three-thirty?' he asked.

'Well, I've got a bet on Solstice. Can't recall the others, but Barrington has a list of the runners, I believe. You aren't going to lay a bet, surely? You haven't paid off what you owe us.'

'Mind your own business,' snapped William.

Barrington was more accommodating. William ran his eyes down the list. Prospero — that was it! And at twenty to one it could solve all his problems. Trouble was, duty prevented him going out to lay the bet. Barrington reluctantly agreed to do it for him.

'But are you sure, old man? Prospero is a rank outsider, you know,' he said dubiously.

'Just place the bet for me and leave me to do the worrying,' William replied, reddening.

Dusk was falling by the time William came off duty. He hurried down to the mess. Rupert Tancred, surrounded by a group of companions, stood by the bar. His animated expression and the rapt attention of his audience revealed that he was regaling them with yet another of his entertaining anecdotes. William pushed his way through the group.

'Which horse won the three-thirty?' he asked eagerly.

Tancred stopped in mid-tale. 'Why, Prospero,' he replied and, turning back to the group, he carried on talking. William's heart leapt in delight. He had only to find Barrington and the heap of golden sovereigns would be his. Two hundred pounds! That would more than settle his debts and put him on the right road.

He scanned the crowded messroom avidly but there was no sign of Barrington. Elated by his good fortune, William ordered wine and sat alone in a corner to wait. No one else came to join him. As the minutes ticked by William noticed how the other fellows averted their gaze when his eyes met theirs. He shrugged. Why should he care if he was not popular with his brother-officers? He was solvent again, and that was all that mattered.

He tossed off the glass of wine and signalled to the waiter for more. By the time the supper bell sounded Barrington still had not arrived. William was beginning to feel a little muzzy-headed.

Much later, when William was irritably preparing for bed, the missing subaltern turned up in the dormitory and was greeted by ribald teasing. William, standing shirtless before a washstand as he shaved, paused with the open razor suspended in mid-air when he recognised Barrington's angry voice. He turned eagerly, already visualising the great golden heap of coins.

'Well?' he demanded. 'Where's my winnings?'

Barrington's gaze slid away from his to stare at the floor, and a sudden silence fell over the room. William was unaware of the half-dozen faces staring intently at them. 'Well? Two hundred pounds, isn't it, at twenty to one?'

Barrington coughed and made a slight apologetic movement. Rupert Tancred sauntered towards them. 'Listen, Willie,' he drawled, 'don't blame Barrington. It's not his fault.'

Cold fear settled over William's brain as he stared at Tancred, silently imploring reassurance.

Barrington coughed again. 'That's right, Willie,' he muttered. 'We were trying to help.'

Tancred lay a hand on William's shirt sleeve. 'You know how you have a gift for backing the wrong horse as a rule, Willie,' he said. 'We agreed it best not to back that nag because Prospero was hopeless, we thought. . .'

William blenched and felt his knees grow weak. 'Are you saying you didn't lay the bet after all?' His voice was thin and weak, no more than a whisper.

'That's right,' agreed Tancred, 'but we were only trying to save you losing any more cash when you're so much in debt already.'

'But it won!' William croaked. 'I should have more than two hundred pounds!' The fear in his heart was turning rapidly to rage. He clutched the razor, beads of sweat breaking out on his palms.

'I'm sorry, old man,' said Tancred urbanely. 'We have your ten pounds, of course. I'm truly sorry — we had no right to interfere but we honestly meant well. Acting in your best

229

interests, so we thought.'

William was speechless with rage. What right had they to interfere, to ruin his chances of redeeming his plight! That bumbling, arrogant Tancred, idol of the mess — how dared he dictate William's destiny? His meddling had destroyed everything.

Before William had time to think, his right hand leapt in the air and he saw a flash of steel under the lamplight. A horrified gasp filled the room. Barrington was standing, his arms limp at his sides. Tancred's left arm was outstretched, and through the long rent in the sleeve William could see blood blubbling crimson to the surface.

'My God!' said Tancred. 'My God!'

William could only stare, dumbfounded. He had no recollection of planning to lash out nor of raising his arm to strike, only of the blind rage that engulfed him and of Tancred's arm rising to ward off the blow. William looked down at the razor in his hand. Scarlet droplets adhered to the gleaming blade. He flung it from him in a swift movement of revulsion.

Barrington seized a towel and wrapped it around Tancred's arm. Another officer ran to fetch the physician. Tancred cast William one blistering look and let himself be led away to his bed.

The physician came, dressed the wound and left. No one spoke to William. Numbly he prepared for bed, one half of his face still unshaven. He climbed between the sheets, still shaken and only half-believing what he had done. Not one ember of his anger remained now; only bitter disappointment and misery.

After lights out, William heard Barrington's voice close by his bed, harsh and hostile. 'Lucky for you, Lumb, that Tancred is a decent sort. There won't be an enquiry. He told the doctor he had fallen on his sabre. You should count your blessings, Lumb, for you don't deserve such consideration.'

As William drifted into sleep that night he had only one vision: a heap of golden sovereigns, just out of his reach. But in his last hazy thought before sleep engulfed him it seemed to him that the shiny golden surface was marred by droplets of crimson blood.

Easter was approaching, and Constance felt weighed down with guilt. Suppose Miss Platt invited her to Thwaite Lodge – how would she explain away the old leaky boots she still wore? Confessing her deception to Father Lawrence would bring no absolution if she did not agree to put the matter right – and how could she? Miss Platt's fury at finding her deceitful would be unbearable, and her fury would be intensified on learning the money had gone to William.

'Have you made your preparations for Lent yet, Constance?' Sister Mary enquired. 'I haven't seen you at Confession.'

'Not yet, Sister,' Constance replied meekly, knowing that she must confess, and do whatever Father Lawrence ruled; that was the only way to purify her soul in readiness to receive Our Lord's Body on Good Friday.

She was steeling her resolve when a letter arrived from Miss Platt. Constance opened it with reluctance.

> *'My dear Constance. The most surprising news from William arrived today which I understand he has not yet communicated to you. By some means, presumably his affable charm, he has prevailed upon the daughter of a senior office to accept his proposal of marriage. He tells me he plans to wed Miss Cynthia Baverstock in the summer.'*

Constance reeled, as though someone had plunged a knife in her heart. William to marry? Impossible!

> *'I am quite sure,'* Miss Platt went on, *'that this is only a means to procure his inheritance before he comes of age. I do not know exactly how large a sum he owes in debts but I fancy the two thousand he will receive will soon be dissipated. It saddens me that he is to take this reckless step, but I have no power to prevent him.'*

Constance let the letter fall from numb fingers, despair closing about her. *Willie, oh Willie! How could you let any woman take precedence over me, who loves you more than life itself!*

Flinging herself on the bed she sobbed unrestrainedly until her temples throbbed with pain. Even when she had wept bitterly for so long that it seemed there was not a tear left in her body to shed, she sat weakly on the bed and felt the burning ache of misery and disillusion. She was betrayed, abandoned in a terrifying desert of desolation. But despite his betrayal she could not hate William. How could she, when he was the only creature she had loved so desperately and exclusively? Poor William, weak and alone. He had been driven to it by circumstances; he was not to blame. Trapped in a corner he sometimes did desperate things he regretted later.

There was no point in writing to plead with him, she supposed, for he had clearly made up his mind. He would resent her interference, unless she could offer an alternative way of raising cash. A loan from Elizabeth or Mary Jane, perhaps? Willie had possibly already tried that, and the girls' husbands were unlikely to respond to a brother-in-law they clearly considered a ne'er-do-well.

No, she was forced to admit that she was powerless to help, and the aching misery in her heart grew. In his panic William had betrayed her. Dully she picked up Miss Platt's letter and read on:

> 'He is far too young in my opinion to consider marriage but there it is. He will just have to learn to mend his ways and live within his income. I understand Miss Baverstock has expectations, and this is undoubtedly what William is relying on. Such a pity. The one consolation is that your papa was spared this.
>
> 'I think in the circumstances, acting in your father's place, it would be as well if I were to write to Major Baverstock concerning this proposed marriage and expressing my reservations. I hope the news does not distress you unduly, knowing how close you and he were, and remember that you are welcome to come and stay at Thwaite Lodge whenever you wish.
>
> 'Your loving Stepmama.'

Constance took hold of the letter in both hands and tore it across, again and again, then flung the shreds on the floor. Fire was burning in her brain, crimson and all-consuming, like the rage that had enveloped her that time in Weatherhead. Miss Platt had humiliated Willie then, making him push Francis out and use the back stairs. Now she was doing it again. Rage, hate, frustration and betrayal boiled in Constance's head and, flinging herself across the bed, she sobbed hysterically again.

Throughout the night she wept, slept fitfully and woke to weep again. Her dreams were a jumble of images — William with a pretty, dark-haired girl in his arms; Miss Platt sitting on a dais like a judge; Papa rising from his coffin to come and join her; and Constance herself alone in a vast, black void where only the cries of women in childbirth could be heard. Then a baby, its head severed, and a bloody razor by its side.

She awoke trembling and bathed in cold sweat. The dawn was near and the nuns would soon be astir to begin the day's work. It was Ash Wednesday, the day of repentance and contrition. Constance stumbled out of bed and fell to her knees on the cold stone floor, but the words of prayer would not come. God was not listening and she was truly alone. Despair engulfed her.

There was no solitude more terrifying than feeling that one belongs to nobody, neither man nor God. She had no mother, no father, her sisters were married and self-involved, her stepmother capable but cold — and now William was allied to another girl. Not a soul in the world now placed her above all else. Constance was panic-stricken at the aridity of life ahead. She seized a pen and wrote feverishly to Tom:

> *'Oh Tom! I can hardly believe it! I feel so lost and alone — if only someone would take me away to peace and tranquillity!'*

The bell was ringing. She dressed, and bathed her swollen face in cold water, conscious of the pallid, red-eyed appearance she would have to present to the sisters. But if anyone noticed, they forebore to comment. After a morning spent labouring amongst the beaten, hollow-eyed women in the hospice she began to feel calmer and reproached herself for wallowing in self-pity. Who was she to feel sorry for herself when these poor souls were in a far more wretched plight?

Ash Wednesday. It was high time she made her peace with God. She must go to Him truly contrite for her selfishness, acknowledging that His suffering for mankind was far above anything she had endured, and beg His forgiveness. If it were granted then she would indeed dedicate her life to Him. To be a Sister of Charity, a bride of Christ, would give meaning and purpose to life. Then she would belong to someone at last, totally and irrevocably. Yes, that was what she must do, even if it meant having to confess that terrible sin which had lain so heavy on her soul for so long. . .

The impulsive letter to Tom still lay in her pocket. She hesitated, trying to recall the words and wondering whether to post it. Then she decided; however rash and unconsidered her words, he would understand. Tom was a friend, a very dear friend, to whom she could communicate any incoherent thoughts just as they tumbled out, and he would unravel them and understand. The letter would be posted, along with another to Miss Platt written in more sober mood.

Cecily Lumb tucked a stray wisp of hair back into her bun and sighed as she re-read her stepdaughter's letter. Constance was being tedious again, and just when there was enough of a palaver over William's antics. Still, if the girl had made her mind up to it, Cecily knew better than to try to dissuade her; the girl had always been wilful.

Taking up her pen she wrote neatly and thoughtfully, then paused to reflect. Under the terms of Samuel's will, Constance was due to inherit her portion on reaching her majority or when she married, whichever was the sooner. No stipulation had been made for this particular situation because, naturally, Samuel had not anticipated it. She would have to consult the solicitor, but the answer seemed clear.

'Concerning your dowry, my dear, the two thousand your papa left you, I see no reason to wait until you reach twenty-one if you are to carry out your plan to enter the sisterhood. It will follow, of course, that you will never marry once you have taken the vow of celibacy, but since you are to become, as the Catholics quaintly term it, "a

bride of Christ," then I think it reasonable that you receive your dowry just as soon as you take your final vows, whenever that may be. I shall confirm this after I have talked to Mr Bartholomew, the solicitor.'

There, now conscience was satisfied. And before releasing the money Cecily made a mental note to add a stipulation that it was not to be used to settle William's debts — but that could wait.

As Cecily Lumb was signing the letter before the fire in the comfort of her parlour, her stepdaughter was kneeling in the darkness listening to Father Lawrence's voice beyond the grille.

'I think I misheard you, my dear,' he said stammeringly. 'I thought you said murder.'

'I did, Father. I am responsible for a murder.'

There was a long pause and a deep breath. 'When?'

'Four years ago.'

There was a gasp of shocked surprise. 'Then why have you not confessed it before now?'

'I did not feel free to do so.'

'Free? What nonsense! What freedom does your soul have while it is weighed down by a sin so terrible! Murder is a mortal sin, condemning you to everlasting Hell!'

'Can you absolve me, Father?' Constance's voice trembled. 'I want so much to cleanse my soul and be worthy to take the veil.'

'Take the veil? Impossible, until you have expiated your sin. Confession is not enough; you must pay the penalty the state exacts for such a crime.'

'Tell the police?' Constance whispered.

The priest sighed deeply. 'I fear that is inevitable, much as I dread to see the hospice brought into disrepute.'

Constance wavered. To tell the police meant hurting others. 'Can't I be forgiven just by confessing to you, Father?'

She knew by his lengthy silence that this was a situation new in his experience. Was he debating with his conscience whether he should involve the hospice in such a scandal, or deliberating whether to discuss it with his bishop?

'Go, my child. I cannot give you absolution until you have made amends,' he murmured at last. 'Do not come to the altar rail to receive Communion again until you have done so.'

Miserably Constance left the chapel. She alone, of all the inmates of the hospice, would be left standing solitary tomorrow in the pew while all the others partook of the Body of Our Lord on the day of His supreme sacrifice. In all her years of loneliness she had never felt so desolate and befouled as at this moment. And the thought brought terror. No William — and no God! The future stretched ahead, terrifyingly bleak, shapeless and without purpose. Constance felt giddy with fear.

Tom's reply was swift but brief:

'Have no fear, beloved Connie, you are not and never have been alone, whatever happens. I am here as I have always been. Very soon I shall be with you.'

The vertigo of fear in Constance subsided a little. Dear Tom, dear faithful, loyal Tom. He was right — his presence helped to alleviate the pain of William's betrayal, to remind her that she was not completely alone, and she thanked God for His grace in allowing her this one fragment of consolation.

The mother superior glanced at Father Lawrence's stocky figure seated by her fireside. He looked older and more tired than usual and concern filled her heart. 'You say something is troubling you, Father? Can I possibly help?'

He shook his grey head. 'I fear not. Tell me, what do you think of your young assistant, Constance Lumb? She's always seemed a quiet, conscientious creature to me.'

'And so she is, Father, liked and respected by all the sisters. And our patients respond to her because she's so good with the children. A most devoted girl. I've always been impressed by her diligence and her piety. I truly hope she will join us one day.'

236

'Do you now? You would recommend her without reservation?'

'Absolutely. A quiet girl, as you say, not given to talking about herself or her feelings, but her concern for others is plainly deep and genuine. She has all the makings of a true Sister of Charity.'

The mother superior saw that the priest's eyes were clouded with worry, but she was too discreet to probe. He would tell her if he wanted, or was able to; it might be a matter of the confessional, a secret he could never betray. But whatever it was, it could not be Constance Lumb who brought that sorrow to his eyes. She was a paragon of virtue and with luck would very soon become one of her flock.

Tom Lawson found the hospice at last, in a derelict part of London where haggard faces watched him incuriously as he walked. The hospice of blackened stone like the neighbouring buildings, nevertheless appeared neatly painted and its brass door knocker gleamed brightly in the pale sunlight.

The sister who opened the door asked no questions but simply led him to a barely furnished room with a deal table and a couple of wooden chairs.

'If you would like to wait, I'll tell Miss Lumb you are here, Mr Lawson,' she said quietly before she left. Within moments Constance stood in the doorway, staring at him in surprise.

'Tom! Oh, how wonderful to see you!' She looked pale and somewhat drawn. All the physical work was clearly taking its toll of her gently-bred frame. He moved forward to take the hands she held out in greeting. They were reddened and rough to his answering touch.

'I came because of your letter. I told you I'd come. What is it, Connie? Why are you so upset? Your letter didn't explain why you were very distressed.'

'Oh, Tom!' Letting go of his hands she sank wearily on to a chair. He sat opposite her, the table between them, and he recalled their last meeting across a table on Leeds station.

She looked drained, exhausted. 'Tell me,' Tom said softly. 'You can talk to me. What is it? Has someone hurt you?'

'Nothing's wrong — no, everything's wrong!' she murmured, and then her face crumpled into tears. Tom leapt up and came round the table to her, kneeling to put his arm about her slim shoulders.

'There now, there, my love, nothing is ever so bad as it seems. Tell me about it and then you'll see how much less of a problem it is already. You're not really distraught over your brother getting married, are you?'

She broke loose from his hold and rushed across to stand by the window. 'It's worse than you think, Tom.' Her small voice drifted back to him. 'My world is over, ended.'

He came closer, trying to resist a smile. She spoke like a heroine in a twopenny novelette such as his sister read. 'You know the old saying, Connie — a trouble shared is a trouble halved,' he prompted. 'Come now, let me into your terrible problem.'

She turned slowly, a slender silhouette against the pale gold of sunlight framed by the window. He could not see her face.

'Tom, dear Tom,' she whispered. 'Thank you for rushing to my side like the chivalrous knight-errant you are, but even you cannot help me, my dear friend. I have talked to the priest and I know what I must do.'

He shivered slightly. There was a note of desperate finality in her voice that presented a threat. Imaginative, highly-strung — but surely she would not contemplate suicide whatever disillusion she might have suffered! He touched her hand, but she remained immobile, impassive as one of those Greek marble statues in the museum.

'What must you do?'

She took a deep breath and he felt a shudder of presentiment. 'I must tell the police. . . Oh, Tom! It's the only way! I cannot receive Communion, and if I have not God's grace, I have nothing left!'

He frowned in puzzled concern. 'What has all this to do with William, Connie? What must you tell the police?'

She came closer, looking up into his face. 'That I am responsible for little Francis' death. You remember, Tom, you were there.'

238

He stared at her in horror, then seized her shoulders. 'You can't do that! You didn't do it, I know you didn't! I've always known you were innocent!'

He had clung tenaciously to that belief whatever Inspector Garlick and Inspector Wheeler thought, and though he heard it now from her own lips he could not believe it. He *would* not believe it. She was still looking up at him, the wild light gone from her eyes.

'I must, for I am responsible, Tom, and I must find peace. After I've paid the penalty I can join the order — unless they hang me. Oh, they won't hang me, will they?'

She looked up fearfully and his arms slid about her shoulders. 'No, of course not. It was all so long ago, Connie — there is no need to re-open the case now. Let it rest, Connie, I beg you.'

She shook her head gravely. 'I shall not rest if I do. Father Lawrence says I must tell the police.'

He saw a glimmer of light. 'Very well, so you have. Tell your priest you have informed Sergeant Lawson and that he is making enquiries. Will you do that?'

Light gleamed in her eyes. 'So I have — yes, I'll go and find him and ask him to give me absolution now. It's not too late to receive Communion yet!'

'And tell no one else, Connie,' Tom urged. She looked at him, eyebrows raised. 'It could impede my investigations,' he lied. 'Promise me you won't speak of it.'

She looked up at him trustingly. 'Tom, will you do something for me?'

'Of course, if I can.'

'Go and find William. He may not want to see you but please, find him, Tom, and tell him I love him still.'

'Does he doubt it?'

She shook her head slowly, a gentle expression of tenderness playing about her lips. 'He knows he has hurt me, cut me to the quick. He must have known I would feel betrayed, but I want you to see him and tell him that nothing has changed, that we are still united and I love him above all else.'

'Very well.' She looked so beautiful, so submissive and dutiful he wanted to seize and kiss her, protect her from the world and its hurts. She was no murderess, he would stake his life on it. He must play for time.

She was clearly restless to go and find her priest. Good Friday had already passed its noon and she was anxious to placate her God. Reluctantly he prepared to leave. At the doorway she took his hand and smiled up at him.

'Thank you, Tom,' she murmured huskily. 'Thank you for being such a dear, kind friend. What would I do without you?'

It took all his will-power to break away without taking her in his arms. She was so pure, so honest and honourable that it seemed to him she was a nun already and to touch her the way he yearned to would be tantamount to sacrilege. But not completely honest, he reminded himself as he crossed the cobbled yard to the street, for she was lying about murdering that child. She would not swat a pestering fly, let alone lift a knife to a defenceless child.

And her obsession with her brother — that was odd. She had spoken little of him, but her wild, incoherent letter had revealed the depth of her passion for him, her bitter hurt and betrayal by his marriage. Poor Connie. It was an unnatural love — could it be that Inspector Garlick was right all along when he spoke of her tainted blood, her heritage from a mad mother?

No! Tom refused to believe it. Crazed to a degree, perhaps to idolise her brother so, but not a killer, never! Outside on the garbage-strewn street he hesitated. How could he begin to clear Constance's name so that her confession never became public?

William — he must know something, since the two were so close. And his barracks were not far away, on the south side of the city. By enquiring he found the way by horse-bus. At the gates, Tom took a deep breath. What he achieved now would seal his own fate as well as Constance's. By keeping her confession to himself he rendered himself an accessory after the fact if ever she were proved guilty. His neck, too, would feel the noose. Without hesitation he strode towards the guard on duty. A distant clock was striking three. Tom glanced up. The sun had vanished and yellowing clouds had

240

gathered. Already heavy drops of rain were starting to fall.

The fair-headed young man standing by the bar, glass in hand, was William Lumb. Tom recognised him, for he had changed little since he was fourteen. Taller perhaps, more haggard, but otherwise very similar in height and colouring to Tom himself. Young William Lumb was clearly the worse for drink, his collar all askew and his eyes bloodshot.

'Lawson? I don't know you, do I?' he demanded. His aggressive manner was understandable. An officer and gentleman does not like to be bearded in his own mess by a stranger who is clearly of the lower orders, even if he was wearing his best suit and greatcoat and a neatly-brushed hat.

'We met once, sir, at Weatherhead some years ago,' Tom replied politely. He would have to lure William to a more private place to talk. Not that he actually appeared to be in company with any of the other officers but they were within earshot.

'Shall we go outside, sir?' Tom enquired.

The youth glared at him. 'Outside? In the rain? You'll say what you have to say here.' He was regarding Tom blearily but obviously trying to remember. 'Let's go and sit in the corner. Have a drink?'

'Thank you, no, not on an empty stomach.' Tom followed his lead, noting how the youth's step faltered as he made his way to a corner table. Once seated, William raised his glass to his lips.

'Your very good health, Dawson. Now what's it all about?'

Tom ignored his mistake. 'I'm a police officer, sir. It's your sister Miss Constance. . .'

'Connie? What's she done?'

'She's upset — about you, sir.'

'About me?' Tom saw a light of suspicion leap to the other man's eyes. 'What about me, that should involve the police? It's not that wretched woman Dolly Larkin who's complained, is it? Or Tancred?'

'What should they complain about, sir?' Tom's tone was mild, designed to lead the befuddled youth on, but the boy was quicker-witted than he thought.

241

'Nothing. Police officers don't travel around because silly girls are upset, so what really brings you here?'

'As I said, your sister. She claims to know about your half-brother's death four years ago.'

William set down his glass so abruptly that some of its contents slopped over. 'Does she now? Does she indeed?' Tom noted how his red eyes flickered. 'Well, that's the mystery solved.'

'Is it? Do you believe she did it?'

William shrugged. 'If she says so. Who else could it be? Hardly my father or the child's mother.'

'But why your sister? She loves children.'

William laughed hoarsely. 'Not Francis though. She was always reminding me how our parents preferred him to me. She hated him for that.'

'Resented it, possibly, out of loyalty to you. It does not appear to us that she is capable of hate.' Tom deliberately used the plural to imply he spoke for the police force.

'Well, perhaps she didn't do it consciously – she did walk in her sleep a lot, you know. She often found mud on her nightgown and sometimes flowers she'd picked in the garden, yet she never remembered going out,' William muttered.

'If it was done unconsciously, how could she remember now to confess it?' Tom's voice was quiet and the younger man blushed. 'Is there any more of that night you can recall which might help us, sir?'

William snatched up his glass irritably. 'I was only a boy of fourteen at the time – slept like a log like all boys of that age. Wish I could do the same now,' he added fretfully. 'So many problems. . .'

'Problems, sir? What kind of problems?'

'Nothing your sort would know about.'

Tom ignored the jibe. 'Your stepmother, is it?' It was a calculated guess that by outliving her husband she had thwarted the boy's expectations. He clearly drank far too much and perhaps excess had lightened his pocket.

'The bitch!' William exclaimed bitterly. 'She won't let me have a penny of what I'm entitled to! I need it now, not in three years' time, but will she relent? Not she!'

Tom clicked his tongue in a sympathetic sound. 'She was always hard on you,' he murmured.

'That's right, she was! Always putting me down in front of the servants and she no more than a jumped-up servant herself! She's a heartless, callous bitch and — '

He broke off suddenly. Tom could see the muscles at the corners of his mouth twitching.

'You were saying, sir?'

'Nothing. Only that my stepmother and I don't see things in the same light, that's all. Just what has Connie told you?'

'I can tell you no more than I have already, sir, I'm afraid. We mustn't influence what witnesses might say in the witness box.'

He saw the youth's ruddy face grow pale. 'Did she tell you about the razor?' William muttered.

'Razor?'

'Yes, the one she found by her bedside one morning just a few days before the murder. She must have been sleepwalking again. Didn't she tell you?'

Tom evaded the answer. 'No razors were found to be missing at the time of police enquiries, sir,' he pointed out quietly.

'No — it had been cleaned and returned to its box in Papa's dressing room. That's just it, you see — no one knew it had been missing, only Connie.'

'And you, evidently.'

A flush crept over William's face. 'Only because she told me — oh, surely she told you that! Connie would protect me to the death!'

'A sentiment you do not share, it seems,' remarked Tom, trying hard to disguise his anger and disgust.

'Now look here, who are you to pass judgement on me?' William snapped, his knuckles whitening as his hand clenched the glass. 'I would do anything for Connie, even though she can be a bit intense. Now I've no more time to spare for you — I've an appointment with my commanding officer at four.'

Tom rose slowly, reluctant to leave before his mounting

suspicions were satisfied. 'Perhaps we could meet again later, sir? I'll stay at that little inn down the road — what's it called?'

'The Cock,' muttered William. His mind was evidently already elsewhere.

Tom noticed that the other officers were standing silently by the bar and had probably overheard the last few words. 'I'll say goodbye for the moment then, sir, and perhaps we can meet again soon. Your sister's statement leaves many questions which I hope you may be able to help us answer. And by the way, she sends you her love. Goodnight, sir, and don't forget, Sergeant Lawson, staying at the Cock Inn.'

He could see the eyes alight with curiosity around the bar but he simply nodded in a deferential gesture before leaving. Outside it was still raining. He put on his hat and, turning up his coat collar, made for the inn, where he could eat something to satisfy his rumbling stomach and think over his plan of action.

Later, as he sat in the neat little dining room of the inn polishing off the last of the landlady's apple pie, he began to feel his brain could function again. Pushing his plate away and re-folding his napkin, he sat back.

It was clear from William's inebriated, careless words that he knew more about the night of the murder than he had ever revealed at the inquest or subsequently. The razor had never been mentioned before, and if he spoke the truth, Constance knew more, too. So which of the two had done the deed? Not Connie — of that he was convinced. Was it William, then, and she was shielding him? It was by her bedside, however, that the razor had appeared — and from where it had disappeared again. That was enough to cast doubt in any jury's mind against her.

But William could be lying, fabricating the story to divert suspicion from himself to his sister. He was weak and self-centred enough to do it and Tom could only wonder at Constance's utter devotion to such a creature. Blind, trusting faith such as she had for her religion, too. Tom felt a rush of protective love for her. Dear, sweet Connie, too far above him ever to allow him to declare his sentiments, but she had acknowledged him as a trusted friend. He could not betray that trust. For love of her, he did not count the cost of contravening police practice and thereby risking his job. He would be leaving the police force soon anyway, he argued with himself.

But could he maintain the silence? The priest could be relied upon not to break confessional secrecy, but what of William, and Connie herself? Either might make her confession public. Speed was essential.

So what next? Tackle William again, or go back to Connie to confirm the razor story? He hesitated to go back until he had something positive to tell her, and besides, he remembered, by now she would have received her precious Communion. He could not hasten back to spoil her happiness at being in grace again.

He sighed deeply. If Constance insisted on confessing, she would almost certainly be found guilty, even if her defence pleaded inherited insanity. No evidence such as bloody razors or blood-stained nightgowns would be needed to convince the jury — her word would suffice.

He must find a way to stop her — but how? Only a miracle now could save her life. In those stories his sister Jessie used to read out to him, the hero would easily find a way — kidnap his love and whisk her away to foreign parts where the law could not reach her. Heroes had no problems over money, it seemed. Tom leaned his elbows on the table and buried his face in his hands, willing inspiration to dawn.

The landlady appeared suddenly in the doorway. 'Excuse me, Mr Lawson, but there's a gentleman to see you. I told him it was late but he said it was important. Shall I send him in here?'

Tom looked up. No one but William knew he was here. 'Did he give his name, Mrs Derby?'

'No, sir, but he's wearing army uniform. An officer, sir.'

'Ah, yes. Please send him in, Mrs Derby.'

Tom was expectant, hopeful. This could be the miracle he prayed for, God willing. A tap came at the door and Mrs Derby's plump figure was followed by a taller one. Tom rose to greet him.

'Here's Mr Lawson, sir. I'll leave you both in peace,' Mrs Derby said, closing the door after her. Tom stared at the uniformed figure, speechless. It was not William.

'Forgive me for disturbing you, Mr Lawson,' the stranger said quietly, 'especially at this late hour, but I believe you are a police officer.'

'That's right. What can I do for you?'

'The major sent me to fetch you. William Lumb is dead.'

17

Tom stood for a moment, bereft of words. The officer removed his cap and waited for the message to be absorbed. 'As I say, Lawson, I'm sorry to trouble you but the major insisted when he learnt you had been with Lumb today. My name is Barrington, by the way.'

'Very good of you to come, Mr Barrington. Please be seated.' Tom was finding it hard to assimilate the news; his mind leapt to the consequences: the improbability of ever finding out the truth, the ghastly prospect of breaking the news to Constance and causing her unbearable grief. At this moment, the manner of William's death was of little interest.

'Fortunately one of the chaps heard you say your name and that you were staying at the Cock,' Barrington said amiably. 'I think you said Inspector Lawson, and he gathered you were a police officer.'

'Sergeant, actually,' Tom said numbly.

'And the major thought you should be contacted, as it appeared you had an interest in Lumb's activities. Up to no good, was he? Odd sort of chap, merry on occasions but damned tetchy and secretive at others. Too much drink lately, if you ask me. Not accustomed to it, either, so it's not surprising if he got out of hand. Some prank, was it? Whatever it was, I hardly think it could have been reason enough to kill himself.'

Tom looked up sharply. 'Suicide?' he exclaimed. William had been irritable, surly even, but not so depressed that one would think he would be contemplating ending his life. 'How did it happen?' he asked.

Barrington shrugged. 'No one knows for certain. All we do know is that he was found in an alley a mile or so from here and his pistol lay by his side. A hole in his chest you could put your fist in.'

Tom reflected. Suicides rarely shot themselves in the chest; the death could be lingering. They usually chose the ear or temple or the mouth. William knew about pistols.

'This was in a poor area, I take it. He could have been attacked by a robber.'

'Who seized his pistol from him? Very unlikely, Lawson, if I may say so. Lumb was a trained soldier and a strong man.'

'He had been drinking heavily, and thus his reactions would be slow. Was there anything missing from his pockets?'

'Hard to tell. He had no money before he left — that I know because he'd been trying to cadge from us all.'

'Watch, ring, anything like that missing?' Tom enquired.

'He'd pawned his watch weeks ago. He wore no ring.'

Tom sighed. 'So his assailant got away with nothing. A pointless murder, if you ask me.'

Barrington pondered a moment. 'Murder, eh? So you don't think he shot himself, then?'

'In the chest, sir? Would a trained soldier do that?'

'Ah, I see what you mean, yes. Well, Lawson, will you come back to the barracks now to see the major, or shall I tell him you'll be round first thing in the morning? It's nearing midnight, I see.'

Tom rose. 'I'll come now.'

On the street, where the wet cobblestones gleamed under the yellow light of the gas lamps, Barrington fell in step beside Tom. For a time they walked in silence.

'Such a pity,' Tom murmured. 'The young lady he was to have married must be very upset by this. I know his sister will be devastated.'

'Pity,' agreed Barrington. 'Though I doubt if Cynthia Baverstock will grieve over-long. She took it quite well when the major refused to allow her and Lumb to marry.'

Tom stopped dead in his tracks. 'Refused?' he repeated. 'When was this?'

'Oh, I think the major told Cynthia yesterday, after the letter from Lumb's stepmother arrived. He told Lumb this afternoon.'

'After I had left?'

'I believe so. I say, you don't think that's why Lumb killed himself, do you? I mean, he didn't really seem to love the girl at all. Cynthia is no beauty, I can tell you. Oh, he couldn't have shot himself out of heartbreak, do you think?'

'No, I do not,' said Tom emphatically. 'He was murdered.'

Major Baverstock was in his dressing gown, but he sat at his desk and glared at Tom with all the dignity as if he were in full dress uniform.

'Nasty business this, Sergeant,' he snapped. 'Would be obliged if you could see your way to keep the matter as discreet as possible, for the regiment's sake.'

'I'll do what I can, sir, but murder must be reported so that the villain may be apprehended.'

'Murder, eh? Thank God for that. Suicide would be a bad advertisement.'

'I believe you saw Lumb this afternoon. Did he strike you as being — shall we say, deranged at all?'

The major rubbed his chin. 'Ah, no, not deranged, though he was a little angry, but I put that down to the drink. These young fellows never learn when to stop.'

'Exactly, sir. He was angered by your refusal to let him marry your daughter, I take it.'

'So you know about that. Yes, I had offered no objection when he began to pay court to her because I knew Lumb senior was comfortably-off and thought young Lumb could

248

maintain Cynthia in the way she has been accustomed. Then this letter arrived from Mrs Lumb.'

'And that changed your mind?'

'Well, let's say it confirmed the misgivings I was already beginning to entertain. Mrs Lumb said she considered the marriage unsuitable on a number of grounds. Shall I show you the letter?'

'Just tell me what Mrs Lumb said.'

The major frowned. 'Is all this really necessary for a murder enquiry, Sergeant? Shouldn't your men be out searching the streets?'

'The fellow is far enough away by now, and my questions are just to confirm that Lumb had no possible reason for suicide, then we can concentrate on murder procedures. The letter, sir?'

The major sighed. 'Mrs Lumb did not spare her stepson. She told me he had always been weak and ineffectual, easily led by people of stronger characters, and that he was foolish and feckless with money. He was badly in debt, she said, and had only a modest inheritance to look forward to. My daughter was a means to an end, and she would strongly advise me to oppose or at least delay the marriage until such time as Lumb could make a man of himself.'

'So you told him the wedding was off. Did he know why?'

'Oh, yes. I told him of the letter, but I must say it only confirmed my own suspicion that the fellow was weak. Not really suitable for an officer at all. Should have asked him to resign his commission but I felt he'd had enough bad news for one day.'

'Thoughtful of you, sir. How did he take it?'

'As I said: angry at first, saying Cynthia loved him and I was being hard and so on. I reproved him for insolence, of course, and when he saw I was resolved he calmed down. Looked pretty fretful when he left, mind you. But what adventurer wouldn't after seeing a rosy future slip out of reach?'

'Quite right, sir, but clearly not so crushed and heart-broken that he would contemplate suicide. Well, that disposes of that,' said Tom, rising to go. 'In the morning, perhaps you would send someone round to the local police station so we can carry on from there. Thank you so much for your help, Major. I'll see myself out.'

'Oh, very well.' As Tom left, Major Baverstock looked mystified but impressed. If it crossed his mind that the police force was taking its time, it probably also appealed to his military nature that they showed no sign of panic but stuck religiously to the rule-book.

In the early morning Tom left the inn and made for the hospice. A serene, gentle-eyed young nun led him down to the laundry, where Constance was at work. At first she did not see him and carried on rubbing clothes against the wash-board. He watched the rhythmic movement of her slim body and his heart felt heavy. He had left this place yesterday in search of a miracle, a knight in armour braving all to rescue his lady-love, and today he came back not with a miracle to lay like a trophy at her feet, but the bearer of evil tidings which would break her heart. He had failed her.

'Constance.'

She looked up, and her flushed face broke into a smile. 'Tom!' Drying her hands on a cloth hurriedly she crossed to him, looking up expectantly. 'Oh, Tom! I'm so happy to see you again! I took Communion last night. Did you see William?'

Her rapturous expression spoke her happiness more eloquently than words and Tom felt a stab of agony. To have to shatter her happiness was more than human flesh could bear. But it had to be done. 'Constance, I fear I bring you bad news.'

For a moment she looked puzzled. Then, looking round at her white-robed companions busy at their work, their faces only dimly visible through clouds of steam, she drew him to a corner. 'What is it, Tom? I can see by your face that it's bad.'

He took a deep breath. There was no way to soften it. 'Connie, I'm afraid it's William. He's dead.'

Her mouth fell open, her dark eyes widened in horror and disbelief, and he waited for the cries, the screams, the protestations. Instead she just stared at him for several long seconds, then turned away.

'How?' he heard her whisper.

'Shot. His pistol lay at his side.'

More long seconds passed and she did not move. Only her shoulders moved slightly, as though she was fighting a great battle for self-control. He could only stand helplessly filled with humble admiration. Without turning she spoke. 'Come with me in here.'

She led the way into a smaller stone-floored room off the laundry, where an elderly nun sat patching a sheet.

'Sister Beatrice, would you mind if I spoke with this gentleman here alone?' Constance's voice was calm, controlled. The older nun rose stiffly and smiled before she left. Constance stood looking out of the little window. Tom did not dare intrude on her grief. He, too, was enduring agonies, longing to take her in his arms and caress and comfort her.

'Did he leave any message – a note, perhaps?' Her voice was a whisper.

'No.' The anguish she must be suffering; he whom she idolised had left her without a word.

'It must have been an impulsive decision, then. He was like that, you know,' she murmured. 'He needed me beside him to restrain him at times. Oh, Willie! Where was I when you needed me most!'

Tom took a quick step forward, fighting down the impulse to seize her. Instead he only rested his hand on her shoulder. He longed to cry out in protest that her guilt and remorse were groundless, that her idol would have sacrificed her life to save his own, that her love was misplaced and her dream hollow. But he held his tongue.

'The world was too hard for him, poor love.' She was speaking to herself, Tom realised. He was forgotten. 'Always too hard. Bullied at school, rejected by Papa and humiliated by Miss Platt, and torn away from my side – he never got over that. He needed me so much, my strength and support, and without it he could not cope. That's why he got into debt – Oh God! He asked me to help and I couldn't!'

Tom's hand tightened on her shoulder, charged with unspoken compassion. Her back towards him, she went on talking to the unheeding yard beyond the window. 'And

251

above all, he carried that terrible burden on his conscience. That was too great a load to carry alone. That is why he died.'

For a moment she paused. Tom was listening, suspicion slowly crystallizing to certainty. 'I would never have betrayed you, beloved Willie,' she whispered, 'for I loved you too much and my responsibility was as great as yours. God grant you have found peace now at last, my darling.'

Tom caught his breath. There it was – the hint that William had done the deed that night and she, poor misguided soul, felt responsible because she believed that she, and she alone, guided his actions. What was it she had said? 'I am responsible for Francis' murder,' she had said, not 'I murdered him.' Poor child. If any trace of her mother's madness persisted in her it was surely her obsessive love for her younger brother which excluded everyone else from her world. Was it possible she might in time forget and be cured? If any treatment, however slow and laborious, could bring her back to the world of normality he would stand by her, tending and loving her back to health. If only she would let him. . .

Suddenly she seemed to remember him. She turned towards him, unshed tears glistening in her eyes. Such mastery of herself, such self-control! He marvelled at her. There had been no sudden wracking sobs, ny hysteria, no swooning. A woman of strength and courage indeed. Like the child on the cliffs to whom he had been drawn by her solemn-eyed magnetism, her air of subdued strength and intensity. She had fascinated him then, a fascination which had later grown to love.

'As I told you, Tom,' she said quietly, 'I am in grace again and for that I thank God. But Reverend Mother told me today that she is unable after all to accept me as a novice in the order. That is sad.'

'But why, Connie? I thought it was settled.'

She nodded slowly. 'So did I. We should learn never to take things for granted. She gave me no clear reason, only that after discussion with Father Lawrence she had come to that conclusion. That is all. It is God's will.'

Tom touched her arm. 'But what will you do now, my dear

– I mean, after the funeral? Will you stay at Thwaite Lodge?'

She shook her head slowly and the wistful sadness in her eyes made his heart lunge. 'No, I cannot. Miss Platt does not want me. Oh, Tom, what shall I do? I can't stay here and I must work for my living! Do you know of any work I could do?'

He took her firmly by the shoulders. She looked up into his face, her eyes full of trust and hope. 'Still the spindrift, Connie, tossed about and lost, seeking its element? Could you bear to come home to the moors. . .?'

'Oh no! Not to Thwaite Lodge!'

'No, not the lodge but the moors. You told me you loved the moors.'

'Oh, yes. Such freedom to breathe.'

'Then come back, Connie. Come to our farm and rest and restore your strength. You can walk on the cliffs and climb the moors in summer with me when the heather is sweet and heavy with honey.'

'Ah, Tom, it sounds like paradise,' she breathed softly. 'But I must work and earn my keep.'

'When you are well. You can keep the house clean and cook and wash for us all – you'll work hard, I assure you. Will you come?' He gazed at her, hardly daring to hope. A faint smile hovered at the corners of her lips but grief prevented it forming.

'Give me time, Tom, but thank you. I am blessed with a truly loving friend and I thank God for sending you to me when I needed you.'

'I'll always be close, if you'll allow me. There is nothing in the world I could wish for more.'

The door opened and Sister Beatrice's face appeared round the door. 'Excuse me, Constance. May I take my sewing?' She hobbled to the table and took up the torn sheet and went out again, leaving the door ajar. Tom realised he should leave. Reluctantly he let go of Constance.

'Tomorrow is Easter Day,' he commented. 'I'll come again on Monday to see if you have made your decision. If you will accept it, Connie, my home is yours and I'll take you as soon as you are ready.'

She was smiling now, he realised with a start. She came closer. 'The third Monday, Tom. I'll have my answer ready.'

She turned away. She needed time to be alone with her grief, and he, too, turned to leave. Soapsuds flying from a nearby washtub floated in the steam-laden air, and as he walked quickly down the corridor he noticed a fluffy white puffball on his collar. He removed it carefully, looking down at it nestling on his fingertip.

'Spindrift', he murmured. 'Come settle on my collar, little spindrift, and no more turbulence will toss your life on the rocks. Only come to me, for I have loved you for so long.' He strode on outside, where a pale sun was just breaking through grey skies.

He did not see Constance standing at the window to watch him cross the cobbled yard. Nor did he see her turn to the table where Sister Beatrice's sewing materials lay. She picked up a stout darning needle and stood for a moment looking at its sharp tip. Then, averting her gaze, she plunged it into the index finger of her left hand.

The blood spurted. She watched it flow, trickling down the side of her finger into the palm of her right hand cupped beneath. Her expression was peaceful, resigned.

'There,' she murmured at last. 'It is over, Willie. You have found peace and, God willing, so shall I. I kept faith with you, Willie, as I promised. I did not betray you. But it is over now, and we are no longer one. We are freed from each other. I loved you well, dear brother, but now my life will be my own again. I kept faith, Willie, but now it is over.'

She replaced the needle on the table and stood again at the window fingering the rosary beads in her pocket and watching the smoke rising like a prayer from the infirmary chimney. The sun had found strength to shine brightly over east London at last.

FICTION

GENERAL

☐ Chains	Justin Adams	£1.25
☐ Secrets	F. Lee Bailey	£1.25
☐ Skyship	John Brosnan	£1.65
☐ The Free Fishers	John Buchan	£1.50
☐ Huntingtower	John Buchan	£1.50
☐ Midwinter	John Buchan	£1.25
☐ A Prince of the Captivity	John Buchan	£1.25
☐ The Eve of St Venus	Anthony Burgess	£1.10
☐ Nothing Like the Sun	Anthony Burgess	£1.50
☐ The Memoirs of Maria Brown	John Cleland	£1.25
☐ The Last Liberator	John Clive	£1.25
☐ Wyndward Fury	Norman Daniels	£1.50
☐ Ladies in Waiting	Gwen Davis	£1.50
☐ The Money Wolves	Paul Erikson	£1.50
☐ Rich Little Poor Girl	Terence Feely	£1.50
☐ Fever Pitch	Betty Ferm	£1.50
☐ The Bride of Lowther Fell	Margaret Forster	£1.75
☐ Forced Feedings	Maxine Herman	£1.50
☐ Savannah Blue	William Harrison	£1.50
☐ Duncton Wood	William Horwood	£1.95
☐ Dingley Falls	Michael Malone	£1.95
☐ Gossip	Marc Olden	£1.25
☐ Buccaneer	Dudley Pope	£1.50
☐ An Inch of Fortune	Simon Raven	£1.25
☐ The Dream Makers	John Sherlock	£1.50
☐ The Reichling Affair	Jack Stoneley	£1.75
☐ Eclipse	Margaret Tabor	£1.35
☐ Pillars of the Establishment	Alexander Thynn	£1.50
☐ Cat Stories	Stella Whitelaw	£1.10

WESTERN — BLADE SERIES by Matt Chisholm

☐ No. 5 The Colorado Virgins	85p
☐ No. 6 The Mexican Proposition	85p
☐ No. 7 The Arizona Climax	85p
☐ No. 8 The Nevada Mustang	85p
☐ No. 9 The Montana Deadlock	95p
☐ No. 10 The Cheyenne Trap	95p
☐ No. 11 The Navaho Trail	95p
☐ No. 12 The Last Act	95p

WESTERN — McALLISTER SERIES by Matt Chisholm

☐ McAllister and the Spanish Gold	95p
☐ McAllister on the Commanche Crossing	95p
☐ McAllister Never Surrenders	95p
☐ McAllister and the Cheyenne Trap	95p

SCIENCE FICTION

☐ Times Without Number	John Brunner	£1.10
☐ The Dancers of Arun	Elizabeth A. Lynn	£1.50
☐ Watchtower	Elizabeth A. Lynn	£1.10

WAR

☐ The Andersen Assault	Peter Leslie	£1.25
☐ Killers under a Cruel Sky	Peter Leslie	£1.25
☐ The Serbian Triangle	Peter Saunders	£1.10
☐ Jenny's War	Jack Stoneley	£1.25

FICTION

GENERAL

☐ The Free Fishers	John Buchan	£1.50
☐ Huntingtower	John Buchan	£1.50
☐ Midwinter	John Buchan	£1.25
☐ A Prince of the Captivity	John Buchan	£1.25
☐ The Eve of St Venus	Anthony Burgess	£1.10
☐ Nothing Like the Sun	Anthony Burgess	£1.50
☐ The Memoirs of Maria Brown	John Cleland	£1.25
☐ A Man	Oriana Fallaci	£1.95
☐ Savannah Blue	William Harrison	£1.50
☐ Duncton Wood	William Horwood	£1.95
☐ The Good Listener	Pamela Hansford Johnson	£1.50
☐ The Honours Board	Pamela Hansford Johnson	£1.50
☐ Buccaneer	Dudley Pope	£1.50
☐ An Inch of Fortune	Simon Raven	£1.25

HAMLYN WHODUNNITS

☐ Some Die Eloquent	Catherine Aird	£1.25
☐ The Case of the Abominable Snowman	Nicholas Blake	£1.10
☐ The Widow's Cruise	Nicholas Blake	£1.25
☐ The Worm of Death	Nicholas Blake	95p
☐ Thou Shell of Death	Nicholas Blake	£1.25
☐ Tour de Force	Christianna Brand	£1.10
☐ King and Joker	Peter Dickinson	£1.25
☐ A Lonely Place to Die	Wessel Ebersohn	£1.10
☐ Gold From Gemini	Jonathan Gash	£1.10
☐ The Grail Tree	Jonathan Gash	£1.25
☐ The Judas Pair	Jonathan Gash	95p
☐ Spend Game	Jonathan Gash	£1.25
☐ Blood and Judgment	Michael Gilbert	£1.10
☐ Close Quarters	Michael Gilbert	£1.10
☐ The Etruscan Net	Michael Gilbert	£1.25
☐ Hare Sitting Up	Michael Innes	£1.10
☐ Silence Observed	Michael Innes	£1.25
☐ The Weight of the Evidence	Michael Innes	£1.10
☐ There Came Both Mist and Snow	Michael Innes	95p
☐ The Howard Hughes Affair	Stuart Kaminsky	£1.10
☐ Inspector Ghote Draws a Line	H. R. F. Keating	£1.10
☐ Inspector Ghote Plays a Joker	H. R. F. Keating	£1.25
☐ The Murder of the Maharajah	H. R. F. Keating	£1.25
☐ The Perfect Murder	H. R. F. Keating	£1.10
☐ A Fine and Private Place	Ellery Queen	£1.25
☐ The French Powder Mystery	Ellery Queen	£1.25
☐ The Siamese Twin Mystery	Ellery Queen	95p
☐ The Spanish Cape Mystery	Ellery Queen	£1.10

NAME ....

ADDRESS ....

....

Write to Hamlyn Paperbacks Cash Sales, PO Box 11, Falmouth, Cornwall TR10 9EN.

Please indicate order and enclose remittance to the value of the cover price plus:

U.K.: Please allow 45p for the first book plus 20p for the second book and 14p for each additional book ordered, to a maximum charge of £1.63.

B.F.P.O. & EIRE: Please allow 45p for the first book plus 20p for the second book and 14p per copy for the next 7 books, thereafter 8p per book.

OVERSEAS: Please allow 75p for the first book and 21p per copy for each additional book.

Whilst every effort is made to keep prices low it is sometimes necessary to increase cover prices and also postage and packing rates at short notice. Hamlyn Paperbacks reserve the right to show new retail prices on covers which may differ from those previously advertised in the text or elsewhere.